KT-226-528

BORDERLINE

Colin Ainsworth Sharp

A STAR BOOK

published by

the Paperback Division of
W. H. ALLEN & Co. PLC

A Star Book

Published in 1984
by the Paperback Division of
W. H. Allen & Co. PLC
44 Hill Street, London W1X 8LB

First published in Great Britain by
W. H. Allen & Co. Ltd, 1983
Reprinted 1984

Copyright © Colin Ainsworth Sharp, 1983

Printed in Great Britain by
Cox & Wyman Ltd, Reading

ISBN 0 352 31465 6

This book is sold subject to the condition that it shall
not, by way of trade or otherwise, be lent,
re-sold, hired out or otherwise circulated without the
publisher's prior consent in any form of
binding or cover other than that in which it is published
and without a similar condition including this
condition being imposed on the subsequent purchaser.

DEDICATION AND ACKNOWLEDGMENTS

This book is for my Mother and Father – Poppy Cynthia Ida and John Ainsworth Sharp.

BORDERLINE could not have been written without the help of many friends and colleagues including Al J Venter from whose book 'Coloured – a profile of 2 million South Africans' (Human & Rousseau, Cape Town 1974) I culled much valuable information. Some important facts were also taken from Jillian Becker's work 'Hitler's Children' (Michael Joseph 1977).

My thanks also to the Officer Commanding Sector 70, SA Defence Force, Katima Mulilo, Eastern Caprivi. Commandant Eddie Wesselo, Captain 'Liep' Bester, Alan Bushell and Hendrik Roelofsen.

This book is based on fact although the organisation AFRA is totally fictitious as is the DFB and ASG in West Germany. However, any resemblance to any persons living or dead is coincidental and any offence or embarrassment so caused is regretted.

Colin Ainsworth Sharp
Johannesburg, January 1983

PROLOGUE

Umgungundlovu is a Zulu word, meaning the secret place of the elephants and in February 1838, this was the name of Dingaan's capital city in what is now Natal South Africa. The city was founded shortly after Dingaan assassinated his famous half-brother King Shaka, the man who had been responsible for welding the Zulu nation into the fearsome fighting force which for decades terrorised much of the southern region of Africa.

Overlooking this sprawling hut-city was a befouled height haunted by hyena and vultures, a ritual killing ground where condemned persons were put to death by various bizarre and horrifying methods. This hill of execution, called KwaMatiwane (place of Matiwane, an unfortunate chief who fell from favour and was despatched there) was where Dingaan lured the Voortrekker leader Piet Retief and his seventy or so followers in the late afternoon of 4 February 1838. The king's pretext was that of an indaba (conference) to discuss peace terms but the Europeans were wary and kept a hold on their weapons as they took their places in the fetid heat of the stinking killing area.

As evening fell, the shrewd Dingaan managed to place the white men at their ease, cosseting them with food and drink and a display of dancing by comely Zulu maidens. But when the visitors eventually relaxed and put aside their rifles he gave the pre-arranged signal for the slaughter to begin and Retief was caught completely by

6

surprise. He and his men were butchered unmercifully in a treacherous act that has never been forgotten by the whites of South Africa and which was to be followed by much spilling of blood on both sides.

Less than two weeks later, on 16 February, Dingaan's Impis, encouraged by the easy slaughter of Retief, left Umgungundlovu on another orgy of killing. Attacking the main camp of the surviving *trekker* families at a small stream, later to be called *Moordspruit* (stream of murder), they massacred women and children and pillaged livestock and supplies. In a few hours the blood lust was sated and Dingaan returned to his kraal, once more the total master of his vast territory.

It was to be ten months before Retief's successor, Andries Pretorius, was able to rally sufficient support to challenge Dingaan. The spiritual leader of his punitive commandos gave an inspiring address on the morning of the seventh of December of that same fateful year and standing on a gun carriage he made a promise to God, his brethren and fellow countrymen. The words uttered were for posterity and the expression that was noted particularly was 'The Covenant'.

On 15 December the Pretorius commandos reached a small river known to the Zulus as Ncome (praiseworthy one) and the following day faced the massed Impis in what they regarded as the hour of destiny for the Afrikaaner nation.

The battle was joined and the handful of tenacious Boers won the day with a few howitzers and their accurate rifle fire which took terrible toll of the ranks of spear wielding Zulus. Many of the black warriors were trapped in the river which eventually ran red with blood as the Europeans exacted their long-awaited revenge. This conflict was to become known as 'The Battle of Blood River' or 'Dingaan's Day' and marked the first major defeat of the Zulus in their many uprisings against the Boers. It heralded the beginning of an era of absolute white power in South Africa.

7

To this day that memorable occasion is still celebrated annually by a national holiday when present-day Afrikaaners, the descendants of the Boers, meet to thank God for their deliverance in the epic struggle. A strangely enigmatic and highly religious race, the Afrikaaners still believe that they are a divine people whose destiny is closely linked with bringing God's word to the heathen tribes of Southern Africa. The word *kaffir* (caffre), actually derived from the Arabic and meaning 'unbeliever', was incorporated into old Dutch. Today the word has become a derogatory term for black and coloured people and is even understood in western countries far from South Africa. For this reason, it is seldom used in contemporary circles, even among Afrikaaners.

The historical celebration of 16 December involves a gathering of the old ox wagons and other period paraphernalia on the banks of the river where the battle was fought and many devotees dress up in the costumes of the time. To the 'orthodox' Afrikaaner or *verkrampte,* it represents the one day in the year which characterises their history, and all they hold dear is graphically represented in the remembrance ceremonies. However, to the sixteen million blacks and almost three million coloureds of the country, it is a blatant reiteration of the ancient and hated policy of white supremacy. It was known as 'The Day of the Covenant' or 'Dingaan's Day' but recently the name has been changed to 'Day of the Vow'.

Approximately one month later, depending on the calendar and its pressure of business, the South African parliament is opened by the State president in Cape Town. This is a ceremonial occasion which signifies the beginning of the Republic's political year. To South African whites it is a re-affirmation of their democratic society and a parliamentary system based on that of Westminster. It is an occasion when throats tighten and eyes mist over. It is the very essence of South African history, and its importance is growing rather than waning.

CHAPTER 1

Gerrit de Kock had an Afrikaans name because, in the early days of the Cape settlement in South Africa, slaves took the names of their masters and were regarded as one of the family – or at least as part of the household. In those days the rapport between slave and master was, in most cases, excellent and similar to that which existed later in the more tolerant areas of the American Deep South in the nineteenth century. Racial tensions did not exist as they do now and so-called colour-bars were unknown.

The owner of this particular name was then twenty-two years old and had rather fine, coffee-coloured skin and tightly curled brownish-black hair. He weighed seventy-three kilos and stood just under six feet tall and was slim and muscular with an athletic physique. He had neat aquiline features spoiled only by a sparse droopy moustache which accentuated rather than concealed his thick lips and contrasted strangely with his springy Afro hairstyle. De Kock was fit and quite powerful for his weight and with a little basic grooming would have been regarded as good looking in London or Los Angeles and as highly desirable in Stockholm or Copenhagen.

In South Africa, however, he was not viewed in this light because he was a hybrid; a living reminder of the white settlers' cohabitation with their indigenous black servants which had been looked upon with more or less a blind eye before the advent of Afrikaaner power and the real birth of apartheid in 1948. De Kock was classified as a coloured and was politely despised by the whites and rejected as being tainted by the blacks. His own reaction to these stigmas had hardened over the years into a suppressed yet bitter hatred of the system which had sired him and almost three million others in the vast territory of South Africa.

In this respect he was different to his parents who had apathetically accepted their miserable existence as long as they had their daily demi-johns of the cheap white and pale red wine. In fact, Gerrit de Kock was one of those not too rare products of a fourth generation Cape coloured marriage. Such inbreeding as had existed in the past had this time produced no runt or cretin for De Kock was a superb physical specimen with an IQ of 138.

Gerry, as he was sometimes called, had always lived with his family in the tin-roofed clap-boarded house in which he had been born. Home was near Goodwood in the windy basin of the flat Cape Peninsula some ten kilometres from the beautiful city and elegant seafront. The family then numbered five and the parents had to work hard to support their alcoholic lifestyle. Gerry's sister Tina at nineteen was a slender light-skinned beauty with the thick raven hair of the Cape Malay, but the younger brother Koos had crinkly hair like Gerrit and a coarse dark complexion, blotched and marred by pock-marks and pimples.

Koos was not very clever and at the age of sixteen desired little more than a new Kawasaki motorcycle and enough money for drinks and cigarettes. Tina was different: she was both attractive and intelligent and had been using her superb body to considerable advantage from the age of fifteen. Her first lover had been a white policeman who had given her many presents of cheap perfume and dresses – but she had soon tired of him and the trashy things he offered her. Now she had established tastes and Gerrit knew that she had had quite a few rich white boyfriends on the go and that she would surely leave home soon. One of her latest men was Willi the German import/export agent who drove her around in his red Mercedes sports car as if she were a European girl. He even took her out to dinner in the Grill Room of the city's elite Mount Nelson Hotel with complete disregard for the law and the Immorality Act which forbade such fraternisation. Tina was actually a borderline case and could quite easily have been classified white. So far, she had never been challenged in a restaurant or public place.

To Gerrit this was very wrong and terribly irritating because he was obviously coloured. His complexion and hair were almost like indelible labels hung around his neck, advertising his mixed blood and announcing his bastard race and heritage. He, like Tina, had gone to a coloured school in nearby Goodwood and had excelled to the extent that he was a full year ahead of his classmates when he matriculated at the age of sixteen, an unprecedented event in his school. His six distinctions earned him a scholarship to the University of the Western Cape in Bellville which accepted gifted coloured students. The scholarship had been all very well but the grant was barely sufficient to maintain him nor to purchase all the books and equipment he would need for the first year of his medical degree. It would require seven to eight years of hard study before he could qualify as a doctor who would be able to go virtually anywhere in the world to work or further his studies.

But this was not to be. On 15 March 1974, a date Gerrit would never forget, his father was wandering drunkenly home from the *shebeen* close to his place of work, when an old but fast-moving Volkswagen had lost control on the wet and greasy road surface of the industrial area near to their home, some three kilometres from Parow. Joseph de Kock had worked here since leaving school, in the assembly plant of a domestic appliance manufacturer but it was pure bad luck that he was in that place at that time. Normally, a friend gave him a lift home but on this day he failed to appear and so Joseph was walking unsteadily to the bus stop in the blustering wet evening. He had his back

11

to the rain, driven by the vicious wind known as the south easter, which howled across the Cape flats, and thus he was hardly warned of the car which mounted the pavement to strike him in the back, flinging him hard against a concrete wall.

Joe had only been forty at the time of his death and surprisingly healthy, despite his vast and regular intakes of alcohol. He had died three minutes after arriving at the nearby Parow Infirmary, his pelvis and spine shattered and his kidneys and spleen torn and ruptured. Joe's heart had survived the impact intact however, and was found to be a healthy vigorous organ. Meanwhile, just a few kilometres away in Cape Town's legendary Groote Schuur hospital, a thirty-seven-year-old South American was close to death, his ailing heart valves hardly able to open and close to drive the vital blood around his body.

Rapid telephone calls were made and within four minutes of Joe's being pronounced dead, the first incision was made in his unmarked chest. Neither Gerrit nor his mother were consulted over the removal of the heart which was transported with a police escort to Groote Schuur. By midnight the following night, the South American was sitting up in bed talking to his incredulous wife and South Africa's famous heart team had performed another miracle.

The distraught Mrs de Kock and her three children became mini-celebrities and the newspapers carried their photographs and those of the dead Joe; husband, father, breadwinner and raging alcoholic. Gerrit's mother soon forgot that her husband's heart had been removed without her consent but to Gerrit it was just another example of the authorities' disregard for the coloured people. But there was little that could be done after the event and the family had no money for expensive legal battles and, in any case, he didn't mind the fact that his father's heart had enabled someone else to continue living. It was just that the absence of consultation constituted a huge indignity and a horrible lack of respect by the whites for a race which was totally their responsibility anyhow.

The accident had put paid to his plans for university and he began work at seventeen in order to support his mother, Tina and little Koos. Gerrit's first job was in a department store in Parow as an assistant to the wages clerk in the general office. His unusual intelligence and excellence in mathematics meant that he was able to handle his work load with almost childlike ease and he was soon promoted to assistant bookkeeper so that by the age of eighteen he was earning in excess of R200 per month. Most of his earnings went on the family but he managed to save a small amount and planned to buy a car.

At fifteen, Tina was already finding her own way with the assistance of various men friends but young Koos was showing little promise at school and would probably leave at the age of fourteen. Their mother had aged tragically since her husband's death and was drinking more heavily and beginning to experience serious kidney disorders. Her continual illness eventually caused her to lose her job at a clothing factory and Gerrit assumed total responsibility for the family on his nineteenth birthday. By the age of twenty-two, he was studying for a degree in business administration at night school and was earning R440 per month as an assistant to the company secretary in the same firm that had employed his father.

CHAPTER 2

If it were not for the whites in South Africa, there would be no coloureds. But ostrich-like, with heads in the sand, many white South Africans maintain that there is little or no white blood in coloured genetics, preferring to think that these people are the result of generations of inter-breeding between the original Bushmen and Hottentot residents of the Cape, supplemented by the addition of slaves imported by the settlers who landed there in the late seventeenth century. This long-established theory is a particularly convenient one for certain right-wing Calvinistic elements present in South African politics and religion.

For centuries the coloureds have been discriminated against and, from the outset, their lot has never been an easy one. Undoubtedly they are true South Africans with a culture and language similar to, and often running parallel with, that of the whites who created them. They are a feeling people, often bright and quick to learn – and occasionally, as in the case of Gerrit de Kock, highly intelligent. Historians have recently hypothesised that these people may be forerunners of the yellow world of the future when individual races and colours will have become submerged and evened out in one huge multi-racial global melting pot.

Eminent South African doctors and anthropologists have confirmed this theory with lengthy research programmes which have shown that the average coloured person possesses a blood-group pattern 34 per cent Western European, 36 per cent Southern African black and 30 per cent Asian. In 1972, a leading Cape medical man announced the startling result of a survey of several years which proved that the four million whites in South Africa were in fact 7 per cent coloured. Thus he obliterated for posterity the previous staunchly held belief that South African whites were racially pure.

An obvious reason for the initial intermingling of blood was the scarcity of women in the early settlements and as early as 1666 almost one hundred indigenous Hottentots became integrated into the first colony and were, to all intents and purposes, regarded as equal to the whites. Eventually, mixed marriages were actually recommended to swell the settlers' numbers and Jan van Riebeeck, the leader of the pioneer band at the Cape Settlement, actually gave such unions his blessing with the result that the colony increased in numbers through sexual activity in and out of wedlock. But the majority of these early yellow people were swamped by the mass of blacks migrating south from Natal, and even as far afield as Zimbabwe. As the black flood increased, the indigenous Hottentots and Bushmen were slaughtered in thousands and in latter years many were to suffer a similar fate at the hands of the Boers.

By the turn of the seventeenth century, the Cape Colony was well established through the auspices of the vigorous Dutch East India Company. Several thousand sailors from all over Europe and the New World would call at the Cape each year and they had little or no regard for the colour or race of the female flesh they pursued after many months at sea. A large number of bastard half-castes resulted.

Most of the early slaves came from Madagascar, whose island peoples are an appealing Creole black race, and these were supplemented later by slave cargoes from Ceylon, Bengal and Indonesia, all trading countries with the Dutch East India Company. The Indonesians, in

15

particular, were attractive and reasonably well presented people and the women were bargained for in earnest by the sex-starved residents of the colony. More bastard half-caste children were produced and all were awarded full civil rights as were those of marriages to 'freed slaves'. So it was that in the mid-eighteenth century, one in sixteen marriages in the Cape involved a woman of known coloured blood.

Strange contradictions involving mixed unions and slaves were illustrated by laws such as that which allowed for the children of a Hottentot or Bushman woman and a slave to be regarded as born free. If however, these offspring were supported by the owner of the father they were held in bond until the age of eighteen. But infusions of white blood continued and after a period of seven to eight generations, a transformation from black to brown to virtually white had taken place. In just after a century since the first settlers had arrived, the foundations of the coloured community of the Cape had been laid and most of these early products of the European settlers were totally assimilated into white society.

The concept of racial intermingling was therefore totally acceptable in the early years but by the middle of the eighteenth century most of the *burgers,* as they were now called, became strongly opposed to further blood contact with people who were not 'racially pure'. Certain slave masters kept the trend going however, because the results of mixed couplings were often hardy and attractive specimens and thus very much in demand.

Finally, a respected missionary caused wisespread scandal by marrying the daughter of a Madagascan slave woman and this example was followed by several of his contemporaries and co-workers. These acts were severely frowned upon by the leaders among the Dutch colonists who believed that they had been sent to this heathen land to educate and civilise the savages, not to co-habit with them; a practice which was in direct opposition to their religious indoctrination. It had not taken long for racial intolerance to manifest itself in official circles and the seeds of South Africa's future development and policies were irrevocably sown.

Tina de Kock was more than satisfied lately in both body and mind. Her life had become quite fantastic since she had met Willi Heim, the thirty-seven year old blond German who had been her lover for the past six months. On this golden Cape evening they met in the city at Willi's office on the Foreshore and he had poured cocktails from the elegant perspex and steel cabinet contained in his bookcase. The offices were impressive and were situated twenty-three floors above the fascinating Cape Town seafront and Tina looked out of the huge tinted windows to see vistas of Signal Hill and the mountains above Camps Bay and just below a good proportion of the bustling harbour.

She sat on a soft natural suede sofa and her drink rested on a glass coffee table in front of her. She could smell the indefinable rich odours of the office which wafted about in the mild draft of the air conditioning and she lifted her Campari and sipped it watching Willi leaning back in his chair, his feet on the glass-topped cane trestle desk. He was talking on the telephone to somebody in Germany and his quiet intense voice sounded confident and happy as he chatted naturally in his own clipped, yet beautiful language. Tina could follow only the odd word or two but it sounded wonderful.

Behind Willi, the soft cream mohair curtains swayed gently to the hum of the air conditioner encased in a matt black unit which ran along the entire length of the window. A large squat glass of whisky and ice rested close to Willi's hand and a short square Swiss cigar smouldered expensively in the brass ashtray. Tina studied her lover as she sipped her drink. He was tall, almost six feet two inches, but slim and hard with skin tanned a wonderful golden colour·from weekends at the beach. The contrast with his white-blond curly hair and eyebrows was marvellous and she watched him smiling as he talked and heard the chink of ice as he lifted the glass to his lips. She sipped her own dark pink aperitif. I don't really like Campari, she thought, but it's reckoned to be terribly chic to drink it.

Willi finally put down the receiver and looked across to her, drawing on his cigar and puffing a blue cloud of smoke towards the ceiling. With the sun setting behind him and the blonde ring of hair around his face, the effect on Tina was that of a halo and he seemed almost Godlike. He was so beautiful, she thought, totally irresistible and a wonderful lover – she adored it with him all the time. Willi Heim's sentiments were much the same as those of the striking coloured girl. To him she was a gorgeous, fascinating and intelligent creature very different from Hildegard, his previous German girlfriend who was a plump, stolid sandy-blonde with freckled pinkish skin.

'Another drink, *schatz*,' he said to the lithe brown girl who lay back gracefully on his De Sede couch. She shook her head and patted the cushion beside her and he rose and walked across and sat down, drawing her to him so that her wonderful blue-black hair flowed onto his shoulder. She smelled amazing, a sort of powdery flowery fragrance overlaid with the peppery, spicy natural odour of her skin. She wore a simple cotton seersucker dress in cream with a thin red leather belt and matching sandals and a little mother-of-pearl heart hung around her slim neck on a silver chain. He had given it to her and it had cost little but she wore it constantly and loved it because it had come from him.

As Tina lay against him he saw the long slim legs and thighs and he knew that under the cotton dress she wore tiny white cotton panties and nothing else because her small firm breasts needed no support. Her elbow pressed into his groin and he began to harden and the girl felt him and moved her upper arm in a gentle squirming motion.

'Come on,' she said softly. Willi got up and locked the door and together they moved to the soft cream wool carpet between the couch and the desk. First she took him in her mouth and he moved down to kiss the warm spiciness of her, knowing that she would be wonderfully clean and fresh, as she always was. But soon their movements became urgent and they moved together and found each other. It was 6.30 on a Friday in March; a glorious late summer evening in what Francis Drake had called 'The Fairest Cape in all the world'.

Heim Import-Export was a successful business run solely by Willi and his elderly German secretary. The imports were mostly German delicatessen items, much sought after by South Africa's considerable German population, and among the exports were hand-knotted Karakul wool carpets from the north-eastern Cape and Lesotho which were equally appreciated by interior decorators in Germany, Switzerland and the Scandinavian countries. These two basic bread and butter lines netted Willi well over sixty thousand rands per annum and he thus enjoyed all the good things of life that the Cape had to offer; among these were the South African assembled Mercedes Benz 350 SL and the penthouse he owned between Clifton and Camps Bay. Food was another great joy to Willi – despite little real exercise he never put on weight. He found great pleasure in introducing Tina to the delights of good living, especially after she had subsisted for most of her life on small portions of rubbishy stewed meat and fish and practically no vegetables. Tonight they had decided to go to the Langoustine, a small sea-food restaurant in Hout Bay, across the other side of the mountain from Cape Town.

The Mercedes purred through Seapoint and onto the long winding coast road and Tina lay back luxuriously against the sheepskin covers of the comfortable bucket seat. She was sated from their lovemaking but hungry with a pleasant anticipation for the meal that she knew they would be enjoying within half an hour. It was just after

7.30 and the top was down on the car and although the sun was sinking fast towards the sea, it was still mild and windless. People were leaving the beaches at Clifton and Camps Bay to go home or to the pubs for a drink and perhaps a meal later in one of the city's many superb bistro-type restaurants. Willi hummed as he drove and smiled thinking that Cape Town in the long summer was much like the French Riviera only less expensive and, thankfully, not so crowded.

Effortlessly the 350 SL smoothed out the many bends along the coast road and began the climb towards the mountains, leaving the sea behind. As the sun set, the rocks and indigenous mountain plants were bathed in a wonderful rosy glow which matched Tina's mood perfectly and, as they crossed over Constantia Nek above Llandudno and the sun disappeared, she drew closer to her lover who drove with an easy fluidity that complemented his beautiful car. He smelled wonderful too, a mixture of Givenchy cologne and masculinity and she placed her hand high up on the inside of his thigh so that he squirmed and glanced left towards her cat-like face. Christ, she was beautiful, thought Heim; he wanted her again already. Tina continued to stroke him until they drew up by the tiny cottage restaurant in the gathering dusk; ahead was the broad dark expanse of Hout Bay in the shadow of the mountains. It was one of the most beautiful places in the world.

Their meal was a simple one; lobster bisque and fresh line fish. Willi chose a steenbrass and Tina the moist and tasty kingklip and they munched on a side dish of crisp calamari and home-made garlic bread. Tina's mood was now bordering on euphoria and her adoration of the slim handsome German was very obvious. She failed even to notice the other patrons of the small restaurant because she was so totally relaxed. And she was completely oblivious of the fact that she, a coloured, was actually forbidden to drink with whites let alone frequent a white restaurant.

Willi Heim's reaction to Tina was beyond infatuation. He had first picked her up four months earlier in a Seapoint coffee bar and had realised from the outset that she was possibly coloured. The girl's incredible looks and body coupled with her animated conversation had cancelled out all his inhibitions however, and he had driven her home to his flat where they had made love without any hesitation on either side. It had been like that ever since so that now, incredibly enough, he was considering marrying Tina. He hadn't told her yet though, because it would mean that they'd obviously have to leave South Africa.

After the bottle of fruity Cape Riesling and two Smugglers Grogs of coffee, rum and cream, they were both mildly drunk yet still bathed in the magic of each other's company. Willi looked at his watch.

'Let's drive back slowly along the coast, *liebling,* and maybe stop and paddle. It's a wonderful night and we mustn't waste it.'

'You're so good to me Willi,' Tina answered softly, leaning close to him across the narrow table and she felt sudden tears spring to her eyes at the tenuous nature of their relationship. 'I can't bear to think what I'd do without you, darling. I think I'd die if you left me.' The great liquid black eyes gazed into Willi's blue ones and he couldn't look away and knew that he could never give her up either, not now.

'We'll talk about it my sweetheart, we'll talk about it tonight, I promise,' he said softly.

They parked the Mercedes between Llandudno and Camps Bay, finding a quiet cove concealed from the road, and walked down through the bright moonlight to the rocks and the great silver-lit expanse of the sea. They sat close together, his jacket around her slim shoulders, holding hands and talking of the problems of their relationship and of the uncertain future and such things as throwback yellow children. On the right, some two hundred metres away, lay the partially dismantled wreck of the Greek tanker which had run aground on the rocks during the previous winter. The dead ship looked huge and ghostly, silhouetted against the moonlit sea and Tina wondered absently what had happened to her captain who must have watched his ship being driven helplessly onto the rocks. She marvelled at the cold splendour of the ocean and loved it now as she always had ever since she had been a little girl scampering on the white sand, out of reach of the cold Atlantic waves. She shivered and drew closer to Willi who was not speaking. It was past midnight and they had said so many things to each other, so many things.

It was Willi who first heard the creak of brakes and he stood up quickly, his cream shirt and slacks pale in the moonlight. He could see that an old Chevrolet had stopped next to the Mercedes which was parked well off the road, slightly hidden by rocks and bushes. Four young coloureds left the old car and walked towards the Mercedes, one vaulting over the door to settle in the driving seat. The youth turned on the radio and rock music blared loudly into the stillness of the night, shattering the pleasant hiss and rumble of the waves.

Heim knew that they were in grave danger because these young coloureds or *skollies*, as they were called, were violent and often pathologically deranged people who lived solely for the knife and the bottle. He pushed Tina behind him and walked forward confidently. Mustn't let them think I'm frightened, he thought desperately above the pounding of his heart.

'You like the car, eh,' he said gaily and walked casually up to the four youths and then stopped abruptly as one broke off the radio aerial with a savage wrench and then proceeded to scratch the jagged end across the bonnet.

'Oh yes mister, we like it OK,' said the one in the driver's seat with a sickening toothless grin. His eyes were flat and hard and in the silvery light he looked almost reptilian.

All of them were dressed in jeans and T-shirts and now they ringed Willi, the one in the car leaping out suddenly over the door. He walked round to the front of the Mercedes and kicked at the grill twice, breaking off the three-pointed star and denting the chrome trim. Willi Heim watched the mindless destruction of his car and began to lose control, feeling anger overcoming his initial fear.

'You nasty little shit,' he said and moved fast towards the slim young man who was the leader. It was then that the knives appeared.

Tina had hung back on the rocks but now she moved up closer to Willi. Seeing the knives and knowing the mentality of men such as these, she was pale and trembling visibly with terror. Willi saw this and felt his anger rising to uncontrollable levels.

'What do you want, you bastards?' he shouted. 'I've got about thirty rands in my jacket,' he said grabbing the garment from Tina and pulling the cash from a pocket. 'Do you want my watch too?' he screamed, taking it off and tossing it to the leader who caught it easily and slipped it into his jeans.

'Oh yes, mister, we want what you got alright. All us coloureds want what you whites got but we never get the chance, do we? Well, now we got the chance my mate and what we want is your woman too because she looks a right cherry.' Tina cringed back and gasped and they all leered at her appreciatively and sniggered.

Willi felt his stomach turn and his resolve hardened so that he no longer felt afraid. 'You'll have to kill me first,' he said, and at that moment he meant it.

Tina screamed as the man to the left of Willi suddenly swung at him with a soft-looking object which thumped sickeningly into his neck between chin and shoulder. The sock, filled with wet beach sand, felled the German like a bullet and he dropped to the gravel without a sound. The four youths moved in on Tina who backed towards the beach again and then broke into a headlong run. In her sandals, she had little chance and they caught her within twenty metres and flung her down between the rocks, the leader standing over her, his eyes crazed with lust and excitement. He knelt and ripped the dress from the whimpering girl and saw the dusky skin, recognising her race as only another coloured could.

'Well, look what we have here my mates, a *lekker* coloured *meisie* who likes the rich white boys eh.' He kicked Tina viciously in the thigh and the others held her legs as their leader readied himself, undoing his belt and pulling down his soiled jeans.

The girl screamed again briefly, a shrill animal sound in the soft beach-quiet of the windless night. The leader smiled, his coarse yellow face splitting to display blackened teeth and he covered her mouth with one hand whilst the other roamed between her legs, tearing her panties and pulling her apart. Greasy with sweat now and mouthing obscenities, he forced his way into her.

'Oh she's nice and wet, eh. Probably had a bit of the white boy already. Oh it's lovely, what a lovely bit of *poes*.' His breath smelled of cheap wine and tobacco and she began to retch as he tried to kiss her and then one of the others was at her head, fumbling with himself and a rank, fishy almost fetid smell filled her nostrils as the man tried to force himself into her mouth. She gagged and tried to close her teeth but one of the others grabbed her long hair, holding his knife to her neck so that she could feel the point just piercing the skin. She froze and opened her mouth obediently. The nightmare went on and on.

It was almost half an hour before they had all finished with her and she had stopped any real resistance after the first few minutes. The last to violate her had been a slim young man, hairless and panting with excitement. He had turned her over and the others had held her legs apart whilst he had invaded her body from behind, his friends cheering him on and she lying face down, almost smothering in the sand as he battered into her. The pain had almost made her faint but he had been quick and suddenly there had been the hot feeling inside her and miraculously it was finished. Then the pock-marked leader stood over her again and spat onto her naked breasts.

'There you are my sweetie,' he said in a cruel whisper. 'Now wasn't that lovely, eh. Now you know what some good coloured boys is like, eh. Just you remember your place *meisie* and be lucky we didn't knock your teeth out like they should be if you was a good coloured girl. Old Paulie would have had it a bit easier then, eh,' he said gesturing graphically with his curled fist and opening his mouth crudely.

They left suddenly and Tina lay looking at the stars and feeling the sand gritty underneath her naked back. She thought of those stars, twinkling everlastingly in the deep navy blue infinity of the night sky. Dimly she could hear the radio still playing in the Mercedes and the sound of the Chevrolet roaring away and she felt like closing her eyes and just lying there, shutting out the horror and pain and humiliation, feeling that the beauty of the beach might somehow absolve the filth and dirt which had penetrated her mind as well as her body. Eventually, she stood up and stumbled down the narrow beach to the sea and sat down in the surf to try and wash the mess from her body. The water was freezing and salty but she sluiced it over herself until she felt reasonably cleansed by the numbing cold. Scarcely feeling her feet, she staggered back to her torn clothes and within minutes was bending over the prostrate Willi who still lay where he had fallen.

Tina rushed to the Mercedes and found the little flask of brandy which Willi always kept in the driver's seat pocket for his fishing trips. She tilted the flask, trying to dribble a little of the spirit into his partially open mouth and after a few seconds he stirred and coughed and began to mutter in German.

Willi's head felt as though it had been pushed sideways on his neck and the left side of his face was completely numb, making his speech incoherent. The whiplashing sandbag had smashed into his cheekbones and jaw, compressing the bones and narrowing the channels by which the facial nerves linked up to the muscles. The result was that one side of his face was temporarily paralysed and the left eye began to water because it was continually open. The left side of his neck and shoulder had also suffered from the single massive blow and the skin was already turning bluish-purple.

Willi felt totally disorientated, there was an odd ringing noise in his ears and he saw double. He swallowed some brandy and tried to shake his head but the pain was excruciating and he fell back moaning until the liquor burned deep into his vitals bringing back warmth and a little reality. Slowly he sat up again and after a while his vision cleared a little and he tried to speak.

'Did they hurt you?' he mouthed to the watery image of Tina that he saw peering closely at him. She shook her head and looked away and then in a rush the realisation hit him that she had been raped.

'Oh Christ, no my darling,' he moaned, 'not all of them, they didn't did they?' Tears began to spill from the girl's big black eyes and Willi Heim broke down and wept in his frustration and impotence, shattered by his uselessness and the shaming inability to protect his woman.

They clutched each other and then Willi stumbled to his feet and they managed to get to the car. Soon they were moving out of the lay-by and back onto the coast road heading west towards Cape Town. It was well past one o'clock and no traffic passed them in either direction as they slowly drove down to Clifton and the apartment. Willi turned straight into the parking garage and Tina protested that she should go home so that he could call a doctor and have his bruising attended to but the German insisted that she stay with him and soon they were inside the big apartment, safe and warm in the comfortable lounge. Willi's jaw was hurting a lot, a steady dull ache which throbbed through his head, but they showered together, the hot clean water driving some of the horror and pain from their bodies. Tina brushed her teeth five times and then took the brandy bottle and fell into the big bed, followed by Willi after he had swallowed a handful of aspirin with a glass of water.

In the warmth and comfort of the bed it all seemed a horrible dream and they lay in each other's arms talking quietly. After two brandies the pain in Willi's jaw slowly diminished and he knew that he could see the doctor in the morning and have the bruising attended to. The girl felt the soreness in her body where she had been violated by the three men and swallowed again instinctively, trying to drive the revulsion of the fourth from her mind.

It did not take Willi long to arrive at a decision and he talked softly to the dark head buried on his shoulder.

'I want to marry you Tina darling,' he rushed on before she could answer. 'We must leave here next month and we'll first go to Germany and maybe London where I have some good friends. Then perhaps we could try the States or Australia. There's so many places *schatzie* and I just want to be with you always.' He was silent for a moment thinking that Tina had fallen asleep, almost to himself he said, 'Nobody will hurt you again like those animals tonight my pet, I'll look after you properly from now on.' He kissed her tenderly on her wet black hair.

Tina had listened unbelievingly. It was all a dream, this terrible and now wonderful night. She had never dared to think that Willi would ever actually want to marry her and was quite content to be with him when she could, although she had known recently that he felt more for her than just a casual sexual attraction.

'Oh Willi, do you mean it?' she said breathlessly. 'But what about your work?'

'To hell with that,' said Heim. 'I can start again anywhere with the contacts I've got and we'll keep the Company going here, old Gunther can take over, he's very capable and I'll come over once or twice a year. Don't worry *liebling*, I can look after us well enough anywhere, I've got quite a lot of money in Germany still and the family is not short you know.' He paused, thinking quickly of all he would be giving up in South Africa and the idyllic life he had had for the past four years in Cape Town.

'We'll both miss South Africa, Tina, but we'll find other things and we could never risk getting married here or even living together permanently because of the stupid fucking laws.' He continued to talk quietly of all the things she had never seen and Tina murmured a few words and then fell asleep contentedly curled on his shoulder.

After a few more minutes the pain in his neck and face slackened to just a dull ache and Willi too fell asleep, drifting in a shallow exhausted state, dreaming of faceless coloureds thrashing around on top of a prostrate, screaming Tina. Despite himself, these images proved strangely erotic and he awoke as dawn was breaking and a dim grey light filled the apartment. He was hard and aching for the girl who lay asleep beside him and gently and patiently he began to stroke and caress her into semi-conciousness. Soon she began to move demandingly in her state of half-sleep and he entered her carefully from the side and then lay still, holding himself back and feeling her moving involuntarily, drawing him deeper inside her. In the cocoon-like softness of the big bed the happenings of the night were driven away as they made love in sleepy abandon, yet with great tenderness.

Thankfully it was Saturday morning and they stayed in bed until after eleven when Willi got up and went to the doctor in Seapoint. The entire side of his face and neck was a yellowish purple mass of bruising yet the pain had almost subsided and it looked far worse than it was.

Two hours later he drove the scratched and dented 350SL along Main Road Seapoint heading back to the apartment and Tina. On the seat beside him were two bottles of Moet et Chandon, six Kronenbrau lagers, crisp French bread and a pot of pâté de foie gras. He'd got some nice Brie too, plus grapes, spring onions, lettuce, individual creme bruleés and chocolate ice cream. For Sunday he had some thick fillet steaks and two bottles of

Nederburg Cabernet Sauvignon '73. They would stay in the penthouse, sunbathe on the terrace and watch the new videos. Perhaps they'd go to the beach late on Sunday afternoon and then on Monday he'd start organising the move back to Europe.

Willi's face was hidden by large goggle sunglasses which belonged to Tina and a bunch of young girls in tight T-shirts and tiny shorts smiled and giggled as the slow-moving Mercedes stopped to allow them access to a pedestrian crossing. Willi smiled back because he was happy inside, somehow he felt that from here on his life was taking on a new meaning and he thought of all the beautiful things that he could show Tina – who had been raised in poverty and had always been regarded as a second-class person. The smile hurt his jaw and he thought of his doctor's questions and the answers he had given about the fight in a bar at the harbour. The old German doctor had asked if Willi had reported the matter to the police. No, Willi had said, explaining that he had been with a bunch of coloured girls. The old man had shaken his head in amazement.

Gerrit never learned of the rape of his beautiful sister. Now she had virtually left home and he presumed that she was living with the German in Clifton. They were taking a risk, he thought. Although a lot of continentals craved the Malay girls and lived with them quite openly, it only needed one or two complaints or a bit of a riot situation to develop and the police would have the lot in gaol, or out of the country if they were foreign passport holders.

He despised Tina's preoccupation with wealth and materialism and never realised that, in her own way, she loved Willi Heim. Most weekends she still came out to Goodwood to visit their mother and sometimes Willi would bring her in the car and hang around, arrogantly ignoring both Gerrit and Koos and behaving condescendingly towards their mother and her tatty hovel of a home.

Tina always brought money, sometimes twenty rand at a time, and the old woman would spend it all on the liquor and wine which kept her in a permanent alcoholic miasma for most of the week. Gerrit knew that there was no chance for his mother now and realised that she couldn't live much longer – deteriorating kidneys forced her to the hospital every three days.

Gerrit had progressed quite well at work and was now earning enough money to save quite a significant amount each month and had bought his car, a 1972 Audi 100 which was all he needed and fairly economical on fuel. Koos had left school at Christmas and was working as an apprentice motor mechanic at a Parow Ford dealers. He too had bought his Kawasaki motorcycle, on hire purchase, and was seldom at home before midnight so that Gerrit had to sit each evening with his alcoholic mother, bearing the brunt of her ramblings and waiting for the day when she died so that he could be free to sell the shack-like house and split the proceeds with Koos. Then he would move away from the depressing place in which he had been born.

One Saturday, in April, Tina failed to appear for the second week running and Mrs de Kock began to whine that her children no longer cared for her. The old woman identified strongly with her beautiful daughter, seeing in her, her own wasted youth now transformed into material successes which manifested themselves in wonderful clothes and French perfumes. Her addled mind regarded her daughter as the most successful of her children and although Tina had only worked as a receptionist, it had never occurred to her mother to question the origin of the girl's plentiful supply of cash.

Gerrit silently tolerated his mother's complaints all weekend and on Monday he telephoned Heim Import Export and asked for Mr Heim. A Miss Winkler told him that Mr Heim had left for Germany for an unspecified period, would he like to speak to Mr Gunther Fuchs who had taken over from Mr Heim in the interim? Gerrit replaced the receiver and knew then that Tina had gone too; Heim must have organised a passport for her and she had left South Africa, probably forever.

This would kill his mother, he thought, and he did not relish breaking the news to her. As far as he was concerned, he was pleased to see the back of Tina because he had never been close to his sister, especially since the day when he was fifteen and she had walked into the bathroom without knocking and caught him masturbating. He regarded her as a money-hungry slut and dismissed her from his mind, closing her off like an obsolete piece of equipment in the factory downstairs. The same applied to his stupid brother, he thought, as he busied himself with the plant-maintenance budgets for the coming year.

The sooner he was rid of all of them the better because he couldn't be hindered by a dependent family in what he knew he was destined for in life. So far the details had not crystallised properly but he knew that he was going to make his mark and in the meantime he had plenty of time. He glanced across at Gail, the financial director's pretty blonde secretary and noticed the black sweater displaying her prominent breasts to perfection. He wondered what she'd be like in bed. Oh yes, he thought, I'll have that too soon enough. He smiled to himself. Everything comes to he who waits, he quoted silently and bent to his work.

Major Hendrik Vosloo of the South African Police, Seapoint, was pleased that Heim had left the country with the coloured girl de Kock. He had received three complaints about them in the last two weeks and they had all come from the Jewish residents of the apartment block overlooking fourth beach Clifton where Heim had rented the penthouse. Of course, he had known of Heim's relationship with the girl for a lot longer than that but such things were happening so often these days in the Cape that there was an unwritten instruction from Pretoria virtually to ignore all but the most blatant cases. As little publicity as possible, that was the official view these days.

In the old days of course it had been quite different. Vosloo remembered the famous case in the early seventies of the German immigrant Ruediger Krebs who had fallen in love with the young coloured girl, Veronica Williams. The couple had lived together quite openly in Barberton, up in the Eastern Transvaal and after a time the girl had produced a child which they had called Uta. This had been too much for the local residents and action had been called for.

Somehow, the young couple had got wind of the fact that they were about to be charged under the Immorality Act and had taken off without warning, heading for the bush with their baby daughter in tow. They were finally arrested just over the Mozambique frontier after a long hike through swamps and thick bush and the then Portuguese authorities had returned them to the South African police. After a brief hearing they had been transferred to jail in Barberton.

When the matter finally came to court, it was revealed that Miss Williams had applied for a passport to leave the country legally but this had been rejected by Pretoria without reasons being given. Mr Krebs' father had written to the Minister of the Interior appealing for a passport for his son's fiancée or at least an exit permit. He offered all expenses and air fares for the couple and their child so that the South African government would not have to be responsible for any financial outlay. Eventually the three were released from prison on direct instructions from the Attorney General and allowed to leave the Republic on exit permits; never to return.

Vosloo had records of all these meaty cases and had been instructed to bear them in mind when making any arrests in the sensitive Cape region, especially in the case of foreign nationals who were permanent residents of South Africa. His job in this area was not an easy one because so many of the bloody coloureds looked white anyhow and some applied for re-classification and in fact became whites so you couldn't really tell where the hell you were. He had to admit that some of the Malay girls were bloody fantastic looking though, and he had tried a couple in the past himself, and by Christ did they only love it. The one Heim had was a real cracker and he'd have loved to give her one personally. It had been six years now since he'd had a bit of chocolate.

He continued to glance through the thick file considering the risk involved in cohabitating with a coloured girl. To be caught in the act was an unthinkable scandal and there had been a lot of blokes who had committed suicide after being charged under the Immorality Act because the publicity and shame of the trial had been just too much for them. Of course, foreign nationals just got sent out of the country on exit permits which meant that they were banned for life from the Republic and quite a few Germans had been handled that way without the bloody English language press getting onto the stories.

There had been another German case involving a white German girl and the son of the coloured politician, old M.D. Arendse. They'd got married in Freiburg, Switzerland, in 1972 despite the refusal of the South African Embassy in Switzerland to issue a certificate of marriage for a foreign country to the Arendse boy. Vosloo supposed that the Ministry of the Interior were worried that young Arendse might bring the German girl back to South Africa and start strolling about Cape Town with her. Christ, that would have only caused the shit to hit the fan; but the couple had had the last word anyway by reproducing the South African letter of refusal on their wedding invitations. It had read 'Due to the prohibition of mixed marriages act of 1949 (amended Act 21 1968)' etc., and had resulted in the three hundred guests at the reception in Switzerland being given first-hand knowledge of the Republic's apartheid policy. It had caused a lot of very bad publicity and, for reasons like this, Vosloo had held back on Heim and the de Kock girl.

Vosloo closed his file on the most publicised Immorality Act cases of the past fifteen years and picked up the

33

photographs of Heim and the girl. They pictured them holding hands in Main Road, Seapoint, driving in the Mercedes and leaving Heim's apartment block together at 7.30 in the morning. Young Frikkie de Beer had taken the shots from a patrol car with a telephoto-equipped Nikon and they were very clear and could have been used successfully as evidence had Vosloo decided to open a docket against the couple. He had Tina de Kock's full record and family details and noted that she had an elder brother, a copy of whose identity document was included. Even the Xerox showed that the youth was quite good looking although he had the coloured's typical crissy hair and darker skin than his sister. Vosloo thought he looked intelligent and his policeman's mind was satisfied to discover that the young man was described as having an IQ 'in excess of 130'. The major closed the file and returned it to the cabinet thinking that some of these Capeys were clever, in fact a few were exceptional. The information he had just read slotted into his subconscious – Gerrit de Kock, IQ 130 plus. An unusual coloured alright.

Later that night there was a disturbance reported in the coloured settlement south of Hout Bay where a group of particularly violent fishermen and fish processing workers lived. The Seapoint catcher van which was patrolling the Clifton area was contacted and told to make an investigation; the time was 2205 hours exactly. A police reservist, Roger Wright was sharing the van with Jeannie Walker, an experienced regular policewoman of which there were quite a number in the Peninsula area. Wright enjoyed his police duties, which were purely voluntary, and each Friday he looked forward to the unusual experiences he often came across. It was quite different from selling insurance all week.

The three-gear Chevrolet van thundered up the coast road towards the dark bulk of the mountains on the same road that Willi Heim and Tina de Kock had taken exactly six weeks earlier en route to the Langoustine restaurant. But on this night, the sea was grey and angry and blustering winds rocked the vehicle so that Wright had to grip the wheel hard as the big van cleared the neck of the mountain and rolled down into Hout Bay.

'What a shitty night,' said policewoman Walker who was able to swear and curse with the best of the Seapoint regulars, and Wright nodded, smiling, as they drove out along the harbour to the coloured area past the fish factories.

Wright slowed the van as they approached the collection of tin huts, clapboard shanties and small brick houses. It was immediately obvious that the situation was ugly and he felt the reassuring bulk of the police issue Smith and Wesson .38 revolver, holstered securely in the old-fashioned Sam Browne combination belt. Jeannie Walker was out of the cab in seconds, without even calling in on the radio, and Wright followed, grabbing his truncheon and running after the sturdy figure of the policewoman. He slowed indecisively when he saw the mob of coloureds, reading the mood accurately and wondering whether to return to the van and call the station.

'Come on Roger, for fuck's sake,' shouted Walker and so Wright carried on, knowing instinctively that he was walking into something rather dangerous.

As usual, on Friday night, the fucking coloureds have to get motherless, thought Wright as he surveyed the sullen muttering mob who had now encircled the two police officers and cut off their retreat to the van. He looked around nervously, Christ, now I can't even get back to the radio, he thought, and touched the butt of the Smith and Wesson, wishing that he had the sergeant with him instead of Jeannie Walker, tough old bird though she was.

It appeared that a drunken coloured woman had smashed a wine bottle and ground it into the face of her equally inebriated husband. The effects were terrible and the husband, a man of about forty, was horribly lacerated with his entire face ripped open and great flaps of skin hanging from his cheeks displaying his top jaw in a grotesque mask.

Sickened, Wright approached him and saw that the man appeared to be in shock and merely sat, holding one hand to his face, the blood pouring down his arm. One of the eyes had gone and was a raw bloody socket but the other eye stared palely out of the gory mess of a face and a low continuous moan issued from the mangled lips.

There were now about fifty coloureds of assorted ages surrounding the stricken man and Wright felt real fear as he saw Jean Walker grab the accused woman and start dragging her towards the van.

'Call for an ambulance Roger,' she shouted pulling the screaming woman along behind her. The crowd reacted with a growl and the young daughter of about thirteen who had been clutching her mother's arm rushed over to Wright and lifted up her skirt to reveal skinny thighs and naked hairless pubes.

'You can fuck me mister, so long as you let my Ma go,' she shouted, thrusting herself at Wright who recoiled in horror. Policewoman Walker belted the girl across the head.

'You rude little bitch, cover yourself and get into the house,' she roared, but instead the child rushed at her screaming and trying to claw her face. Wright still hung back helplessly as the child was smashed to the ground again by the enraged policewoman. Then the crowd seemed to go mad and everything happened at once.

First they started on Jeannie Walker. A man swung at her with a bottle, catching her on the shoulder and breaking the collar bone, effectively immobilising her left arm. Despite the pain, Walker grabbed for her revolver in its waist holster but the man struck again, connecting with the back of the big woman's head so that she fell onto the filthy cobbles and disappeared under a horde of bodies, all trying to kick and punch her. Wright saw blades flash and screamed for them to stop and then drew his Smith and

Wesson and fired into the air so that they all suddenly fell back from the woman and turned towards him. He had a glimpse of the policewoman's half-naked body, displaying an old-fashioned brassiere and garish pink suspenders. Somebody had stabbed her twice already and she seemed to be unconscious, blood covering her stomach and thighs.

'Keep back or I'll fire,' he said hopelessly, knowing instinctively that he had no chance now.

A group of youths charged Wright who fired into them wildly, dropping one, before the rest were onto him and he felt jarring blows on his head and chest. He fell, feeling feet pounding him and blows raining down on his head and he began to feel less as the intensity increased. Then suddenly there was the hot and cold searing pain in his stomach and he saw the long skinning knife drawn out from just below his waistband and plunged in again. The agony hit him and he screamed and then a man pulled back his head from behind and he felt the cold slicing movement stroking across his throat and then the blackness came and funny little red and yellow dots filled his vision. Soon, they went out and he couldn't seem to hear or see anymore and then a big black curtain enveloped him and it didn't matter that he couldn't breathe.

The Hout Bay riots sparked off minor racial confrontations in the Cape which spread throughout the Peninsula to all coloured areas and would have been taken up by the coloureds and blacks in the Transvaal, had not the authorities acted swiftly. It had been ninety minutes before a second police vehicle had approached Hout Bay that night and by then the outbuildings of the fish processing plant were blazing and the fires had been reported by sixteen independent residents in the village some four kilometres across the bay.

The second patrol van had sensibly stopped short of the conflagration and radioed for assistance so that a contingent of camouflage-clad riot police, led by a young lieutenant, were dispatched from the central police station in Cape Town. Nearing the scene in their Hippo armoured personnel carriers, these paramilitary units were immune to the bottles, stones and occasional Molotov cocktails which were thrown at them. The riot police had strict instructions not to use anything but established riot techniques and, after some fifteen minutes, they had successfully driven back the mob of around three hundred people, using teargas and the occasional volley of rubber bullets.

By one o'clock in the morning the whole matter seemed to be well in hand and the lieutenant was congratulating himself on his restraint when, without warning, there were two loud cracking explosions and several of his men dropped, blasted off their feet by what were later found to be Chinese fragmentation grenades apparently lobbed from the hill behind the fish processing plant. There was utter silence for a few seconds and then the flat whiplashing sound of a Kalashnikov AK 47 rifle galvanised the shocked police into action and they scattered, frantically changing the magazines on their R1 rifles and taking up defensive positions in and around their vehicles.

The crowd fell back in panic as the police opened up, their 7.62mm bullets punching great clouds of dust and dirt into the air as they blasted the hill and the upper floors of the processing plant, illuminated by hastily erected searchlights. Inevitably, some non-combatants were struck by ricochets and wild shots but still the AKs kept firing at the Hippos, bullets clanging off the metal sides and whining away into the night. Eventually, the situation became chaotic with the police firing their rifles on full automatic, expending the magazines in seconds. This caused the shooting to become more inaccurate because the R1, a copy of the NATO FN, is not ideally designed for such use and the barrel rises up in an arc from left to right.

Towards two o'clock Vosloo arrived with his riot police opposite number and together the two officers managed to halt the firing. By then it was raining steadily and the area was totally deserted except for the nineteen coloured dead who lay sprawled on the greasy cobbles. Amongst them were four women and three children including the daughter of the woman who had started the trouble. In addition, six people were badly injured and three policemen had died from bullet wounds and grenade fragments whilst four others had serious injuries.

Walker and Wright had of course been dead for some hours. Vosloo knew that the situation could explode again at any moment and called for reinforcements to patrol the area. He also requested a forensic detachment to examine the grenade fragments and spent bullets. It was unbelievable that communist weapons had somehow managed to be cached here in Hout Bay and used against the police. Oh Christ, he thought, as he saw the bodies being carted away into the ambulances, now we've really got a fucking problem to handle.

'What a fucking lousy night,' he said aloud to Johann Mostert, the riot police major, and walked off disgustedly towards his car.

CHAPTER 3

Gerrit read the early reports in the *Cape Times* which was lying on his desk when he reached the office. Few details were given, other than an embroidered account of the police bulletin which he had heard on Radio Good Hope whilst driving the Audi into Parow. By lunchtime a few more facts had been revealed, primarily the shocking news that twenty-one coloured people had died, amongst them women and children. It was also stated that in total, six police officers had lost their lives, one of these being policewoman Walker who had been brutally slaughtered with reservist constable Wright when they had first investigated the matter.

No mention had been made of the attack on the police with grenades and automatic weapons, now established as being two AKs, and the lack of these facts being made public served to fan the flames of outrage against the authorities who were accused of using armed troops against defenceless civilians. Nobody seemed to know how the policemen had died, except for Wright and Walker, and the Commissioner of Police for the Cape Peninsula was not telling either. The report added that the Hout Bay harbour area had been sealed off whilst police continued with their investigations into the basic cause of the unrest. Riot police units were continuing to patrol the area.

Feeling desperately angered by the shootings, Gerrit read of the useless statements of regret made by the leaders of the Coloured Representative Council and other coloured political figures. That was not the way to solve these things, he thought, as he busied himself with his work, trying to ignore the solicitous behaviour of his white colleagues in the office. Some had patted his shoulder, murmuring inanities and others had called him on the internal telephone to offer stupid words of sympathy, presumably because they regarded him almost as an equal. He had muttered polite thanks and agreed with their allegedly sincere statements about uncontrolled use of police power and overt brutality against unarmed civilians. There were others of course who did not mention the shootings and Gerrit actually admired them because they at least were not hypocritical like his so-called friends.

He knew quite well that many of the average English-speaking white South Africans would always decry such shows of force by the police and military, seeming to identify themselves tenuously with the caucasian critics of South Africa in Europe and the United States. In actual fact he maintained that a large proportion of these so-called liberals continued to vote Nationalist, thus keeping the government in power by an overwhelming majority. By these means, they secured their superb lifestyle whilst excusing their actions by explaining to their circle of friends and to themselves, that, with the advent of such enlightened men as Foreign Minister Pik Botha, things were changing fast. Gerrit reckoned that most thinking white people in South Africa would see Botha as the country's man of destiny but to Gerrit he appeared as an unusually silver-tongued Boer whose psuedo-sincerity was so apparent that it almost seemed to be sprayed on like a deodorant.

With his immediate superior away in Johannesburg, Gerrit was again working in the big office with the financial director's secretary Gail Wilson. The girl was unusually silent today, seeming to be personally embarrassed by the Hout Bay situation and unable to discuss it

41

with the young coloured man with whom she normally chatted quite openly. Gail considered Gerrit to be good looking in a way and she admired his indisputably excellent brain without the help of which her boss would be somewhat lost.

In line with the clean executive look that he now wished to portray, Gerrit had recently shaved off the wispy moustache and cut his Afro hair down to a neat rounded style which just touched his ears and the collar of his white shirt. Unlike the other coloureds downstairs in the plant, he wore conservative colours, neat shirts and ties and had taken to spraying himself with cologne after shaving each morning. It was one of the little luxuries he allowed himself, like the John Player Special cigarettes of which he smoked ten a day. Next on the list of possessions was the gold Dunhill lighter which he intended to buy at the end of the month. He could in fact afford it easily right now but preferred to wait; that way he would appreciate it more.

Today Gerrit had smoked four cigarettes by ten o'clock and Gail Wilson noticed his obvious distress and eventually plucked up courage to raise the matter.

'Don't take it to heart Gerry,' she said softly, instinctively knowing what was troubling him. The intense brown eyes looked up from the computer playouts and regarded her steadily, running up and down her body from face to waist so that she suddenly felt hot under his gaze.

He replied equally softly, 'I'm not taking it to heart Gail. I just feel so hurt because of the way my people are treated.' He failed to recognise the fact that he had said 'my people' and continued in a voice at once emotional and compelling. The girl listened spellbound.

'You don't know what it's like to be coloured, Gail. How could you know, when you are blond and beautiful, an obvious white, almost like an advertisement for strong and healthy South Africa.' Gerrit knew that in fact Gail was English but she did not deny the description. 'I am fortunate to have been blessed with an above average brain,' he continued, 'but undoubtedly I could have gone further and faster up the ladder had it not been for my colour and the way it's regarded by the whites in this country.' He laughed harshly. 'With my sister it was different. She too was of above-average intellect, but it was her looks that got her started on the road to success. Now she's disappeared overseas with a German leaving a dying mother behind. I can't imagine that she'll be coming back, can you?' The intensity of his voice had increased, although the pitch was low and the girl was transfixed now, hanging on every word. This was Gerrit's first attempt at oratory and he could appreciate the effect of his words, even as he was saying them.

'Let us imagine that I wanted to ask you, Gail, out to dinner.' The girl reddened again and looked down at her desk. 'Don't be embarrassed,' said Gerrit. 'I can easily afford to take you to any restaurant in this city and I can tell you that I find you very attractive. I'm quite a normal man you know, although some people here think I'm a sort of coffee-coloured book-keeping and cost-accounting machine. Now I know, as you do Gail, that there are quite a lot of continental guys here in Cape Town who take out coloured girls quite openly and some even live with them. But you don't see that many white girls with coloured men, do you?'

Gail Wilson trembled, strangely fascinated by this man who totally captured her with his words. As if for the first time, she noticed his strong chin and brilliant white teeth and the fine features bordered by the tightly curled black hair. But it was the eyes that bored into her, seeming to strip her physically and mentally, leaving her drained and unable to resist. This man has power she thought, and he's quite brilliant. I don't think I could say no to him whatever he asked of me.

The moment was shattered by the telephone which rang softly on Gerrit's desk. He picked it up and muttered a few words of thanks and then turned to Gail again, his eyes burning. 'We'll talk again Gail, won't we.' It was a statement, not a question, and she nodded mechanically.

43

He smiled, a wonderful winning smile which lit up his whole face, making him boyish looking and almost beautiful. Then it was gone, but the feeling was there now between them and both recognised it like a tangible thing that was electric to the touch. Koos would call it a vibe, thought Gerrit, feeling warm inside and excited by his effect on the girl.

That night in her small flat in Gardens, a suburb below Table Mountain, just north of the city centre, Gail lay awake thinking of Gerrit de Kock. She had none of the ingrained congenital horror of race mixing which was inherent in most South Africans, because she had only been in the country for two years. In London, she'd had an Indonesian boyfriend who was slim and beautiful and the most marvellous lover she'd ever had. He had left London eventually, to go back to Bangkok or somewhere, and for some time afterwards European men had seemed clumsy, repellant and boorish to her. Gail stroked herself under the light duvet, imagining Gerrit's slim muscular body, and her hands began to move faster as she closed her eyes and lost herself in her own erotic fantasies.

CHAPTER 4

Major Mostert's men had found the ejected cartridge cases and ballistic tests had established that they had been fired from two different AKs. The team had recovered 118 cases which indicated that four thirty-shot magazines had been fired, probably two to each rifle. The terrorists, as they were now labelled, had been on the roof of the processing plant and very few police bullets had come anywhere near them. There was no sign of the weapons or magazines and, despite the fact that a cordon had been thrown around the entire Hout Bay area and every house, white and coloured had been searched, nothing had been found.

Although the police had tried to keep the matter suppressed, the cordon had raised many questions and the story had got out to the press after only two days. Now it was Tuesday and an official statement was made by the Minister of the Interior to the effect that a group of terrorists, probably not more than four, had taken advantage of a domestic incident to incite unrest. Police were investigating the matter thoroughly and it was expected that the terrorists and their supply organisation would soon be discovered. In the meantime, said the Minister, the incident only served to illustrate that the Republic of South Africa was under constant attack by an increasingly well organised network of ANTISA forces, as they were now called. All the people of the country must strive as one to unite against the enemies of South Africa's

45

sovereignty, he had said and had finished by saying that anyone who had even the slightest and most innocuous piece of possible information about the Hout Bay attack must please come forward in the interests of national security.

Mostert watched the television news bulletin in his comfortable three-bedroomed home in the Cape Town suburb of Rondebosch but his mind did not absorb the announcer's words. He knew that by now there were probably several such caches of communist weaponry within the country's borders and that the police and military discovered them quite regularly up in the Transvaal. He'd heard it said that there were enough grenades in Johannesburg's Alexandra coloured township to start a war; and other information that intelligence had revealed, back in the early seventies, indicated that sufficient AKs had been exported to Africa to equip every man, woman and child on the continent. In anybody's terms, that was a hell of a lot of weapons.

He had handled and fired the AK which was a superb guerilla weapon, light, easy to fire and virtually indestructible. Up on the South West African border a few years back, they'd found a cache after an informer had tipped them off, and dug the rifles out of a stinking waterhole where they must have been hidden in the dry season and never collected. The weapons were rusted up and encrusted with mud and the men had not believed what he had proved to them. Back at the base, they had taken two of the AKs and hosed them down and then jumped on them a few times and bounced them on their butts to loosen the actions. Then he'd taken two fresh magazines from a pile they'd captured earlier, and fitted them to the rifles without any trouble. While the young troopers had looked on unbelievingly, he'd set the actions on auto, cocked them and pressed the triggers, holding one rifle under each arm. Both had fired their entire thirty-shot magazines without jamming and were examined carefully afterwards for corrosion or damage. There wasn't any. That's what the terr's did with AKs that had been hidden or stored for long periods – they fired the fucking things to clean them and after that they hardly ever touched them again. It was a bloody amazing weapon.

Mostert poured himself a drink. There was the other advantage that the Kalashnikov had over the South African R1. It was incredibly accurate on automatic fire, up to two hundred metres, an unprecedented performance for a hand-held automatic rifle. It was largely due to the flash eliminator which was sliced off diagonally on the AK, making the weapon very stable. They'd experimented with R1s, cutting off the eliminator in the same way and it had improved the auto fire accuracy a bit, but it wasn't the same as the AK. All things considered, the AK was streets ahead of the R1, except for its hitting power which was some thirty per cent less due to the shorter bullet.

Mostert sipped his Oude Meester brandy and ginger ale and watched the ice cubes clinking in the amber liquid as he held it up to the table lamp. Thank God for the odd pot, he thought, or life would be bloody unbearable. He considered the weapons problem of the South African armed forces and thought longingly of the new R4 rifle which was rumoured now to be in limited production and had supposedly been supplied to some of the units on the South West African/Angola border. The new weapon was a 5.56mm job like the American M16 but was largely modelled on the Israeli Gallil multi-purpose assault rifle. It was a bit lighter than the AK and phenomenally accurate on full auto and you could change the barrel for a heavier one, which had a bi-pod and belt-feed, making it into a superb light machine gun. Mostert had seen recent films which demonstrated the new rifle in comparison tests against the R1. They'd used a sheep's carcass at one hundred metres and the R1, which was fired first, had left an exit hole about the size of an orange. Taking a fresh carcass, they'd tried the R4 and the hanging sheep had

47

almost been blown in half by the 4000 feet per second muzzle velocity of the tiny, tumbling .220 bullet. The exit hole had been as big as a football.

The other great communist bloc weapon was the RPD light machine gun which was accurate on full automatic at an incredible eight hundred metres. It used the same 7.62mm short bullet as the AK and Mostert had not believed it until he'd tried it out himself on the range in Ovamboland and riddled a jeep silhouette target at six hundred metres. If SWAPO knew how to handle these weapons properly, they'd really have their hands full up on the border but the possibility of their being used in suburban areas was really frightening. He still couldn't work out why the AKs and grenades used at Hout Bay had been there, in that small coloured township, ready for action when the stupid scene between the drunken woman and those poor bloody cops had erupted.

Things like this made one think that the buggers had similar caches all over the country and it was bloody unsettling. No wonder the government hadn't wanted to release the information to the public via the press because it was pure fucking dynamite and must have already caused a great deal of alarm. Mostert knew, however, that the public had short memories and that, barring further incidents of unrest, the whole thing would be forgotten within a week or so. By the whites of course.

He drained his brandy and poured another and a gin and tonic for his wife and wondered how his men were feeling out at Hout Bay. So far they'd managed to suppress any further trouble both there and in other coloured areas throughout the Cape and had even showed a presence in Langa and Guguletu, the two black townships, just to be on the safe side. It was all in the game, he thought. The trouble was, the bloody game was getting a bit rougher.

Not that the coloureds had always remained passive, thought Mostert moodily. Long before the first bloody Soweto riots in June 1976 and the subsequent unrest in the

Cape right through to early 1977, sporadic rioting had occurred as early as 1959 in Paarl, an old Afrikaans wine-growing area almost forty kilometres north of Cape Town. He remembered what the police had regarded as the first really political confrontation, which had taken place in March 1971 at a coloured township called Gelvandale near Port Elizabeth in the Eastern Cape. On this occasion, about ten thousand people of all ages had met at a sports field on a Sunday afternoon ostensibly to protest about the recent increase in bus fares by a commercial transport company which serviced the coloured areas of the city.

In spite of official lack of interest in what they regarded as a domestic issue, the police had patrolled the perimeter of the field in vans and also kept an eye on the bus routes to ensure that the protestors did not decide to vent their displeasure on the property of the bus company, namely the shabby single-deck buses. At this time, Mostert was heading up the newly formed riot police unit in the northern suburbs of Port Elizabeth and had been promoted to captain some months earlier. He had been off-duty at the start of that Sunday afternoon but had been called later and would never forget the scenes which had erupted.

Apparently it had all started when a police van had driven through the entrance to the sports field in order to arrest a drunk who was making a nuisance of himself on the perimeter of the crowd. The man had put up a struggle and the crowd became incensed and began to scream 'Kill the pigs' and then a few stones began to fly. One of the policemen had managed to get the man into the van and then leapt up onto the roof in order to try to harangue the crowd into calmness. The mood became even more ugly. A hail of rocks met this ploy and forced the constable into drawing his revolver which he fired into the air in an attempt to restore order. This act seemed to provoke the mob even more and the van hastily left the field pursued by stones and bottles, the constables inside shaken and bleeding.

Sensing a victory in the offing, a mob of some two

thousand had run after the police and chased them to nearby Gelvandale police station where they demanded the release of the man who had been arrested. By now, Mostert had been informed and was en route to the area from his home in central Port Elizabeth but he never reached Gelvandale station because of the peripheral activities of the crowd who recognised his vehicle by its SAP number plate and immediately attacked with rocks and bottles.

Mostert had then pulled back and described the situation to headquarters on the car radio. He could not see much of what was going on but got all the accounts of the subsequent events later when an in-depth enquiry was held. Apparently, the mob had demanded the drunk's release and began to set up roadblocks around the police station to prevent reinforcements arriving. Despite these efforts, a few patrol vans managed to reach the marooned officers within the station and eventually several police with pistols drawn faced the mob from behind the fence which surrounded the police buildings.

The rioters had become frustrated and began to stone the police and their Alsatian dogs, and missiles crashed into the buildings and parked vehicles, smashing several windows. Realising that the matter had gone far enough, the police fired teargas into the crowd but the brisk evening breeze dispersed the gas without doing much harm to the rioters who were now beyond reason. The police then decided to try a baton charge and a pitched battle broke out with the officers outnumbered by about one hundred to one. Eventually the situation became very serious and several of the police fell and then a shot was fired and suddenly all the police officers began to empty their .38 revolvers into the crowd at point-blank range.

The mob had fallen back but continued to jeer at the police, exhorting them to fire again. Incredibly there had been no deaths. The final total was nine coloureds seriously injured, one a fifteen-year-old girl and another, a pregnant woman, and there were fifteen casualties among the police, none of which was serious.

Unrest had continued for almost two weeks and Mostert remembered the various faces of the mob and recalled vividly the hatred and thirst for blood that had been so plainly obvious among the coloureds of all ages. Now that they had access to guns, the slaughter could be horrendous and one man with an AK could cut down unarmed civilians in their dozens. It was a horrifying possibility and one which had often happened in Rhodesia, but that was a different situation entirely. It could surely not happen here, in the Cape of all places. They'd have to make bloody sure that it didn't and find the weapons – if there were any more – which he knew there must be. Then there were the lines of communication that had supplied the things, they'd all have to be found and eliminated. Mostert drained his third brandy and watched the very reverend gentlemen who was reading the epilogue. He didn't hear the man or see him consciously because he had just convinced himself that the shit was about to hit the fan. It was all just beginning. He could feel it and it frightened him.

CHAPTER 5

Gerrit felt increasingly restless in the weeks following the Hout Bay riots. His mother had reacted badly to the disappearance of Tina and had begun to drink even more heavily so that recently she was almost permanently paralytic, only rising from her bed for the toilet and to make the twice-weekly visits to the hospital which Gerrit now considered to be useless.

She depended on him totally and he gave her the money for her alcohol without question or comment. Koos bought her the odd bottle too but the African woman who came in to clean bought most of it so that Gerrit didn't feel responsible for obviously promoting his mother's eventual demise. These days, the old woman was either asleep or rambling drunkenly, her speech incoherent and self-pitying. Gerrit would sit with her in the evenings and watch as she drank straight from the bottles of cane spirits or wine, depending on whether it was the beginning or end of the week. Often she soiled herself or vomited in the bed, turning the small bedroom in which she now lived into a stinking hole of filth and decay. Gerrit would try and ignore the smell, knowing the black woman would be in to clean up in the morning. He had to pay her twenty rand a week for these services, but it was worth it.

For the first time in months he was having a night out, leaving his mother to her own devices and justifying himself by maintaining that she probably would not be aware that he was absent anyway. The arrangements he had were with Gail Wilson and they had been carefully made with the blonde English girl who had moved into a tiny cottage at Tamboerskloof on the lower slopes of Table Mountain in Cape Town. There were a few coloureds living close to this area and a number of whites and coloureds lived together quite openly, apparently without interference from the police. He and Gail had discussed the matter at length and decided that he would not be taking any undue risks if he went to the cottage for dinner. She would cook and he would bring the wine, it was all arranged. Gerrit looked at the gold Longines watch he had bought a few days earlier in a Parow jewellers sale and quivered inwardly. It was 4.30 exactly; in three hours he'd be alone with her.

Gail too was feeling a little apprehensive about the dinner that evening. She had no qualms about the fact that Gerrit was a coloured because, to her, coloureds were human beings like anyone else. She did recognise, however, the strong attraction that she felt for this intense young man and it was this fact that was making her stomach contract with anticipation. At lunchtime, she had gone out to the nearby shopping centre and bought a small saddle of lamb, fresh green beans and field mushrooms from the mountains. With this they would have a green salad and, afterwards, apricots in brandy which she had bottled herself last season.

By 5.45 she was home and quickly seasoning the lamb, adding fresh rosemary and a little thyme. Then she made small slits in the skin and inserted half cloves of garlic and lastly poured a little red wine over the joint. In five minutes she had the lamb in the oven and had chopped a little more garlic to brown in butter and pour over the beans; next she placed a dozen new potatoes in a saucepan and then sliced onions and tomato for the salad. Feeling unusually happy, she changed into a housecoat and pottered about, arranging the table and laying out her French crystal glasses and the old silver cutlery she had found in an antique shop in Wynberg. Finally she was satisfied that everything was perfect and ran her bath. It was already 6.30 and she had only an hour in which to get ready.

Gerrit drove across Cape Town in the Audi feeling excited, yet outwardly calm. He wore a beige cotton cheesecloth shirt and dark brown corduroy slacks with a natural canvas and leather belt. On the seat next to him was his soft suede zipper jacket and on his wrist the new gold square-faced watch. He lit a John Player Special and thought of the Dunhill lighter that he had decided to forego in favour of the Longines which was undoubtedly more of a bargain. What the hell, he thought, there was plenty of time for the lighter. All the time in the world.

At 7.40 precisely he locked the car and, carrying the wine, walked back down the hill towards the flickering light from the curtains of Gail's little corner cottage. He knocked and she opened the door immediately and he stepped quickly inside. Despite himself Gerrit gasped with a short audible intake of breath. He looked in amazement at the simple tasteful furnishings of the compact room and the elegant little table set for two. He had never seen anything so intimate and appealing or just so wonderfully correct as the interior of this minute sitting room and dining area. Gail pushed him towards the two seater sofa and pressed a button on the cassette recorder in the pine wall unit. Cat Stevens' voice filled the cosy room which glinted in the candlelight and smelled of a strange, musky perfume.

'God this is too beautiful,' said Gerrit in awe. 'How did you manage to make it so incredibly appealing?' He paused. 'No, that's not the right word Gail, it's just wonderful and so tasteful. It's you,' he added as an afterthought.

The girl glowed with pleasure at these obviously genuine remarks. As if for the first time, Gerrit noticed her and thought immediately that she was as beautiful as her little house. She wore a white cotton full-length kaftan which was slit up the sides and at the throat to reveal expanses of bronzed skin, and her corn-coloured hair was piled up on top of her head in a seemingly careless style which allowed ringlets to escape from the plain white ribbon that held the shining mass. She smelled of oranges and, as she walked in front of the table lamp, Gerrit saw her body outlined through the thin cotton. He was sure that she wore nothing underneath the kaftan and he felt himself move as he sat very correctly on the sofa.

Gail was very relaxed because she had smoked a small joint in the bath, the steam and bath-oil aroma having removed the tell-tale smell. Just to make sure though, she'd lit the sandalwood incense stick and it still smouldered in the planter behind the lamp. The grass had made her feel wonderfully tranquil but had heightened her awareness as it always did. She heard every note and nuance in the music and could smell Gerrit's cologne which she had come to know well from the office. She smiled at him and took the wine from the bag, skilfully opening the red so that it could breathe.

'What can I offer you, Gerrit?' she said huskily, taking a squat glass from the wall unit. She realised that he was still young and had obviously never experienced anything like this before. Even though she was only two years older, she felt masterful and worldly and far more experienced than this rather beautiful young coloured man who sat rigidly on her sofa, so obviously taken aback by his surroundings.

They both had a whisky and then she served the dinner which began with hot wholewheat rolls and some rather nice smooth terrine she had bought at the delicatessen on the way home. Gerrit had watched her with the pepper grinder and followed suit, marvelling at the tastes and smells he was experiencing. In a moment of truth he realised that his sister had discovered these things long before he had and that these discoveries had resulted in her single-minded ambition for advancement and her eventual disappearance with Heim.

Gerrit had never learned about the subtleties of good food and although he had never gone hungry in recent years, he had not developed any imagination for anything even resembling *haute cuisine*. Although this meal was far from that, the quality and finesse of flavour of the lamb caught him totally unprepared and he ate five of the deliciously tender loin chops, virtually without speaking for more than ten minutes. The girl watched him with pleasure and refilled his glass with the good red wine he had brought. She loved to cook and the appreciation of her food by others gave her as much pleasure as eating it.

Eventually they finished what was undoubtedly the best meal Gerrit had ever eaten and relaxed on the sofa with coffee and brandy. Slowly Gerrit began to unwind and stopped trying to watch his manners and general behaviour. After the second brandy, he became even more articulate than usual and the charismatic intensity of his voice and eyes returned to transfix Gail whose own mastery of the situation evaporated swiftly.

Gerrit could feel his effect on the girl again and eventually, he casually slipped his arm around her shoulders and was not surprised when she fell against him tremblingly. Slowly, he put his hand inside the throat of her loose gown and cupped the firm naked breast which seemed to harden at his touch. Unbelievingly, he carried on and pushed up the long skirt, moving sideways so that the girl now fell back along the length of the couch, her legs and thighs exposed. Gerrit kissed her and tasted the exquisite sweetness of her breath, and the warm citrus smell of her enveloped him. As if in a dream, he saw himself uncover her and then his face was on her naked stomach and she was pushing him down towards herself and then she opened like a flower and he smelled the clean, incredible female scent of her and he couldn't believe that it was happening to him.

In the tiny bedroom she undressed him and then took him in her hand, fascinated by his body, cupping and rubbing him until he felt he must explode. Like a cat, she rolled over on top of him and straddled him, holding him upright and sinking down slowly so that the incredible feeling seemed to go on and on as he penetrated her warmth. She seemed to move gently and then faster and suddenly it was coming and she pressed down harder and opened her mouth in a soundless scream and everything was wonderfully warm and bursting and she collapsed on his chest, her beautiful breasts pressed hard against him and her kisses covering his face like the fluttering of butterfly wings.

'You are a lovely man, you know,' she said wonderingly and settled down beside him on the pillows, her eyes poring over his face.

Sex had always been a somewhat furtive, and dirty experience to Gerrit who was by nature a person of great fastidiousness. He had been with the coloured girls in Goodwood from time to time but had found them giggly and inexperienced and above all, unwashed. There was no comparison between them and this immaculate young woman whose body was as fresh and sweet-smelling as a dew-covered field and whose lovemaking was both wanton and yet naturally beautiful. They made love again and he had fallen asleep to awaken at well after two o'clock, feeling nervous and guilty and wanting only to get away.

He knew that it was the old stigma again, of being coloured and feeling out of place in white surroundings. But here he was, in a white girl's bed lying next to her after enjoying her wonderful body. He had crossed the barrier, just like Tina had done and he knew that nothing would ever be the same again. Now, there would be no going back.

He pushed aside the tumbled blonde hair and kissed the soft cheek, beside him on the pillow, and she stirred and opened her eyes.

'Don't go, darling Gerrit,' she said softly, but he knew that she would prefer him to go, would not want to take unnecessary risks. It was unspoken between them and existed as a fact of life in the society in which they lived but he said the words anyway.

'I must go Gail, you know I must. Thank you for the most wonderful night of my life.' He rose and dressed quickly and kissed her again and already she was almost asleep, but she smiled through half closed eyes.

'Bye darling,' she murmured. 'See you tomorrow at the office.'

Gerrit drove home in total euphoria. Despite the exertions of their lovemaking, coupled with the unaccustomed wine and brandy, he felt wide awake and flung the car around the curves of the superb Cape freeways as he headed east towards Goodwood and his squalid home. As he reached the street in which he lived, he saw lights and vehicles drawn up outside his home and knew instinctively that something must have happened to his mother.

Koos greeted him curtly as he leaped from the car. 'Don't hurry Gerrit, she's dead a long time already, I came home at 12.30 and she was already cold. The doctor said it must have happened between nine and ten.'

As he pushed his way into the dingy tin-roofed nonentity that had been his home since birth, Gerrit could not help noticing the difference between this place and the beautiful little cottage he had just left. Gail's house was in fact smaller and had only one bedroom compared to the three in his home but there was no comparison in appointments, finishes or even basic cleanliness. Gail had told him that she had furnished her place for only R1200, picking up bargains here and there and putting it all together with taste and panache. That was what was lacking here, he thought, as he tried to imagine the improvements that could be made to make the place more homely and attractive. It would not be worth it though, he hated the hole and would sell it as soon as his mother had gone and then he remembered – he saw her – and his mind emptied of everything except her gaunt and hideously ravaged face.

Later the coloured doctor took him to one side and

explained that she had suffered severe renal failure and had obviously died in great pain. The body had been found doubled up on the floor of the bedroom and the agony must have been considerable because she had chewed her lips and bitten clean through her tongue. The neighbours had been unable to do anything and had called the hospital but it had taken an hour for the ambulance to arrive and a further twenty minutes before he, the doctor had managed to get there. By then she was dead because the black ambulance men had been afraid to move her, but they had given her some morphine to try to ease the pain. She hadn't said much, just screamed for Tina all the time and had not mentioned Gerrit or Koos' name. The doctor looked serious and said that she would have died anyway because he had checked the case history and seen that the kidneys were badly diseased. He was prepared to bet that one, if not both, had failed completely and even one remaining kidney could never have sufficed on its own.

Gerrit arrived at the office as usual the next day which was Wednesday. He told none of his colleagues of his mother's death and even concealed the news from Gail whom he didn't see at all in the morning. In the afternoon she called him on the internal phone, her voice soft and concerned.

'Is something the matter Gerrit?' she asked quietly. 'What's the problem, don't you like me now, or something? You could at least have called me this morning and said hello.'

He could hear the hurt in her voice and could not hide the reason for his silence from her. His feelings were mixed, even confused. He had loved his mother as a child but, as is often the case with old and ailing relations, had lost a great deal of respect for her as he grew into adulthood and despite himself, began to despise her lack of intellect. Her incapacity and ill-health, which was largely self-induced, seemed to engender increased lack of feelings rather than sympathy. They had grown apart and

59

he did not really regret her death because in a way he had been waiting for it, even looking forward to it, although irrationally he had somehow never believed it would happen.

'My mother died last night, Gail,' he said quietly and heard her gasp.

'Oh Gerrit, oh God how awful, Gerrit.' She paused. 'Then I must see you very soon, tonight please, oh please say you can make it tonight Gerrit, you need someone who cares for you at this time.'

Gerrit paused and heard the sound of a door opening on the other end of the line and a male voice speaking and then Gail's tone changed completely.

'OK, Gerrit,' she said. 'I'll look for those schedules and I'm sorry to hear about your mother, really. I'll call you when I've located the pages, bye now.'

She called again just before five and he could tell that she was not alone for long because her tone was guarded and hurried. 'Please come tonight Gerrit, I need to see you.' She paused when he failed to answer. 'I'll be waiting after eight then,' she said swiftly and the phone clicked and went dead before he could answer.

Gerrit did not go to Gail that night because he had to try and think, try to work out his life of which she now seemed to have become an indefinable part. He waited for Koos to come home and his younger brother arrived at 9.30 and it was obvious that he had been drinking. The black housekeeper had cleaned up his mother's room and they had taken her away to the mortuary and he and Koos sat alone at the shabby dining table where they had eaten all their meals with Tina and their parents since they could walk. Gerrit produced his mother's last bottle of cane spirits, some orange cordial and water.

'We have to talk Koos,' he said seriously. 'I intend to sell this house and you will get one third of the proceeds, as will Tina and myself. I shall keep Tina's share until she collects it and have already hopefully contacted her via Heim's Company who must know where he is.' Koos nodded blankly and Gerrit continued.

'I expect we'll realise about nine or ten thousand for the house so you should get around three thousand rand and with that money you've got to sort out somewhere to live and try to save or invest the balance. I'll happily handle that for you if you want.'

Koos nodded again. 'It will be funny not coming home here anymore Gerrit,' he said hestitantly, taking a long pull from his cane and orange. Suddenly his eyes filled with tears and he slumped forward, sobbing onto the table top. 'Oh God, we should have looked after her better, she was the only mother we had and we let her die like that, oh Christ, I'll never forgive myself for her pain, that terrible pain that she must have gone through last night.'

Gerrit stood up and walked around the table and put his arm around his brother's thin shoulders. 'Koos,' he said quietly. 'You know she couldn't have lived much longer. Her kidneys were finished and neither of us could ever have stopped her drinking. Believe me, it's not our fault, it was the first night I had left her for months but even if I'd been here, she would have gone anyway. I spoke to the doctor and the results of the post mortem confirmed his original diagnosis. She had no chance Koos, no chance at all with kidneys that had failed completely.'

This information seemed to make Koos even more upset and he broke down, sobbing like a child and holding onto Gerrit's arm. After some minutes he stopped shudderingly and stood up, shaking his head as if disgusted with his emotional outburst.

'Do what you think is right Gerrit,' he said roughly. 'I'll leave it all to you. Now I'm off to bed because I've had enough for one day. I'll see you in the morning probably, and if not at the funeral, OK.'

Gerrit went to bed soon after but could not sleep. His mind seethed with a maelstrom of tangental thoughts and it was as if he were unable to turn off his over-active brain. Eventually, bleary-eyed, he took a notebook and pencil from his briefcase and jotted down the various things that he had to attend to and towards dawn he finally fell into a shallow sleep and dreamed of Gail and her firm tawny body. He would send her flowers to the office because he wouldn't be going in that day. His reminder to himself about the flowers was one of the first things on the list.

Tina de Kock received the news of her mother's death an hour before she was due to be buried in the coloured cemetery at Elsie's River, Cape. The telegram arrived without warning at twelve o'clock German time whilst she had been waiting for Willi to come back for lunch from his various meetings in Munich. The communication was couched in Gerrit's typically terse prose and merely said, 'Mother died 20.00 hours last night stop funeral Thursday at Elsie's River cemetery stop more news later stop Gerrit.'

Tina's eyes had prickled but no tears had formed and when Willi came back at one o'clock to their hotel, she had showed him the cable quite dry-eyed and he had marvelled at her poise.

'There's no point in me dashing off back immediately Willi,' Tina said calmly. 'I can't get there for the funeral anyway and tomorrow we're off to London. I'll wait until Gerrit writes and then see what's happening with the house etcetera. He's good at that sort of thing and he'll handle it alright.'

Willi nodded and smiled at his beautiful wife. All his friends had raved about her and some had made obvious passes because they were so captivated. They certainly made a fantastic looking couple, everybody had said, and even his parents had adored her after a week or so.

In the four short months since they'd left South Africa, Tina had changed fantastically, becoming fabulously well-groomed with the new clothes he'd bought her. She'd always been a great dresser, of course, and on her body everything looked superb, but now she had more than just looks. It was as if Europe seemed to have instilled in her an instant sophistication, as if all the culture and breeding that she had missed in her life had now been found and retained instantaneously. Already she spoke a bit of conversational German and as soon as they decided where they were going to settle she'd learn it properly at a language laboratory.

So far so good, thought Willi. He'd made some great new contacts since they'd been back in Germany and the economy was booming with the Deutschmark never stronger. There seemed to be many and varied opportunities everywhere and already he'd found some new winners for the Cape Town office and had sold about eighty thousand marks' worth of karakul rugs to a carpet wholesaler in Munich. Tomorrow they were off to London and various new possibilites and then he'd tentatively planned a visit to the States in May and in between they'd live in Dusseldorf in the block where his parents stayed. The old people owned the entire block and always kept a flat free for guests or family.

Willi took his wife's hand and pulled her to him. There was perhaps a little more moisture than usual in those fantastic liquid brown eyes but the incredible mouth smiled with only a tiny tremble of the lower lip.

'When I go back to Cape Town, you will come with me won't you, Willi?' she said with a slight catch in her voice. 'I couldn't bear to be apart from you and halfway across the world.'

Heim smiled and kissed Tina. '*Schatz*' he said warmly. 'I will never leave you alone unless it's absolutely necessary, you know that. Of course I'll come back to Cape Town, I love the place and you are my wife now and hold all the privileges of a citizen of the Federal Republic of Germany.' Tina smiled happily now and pulled his mouth down to hers. They had lunch in the room and spent most of the afternoon in bed.

In Elsie's River it was raining and the southeaster lashed the small group of mourners as the remains of Nelly de

Kock were lowered into the damp brown earth in a simple pine coffin. Gerrit and Koos stood together, heads bowed and shoulders hunched as the rain spattered against their bent backs and the coloured minister droned on interminably. Koos had been drinking again at lunchtime and swayed a little on his feet so that Gerrit had to nudge him into full consciousness from time to time. His younger brother did not possess a suit and wore a white shirt and thin black tie which had belonged to his father. Over these he wore his black leather motorcycle jacket, and narrow black corduroy jeans and greasy boots completed his garb making him look somewhat inferior to Gerrit who wore a navy suit, arm band and black tie.

The rain started to fall harder and the mourners began to get restless as the wasteland of a windswept cemetery offered no shelter. Eventually it was over and Gerrit gave the minister ten rands and the two brothers drove home together without speaking. There didn't seem to be anything to say. A telegram of condolence from Tina lay on the dining room table and this time Koos produced a bottle of brandy and a litre of Coca Cola. By six o'clock in the evening they were both very drunk and Koos fell asleep on the threadbare settee. Gerrit had never been drunk before and sat in his father's old chair completely stupefied, one of his John Player Specials burning a long scar into the cheap walnut veneer of the sideboard.

At 1.30, he awoke in the chair, cold and wretched, his head burning and his mouth terribly dry and foul-tasting. He staggered into the kitchen for a glass of water but this seemed to make him feel drunk again and he reeled, vomiting painfully into the sink, heaving and coughing up the cheap brandy and syrupy cola until finally he retched drily and managed to stand upright, looking at himself in the old cracked mirror where his father had shaved every morning of his working life.

His eyes were thick and red and there was no brightness in them as they stared back at him disgustedly. He stuck out his tongue and saw the yellowish-white furry coating which was the basis of his foul-mouthing feeling. Head aching horribly, he went to the tiny bathroom and brushed his teeth long and hard, continually rinsing his mouth until he felt a normal flow of saliva. Returning to the kitchen, he boiled some milk and made a strong cup of cocoa which seemed to go down and stay down alright, settling the disturbance in his stomach.

'Oh my God,' he said aloud. 'I'll never let myself get like this again' and he stumbled off to bed and slept deeply until seven o'clock when Koos woke him with a cup of coffee. He marvelled at his brother's appearance.

'How do you feel, Koos?' he said wonderingly.

'Fit as shit,' said the younger man and left in a hurry, his helmet over his arm. 'You're just not used to it Gerrit,' he said and then the Kowasaki roared briefly and howled off into the distance.

Gerrit reached the office at his usual time of 8.30. There were various condolence cards and little handwritten messages on his desk. He telephoned his thanks to most of his colleagues on the internal phone and sat drinking his third cup of coffee of the day whilst he perused his copy of the *Cape Times*. The headlines read: 'New drama with SWA agreement – FIVE back UN on SWAPO bases.' He read the small columns of type, quickly taking in the gist of the article which seemed obviously anti-government as most of the country's English language newspapers were. Since the scandal involving the now defunct Department of Information, and the resultant underpinning of Nationalist Party credibility, the English press had been having a field day and even thinly veiled threats by the Minister of Justice had failed to silence them. Just recently, in fact, the Johannesburg based *Rand Daily Mail* had won a government-inspired interdict against it in the Supreme Court. Things were changing alright.

Gerrit continued to read of the South-West African situation and wondered what Windhoek was like as a city. He knew that the company had an office there and quite suddenly he felt that he wanted to go there, get away from

Cape Town and see this transitionary State of Namibia at first hand. It would give him a chance to think things out and he would ask for a transfer, now, today, whilst the idea was still fresh in his mind. He lifted the internal phone and dialed. Gail answered.

'Mr Marais' office.'

'Hello Gail, it's Gerrit,' he said quickly. 'I want an appointment with Mr Marais today and it doesn't matter how late.'

Gail's voice became distant. 'I'll try and see what his diary is like,' she said. 'Perhaps later this afternoon there may be something.' Suddenly her tone changed and she said, 'Why didn't you come last night or the other night Gerrit? I waited for you and didn't sleep the whole night because I was sure you'd come, you are a bastard.'

Gerrit didn't speak for a moment and then his voice became soft and intense. 'Gail,' he said. 'I would love to have come but you must realise that I had to talk things over with my brother. Then yesterday was the funeral and it was pretty upsetting, so much so that I got blind drunk last night.' He paused. 'Didn't you get the flowers I sent yesterday morning? Surely you must have got them.'

The girl's voice was softer now. 'Oh yes, of course I got them, they were lovely Gerrit and I took them home to the cottage because I thought you might come last night.' She stopped suddenly. 'Must go now, I'll talk to you later,' she added in an efficient secretarial voice.

Gerrit replaced the receiver and looked blankly at the newspaper. He could not imagine why or how but Gail seemed to have fallen in love with him. He felt for her and she was undoubtedly the most incredible woman he had ever had but it was impossible to imagine complicating his life with her at this stage. Now it was even more important for him to leave Cape Town and South-West Africa seemed the natural choice. Nobody knew him there and he could watch the political happenings and form his own conclusions right on the spot.

Just lately he had begun to follow politics closely and

the more he read magazines like *Time* and *Newsweek*, the more he thirsted for political knowledge, especially with regard to the rights of black and coloured people. South Africa would have to change one day and he saw a place for himself within this sphere when the time came. But in the meantime there was a lot to learn and what was happening now in South-West would happen here in South Africa sooner than the whites expected. If he could absorb the mechanics of the South-West Africa–Namibia plan it would provide him with an excellent grounding.

Late that afternoon he managed to see his boss Bob Marais, the financial director, who listened to his story without comment until he had finished.

'Well, Gerrit,' said Marais heartily, 'I'll see what I can do. In fact I'll get Rothman in Windhoek on the blower first thing in the morning. The Windhoek office will have closed by now of course,' he added, pointedly looking at his watch. 'But you know Gerrit, you're very valuable to me and I would miss you like hell.' Christ, it would wreak havoc with his golf schedule, he thought angrily.

Gerrit knew his value to Marais and realised that this fact would be obstructive as far as a transfer was concerned. Bearing in mind this thought he made his decision, dangerous though it was with a man like Marais who, he knew, hated to be pushed into anything.

'Mr Marais,' he said, 'I know you must have been instrumental in my advancement here but for the reasons I have given you, I must leave Cape Town, must get away. Primarily it's because of my mother's death but there are other personal reasons.'

Marais grinned lewdly. 'Have you got a nice little Malay girl in the club?' he said coarsely and Gerrit imagined, very briefly, what the reaction would be if he, Marais, knew what he, Gerrit, the coloured boy, had done with his beautiful blonde secretary only two days ago.

He tried to smile. 'No it's nothing like that,' he said seriously, 'but if this company cannot assist me with a transfer to another centre, then I shall have to consider moving elsewhere. In fact I have been approached,' he added 'but have seen no reason to leave Metricor as yet!'

Marais' eyes hardened as he regarded his clever young assistant. The bastard had guts alright, especially for a coloured but of course he was far from your average *skollie*, this one, that was for sure. He'd hate to lose him because the bugger did most of his work and was bright enough to realise this would mean that he wouldn't like to let him go. That's obviously why he's threatening to resign, thought Marais, and there would be hell to pay if he was lost to the company because even the MD regarded him as his special pet. He really was something else, this lad.

'Leave it to me Gerrit,' he said brusquely. 'I'll let you know as soon as I have an answer.'

Gail had already left her little cubicle when Gerrit came out of Marais' office. He thought of going home via her house but disgarded the idea as merely aggravating an increasingly escalating involvement. He knew that he was close to loving her, even after only one evening, and felt that if he slept with her again he might not be able to leave – and leaving Cape Town was vitally important now. He felt this inside him and knew that somehow his destiny was linked with getting away and in any case tonight he had to see the estate agent who was to handle the sale of the house at 7.30. He left the now silent Metricor administration building and climbed into the Audi. The evening rush hour had subsided and within twelve minutes he was home.

The following morning Marais spoke to Heine Rothman in Windhoek and was mildly surprised that the South-West African director seemed very keen to have Gerrit de Kock.

'De Kock,' he said. 'That's the coloured who was in the newsletter about six months ago, eh. Shit Bobby, he would be fantastic here, man. With the way things are going in Windhoek, we'd be regarded as very progressive to put in a coloured financial man. Hell man, you're right on target with De Kock, I'd love to have him and in any case he's reckoned to be bloody brilliant isn't he?'

It seemed to Marais that de Kock would get his way and there was little he could do to oppose it, knowing the MD's attitude. But he decided to set up a meeting anyway to make one last effort. He told Gail to arrange it with the personnel manager and ask the MD's secretary when he was free.

Meanwhile Gerrit restrained his impatience and continued with his daily duties in the usual more than adequate fashion. He had arranged to see Gail again that weekend to tell her his plans and explain his feelings about leaving Cape Town. He was determined not to sleep with her again though: it would just make things worse. They were to have supper at the cottage on Friday but, despite his resolve, by Wednesday evening he was desperately looking forward to the date. It was the same stomach fluttering, dry-mouthed feeling he'd felt the first time only now he knew what to expect and by Friday the anticipation had become almost unbearable so that he'd just about forgotten about the Windhoek transfer in the excitement of being with Gail again.

This time she had made an Italian dish of lasagne and, with it there was a superb salad with olives and fresh mushrooms, sliced wafer thin. To start with, there had been a light mousse of smoked salmon and with it, wholewheat rolls fresh and hot so that the butter melted onto them. The lasagne was rich and creamy and heavy with herbs and flavours that Gerrit had never tasted and he enjoyed two large helpings and drank half a litre of Ruffino chianti which Gail had bought especially. She watched him eat and enjoyed his pleasure as before, passing him extra rolls and salad and mixing the dressing of olive oil and grape vinegar.

She had tried to analyse the intensity of her feelings for Gerrit de Kock. He was quite a beautiful man to her but

69

that was not really his main attraction. There was a charisma about him that held her captive and made her heartbeat accelerate when she was near him, even in the impersonal confines of the office. It had been like that with few other men and the feeling seemed as much mental as physical because she loved to talk and allowed him to use her as a sounding board for his articulate views and sometimes angry radical ideas. Undoubtedly Gerrit was well-read and extremely bright but he was terribly naive about many things and especially so in bed – although that didn't matter because he excited her so much. She could have an orgasm just thinking about his body and had experienced quite a few since that first night.

She served a fresh fruit salad and then they sat together again on the little sofa and sipped their coffee. Gerrit was relaxed now and he began to outline his plans for a move to South-West Africa, talking excitedly about the political situation and the tremendous possibilities for the territory. Gail had suspected some such plan because she had heard Marais talking to Rothman in Windhoek and Gerrit's name was mentioned. She was adult enough to appreciate his reasons and was able to conceal her feelings quite effectively.

'Oh Gerry, I shall miss you but I do understand why you feel you must go, I really do,' she said softly. This understanding provoked reactions in Gerrit which he would not have believed possible and he visualised Windhoek as a lonely dusty city where he would be without friends, thrown into a hostile environment by his own choosing. It would not be like that for her though.

'Yes, Gail,' he said sorrowfully, 'but I can imagine that you'll survive alright, there must be dozens of guys who would love to have you,' he added cruelly. His anger rose as he imagined some strange white man with this beautiful blonde girl, touching her and spreading her legs and then heaving around on top of her. The thought appalled him, so much so that he pulled her roughly to him and opened her blouse and put his hands on her wonderful breasts.

'I don't like to think of anyone touching you,' he said hoarsely. 'I'd kill them if I caught them.' Oh Christ, he thought, I'm being bloody stupid and irrational again.

Later, after they had made love, he talked quietly to her and found out that she understood eveything he said and felt for him deeply. He didn't understand why and it suprised him, but it left him feeling warm and wanted.

CHAPTER 6

Mostert's orders had arrived at his office at 9.15 on the Monday morning.

'Report for duty to OC SWA Command 08.00 hours 25th May,' was all the flimsy said. That was in less than forty-eight hours' time, he thought in irritation. But to be truthful to himself he enjoyed the visits to Ovamboland and had never regretted transferring to the Riot Police. He much preferred the occasional bout of soldiering to the drudgery of regular policework, although there was little of that in his unit. Mostert reflected that he had the best of both worlds really and promotion had been fairly rapid.

It was a grey and windy afternoon when he boarded the huge Super Frelon army troop transport helicopter with thirteen other men of various ranks and divisions of the services. There were a couple of photo-journalists there too and they laughed and played cards and drank from hip flasks which they offered around. All the men refused and Mostert noticed that he was the highest rank together with another major from thirty battalion. He thought that if he'd had a swig they all would have had one and the poor bloody journalists would have been cleaned out.

The Frelon had room for up to thirty and Mostert was able to relax with ample room as the big machine clattered north-west for Grootfontein, passing over the north-western Cape and Namaqualand and into South-

West Africa. Mostert knew a little of this territory and its history and thought now of the strange race called the Basters who lived south of Windhoek, the capital of South-West Africa.

They had their own capital called Rehoboth and were staunchly an individualistic race, evolved from an original ninety families who had trekked north from the Cape well over one hundred years ago. Here, Mostert knew, were some of the wealthiest coloureds in Southern Africa and their most striking feature was the whiteness of their skin. He had driven through Reheboth on a previous trip to South-West and had been amazed by the incongruity of English, Scottish and Afrikaans names on shops and stores. He had seen blond, blue-eyed coloureds for the first time in his life and recognised the infusion of German blood from the days of *Deutsches Afrika*. They were a proud almost arrogant people this bloody lot, who even went so far as to bar relations with blacks in order to retain their whiteness and purity of line. To Mostert it was all quite fascinating.

He remembered reading some time back that one of the Cape's coloured political leaders referred to the Baster nation, of some fifteen thousand people, as the precursors of coloured nationhood. This insinuation that the Basters should have total autonomy in their own territory could not have been overly popular with the government or the Department of the Interior, thought Mostert wryly. As far as he was concerned, the Basters were truly bastards, a result of various unions between the indigenous Hottentots of Namaqualand and the early Cape and South-West African settlers, especially the bloody krauts who were world-renowned for liking black and coloured women.

But you had to give the Basters their due. They were tough and hardy bastards alright, he laughed silently to himself at the pun, and had fought various desperate battles to retain their sovereignty in the old days. They'd taken on the Imperial German Army and the South-

African Air Force and army in the days of General Jan Smuts and on both occasions they'd displayed quite an amount of diplomatic, as well as martial skill, petitioning the League of Nations and such like.

The Super Frelon hammered on into the evening as Mostert sat comfortably considering the lot of all the coloureds in Southern Africa. The territory was really as much theirs as ours, he thought. The poor buggers were stuck in the middle and were hated by the blacks for being tainted and looked down on by the whites for much the same reasons, although some whites made liberal noise about them. There were Basters in the South-West African army, shortly to become the Namibian Defence Force, he supposed. The South African army had inaugurated two new coloured battalions, three-four which was coloured and three-five which was actually mostly black and specialised in clandestine ops rather like the now disbanded Rhodesian Selous Scouts. The Cape Corps was the other coloured unit and they had been around for years of course but lately they'd all been doing their stuff well and he'd been with the three-five lot on two missions. They were bloody good.

Since joining the Riot Police and having to do border duty, Mostert had been studying classified documents on the birth of SWAPO and the beginning of hostilities back in '71. At that time it had been just a South African police holding operation, regarded as a problem for internal security rather than a national threat from beyond the country's borders. In 1972/73 under the clever chairmanship of the outlawed Sam Nujoma, who was busy drumming up financial support in Europe and the United States, and political recognition at the United Nations, SWAPO began to come across the border from Angola in more than their previous limited numbers. At this stage the Defence Force was called in to assist the police and this nasty little war began in earnest.

In the early days, the run-of-the-mill SWAPO volunteers received training in Zaire, and sometimes Czechoslovakia, but the brighter recruits were sent to Russia where they were given thorough training in weapons, explosives and the classic Marxist terrorist doctrines of intimidation and control of the local population. Oh yes indeed, Mostert thought, the old SWAPO terr' was a different kettle of fish to the crap they had faced in Rhodesia. Up there, they'd killed all the good ones and the rabble who'd taken over could not be considered as anyone's idea of soldiers. It was just a bloody pity that the Rhodesians had run out of time and money, at the death, so to speak. Zimbabwe had been finished before it started really. Now it was totally ballsed up. He'd spoken to a few Selous Scouts about it – there were quite a few in three-five battalion.

Of course, ninety per cent of SWAPO were Ovambos and he could understand their motives because prior to the Angolan adventure the border had been virtually wide open and passed right through the middle of Ovamboland. He'd met a number of Ovambos whose families were on the Angolan side whilst their sons or husbands were fighting in the South African army.

There was no way those poor buggers could ever see their relations under present circumstances since the army had cleared the Jati Strip. Quite a few reckoned that they might one day blow their brothers to bits in a fire-fight, both being Ovambo but wearing different uniforms. It didn't really make much sense to Mostert but they were volunteers, both groups didn't have to fight, nobody was forcing them.

Of course, Mostert himself had not taken part in operation Savannah, the South African expedition into Angola in early '76 in support of Jonas Savimbi and UNITA, but he'd heard the tales. At the time the present Prime Minister, old P.W. Botha, had been Minister of Defence and he'd been all for it and the bloody Americans had guaranteed support, in terms of arms and war material to both South Africa and UNITA. Gerald Ford had given the plan his blessing and the South African forces had moved, the Tank Battalions Eland armoured car columns going through the MPLA and the Cubans like the Wehrmacht panzers had in the Polish Campaign. The Blitzkrieg had stopped of its own accord only five kilometres from Luanda, the Angolan capital, and then the South Africans had felt the terrible pinch of the United States Congress who reneged on Ford's promise and decided against support. Way out on a political limb, the South African army had tried to retain the advantage for their black allies, UNITA, and planned to lay a barrage on the city, finishing at seven o'clock on the morning prior to their withdrawal. When this was lifted, UNITA would go in alone and take control in a classic *fait accompli* and that would be that.

A friend who had been there had told Mostert that it was all set up for UNITA and then the stupid kaffirs had gone and got totally pissed at a victory party on the previous evening. After the barrage lifted they finally got moving at about 10.30 but by then the MPLA had moved in fresh Cuban reinforcements and what with their hangovers, and the lack of moral and physical support from the South Africans, UNITA had ballsed it all up. That had been the end of that, thought Mostert, a gross and costly embarrassment for South Africa and a political *faux pas* by the West which had resulted in a drastic change for the worse in the Southern African status quo.

It was totally dark by the time the Frelon lumbered down at Grootfontein and Mostert was met by a young sergeant in a Landrover who drove him to TAC HQ some twenty kilometres north of the border between Okavango territory and Ovamboland. He reported immediately to Brigadier Paul Holsworth, a dapper young professional soldier who had been wounded twice in Malaya and Aden when serving with the British SAS. Holsworth was a Rhodesian and had served there until 1976 when he had seen the writing on the wall after a few nasty incidents in the Eastern Border area where he was officer commanding. His wife and little daughter had been shot up on the main Umtali to Fort Victoria road and the little girl had lost partial use of her right arm. Now Holsworth was second in command of Tactical Group Zulu Pepper Two, a force which now included three-four, three-five and the Ovambo battalion.

Holsworth greeted Mostert warmly and offered a bottle of Bell's and the ice bucket. 'How was the flight down?' he said in his loud, high voice. He reminded Mostert of a scoutmaster he had known as a child but the resemblance was purely physical because Holsworth was far from an amateur when it came to soldiering. Mostert saw the 9mm Uzi sub-machine gun hanging on the wall with the Brigadier's camouflage jacket and noted the two magazines taped together end-to-end giving the weapon double the firepower. That was typical of Holsworth. Experience had taught him to cover every eventuality.

In mid 1978 Mostert had been up on the border during his second tour of duty when the Army had carried out the punitive raids against 'Vietnam' and 'Moscow' the SWAPO training bases some four hundred kilometres inside Angola. Holsworth had been on the Combined Operations committee who had planned the raids and insisted on going in himself. He had invited Mostert along as an observer and Mostert had felt unable to refuse. An incident which occurred at 'Vietnam' had resulted in sort of friendship between the two men.

The camps had been well established for almost two and a half years and aerial reconnaissance and intelligence had reported that they were well defended with Russian 14.5mm anti-aircraft batteries. Bearing this in mind, prior to the ground strike, the Air Force had pummelled the bases with American-made 'jumping-jack' anti-personnel bombs. Unfortunately quite a few of these had failed to go off with the result that several of the gun nests and their crews had remained intact and unusually determined.

Mostert and Holsworth reminisced over their whiskys, remembering that day. 'It was a bit of a fuck-up from the start,' said Holsworth his high English public-school accent making the profanity seem almost acceptable.

'You're not wrong Brigadier,' said Mostert, smiling at Holsworth's pronunciation which made the words sound like 'faak op'. 'We were a little fortunate to get out with our arses intact, that's for sure. But I can't remember ever feeling better than we did back at camp that night, even those warm Castles tasted like nectar, and we did stuff them up, eh.'

The raid had been scheduled to start at seven in the morning but due to the tenacity of the surviving gunners and the delayed return of the Canberra bombers, the Hercules had only managed to drop the paras at nine and then they'd been deposited on the wrong side of the river. The men of three-five battalion were to be collected after the action, by Army Puma helicopters and Holsworth and Mostert had gone in with one of them, obviously far too early for the pick-up.

From the chopper they had seen the big Hercules transports veering off before the drop zone and Holsworth then the men were skirmishing in but the SWAPO gunners who had succeeded in ruining his carefully made plan.

'What about the fucking Air Force,' he had shouted at Holsworth. 'Christ almighty, they should have pulverised the monkeys by now.' A few stray tracer bullets had crossed the nose of the Puma and the pilot had sheered away and landed way across on the far side of the river. By then the man were skirmishing in but the SWAPO gunners had craftily set the anti-aircraft guns on maximum depression and were hosing away at the advancing South African forces with the fast-firing weapons.

Slowly the paras had made ground and the defenders began to suffer under a hail of small-arms fire and accurate mortar bombing. By then, Holsworth was well up ahead of Mostert firing the Uzi from the hip, while at the trot, and urging his black troops on. Mostert had never experienced action in his life and had been very frightened in the helicopter but after the first few shots the tension had left him and he had followed Holsworth, blasting away with the R1 rifle and forgetting his fear in the heat and excitement of the attack. After only ten minutes the SWAPO recruits began to falter and the three-five boys carried on, overrunning the carefully dug zig-zag trenches and then the black troops had gone crazy with their usual blood lust, slaughtering anything that moved. Holsworth had let them have their way, knowing that they had need of this terrible sort of relaxation and, indeed, this was what they had been trained for.

Mostert had felt incredibly light-headed standing with Holsworth, winding down and taking great gasps of breath and then he'd seen the movement and the glint of metal in the pile of tumbled sand-bags some twenty or thirty metres from where they stood. The paras had already passed this bunker and had left everyone for dead but the olive drab figure that Mostert saw had seemed very much alive. 'Down sir,' he had screamed at Holsworth and pushed him heavily. They had fallen together in the dirt, rolling over and over as the RPD machine gun opened up, blasting the earth and rocks all over them so that they became concealed behind a low cloud of dust.

Seemingly in seconds, one of the black troopers had got the RPD with a grenade and the single SWAPO soldier had come flying out of his hole, cartwheeling in the air to fall almost on top of Mostert and Holsworth. He had been about eighteen and most of his jaw and right arm had been blown off by the grenade, but he had still been very much alive and had lain there staring up at them, his eyes full of mute appeal and rolling white with terror and pain. Holsworth had shot him in the face with the Uzi.

In the two camps they'd killed over thirteen hundred and some of these had been camp followers, including a few women. About two hundred had been taken back for questioning and they'd found huge ammunition dumps of mortar bombs and RPG 7 rockets. They couldn't take much of it so Holsworth had blown the rest up and then they'd moved out fast in the Pumas. It had only been three hours but to Mostert it seemed like a lifetime. Holsworth had just said, 'Thanks Johann, that could have been a nasty one,' but Mostert knew that it meant more than that.

They finished half of the scotch and then Mostert said goodnight and went off to his tent. It was cool now with the night sounds coming loudly from the dense bush around the camp. Mostert stripped and lay down on his stretcher in the thick darkness formed by the brown canvas of the tent and thought of his wife back in Cape Town and his little five-year-old daughter Janine.

They would be sleeping together tonight, as they always did when he was away, the little girl curled up just like a miniature version of her mother, hands under her cheek. He remembered the prayers she said every night. 'Dear God, thank you for today, make me good at school and make me work well and pass my term. I love you God. Look after all the poor children and keep them safe and bless Mummy and Daddy and all my friends and everyone. I love you God, I love you. Amen.' Mostert smiled as he fell asleep. He thought that his daughter may turn out to be a good lawyer because in a way she was just like them; or Holsworth for that matter. She too always seemed to cover every angle.

CHAPTER 7

'Don't be bloody stupid,' said the managing director. 'I can't see any real reason why de Kock shouldn't go to South-West. It's got to be beneficial to his development and therefore beneficial to the company, ultimately. Surely, we all want him to stay with us, don't we Armstrong?'

The personnel manager, sweating in a pin-striped crumpled suit shuffled his papers uncomfortably. He was a sometime social friend of Bob Marais and saw in him a possible avenue towards the long and winding road that leads to directorships. Marais wanted young de Kock to stay here at Parow and he'd already told him to do what he could to make sure the coloured remained. He looked at Marais and saw the imperceptible nod and cleared his throat in embarrassment and pulled the letter out from the folder in front of him.

'Well, sir,' he muttered, so that the old man looked up at him strangely and Marais gazed out of the window. 'The thing is, sir,' he continued more loudly, 'I have received a letter from de Kock which is in the form of an ultimatum.' He produced the letter and pushed it gingerly across the table 'He has more or less stated that he'll resign unless we transfer him, sir, to South-West that is. Surely that sort of pressure cannot be kowtowed to, sir,' he added lamely.

'Bloody well not, you're right there, Peter,' said Marais hotly. The MD looked from one to the other and cupped his chin in a classic gesture of intense thought. 'I want to see de Kock tomorrow, gentlemen,' he said. 'See that you send him in to me in the morning and I'll talk to him. Until I've done so I'll reserve judgement, but I must say that such a letter is most unlike de Kock, not at all like him in fact'.

Gerrit walked into the big office which was ornately panelled in Cape yellowwood. The MD gestured to a chair and he sat and looked across the maroon leather top of the desk at the slender, immaculately groomed grey-haired man, whose father had started Metricor and whose family still controlled thirty per cent of the shares in what was this year listed as twenty-first of the top one hundred companies in South Africa.

'Now, Gerrit,' said the MD kindly. 'Can you tell me why you want to go to Windhoek so badly? You must know that we're all very fond of you here at Metricor Cape and we'd hate to lose you. But I understand you've put an ultimatum to Peter Armstrong and this strikes me as being rather odd. What's it all about, Gerrit?' The old man seemed fatherly and very understanding, thought Gerrit, but it would be impossible to tell him the real reasons, explain what was deep down inside him, things that he didn't really understand himself. The MD probably knew that Marais wanted to keep him because he was a bloody sight more than an assistant and did most of the financial director's work. But how could he explain about Gail? About his aspirations, political and otherwise, and that weird feeling of destiny? It couldn't be done and so he decided to try the other way and appeal on more or less personal grounds.

'You see, sir,' he started. 'It's difficult for you to understand, I would imagine, but being a coloured is quite unique, and unique, sir, for mostly all the wrong reasons. In many ways, in the most important ways in fact, one is regarded as an outcast in this society.' The MD began to speak but Gerrit carried on, 'I'm sure I don't have to explain all that to you, sir, and I really feel that my future is here with Metricor, that my advancement here will be assured. But I want to see new places, I feel stifled and I want to experience new things in new countries. I believe that South-West Africa is a country that is experiencing tremendous change and challenge. I'd like to be a part of that, sir, as a coloured, because I feel in some way that the challenges are not so great here – at present I mean.'

The MD pondered the statement of the young coloured. Much of what he said was right and he was bloody articulate and quite captivating when he talked. He suddenly felt an odd sort of apprehension about Gerrit de Kock. He was just too bloody bright, too clever, and maybe to get him away for a while could be the answer, it would give him a chance to think about the coloured's real worth. Apart from that, it would force Bob Marais to get off his arse and do some work.

'Well, Gerrit,' he said quietly, 'I accept your explanation and can see no reason why you shouldn't succeed in Windhoek as you have here. In fact you will probably forge ahead.' He smiled benevolently. 'But I can tell you that we don't like ultimatums and whilst I respect your motives, I cannot condone such letters as this. So I can tell you Gerrit that any further correspondence like this,' he held up the letter Gerrit had written, 'will be dealt with in the strongest terms. I'm sure you understand me.'

Gerrit nodded respectfully and knew instinctively that he should not apologise or grovel to the old man's supposed generosity in excusing his unprecendented letter. 'Thank you, sir,' he said and rose, dismissing himself. He walked out briskly and somehow the MD felt that it was he who had been dismissed. Blast the bugger, he thought. We'll have to watch him from here on.

There were so many things to do before he left. The house had been sold for R9750 and the agent was to receive just under R500 which meant that the net figure to each of them would be around R3100. Koos had found lodgings in a flat just outside Belville which he shared with another mechanic from the garage where he worked. He planned to buy a hi-fi rig and an expensive movie camera and reckoned that he would have about R1000 rand left after these purchases. Gerrit knew that this too would be gone within a couple of months.

For his own part, he was going to take his share and Tina's and add just under R2000 of his savings. This sum was to be invested in Wesberg gold shares, a recently listed company on the Johannesburg Stock Exchange and one he fancied as a safe medium-term speculation. Tina had written to say that she would not be coming back to South Africa until the end of the year and had asked him to look after her money and he thought that Wesberg was as good an investment as any. Her letter had been typed on Heim Import-Export letter heading and had a Dusseldorf address. Tina had signed it with her name and underneath had typed Mrs W. F. Heim.

Gerrit had a few personal trinkets and mementos which he had arranged to leave with Gail and he had sold the Audi to her at a very low price on the proviso that he could buy it back if and when he returned to the Cape. This transaction had realised only R1200 but provided a degree of mental satisfaction in that it formed a link between himself and Gail and he could keep the car right up until he left for Windhoek. He felt the need of such contact, however tenuous, and was dreading leaving Gail as much as he was looking forward to his new post.

They had been together quite a bit lately, much more than he had intended, and somehow tongues had started to wag at Metricor. The rumour had reached Marais and he had discounted it as totally ridiculous until the girl had bought de Kock's car. Even then it had seemed a ludicrously remote possibility that Gail Wilson with whom he had attempted a liaison on various occasions, would enter into a relationship with a bloody coloured, clever though he may be. He tried to imagine them together but just couldn't seem to visualise sexual contact between his beautiful blonde secretary and his coffee-coloured assistant. He took to examining Gail and tried to imagine her in erotic situations, with or without the coloured. But his pre-programmed mind, born of an Afrikaans country upbringing, could just not accept the images his subconscious tried to project.

Marais was a bachelor and a highly physical person who loved golf and tennis and had played rugby for Western Province in his younger days. He had an insatiable sexual appetite and his rough-cast good looks had appealed to many women when he was younger. Now with a spreading paunch and only golf for exercise, he was not so attractive but even more ambitious in his attempted conquests. Even now, with his boisterous methods of approach, the unruly ginger hair, ruddy countryman's complexion and 'one of the boys' aura, he had experienced few failures. Gail Wilson was therefore a challenge and although he hadn't tried anything further with her since the last cold rebuttal about six months back, he felt a strong urge to compete with the bloody coloured boy. If he was getting it, however unlikely it seemed, why shouldn't Marais?

Gail had tried hard to reason out what she would do when Gerrit left in June. By nature she was an independent person who had come to South Africa alone and was quite happy with her own company. She'd had few boyfriends prior to this affair and had not felt a need for regular sex. Now she couldn't seem to get enough and always pressed Gerrit to stay the night, but he never did, going off to the empty hovel in the small hours of the morning. He was going to stay there until he left at the end of May.

She felt rather than heard the rumours at the office because nobody had actually said anything to her and she had her answer all ready if they did. Marais had started to be very attentive and sweet to her and kept brushing his leg or arm against her whenever he had the chance. He was a randy old sod and turned her on just about as much as the Irish navvies back home in London. Considering the problem objectively, she thought that she would start looking around for another job and give in her notice at the end of May when Gerrit finished off.

As far as men were concerned, she had no plans and thought that she would take it easy for as long as it suited her. She'd made enquiries about taking up Yoga and could practise two nights a week and perhaps rent a television for the cottage although she couldn't understand the bloody Afrikaans programmes which took up half of each evening's transmission. She hadn't considered any long-term relationships with Gerrit but had dreamily pictured a vague continuity one day in South-West Africa, when it became independent and all the racial barriers were lifted. Or perhaps back in the UK, because he was clever enough to get a job anywhere. They'd never really discussed it but had talked of his sister Tina and her German husband. Gerrit had reservations about that relationship and felt that it wouldn't survive in the long run because his sister was over-ambitious and would leave her husband Willi when she found someone richer or more famous. Gail thought Gerrit was jealous of his sister in some strange fashion.

Tina lay in the sauna in Munich's Bayrischerhof Hotel where they were staying again. She had just had a marvellous massage with a Chinese girl who was very butch and ugly, but a superb masseuse. After the sauna she'd have a dip in the pool and then meet Willi for lunch in the bar of the *Kaffeehaus*. Eyes closed and head supported on the slatted wooden rest, she lay on the thick fluffy white towel and thought of Horst, beautiful Horst, the dark, slim, aristocratic son of Wolfgang Steiner chairman of the Steiner Bäckerei in Berlin and a man of considerable wealth and countless property holdings.

The perspiration rolled from Tina's naked body which was enviously being perused by the other two occupants of the sauna, both blowsy German matrons who indulged in too many lunches in the Bayrischerhof's *Kaffeehaus* and various other fashionable Munich lunchtime restaurants.

86

Tina surrendered to the heat and vaguely heard one of the women saying something about *wasser*. '*Ja bitte*,' she said with eyes still closed and heard the ladle of pine-scented water hiss against the hot stones of the heater. Instantly, the water vaporised and the humidity rose rapidly so that all three women gasped and exhaled slowly in almost an agony of pleasure as the moisture rolled from their bodies.

Tina closed her eyes again and dozed in the cloying heat, heart beating rapidly and vainly making its frantic effort to circulate surface blood and keep her body cool. She had met Horst Steiner in Mampe Stuben in Berlin only two weeks earlier. Mampe's was a sort of coffee house cum restaurant where you could have drinks on the terrace and she'd been there once before with Willi. That morning she'd been shopping on the Kurfürstendamm and had the afternoon free too because Willi was seeing some clients and wouldn't be back at the Bristol Kempinski until after six. It was a warm spring day and she'd been window-shopping idly along the wonderful Ku'damm and had tried on slacks in Horn's and Braun's and eventually bought a gorgeous beige corduroy outfit at Madame in the Europa Centre. Wandering back towards the Gedachtnis Kirche she'd seen Mampe's and remembered it and just walked in to have a sandwich and a beer.

She had been just sitting on the terrace sipping a Carlsberg, savouring the wonder of Berlin in spring and the incredible cosmopolitan, European feeling of it all. The voice had shattered her daydreams and had been deep and respectful.

'*Entschuldigen Sie bitte Fraulein ist hier noch frei*?' Tina had looked up to see the dark handsome bronzed face with smooth aquiline features and incredible bright blue eyes.

Nervously she had replied in broken German, '*Ja bitte nehmen Sie Platz,* er, *mein Herr*.'

'Ah, you are English,' he said immediately in a faultless accent. 'Allow me to introduce myself. I am Horst Steiner and I live here in Berlin, and you *Fräulein*!' Tina smiled remembering his smooth but nonetheless blatant approach. She had told him immediately that she was a *Frau* and not a *Fräulein* but he had not seemed to find this an obstacle and had invited her to lunch in a gourmet restaurant called Le Maître and it had all been wonderful, the food, the 1971 Hock and Horst – laughing, joking, flattering and superbly confident.

In the afternoon they had driven out to Wannsee in his Porsche 911SC and had left the car and walked through the beautiful parkland, fresh and blooming in the matchless glow of spring. They'd sat and looked out across the wide lake to where the red buoys marked the border with the Eastern zone. Then they had walked off through the woodland and there had been nobody around and she had let him kiss her and then it had started and nothing in the world could have stopped it. Afterwards she had lain in the grass, looking up at the beech trees and the oaks, all resplendent in spring-fresh green leaves. She was completely captivated by Berlin and he had completed it all for her in a sort of beautiful sophisticated maleness. Tina dozed in the sauna, visualising the fine laughing face. She would see him again in just under three weeks.

She left the sauna and dropped into the icy depths of the plunge pool, feeling the coldness enveloping the warm outer layers of her skin, quickly beginning to neutralise the latent heat within her. She leapt, tingling from the pool, nipples erect and skin rosy with increased circulation and grabbed the big, warm, fresh towel provided by the attendant.

'Oh God, I feel marvellous,' she said aloud and the attendant smiled, although not understanding English. Tina thought that she had never felt fitter in her life and it was all thanks to Willi. Dear Willi, he was so good to her and she did love him. But I must have my own life sometimes, she thought, because I'm still so young and there's so much to do and see, and experience.

She dried herself briskly and then sat under the hairdryer so that her long blue-black hair would become soft and fluffy before she brushed it into the usual natural full shape. In five minutes it was almost dry and she applied cologne and lipstick and a touch of eye make-up. She pulled on plain white cotton slacks and black silk shirt and put on the new Dior sunglasses she had bought that morning. When she walked into the bar he was already there drinking a lager and she ran over and kissed him like a child would, hugging him and smiling up into his face. There was not a man in the room who did not envy Willi Heim.

After only ten days at home in Dusseldorf, they were back in Berlin where Willi had found three quite keen buyers for South African estate wines. Some sample cases had been sent out from the Cape to Willi's new Dusseldorf office and they'd brought them along on the plane with them. This morning he'd gone off in a taxi to his appointments taking the wine with him and was to have lunch and drinks with two of the clients. He told Tina not to expect him before 7.30 back at the Kempinski and so she had the whole day to herself.

She dressed carefully after her shower, starting with tiny cotton lace tanga panties over which she wore a soft rich brown cotton jersey skirt and a cream silk shirt. She put on a string of coral beads, some of Willi's samples from a contact in Mauritius who'd thought they might be a good line for the German market, and then put all her bits and pieces and make-up into a large wicker and leather shoulder bag. Lastly she sprayed herself with Diorissima and checked her hair in the mirror. She looked back at her image and smiled widely, showing perfect white teeth. 'You're a pretty little bitch,' she said aloud and walked out of the room.

Tina stepped out of the lift into the Kempinski foyer and the hall porter looked on approvingly as she walked lithely towards him. '*Guten Morgen Frau Heim*,' he said politely and Tina smiled and said, '*Taxi, bitte*.' The porter decided to practise his English.

'You go to shopping, *ja,*' he beamed.

'Yes that's right,' said Tina. 'I love the shops in Berlin.'

The porter pondered heavily and tried again: '*Habst du seen Nollendorf Platz, Frau Heim.* It is *fantastiche, Ja fantastiche. Zer chic,*' he added triumphantly.

Tina nodded. 'Nollendorf Platz, eh, well, thanks Herr Feldman,' she said, reading his brass nameplate on the green jacket lapel. She smiled again at the glowing porter and he signalled a page to call a taxi from the rank outside the hotel.

'*Mampe Stuben bitte,*' said Tina and settled back on the worn leather of the old Mercedes.

'Can we go to Nollendorf Platz, Horst,' she said as soon as he had kissed her and they were seated at a table.

He frowned. 'That's a weird place, Tina, it's full of hippies and drop-out left-wing students, it's just a sort of flea-market really like they have in London. In actual fact it's the old U-Bahn station which was by-passed when they changed the Ku'damm line.' He saw her face brighten with interest. 'Well, I suppose you might like it, some of the shops and stalls are in the old railway carriages. It's rather quaint I suppose.'

Horst had completed the last two years of his education at Shrewsbury School in England because his father believed that the English public-school system was the best in the world. Apart from this, he wanted his son to be able to speak English in the way his British business acquaintances did and as a result Horst's accent was impeccable and he relished the correct use of his English vocabulary. Often Tina didn't understand him.

The Porsche purred down the Ku'damm towards Nollendorf Platz and Tina's hand rested lightly on Horst's right thigh. On the opposite side of the wide Mall a taxi stopped and Willi got out with a man and a smart-looking blond woman. The Porsche was stationary now at a pedestrian crossing and Willi looked straight towards them so that Tina huddled down in the seat trying to hide behind Horst.

'Oh my God,' she said, 'there's my husband.'

'Don't worry, *schatz*, he won't see you because of the tinted windows,' said Horst uncomfortably, picturing a violent fight in the middle of the Ku'damm. Willi seemed to stare briefly at the car and frown and then looked away towards the boot of the taxi as the cases of wine were unloaded. The Porsche accelerated quickly and Tina did not dare to look back.

Down in Nollendorf Platz, they walked hand in hand among the stalls of bric-à-brac and handicrafts. Tina's natural bazaar instincts took over and she became entranced with the variety and colour of the goods displayed, many of which were of eastern origin. Pop music bellowed loudly and there was a heavy odour of incense and occasional whiffs of pot and eventually Horst had had enough and pulled Tina off towards the small bar and restaurant.

'God, this is a stinking hole,' he said as they sat down at a small table and a dark young man opposite smiled and shook his head in disgust as if at Horst's lack of understanding. Horst flushed and Tina thought that he was going to get up from his chair. Then suddenly recognition dawned in his eyes and he shouted, 'Manfred, Manfred Meyer *mein freund*,' and jumped to his feet excitedly.

Tina was forgotten as the two men spoke happily in rapid German and then Horst suddenly remembered her and dragged her over to the man called Manfred. 'Tina,' he said. 'This is one of my oldest and dearest school friends, Manfred Meyer. Manfred may I present Frau Tina Heim.' He hesitated. 'A close friend of mine.'

Tina looked closely at Manfred Meyer. He was of average height with a fairly stocky build and sallow yellow skin which had an unhealthy pallor. His face had a haunted look and he wore a wispy moustache, not unlike the one Gerrit had sported at one time, and lank, black hair hung down to the collar of his greasy suede jacket, although his white shirt seemed clean enough. He looked

91

unkempt rather than unwashed and resembled any other professional student type the world over.

Meyer smiled at Tina and his face was transformed into that of a mischievous child although his eyes were dark and penetrating and seemed to bore right into hers. 'How do you do,' he said in correct, yet slightly accented English.

'Pleased to meet you, Manfred,' said Tina pleasantly and Meyer stared again into her face and then his eyes crinkled in recognition.

'Of course,' he said. 'Now I've got it, you're a South African, aren't you, and if I'm not mistaken you're a coloured. Am I right?'

Tina flinched as if she'd been struck. Quite suddenly she felt peculiarly alien, as if she'd been exposed in unaccustomed territory. It was like the dream that she'd often had as a child and even today still had sometimes. She would dream that she was in a crowded place, like a supermarket, wearing only a shorty nightie without panties. She'd always wondered what this dream meant and Willi had said that it indicated the fact that she was a latent exhibitionist. Now she felt that she knew what it really meant.

Manfred continued to smile at her and Horst looked from one to the other, feeling the electricity between them in the smoky atmosphere of the U-Bahn station, although he failed to understand the reasons for it.

Tina's face hardened. 'What do you know about the coloureds?' she said venemously.

'Oh a great deal,' said Manfred lightly. 'More than you could ever imagine. You see I know Cape Town, I was there about eighteen months ago. I had to leave,' he added softly.

'You mean you're a prohibited immigrant,' said Tina and Manfred shrugged his shoulders and the stringy black hair fell down across his forehead. He shook it back with a flick of his head in an unconscious gesture.

'Well, Tina, I was visiting only but I met many coloured

people and there was one, a girl, who I spent a lot of time with. I was forced to leave the country in the end so you're interpretation of the situation was actually correct.'

Horst broke in. 'Manfred was a law student.' He looked questioningly at his friend. 'Are you doing post graduate work now?'

Manfred nodded. 'That's right – criminal law, Horst, and I've handled a few cases against the State, you know, against the police and that sort of thing.' He turned again to Tina. 'When I was at university, I had African Studies as my alternate subject and then after I'd got my degree I decided to drive down Africa in a Volkswagen bus. There were four of us who made the trip and we finished up in Cape Town.' He looked down at the dregs of his beer. 'I saw things on that trip that made me glad to reach civilisation again and Cape Town was just that. It was wonderful to start off with and then I got involved with the coloureds and the police started watching me. I suppose they checked up with the Federal Government and found out about my past and left-wing sympathies and that was it. I was out within forty-eight hours, on an exit permit.'

Until that day, Tina had not really given much thought to South Africa and her home which had been the draughty tin-roofed house, freezing cold during the long wet winter and stinking hot in the summer. She'd forgotten Gerrit and Koos and hadn't even written back to Gerrit about the R3000 he had invested for her. Now she thought of the dirt roads, made almost liquid by the wind-driven winter storms, and the abject poverty of the coloured people who had nowhere else to go.

She remembered the two pairs of school knickers that had to last for two or three days without washing and the greasy fish stew and tough stringy meat. Then there was the foul alcoholic smell of her father's breath when he had come to kiss her goodnight, always insisting on waking her despite the hour, so that she would kiss him and talk to him a bit. She could see her mother's toothless smile and remembered the pride she had in her beautiful daughter and the way that she had always hugged her to the greasy apron which smelled of dirty towels and musty sink odours. And the dusty crinkled hair that was always dyed in a garish red colour and the breath, similar to her father's. 'You'll be my girl, you'll show them Tina my baby' – that had been her mother's sentiments since she was old enough to talk and the old lady had been right because she had shown them and she'd done it and got out of the squalor and filth of Goodwood Cape, and was now the wife of a successful man in West Germany and at least a reasonably wealthy one.

There had been that young bastard of a South African police constable who had picked her up in the van one day when she was walking past the shops on the way home from school. He'd looked like a coloured himself but was clasified white and he'd driven down by the flats and started pawing her in the car and then when she'd refused he'd taken her down to Goodwood police station and said he would charge her with loitering with intent. She'd been very frightened and then the lieutenant had come and asked what the trouble was and the young one had disappeared and the lieutenant had been kind and given her chewing gum and asked her what pop groups she liked. He'd been an amateur photographer and asked if he could photograph her and she'd been flattered and agreed. It wasn't until weeks later that she'd thought it all out and realised that the constable was a sort of talent scout for the lieutenant. She thought that they probably had a racket going for distributing the photographs and remembered how he'd made her dress up in her school uniform with the black stockings and garter belt. He'd paid her two rand an hour and then she'd always had to do it to him after the photographic session was finished.

These thoughts flashed through Tina's mind as she sat, outwardly composed and perfectly groomed, in the old U-Bahn station some two hundred feet under central Berlin. She realised suddenly that Horst was speaking to her and that he was ordering more drinks.

'A brandy and coke with ice, please,' she said and grinned at Manfred who smiled back with an intimacy that went unnoticed by Horst. He was pondering on how anybody could possibly drink Cognac with Coca Cola.

They talked on and the intensity with which Manfred made his points reminded Tina of her brother Gerrit. She soon realised that Manfred Meyer was a political agitator of sorts, a left-winger bordering on the urban terrorist type, but without any of the ranting and raving dramatics that often typified radical students. Manfred was quiet and sincere, captivating to talk to and undoubtedly quite brilliant. He fascinated her and she agreed with everything he said, especially about the liberation of Southern Africa.

Horst tried to make a point from time to time but didn't stand much chance because Manfred and Tina were so engrossed in each other. Eventually he tossed his head angrily. 'Well, my dear friends,' he said acidly, 'you can talk about South Africa for the rest of the afternoon, but I've had enough.' He stood up dramatically and Tina looked up suprised and then smiled at his petulant expression.

'Are you going, Horst? Don't worry I'll find my own way home to the Kempinski. I'll call you tomorrow darling, at the office.' She turned back to Manfred and Horst realised that he had been dismissed, rejected – at least for the time being.

He flung a twenty mark note on the table and bowed to Manfred, a short abrupt movement from the waist. '*Auf Wiedersehen meine freunde*,' he said icily and strode off towards the exit.

They stayed in the bar at the old U-Bahn station, talking for almost five hours more, not wanting to break the spell of each other's company by moving to more comfortable surroundings. He told her of the struggles that he had taken part in against the Federal Government and he graphically described the student riots of 1969 and '70 when the army had been called out. He had been only seventeen then and the students had all taken refuge in an

95

old church and barricaded it, hurling bottles and fire-bombs at the police who had come at them with pistols and teargas. Then the army had sent the panzers and they had fired at the walls with fragmentation shells and two of his friends had been injured. Of course, they'd all lost their nerve then and surrendered. It had been typical fascist power-play and armed-might techniques, said Manfred, but it had worked alright and broken the back of the student rebellion in Berlin. Since then he'd dedicated himself to the support of those oppressed by the State and now that he was qualified, he'd been able to defend victims of such matters as police brutality in court. So far, he'd been very successful.

It was the same here in Germany as it was in South Africa, explained Manfred. Although here there was no apartheid system, everybody was under the control of the police. You had to report to your nearest police station within forty-eight hours of changing your address and had to carry documents called Social Security Cards. If you didn't report, they tracked you down after a while and you were prosecuted.

'West Germany is a card-carrying state,' said Manfred. 'If you haven't got your driving licence with you when you have an accident or commit an offence, they can throw you in jail. That's the way things are here.' He paused and looked directly into Tina's eyes. 'It's going to change though, just the same as it will in your country and all over the world where such systems exist. Western capitalism is doomed Tina, it can't survive because basically it's rotten. West Germany is as corrupt now as it was in the days of the Nazis, the respectability is all a facade, that's all it is.'

Tina considered Manfred's theories. She knew little about the political situation in West Germany, but to her the country seemed prosperous and successful and repre-sented all the things that she personally had yearned for in her twenty years of struggling as a second-class citizen in South Africa.

'But Manfred,' she said, smiling at his serious face,

'Germany seems orderly and respectable and the economy here is excellent, isn't it?'

Manfred smiled back with his mouth only. 'Oh yes, Tina, the mighty Deutsche mark, the strongest currency in the world, based on capitalist chicanery and corruption perhaps, but nonetheless mighty. No Tina, it isn't the wealth of Germany I despise, nor is it . . .' he grasped for the words in English, 'self-important, conceited people that I condemn. It's the political machine of so-called Western democracy that I despise.' He talked quietly but with great feeling. 'I despise that as much as I hate that bunch of fascists in your country, with whom we trade incidentally, to the tune of a few hundred million marks a year.'

Eventually they left Nollendorf Platz and walked to Wittenburg Platz. There they caught the U-Bahn and got off after only a few stations. They were going to Manfred's place, a house he shared with a few other students, artists, musicians and friends. Tina had never been on an underground railway and the fast, rattling trains fascinated her so that she was sorry when they had to get out. They emerged back into daylight in an old part of Berlin called Charlottenburg where the tall apartment buildings were dark with age, some still derelict from the bombing during the war.

By five o'clock there were fourteen people in the ground floor section of 98 Kaiser Wilhelm Strasse and large jugs of Algerian wine were being passed around to fill old china cups and plastic mugs. Two girls were making endless supplies of *Kartoffelpuffer,* the spicy potato pancakes much loved by German people, and these were being fried on an old gas stove and served on paper plates with spoonfuls of scrambled egg. The room was full of smoke from cigarettes, pipes and cooking oil and the pungency of the atmosphere reminded Tina of her mother's kitchen back in Goodwood. It was all very similar to the regular drinking sessions that her father had indulged in on Saturday afternoons. Only the language was different.

There were two Americans and a few Turks, Spaniards and Nigerians, the balance being German. The Turks and

Spaniards were *gastarbeiters* or 'guest workers' of the Federal Government and were in West Germany only as long as they were required. They could theoretically be sent back to their country of origin when the authorities decided that their services were no longer needed. Such people cleaned parks and swept streets, explained Manfred. Often they lived in squalor like the Pakistanis in England or the coloureds in the Cape. For her this comparison with European conditions of deprivation was a surprising one.

Tina found the people happy and friendly and wondered how they could be dissatisfied with such a wonderful place as Berlin. Manfred introduced her to all of them and she was thankful that she wore reasonably inexpensive looking clothes although a few girls seemed to eye her shoes and handbag enviously.

It was a beautiful summer evening and the eggs and pancakes were carried out to the small back garden which was surrounded by a high wall of black stone. Tall apartment buildings towered over the little square of green and stretched away on two sides up and down the street, their roofs bristling with television aerials. A solitary pear tree grew in the garden, majestic and laden with fruit, it formed a sharp contrast to all the dereliction of the ancient grime-coated buildings. They all sat on the grass under the tree, drinking and smoking and watching a few swallows darting about high in the cornflower blue of the sky.

The two Nigerian girls sat with Tina and Manfred and seemed happy to be able to speak English in which they were very fluent.

'Well honey,' said the one called Merle in a slight American accent. 'Down there in South Africa, you really got the problems coming. You're well out of that scene for sure, I'd say.' Her sister Mona nodded seriously but did not add to this statement. They were both very black, big girls with superb figures and wide Afro hairstyles which seemed to grow stiffly out from their heads like barbered ornamental hedges. Merle seemed very friendly towards Manfred and kept touching him when she talked, little fleeting contacts which he totally ignored.

Tina looked at her watch and saw to her amazement that it was almost seven o'clock. 'Have you a telephone Manfred,' she said urgently. 'I must ring for a taxi quickly, God I'm going to be late, I must get back to the hotel right now.' She saw his face fall.

'It's been wonderful, really,' he said and meant it and he smiled his mournful smile and got quickly to his feet.

As they waited in the hall for the taxi, he took her hand and pulled her gently towards him. 'I haven't asked you much about your life Tina, about your husband or anything.' He paused. 'But I would like to see you again before you leave Berlin. There are some places, bars and cafés, where my friends meet and I'd like you to see them so that you'll know that there's another side to Germany besides Henkel Trocken and Mercedes Benz motor cars.'

Tina stepped forward and kissed him on the lips. He smelled of the cheap Algerian wine and Gauloise cigarettes but she didn't find it unpleasant although the moustache tickled. She stepped back as the doorbell rang and they could see the shadowy figure of the taxi driver through the frosted glass. 'I'll meet you at Nollendorf Platz on Wednesday if you like,' she said. 'My husband will be away all afternoon so I can meet you there around 2.30.'

Manfred smiled, the smile that illuminated his whole face and made him look like a child that has received an unexpected gift. 'Good,' he said as he opened the door for her. 'I'll see you there, in the same bar then, *Auf Wiedersehen*.'

CHAPTER 8

Douglas Hoyle was born in 1942 in Wynberg, Cape Town and his family had moved to Johannesburg when he was five years old. Young Douglas attended the exclusive Maritz Brothers College in northern Johannesburg and had entered the University of the Witwatersrand in 1958, unusually early at the age of sixteen. Hoyle studied a BA course with English, Psychology, German and Political Science as his major subjects. He never graduated however, because at the age of nineteen he fled the country after being urgently sought by the Security Police.

Hoyle had been implicated in the sensational Rivonia Trials which were held after a discovery which proved that South Africa was some forty-eight hours away from a very well-planned suburban uprising. Braam Fisher, the white sympathiser of the anti-Government Pan-Africanist Congress and African National Council had secreted away almost 200,000 rounds of ammunition, and several thousand hand grenades and other explosive devices, in the basement of his rural homestead north of Johannesburg. The lesson was learned by the South African government and suspects were rounded up immediately under the Suppression of Terrorism Act. Hoyle was one of the few who cleverly escaped the net.

During the early 1960s he travelled extensively throughout Europe, beginning in Germany and then going on to France where he worked as a casual labourer, picking grapes and learning the language. Portugal, Spain and

100

Greece were subsequent ports of call for the restless young man whose considerable gift for languages combined well with his likeable nature and attractive blond boyish appearance. The result was that strangers welcomed him and would even maintain him for quite lengthy periods and he spent several idle and happy summers in varying degrees of luxury. In 1964, he finally ended up in England and decided to settle in London which he found stimulating and exciting. Disenchanted with the idea of going back to university after so much freedom, he tried many jobs which varied from selling hairspray to acting as a travel courier.

It was not until 1967 that Hoyle eventually found gainful employment of a more permanent kind when, together with a friend, he started a small magazine in London called *Capitalisms*, a sort of underground student rag in the vein of *Private Eye*. In the satirical fever of the late sixties, the little journal prospered and Hoyle was able to indulge himself with his pet hate, writing vitriolic attacks on rich South African whites and the Vorster government. He was approached by the Anti-Apartheid Movement and eventually joined the London group with the result that *Capitalisms* almost became the unofficial mouth-piece of the movement and in doing so, lost circulation at such a rapid rate that it eventually closed down. After this period of relative wealth in the halcyon days of the easy-living sixties, Hoyle was faced with having to exist frugally on the very fringe of British political splinter groups amongst whom he was regarded as something of a radical left-winger. He was largely ignored and often misunderstood because few people seemed to know where South Africa was, let alone being conversant with the lot of the country's black or coloured people

Douglas Hoyle hit the news in July 1976 when he was interviewed on television for his opinions of the Soweto Riots outside Johannesburg. He made minor television history in a live programme by saying that it was about time the world reacted to 'those fucking facists'. The words were calculated to provoke the attention they received but Hoyle's fame was short-lived, for soon world attention moved off South Africa and he was back on the breadline, drawing National Assistance and a small retainer for odd articles written in the Anti-Apartheid magazine.

In early 1979, Hoyle married a South African Zulu model whose professional name was Jane Zomba. Jane's real name was Miriam Mhlangane and she had been born in Soweto in 1958, the year Hoyle had gone to university. Jane had become a model in Johannesburg and then left for Kenya in 1976 at the age of eighteen after saving up her air fare for almost two years and applying six times for a passport. She had worked as a disco dancer in Nairobi and had lived with an English journalist who had made her pregnant and then left her.

Now Jane had an apartment in London's newly fashionable W11 and a cottage at Pagham in Sussex where her three-year-old daughter Glade lived with a white nanny. Marrying Jane was Hoyle's big break because the 'black is beautiful' theme was still very much alive in England, despite the efforts of the National Front, and Jane's face had appeared on various magazine covers and in television commercials. The girl earned upwards on £1500 in the average month and her astute agent had even bigger plans for her in the world of cinema and records. Jane was not particularly intelligent but hated South Africa with an intensity equalling that of her husband and, so far, this year was proving to be a popular one for the haters of her homeland. The Hoyles were invited to many functions in and around London where the pop and fashion society provided valuable black and white contacts. Money was now no object and Hoyle decided to form a new, independent action group that would work for the liberation of Azania, as South Africa was called by the black nationalist movements. He called it AFRA for Azanian Freedom Revolutionary Army and the name caught on nicely in identifying with Africa, Africans and even the

102

black and coloured people of London's weird and fashionable jet-set.

Offices were found in South Kensington and the first AFRA opened its doors in early summer and by the end of a month, there was just over £107,000 in the bank account. Most of this was donated by friends of Jane's who sympathised with the cause. The Press investigated the AFRA set-up but could learn little as both Hoyle and Jane projected low profiles and declined to comment on the activities of the movement. Then, in the early hours of one morning, a National Front vengeance squad threw a bottle of petrol through the window of the ground-floor offices with dramatic results. Hoyle's automatic sprinkler devices coped with the flames after a few minutes but damage amounted to almost £14,000. The insurance company agreed to pay out the claim and a day later two young men from Balham were arrested in connection with the bombing. Hoyle and Jane became mini-celebrities and were to be interviewed on the BBC programme *Action Week*.

The presenter Timothy Norris was an old hand with the enviable reputation of being a hard-arsed bastard who made his subjects say the wrong thing with verbal trickery and innuendo. To him Hoyle and the African girl were just another couple of jumped-up agitators but the girl could be described as attractive, if one liked that sort of thing. Personally, he didn't. He'd been on many of the newsfronts of the world since the early sixties and he'd tried a few blacks and coffee-coloured popsies here and there. They always smelled to him, a sort of mixture of stale onions and shit and he just couldn't bloody well tolerate it, and on two occasions it had given him the old soft half inch, even though he'd been half-pissed. This Jane Zomba smelled alright though, she'd kissed him when they'd gone into the studio and she'd smelled bloody marvellous a sort of peppery fragrance that was undeniably sexy. Perhaps he would make an exception with her, he mused, watching for the red light on the camera which faced him.

103

As always, it went on suprisingly suddenly. 'Good evening ladies and gentlemen,' he said suavely and imagined all the millions settling into their seats in anticipation of the delights that he and the box would bring to them tonight. 'Tonight, in the first part of *Action Week*, we will talk to Mr and Mrs Douglas Hoyle, Mrs Hoyle is probably better known as the model Jane Zomba.' The camera light went off him and another camera moved onto the girl. He could see her on the monitor staring haughtily out of the screen. She wore a startling silver lame cape over a plain sheer silk blouse and he could see her firm dark breasts quite clearly. Norris grinned to himself thinking of the middle-aged men in countless living rooms around the country, leaping up to adjust their sets whilst their wives looked on disapprovingly.

The light shone redly again, almost catching him out. 'This week's fire-bomb attack on the offices of the Azanian Freedom Revolutionary Army, otherwise known as AFRA, in South Kensington, is thought to have been perpetrated by a right-wing extremist group whose policies are in direct confrontation with AFRA's.' Norris smiled knowingly. 'The police have already arrested two National Front members in connection with the attack, but I would like to ask Mr Hoyle, who describes himself as Chief Executive of AFRA, just why he and indeed his attackers, are so preoccupied with events which are happening some six thousand miles from British shores and which have no direct bearing on this country.' Before Hoyle could speak he added seriously, 'Surely we have enough terrorism in Europe without bringing African problems to our shores.' Norris sat back smiling indulgently at Douglas Hoyle who wore a smart grey suit and blue shirt with a dark tie striped in red AFRA logos.

'Mr Norris, you are either ignorant, stupid or both,' said Hoyle icily.

The controller in the glass box tapped his earphones, stared at the monitor and looked up wonderingly. 'Jesus,' he said to his mixing technician, 'did you get that?' The man nodded and the controller put his finger over the erase button. 'The opposition had trouble with this guy once before,' he said, referring to Hoyle's 1976 appearance on Independent Television News. 'He's a bit of a nutter.'

Norris smiled, and said waspishly, 'That is not an answer, Mr Hoyle. And I can assure you that I am not ignorant of events in South Africa. The question was, what bearing do they have on the United Kingdom, what possible good can your organisation do for this country, or indeed for South Africa?' He paused deliberately. 'I beg your pardon, Azania, I believe you prefer to call it.'

Hoyle smiled coldly at Norris and when he began to speak his voice was quiet and clear. 'By your remarks, Mr Norris, I must presume that you are unaware of the millions of pounds per annum of British investments in South Africa and the vast amounts of goods that we import from what is basically a more corrupt fascist state than Nazi Germany.' He looked sideways at his beautiful black wife and the camera followed his gaze dramatically. 'My wife was born in Soweto,' Hoyle continued. 'She wasn't there at the time of the riots but many of her friends were and a vast number were cut down by the police. Her own sister was killed and two of her cousins are missing to this day and are believed to be in detention. Permanently detained, Mr Norris, in conditions of terrible degradation and suffering.'

Norris felt he was beginning to lose control of the interview and was about to reply when the camera moved to Jane and incredibly he saw on the monitor that she was crying, great glistening drops running down her cheeks towards the soft red lips which were trembling pathetically.

Now the controller was on his feet and making signs through the wall of his soundproofed glass booth. Norris ignored the gesticulations and then a camera glared redly at him and another covered Hoyle whilst the third zoomed in on Jane Zomba's dramatic, beautiful face. The producer spoke quietly into the microphone, which linked him with the earphones on the cameraman's heads. He was outwardly calm yet actually very excited. 'Christ all bloody mighty,' said the controller. 'This is bloody fantastic.'

Hoyle continued in his soft crisp voice. 'All these young people did was protest against the appalling conditions under which they are forced to live.' He paused for effect. 'For that they were shot, tortured and treated like animals. I know this for a fact because I have spent time with some of them, have spoken to actual survivors of the Soweto massacres, and I know what goes on in South Africa because I was born there, and lived there for almost twenty years.' He looked hard at Norris and shook his head briefly. 'You can't tell me that you understand the situation Mr Norris and therefore you can't obviously understand why we exist in order to try and bring the true facts to public knowledge. As far as I'm concerned, you're not qualified to ask questions on this subject.'

Norris began to speak hurriedly but Hoyle stood up and took Jane's arm. The camera followed them as they left the studio.

After their exit there was mild uproar in the studio but Norris was too old a hand to be ruffled by even such unprecedented behaviour. He had been amazed by the girl's incredible sobbing and the theatrical tactics of Hoyle and admitted to himself that he had been momentarily non-plussed. When they'd both got up and left he really had been shattered. Now he smiled his knowing smile into the camera.

'Well, so much for AFRA. It takes all sorts to make a world and I suppose these people have apparently decided to use our country, England, as a minor battlefield.' He paused. 'Another battlefield this week was Northern Ireland, where two British soldiers were brutally slain in a Belfast pub. Here's Walter McClintock in Ulster.'

At last the light went off on the camera and Timothy

Norris sat back in his chair. He knew that he'd been made a fool of and that the comments about a minor battlefield would not go down well at all. His head ached and his mouth was dry but he smiled theatrically at the nearby cameraman.

'How did that go?' he said pleasantly, craving a kind word, wanting to be reassured.

'Great Tim, great,' said the callow-looking technician. 'That bugger really saw you off, eh?' Norris swallowed hard and was about to react when the buzzer sounded and the red light went on again over the camera. He smiled with great effort and faced the one-eyed monster.

Hoyle was delighted. They had worked out the tactics the night before and decided that under no circumstances could Jane be subjected to a grilling by Norris. The crying bit had been decided on as a last-minute resort by Hoyle and he had given her the keyword 'Soweto' and she had responded marvellously. Perhaps they hadn't been on all that long but the attacking tactics had worked perfectly and Norris had been effectively ridiculed. The papers would be full of it in the morning.

Forty-five minutes later they poured slim flutes from the litre bottle of Asti Spumante which Jane loved to drink. Taking the bottle, Hoyle carried the glasses through to the bedroom which was decorated entirely in off-white and was very chic. Jane lay back on the silk sheets and opened her white-lace negligee. As always, the black skin against the white sheets and lace, aroused Hoyle incredibly and he fell on her, kissing the beautiful red lips and fumbling with one hand at his trousers and the other on her small firm breasts. She moaned and he felt her legs open beneath him and he surged into her, not bothering to remove his clothes. The bottle fell off the night table but neither noticed and the sparkling white wine frothed out onto the thick cream carpet.

At about the same time, Timothy Norris walked into

the pub in Shepherds Bush, across the road from the BBC studios. His old cronies were there at the bar and greeted him in the normal way, thankfully without any snide remarks or whispered comments. Louie the barman, pulled him a pint of the usual and he congratulated himself that things were not so bad after all. And then the bastard ruined it all.

'Bad night Mr Norris?' he asked innocently and the whole lot of them looked up, grinning and enjoying his discomfort.

In a rage Norris swept the pint off the counter and walked to the door. He turned and they still stared, smiling like bloody Cheshire cats. 'Stuff the lot of you,' he said petulantly and stalked out into the drizzling rain.

The following morning, Hoyle read the papers at the breakfast table. Jane still slept and rarely rose before eleven unless she was working on an assignment. The *Telegraph*'s comment was typical of what Hoyle would expect from the bloody right-wing press. 'South African walks out on BBC,' said its small leader. But the *Sun* and the *Mail* screamed: 'Thin end at last for Norris' and 'TV coup for AFRA'. It couldn't have been much better, the *Mail*'s piece was on the front page and the *Sun*'s on page two. Hoyle drank his second cup of coffee and lit the first cigarette of the day.

Later that morning at the office, he received dozens of calls and by 11.30 the switchboard was totally jammed. Most of the calls were complimentary but the callers' remarks were more gleeful congratulations at the treatment of the hated Norris, than positive comments about AFRA and the cause.

At the South African Embassy in Trafalgar Square, the morning was not going quite so well as it was for Hoyle. The ambassador was holding a staff conference with his personal advisors and the first three secretaries. The six men and one woman wore serious expressions as they discussed what was literally the overnight success of AFRA, an organisation they had regarded as fly-by-night until Hoyle's BBC TV appearance.

Two of those present were operative in the Pretoria-based Department of National Security and were seconded to the London Embassy for an indefinite period. Ambassador Jaap Booysen was particularly interested in their views on the mounting threat of AFRA. The meeting continued until after five in the afternoon and a plan was formulated. Details were coded onto the telex to Pretoria immediately and a positive reply was received before six o'clock, London time.

PART TWO

CHAPTER 9

Selwyn Cohen and Patrick Reilly had struck up an unlikely friendship of sorts, purely because they were both from Johannesburg and were the sole English speakers in the section. 'A tiny light, burning in a sea of Afrikaanerdom,' Reilly had said somewhat poetically. Cohen's parents had suggested that he join the South African police, rather than do his national service in the army. They imagined Selwyn being billeted in a comfortable Johannesburg North police station whilst his contemporaries dodged bullets and ate dust on the South-West African border. In this way, Selwyn would do his two years service for his country without risking life and limb. The decision was taken and Selwyn was not consulted.

His father, Solly, had made enquiries through a friend in Pretoria, cajoling and bribing until the arrangements were made and his son was safely in the police force instead of the army. At the beginning it had all gone as planned and Constable Cohen was ensconced safely in Bramley Police Station only minutes from the family home in Highlands North, Johannesburg. Then, without warning one day, had come the border posting and four days later Selwyn was aloft in the Hercules to Grootfontein. Solly had ranted and threatened but it had made no difference, a new government decree stated that police recruits must do border duty. So ended the yearly rush of volunteers to the ranks of the SAP.

Patrick Reilly's case was a little different. His family

112

had emigrated to South Africa from Liverpool in the early sixties and taken him along as a two year old. Patrick was educated in Johannesburg and brought up in a typical middle-class home so that he expected to do his army duty, as a matter of course. His father had suggested the police, a suggestion which had followed an offer to send Patrick to the UK to his uncle who had a textile finishing factory in Lancashire. There were possibilities of a place at Liverpool University after a year's acclimatisation and a couple of exams, the whole package had been quite well planned. To his parents' consternation, Patrick had refused, maintaining that all his friends were going into the army and that he was quite looking forward to it. The police was a concession to his parents but he hated the boring charge office duties and was delighted when they were posted to South-West Africa.

Cohen and Reilly were billeted with two Afrikaaners named Albertus van der Merwe and Sarel le Roux. Albert was a 'poor white' from the East Rand near Johannesburg and had joined the police at the age of sixteen after gaining his standard eight matriculation certificate six months early. Sarel le Roux was from a rich farming family in the Oudtshoorn region of the Karoo, a vast desert-like area some four hundred kilometres north-east of Cape Town. The ancient family homestead was between Matjiesrivier and Prince Albert and the Le Roux's had farmed ostriches there for three generations. There was a saying among the Afrikaans families of Prince Albert that the Schoemans talked to the Le Roux's and the Le Roux's talked to God.

Jacobus le Roux, Sarel's father also talked to his contemporaries and sometimes took their advice. Major Grobbelar at Oudtshoorn police station was an old and trusted friend from Jacobus' schooldays and he reckoned that the police would be good for young Sarel who was a bit of a hot head. Sarel had little choice in the matter and was packed off to Oudtshoorn and from there posted to George down on the coast. He was only in the station for three weeks when the commandant Captain Kruger decided that he'd had enough of the cocky youth. Sarel was drafted to the border. In fact Captain Kruger had 'volunteered' him, although he didn't know it.

Of the four young men, van der Merwe was the most accomplished in police 'standing orders' having been a regular in Boksburg, East of Johannesburg, for some six months. He took every opportunity to impress this fact upon his three companions, particularly the Jew Cohen who was somewhat slight of build and typically characterised by his large nose and sallow complexion, topped by unruly coarse black hair. Cohen's voice was rather high and nasal with the affectations of the Johannesburg Jew. These points were sources of constant ridicule by Van der Merwe.

'*Ag* you fokking Yid man, you're bloody stupid man,' said Van der Merwe conversationally. 'Hey Sarel, did you ever see such a *doos* as him?' Le Roux smiled but said nothing. They all lay on their beds in various stages of undress because it was already 21.30 hours and lights out was at 22.00.

Cohen looked pained and whined back at Van der Merwe. 'Shut up Van,' he said weakly. 'How must I know that you can't use a red pen in your pocket book, how must I know that red ink is just for officers.'

Van der Merwe sniffed disgustedly. 'Shit, you prickhead,' he said loudly. 'It stands to reason man, elsewise we'd all be using red wouldn't we you arse-hole.'

At this stage Reilly stepped in and told Albert to leave 'The Rabbi,' as Cohen had become known, alone. Le Roux, who was a muscular blond-haired 180 pounds, still did not respond to the bantering of the other two and the baiting of Cohen.

He was thinking of Sylvie Venter, his girlfriend in Oudtshoorn, and of what they had done together in the back of his Chevrolet pick-up. He hadn't had it since his last leave, over a month ago, and Christ he could only give it to her now, he thought moodily, wondering who she was having it with. She couldn't wait, not Sylvie, she liked it too much.

SAP eight battalion was at a forward position near Oshakati, less than forty kilometres south of the Angolan border. The men were sleeping in tents and in Van der Merwe's Alpha section, the four lay close together, their R1 rifles stacked by their kit bags and the SAP leaf-splotched camouflage uniforms neatly folded at the bottom of their beds. The camp was well guarded and protected on the eastern side by a sizeable lake called Witberg dam. So far there'd been no trouble since they moved up from the training camp at Grootfontein fourteen days ago. In any event, this was a so-called soft position, really a sort of continuation of training.

As Patrick Reilly drifted into sleep, he heard the rhythmical rustling in the next bed. Old Van's at it again, he thought idly, every night it was the same. He had to have his bloody hand-shandy and then he'd give a long-drawn-out gasp at the end and settle down to sleep like a baby until morning. Reilly had been disgusted at first, but after nearly six weeks of it, back in Grootfontein, and now here on the border, he'd got used to it. He smiled into the darkness: even a bloody mortar attack wouldn't stop old Van from having his fist exercises.

He thought of poor old Cohen. The bugger was persecuted by everybody – and there apparently wasn't another Jew in the whole battalion; after all, they were pretty rare in the bloody cops. The poor sod was like a fish out of water and had to be excused from church parades and all the other religious clap-trap that the police and army seemed to favour so much. Cohen seemed so weak and over-protected that Reilly sometimes blamed himself for always sticking up for the Jew, defending him in the constant verbal attacks and never-ending baiting by Van der Merwe. Screw it, he thought, Cohen will have to learn to stand on his own feet. A minute later he was sound asleep.

The noise was incredible and like nothing he had ever known. It blasted him from sleep in a mindless terror which was worse than anything he'd ever experienced and it seemed that his eardrums would burst from the unbelievable percussions. The continuing ear-splitting cacophany was actually caused by 122mm rockets landing in the camp, their alloy casings shattering into tiny shrapnel fragments which, with the dirt and rocks caused by the explosions, lashed through the canvas tents peppering the sleeping men. The bangs were colossal and went on and on as the missiles exploded with crashing high-pitched thunderclaps of sound that seemed to make his heart stop. He had to move, had to get away from the terror and the noise, the God awful noise and unreal blasts of sound.

After a few milliseconds of petrified indecision, the four young policemen bolted from their beds and collided in a scrambling gut-wrenching terror at the door of the tent and then they were stumbling towards the narrow, horribly shallow slit trenches. Reilly fell on top of Van der Merwe, burying his head in the other's armpit, smelling the rank sour odour of fright and then suddenly the other richer, animal smell as the sphincter muscles relaxed and Van der Merwe voided into his shorts.

'Oh Jesus,' screamed Van der Merwe as he tried to burrow deeper into the soft earth at the bottom of the bunker. '*Asseblief* Jesus, *assablief* Jesus,' he wailed. 'Oh dear Jesus man, I don't want to die.' In the terror and noise, Reilly sensed Cohen next to him and realised that he was in a prone position, rifle held out in the prescribed manner. The Jew was quiet and his cheek was pressed up against the stock of the R1 as he sighted in the direction of the firing. Reilly realised that Cohen was the only one of the four in the tent who had remembered to bring his rifle. Feeling heroic he leapt up and scrambled back to the tent, grabbed the three R1s and scuttled back to drop trembling into the trench.

The SWAPO attack was lead by a young Ovambo known locally as Bazooka, because of his proven ability with an RPG 7 rocket launcher. His real name was Lucas Lundonze and he was a strikingly handsome rather light-skinned twenty-six year old, not at all typical of his tribe. His twelve-man team had fired the battery of twelve portable Katyusha 122mm rockets in just under thirty seconds and were now following up with 40mm mortars and rapid fire from the two RPD light machine guns they had set up on the flanks of their position. Lucas was located some 250 metres from the South African camp and had cleverly positioned the lake between himself and his target. He knew, from the training he had received with the Cuban instructors in Luanda, that the 122mm rockets, in their disposable launchers, were more a psychological weapon than a really damaging piece of firepower. The mortars were killers though and young Nicholas seemed to have the range because he could see the flashes going off among the South African tents. The RPDs chattered on both sides of the lake. He looked at the tiny glowing light of his digital watch, it was 23.45 hours exactly and the engagement had been in progress for precisely three minutes. In one more minute they must leave.

Cohen could see where the tracers were originating from. They seemed to loop out over the water and then rush past so fast that they disappeared. He squinted down the barrel of the R1 and through the peep sight, could just make out the darkish mass of bushes along the shore line of the lake. The thick front sight seemed to cover the blotch of low undergrowth but he squeezed the trigger gently as he had been taught and felt the rifle thumping into his shoulder. He wasn't frightened at all and although it amazed him, he felt absolute calm, bordering on confidence and the more he fired, the more elated he felt. Somewhere close by the heard the keening mumble that issued from Van der Merwe in a mixture of barely recognised prayers and obscenities. It went on and on.

After the first few tentative shots in retaliation, the South

Africans opened up with 60mm mortars, the guard posts fired their MAG machine guns and scores of R1 rifles joined the orgy of sound. Across the dam Lucas blew his whistle and the RPDs stopped firing and were lifted up smoothly, the belts snapped out and the bi-pods collapsed. The mortars fired a final salvo and were quickly dismantled. The South African mortars, using illuminated tracer rounds, were just beginning to find the range when Lucas's group melted into the bush. He looked at his digital watch and pressed the little button on the side again so that the figures glowed redly. It was 23.49 hours and 49 seconds. The entire action had taken less than five minutes.

Van der Merwe's terror continued long after the others, and the crashing of the rifles caused him to remain crouched in a foetal position at the bottom of the trench whilst the others blasted away hysterically at the line of bush across the dam. It was the noise of the rifles that kept up his level of terror and he continued to moan and shudder in a paroxysm of absolute agony, barely aware of anything other than the terrible fright which made his muscles useless and his stomach contract involuntarily.

Soon all the R1s fell silent because they were empty and nobody had thought to bring many magazine pouches during the mindless scramble from the tents. As it was though, some 150 twenty-shot magazines had been emptied at the unseen enemy and, in addition, over thirty mortar rounds had been loosed before ceasefire was called. At a cost of sixteen and a half cents per R1 bullet and around R260 per mortar bomb and up to R400 for the illuminated rounds, the action had cost the South African tax payer well over R10,000, close to the same amount in US dollars.

Lucas' group sped through the blackness of bush, weapons held high, their unused ammunition carried in pouches and rucksacks. Lucas didn't think that they would be pursued at night and intended to get as far away as possible under the blanketing cover of darkness. In the morning, he knew that the South Africans would come in their helicopters with fresh troops and expert trackers. They would be determined to seek out and destroy the 'bloody kaffirs' that had dared to attack them.

As he ran steadily and without effort, Lucas pondered on the logic of the forces which opposed him. It was the most difficult thing to understand about them and had cost them quite a few lives in Rhodesia when the South African police had displayed various serious shortcomings. On several occasions they had been successfully goaded into revealing themselves in the bush by Afrikaans-speaking African Nationalists who bombarded the whites with obscenities causing them to lose their tempers, charge out of cover and be shot.

He knew that whilst these men of the SAP 8th battalion would not be particularly tenacious in their follow-up operations, others would be and some training camps across the border would suffer in a flurry of air attacks and reprisal raids. As far as he was concerned it was just too bad for those that would die. Fortunately, he, Nicholas and the rest weren't going anywhere near that far. Within three hours they'd pick up the raft on the canal which was a part of the vast Cunene River irrigation scheme and paddle upstream towards the Ruacane Falls.

All being well they'd disembark at the village near Enunda and cache the weapons as usual in the old 'mine workings. They'd become just another group of vagrant, useless Ovambos and that was the secret of this war, thought Lucas. The white men thought that all blacks looked the same and this meant that they could take refuge anywhere in the Ovambo and Okavango area, provided that they had personal documentation which was up to date and in order. It was classic Maoist tactics, strike and disappear.

Back in the camp they were counting the casualties. One policeman had been killed by a mortar bomb which had dropped so close to him, lying at the end of a trench, that it had literally blown him to pieces. He had been

Constable Els, aged nineteen, and fortunately for his companions, his body had acted as a shield and the earth wall of the trench had absorbed the shrapnel on the other side. Two men had been critically injured by the accurate RPD fire and several others had suffered burst eardrums from the deafening percussions of the Katyusha rockets.

These losses were quite intolerable to Holsworth who was informed of the attack within minutes of the ceasefire. He cursed roundly and ordered a conference of officers and NCOs immediately. At first light, three-five's trackers would go after the sods. On no account would they escape, he assured the shaken captain in charge of the eight battalion SAP detachment.

A strange feeling of euphoria engulfed the young policeman who had survived their baptism of fire. Cohen felt fantastic and Reilly and Le Roux joked and laughed nervously, their voice high and shrill with reaction and the emotion of being alive. The exultation persisted and eventually the laughing grew more normal so that Van der Merwe slowly regained his reason and extracted himself from the bottom of the trench. He was stinking and mud-spattered and the others found themselves awkward and embarrassed by his presence because he was living proof of the gut-wrenching fear they had all experienced. He stood up and looked around in a daze and none of them could look him in the eye and he seemed to shake his head like a wounded animal and wandered off to clean up and change. They watched him go in silence.

CHAPTER 10

The attack on the SAP eight battalion camp was front page news in South Africa, and in Johannesburg. *The Star* English language evening paper trumpeted 'Two SAP die in SWAPO attack.' In the *Cape Argus*, the story was similar and Mostert bought a copy from a street vendor as he drove home to Rondebosch in the evening rush-hour traffic. He had been back only four days from the border and had been almost bored with the inactivity during his three week tour of duty. Now, it had all happened again and to the SAP too. He could imagine Holsworth's reaction and the retaliation he would plan with three-five battalion.

The bloody kaffirs were getting better all the time, he thought. Just the other day, three of them had walked into a cop-shop up in Johannesburg at the coloured township called Alexandra. They'd walked in as calm as you like and mowed down four black constables with AKs. Old Visser and his mob up on the Reef must still be reeling from the sheer audacity of the swine, it was pretty obvious to Mostert that things were not getting any easier in this direction. For his own part, his chaps and the Security Police still had not found the sods who had shot up the lads and carved that poor bloody policewoman in Hout Bay. The trouble with kaffirs was that they could just disassemble their weapons and hide them and then walk around free as birds. You couldn't tell one from the other unless they had guns and a uniform and of course they were too clever for that. Often, even the SWAPO bastards didn't have uniforms and the only way to identify them was with other kaffirs and that could be a bit tricky because you couldn't trust any of them farther than you could throw the bastards. In any case, they were only really good as informers, you couldn't get them to risk their lives, except for Holsworth's three-five chaps, of course. They were something else again.

As Mostert crawled along De Waal Drive towards home, the sun was beginning to shine weakly through the rain clouds which had been building up all day and were now beginning to disperse with the onset of sunset. It hadn't actually rained because it was still too early for that but when it did, the cold misery of the Cape winter would be on him for at least four months. That was the trouble with the Cape, thought Mostert, it was all bloody fine in the summer with the beautiful beaches and the cooling breezes. The winter was a different story though, wet and windy and unbelievably cold at times.

He drove automatically, the little Mazda 323 moving a few car lengths forward before stopping again. On the few times that he worked office hours, like today, he would normally miss the bloody traffic by going off to the Townhouse bar in the city, for a pot or two after his duty finished. But today he had to get home because it was Lorraine's birthday and he'd promised to take her out to dinner at the Vineyard grill room. Meanwhile, there was his sweet little Janine to get to bed and he'd seen little enough of her lately.

Two cars in front of Mostert's Mazda was a green single-decker bus which crawled along full of coloureds and middle-class white city workers who sensibly preferred to sit reading their newspapers and let someone else do the driving. They all poured out of their offices and shops on the Foreshore and there were dozens of buses just waiting for them. Then it was a nice rest and the paper or a book all the way home. Mostert watched them all, absorbed in themselves or chattering away to their neighbours. Buses made a lot of sense, he thought.

In actual fact, he hated large vehicles in front of him and longed to pass the lumbering green monster which belched

122

out diesel fumes so that he had to close the window. Soon they'd be at the intersection with Settlers Way, just down from the hospital, and half the traffic would peel off to the left heading for Belville and Paarl. The bus stayed in the right hand lane though, because it was going to Rondebosch like Mostert and his Mazda, this meant that there wouldn't be many coloureds on it, he thought idly; then the right hand lane began moving and the bus moved over to let the faster traffic pass.

As Mostert changed down a gear and pulled out to overtake, there was a blast of sound behind him and he ducked back into the left hand middle lane, as a large battered Holden Monaro thundered past, its V8 engine rumbling loudly. Mostert saw that the car was full of coloureds and it pulled past him and slowed alongside the bus which was still two cars ahead of the Mazda. He noted passengers watching the big car in idle curiosity and then the unbelievable happened and Mostert saw the two black gun barrels appear magically from the side windows; and then fire winked from the ends.

He heard the stuttering rattle of automatic fire above the roar of the bus and his own car, and watched fascinated, unable to do anything in the crush of traffic moving at a steady fifty kilometres an hour. He flinched as copper cartridge cases bounced off the tarmac and struck his windshield and then the bus started to slow up before suddenly stopping dead, causing the Volkswagen Passat in front of Mostert to clang into its rear end. Mostert stopped without hitting the Passat and leapt from the car watching the Holden thundering away in the now clear outside lane.

The line of bullet holes was irregularly spaced along the side of the bus and had made neat punctures through the thin metal skin. The attackers had needed to elevate their weapons and some bullets had gone high, punching through the windows and passing out through the roof. Mostert ran around to the cab and saw that the driver was slumped over the wheel, blood running down the side of his face. His cap had been knocked askew and the effect would have been comical, except for the blood.

Some fifty 7.62mm bullets had drilled through the crowded passenger cab and most of these had passed through both sides of the vehicle and presumably some of its occupants. Screams and wails greeted Mostert as he jumped up into the passenger section. There was blood everywhere and of the sixty or so occupants, around a dozen were already obviously beyond help. It was 7.15 before Mostert was able to telephone Lorraine to tell her that her birthday dinner was off. His had been the best description of the Holden and its occupants and he had noted that it had a CY, Belville number plate.. He told his wife that the hunt was on and to expect him when she saw him. In fact, he didn't get home until after three the next morning.

There was no real connection between the attack on the SAP border detachment and the massacre on De Waal Drive, Cape Town, except that it was safe to surmise that the two groups had much the same motivation and ideals. Slips of paper found at the scene, which had been thrown out of the speeding Holden and blown all over the highway, bore the crudely stamped legend 'Support ANC and UMKHONTO WE SIZWE. Remember June 1976 – TAKE UP ARMS AND FIGHT.'

The five men who attacked the bus were actually not members of the ANC – African National Congress, a banned organisation in South Africa whose ringleaders were rounded up and interned during the sixties. Most of these were still in prison in Cape Town in the maximum security prison at Robben Island in Table Bay.

Although they worked with the ANC and shared headquarters in exile in Lusaka, Zambia, the De Waal Drive attackers were from UMSA – the Unity Movement of South Africa whose military wing APDUSA had been known to the South African Police and Security police as a formidable and well-trained movement in the early sixties. The gang from the Holden had cleverly left the ANC leaflets to confuse the police in their avenues of pursuit and this simple ploy was effective for a little more than twenty-four hours, which was all the time they needed to escape.

With the PAC – Pan-Africanist Congress – these three movements have sworn to overthrow the South African government, by force if necessary. In this aim they enjoy strong support from the Eastern Bloc and many of their members in exile have received valuable and sophisticated guerilla training in Russia, China and more recently, in certain militant black states. A surprising number of hard-line leaders among these groups are known to be coloured and this fact has caused great concern among South African security personnel because they respect the radical coloured as a dedicated and intelligent enemy rather than a sort of poor relation of the whites, which is what the coloured man has traditionally been regarded as for centuries.

Back in his office early on the morning following the De Waal Drive incident, Mostert began to pore over the SAP files of known coloured militants from the beginning of the sixties. A classic star of this group had been Basil February, originally from Cape Town, who at the beginning of the decade had obviously rejected the restraining cloak of blind acceptance which typified the average coloured person in South Africa, a person doomed from birth to be regarded as racially inferior.

February had headed north into Zambia during those ten years when the wind of change had blown down the continent of Africa. Eventually he had met up with a group of guerillas intent on invading South Africa and had joined them.

On his first mission with his associates, south of the Zambian border, he had encountered a strong group of Rhodesian security forces and a protracted battle ensued, involving hundreds of troops and fighter aircraft of the Rhodesian Air Force. Driven into a last-ditch stand in the remote and blistering heat of the Zambezi Valley, February and his colleagues – many of them Russian-or Chinese-trained – had put up a tremendous fight until their ammunition was expended. February and most of the group were killed, only a handful surviving to be captured when they had nothing left with which to fight.

There had been no voluntary surrenders and the Rhodesians had commented, after the fire-fight, on the tenacity of the enemy. This admiration from one of the world's finest anti-terrorist armies had made February's name a legend and eventually he had become one of the more famous martyrs to the coloured cause. Mostert sat back in his chair imagining the bitter fight in the sweltering heat of the Zambesi basin and the young Rhodesians and insurgents who had lost their lives. He read the pencilled notation; 'Basil February is still highly regarded among politically-aware coloureds, especially among those in the Western Cape. February was a member of UMSA.'

Mostert, now very interested, read on from a press release handed out to African heads of state at a summit meeting in Ethiopia in mid-1971:

The Unity Movement of South Africa was formed in 1943 when the Second World War was in its crucial stages and General Jan Smuts was the Prime Minister of South Africa. The year before, Smuts had declared the death of 'Segregation', the cornerstone of his policy, when the Japanese were menacing the shores of South Africa in the Indian Ocean. But we of the Unity Movement did not swing the non-whites behind Smuts' imperialist war wagon; we resolutely opposed the *baasskap*(masterhood) of his 'Segregation' policy, out of which the Unity Movement was born in 1943. We wish to emphasise this point, that the All-African Convention ('largely African' had been pencilled in) and the National Anti-CAD Movement ('largely coloured') which were jointly responsible in 1943 for the formation of the Unity Movement, arose against the Colour Bar system which existed for many years before the Nationalists came to power in 1948.

Our Movement against operation and exploitation by the Herrenvolk goes back as far as 1935–6 when the All-Africa Convention was formed. This federation of organisations and committees of peasants was largely a rural one and arose out of the disfranchisement of the African people in 1936 and the granting of separate dummy representation and a so-called Representative Council. The next step in our march, both against oppression and towards the unity of the oppressed was the formation in February 1943 of the National Anti-Coloured Affairs Department Movement, Anti-CAD, another federation of organisations of mainly the coloured population, to oppose dummy representation and the eventual disfranchisement of the 1½ million coloured people of South Africa (here was another pencilled note stating 'now almost 3 million'). And the third was the formation of the Unity Movement in December 1943 against a federation of federations and their constituent organisations and branches. It was at this inaugural Unity Conference that the 10 point programme of democratic demands was adopted as a policy for the whole non-white population, the first time in the history of South Africa that all the oppressed had made such a clear demand for full equality and full citizenship in the land of their birth. The demand was unequivocal and uncompromising. Our slogan became 'Nothing less than full democratic rights . . .'

Mostert sat back again in his chair marvelling at the brain that had put together this load of claptrap. But despite his instinctive ridicule of such statements by blacks and coloureds he knew that this was no small band of bar-room politicians and bottle throwers. As if to reinforce this thought he saw the additional pencilled note at the bottom of the page.

Although it has been forced underground and virtually destroyed within the borders of South Africa, the original Unity Movement's spirit and morale is still in existence today among certain coloured leaders. Some quite prominent coloureds disassociated themselves with the movement when violence became the accepted method of enforcing change in Government policy and APDUSA was formed. Thus they resigned their interest when it became impraticable and dangerous.

Lighting a Benson & Hedges Luxury Mild, with which he convinced himself that he was doing his lungs less harm, Mostert considered for the first time, that the De Waal Drive attackers could be UMSA men rather than ANC who themselves were known to have many coloured followers. Sucking deeply on the almost tasteless cigarette, he turned back to the file and grabbed another thick folder entitled 'Trials and history of Coloured members of the ANC'. He would read this and try and make some sort of conclusion as to whether those murdering bastards last night had been UMSA or ANC – already his Security Police colleagues were out rounding up all the likely suspects anyway, it wasn't really his business but he felt that he was close to a real breakthrough, perhaps more reading would crystallise his thoughts in one direction.

The five UMSA men who had done the killing on De Waal Drive crossed the border into South-West Africa some three hours before Mostert began pondering the political identities of the group. They had continued along De Waal Drive and turned off at Claremont to run down Lansdowne Road alongside the Kenilworth race course. Crossing over the Eastern Freeway of Settlers Way, they had then circled back through Kuils River, Belville and Parow and joined the main N7 freeway to the north near Goodwood. By 7.30 that evening they had reached Piketberg some one hundred kilometres north of Cape Town on the direct route to South-West Africa.

During the night, whilst the police in the city were vainly combing the coloured townships from Nyanga to Elsies River, the Holden had roared north at a steady 90kph. The border was about 800km distance and it took the fugitives just on nine hours, including the stop to re-fill the tank from the two 25 litre containers in the boot. During this stop they disposed of the AKs in a water culvert which passed under the road.

The coloureds had decided that there would be little chance of interception because the South African Police would fail to consider a dash for the border as a feasible escape route. In fact, Mostert had ordered a road block set up on the N7 about ten kilometres before Malmesbury but by the time it was erected the Holden had already passed the point forty minutes previously. The road block had taken a bit longer than usual because the officers in charge had not thought that the terrorists would be travelling in that direction. Mostert himself had thought about it a bit late in the day in any case.

Once inside South-West African territory the group relaxed and changed the Belville number plates for the characteristic SW ones of South-West Africa. By mid-afternoon they reached Windhoek and split up, the driver and one of the gunmen heading on north for Tsumeb and Oshakati, close to the border with Angola. They talked happily and smoked Lexington cigarettes non-stop as the Holden thundered on through the flat countryside and the windless heat of the dying afternoon.

CHAPTER 11

Almost ten thousand miles away in London it had been an excellent day for the chief executive of AFRA who was congratulating himself on his achievements. Hoyle had enjoyed a superb lunch with Julius St George, the black fashion designer whose new collection included an AFRA dress in ivory fabric decorated in a geometric pattern with countless tiny red AFRA logos. This garment was to be modelled by Jane at a gala showing of the collection during the following week, at the Hilton Hotel on Park Lane. Hoyle was to be the guest of honour and it was all going to be marvellous publicity. AFRA was succeeding beyond Hoyle's wildest dreams and the trust account had accumulated an additional two hundred thousand pounds in donations. Furthermore, there was a great deal of new interest from abroad and, just yesterday, Colonel Gadhaffi's London representative had called on Hoyle personally. The future was looking incredibly rosy.

Hoyle consulted his gold Patek Phillipe and saw that it was well after 5.30. The traffic roar from the busy South Kensington intersection was muted by the double glazing of armoured glass and the thick velvet curtains in the office. And the air conditioner had coped well with an unusually hot early summer day. Hoyle sat back at his leather-topped oak desk and opened the cupboard at his elbow which supported a battery of telephones, the intercom, a dictating machine and a few 'executive toys'. He withdrew the dark green triangular bottle and poured a measure of the amber liquid into a chunky crystal glass. With pleasure he looked around the room at the beige silk clad walls and matching Wilton carpet and appraised his collection of David Hockneys and the two magnificent tribal masks from Ghana which had been given to him personally by the Minister of Foreign Affairs of that country.

Hoyle sipped the Glenfiddich and then added two cubes of ice from the silver bucket and a little water from the Waterford decanter, his secretary Mary always brought the makings through before she left at 5.15. Hoyle thought pleasurably about Mary and what he had done with her in this very room on the brown velvet couch under the window. She was a coloured American from Dallas, Texas, and her drawl was soft and warm like milk chocolate melting in the sun. He had managed to have her three times now and each time it had been a calculated risk he considered very worthwhile. All he would have needed to to do tonight was to ask her to stay behind for dictation because she knew the score and would have disappeared into the toilet for ten minutes and come out smelling like a rose, freshly washed and perfumed. He'd thought about it tonight but had felt a bit jaded after the long boozy lunch at the Grosvenor House; and apart from that, he and Jane had planned an evening at home and he'd need all his strength for her. She was bloody insatiable.

It was after six by the time Hoyle finished day-dreaming and musing pleasantly on his good fortune. He'd left the Rover at the flat that morning because Jane had been up early for a modelling job and her taxi had dropped him en route to Knightsbridge. Now he would catch the train from South Kensington underground, just across the road and get off at Notting Hill Gate to catch a cab home. That way he'd beat most of the traffic and the snarl up in the Park which was impossible to cross at this time of the evening.

As Hoyle locked the doors to his offices and turned to

cross the busy crescent to the underground station, he failed to see the attractive dark-haired woman who was watching him in the reflection from the sports-shop window across the road. Jenni Theron had been following Hoyle for five days but she was a professional and he hadn't noted her surveillance. The young woman was one of the two special operatives at the South African Embassy in Trafalgar Square and she relished the task and the responsibility that had been given her. As far as she was concerned, Hoyle was vermin and needed to be exterminated.

Tonight she saw that Hoyle was not walking away down the crescent to collect his car, as he normally did. Now he was coming across to the tube station and she felt a gut-wrenching excitement. Tonight could be the chance and she hoped to hell he wasn't just going to buy a paper or cigarettes.

As she watched, Hoyle crossed into the station arcade and joined in the queue at the ticket office. She fell in behind him and examined him critically. He was quite good looking in a blond boyish sort of way and she tried to imagine him in bed with that flashy kaffir bitch he was married to. The vision just wouldn't crystallise. She watched as he bought his ticket and crossed to the news-stand to buy an *Evening Standard* and then passed through the automatic barrier following the yellow and green signs to the District and Circle Line trains. She walked behind him unhurriedly, about twenty metres back and prayed fervently to herself that a train would not arrive as they reached the platform.

Nose buried in his paper, Hoyle stood on the edge of the concrete lip below which was the burnished steel of the rails. The indicator board showed that the first train was Circle Line and he knew that it would be here literally any minute. To make sure he would get on, he had shouldered his way through the crowds and walked down the platform a bit where the numbers were a bit thinner; even so, they'd built up to four deep behind him already.

In the rush hour, the most regular of London Underground trains hurtle through the myriads of catacombs under the central city every two to four minutes. The Piccadilly Line which serves the West End and City has the fastest frequency with trains every two minutes but the Circle Line comes a close second. Jenni Theron knew that she wouldn't have much time and she sidled and pushed her way through the crowd until she was located directly behind her target. She loosened the strap of the bag on her left shoulder and took a deep breath as she heard the muted rumble of the train's approach. Hoyle stood unsuspecting, his nose still buried in the newspaper.

The girl waited and judged her moment perfectly. As the lights of the train hurtled out of the black maw of the tunnel, she dipped her left shoulder so that the handbag dropped to the platform giving her the excuse to bend and try and catch it.

In bending forward, her right shoulder struck Hoyle squarely in the small of his back, propelling his forward over the edge of the platform. Hoyle had sensed the movements behind and felt the soft yet solid push in disbelief. He tottered on the edge of the concrete lip of the platform and his mouth opened soundlessly in terror and as he fell he half turned and saw the face of the woman.

Although her hair was dark and thick, her skin was sallow and almost pale and her eyes were large and brown like liquid pools. The lips were full and red and they were drawn back now in a sort of smile, the teeth parted with excitement, and he knew then with absolute certainty that she had murdered him and in that one millisecond recognised her as a typical Afrikaans beauty from the country of his birth. As if to confirm his suspicions, in the seemingly eternal space of time as he was poised there in space, she spoke two quiet words which only he heard, he was sure, 'Totsiens veraaier.' These were the Afrikaans words for 'Goodbye traitor'.

He fell screaming into the well of the track, his body slipping miraculously under the central electric rail and then his wail of terror was swallowed up by the thunder of the train and the horrified screams of the crowd. The girl shrank back quickly into the mass of jostling humanity, hand to mouth and screaming to camouflage possible reaction from anyone who had noticed her movements prior to Hoyle's plunge from the platform. For the Jamaican driver of the train, it was the second such incident he had experienced and he simply hit the emergency brake. Passengers inside the carriages were sandwiched together in any event and thus there was minimum injury except for a few seated old people who were flung on top of each other.

The driver communicated with the London Underground control at St James Park and the power was cut off on the South Kensington section of the Circle Line. As the train screeched dramatically to a halt, the more ghoulish among those on the edge of the platform tried to view the mangled remains of Hoyle through the tiny gap between carriage and platform and others pressed forward from behind them.

With the cutting of the power the train's emergency generators were used to operate the doors and after a hurried discussion with the station inspector, the driver opened the doors in the carriage under which Hoyle lay. This released more fascinated spectators onto an already packed platform and the station officials began to clear the area by ushering the masses of commuters towards the exits. The other doors were left shut until the platforms were reasonably clear and then the remaining passengers were let out and they too were shooed away, many protesting loudly and indignantly to the grinningly important porters.

As he had fallen, Hoyle had somehow managed to slip horizontally below the feeder rail carrying tens of thousands of volts of direct current which would have literally crisped him in less than a second. After the initial stunning from the headlong fall, he had tried in horrified panic to scramble his body below the level of the track but in the half second left for this manoeuvre, the train was on him with fearsome speed and one leg and arm remained above the level of the rails when the first carriage roared overhead in a terrible cacophany of sound.

Hoyle felt the blow beneath his left knee and a great pressure on the same forearm, and then somehow he was released and forced down into the foul oily smelling gravel and debris beneath the rails. Mercifully he passed out with severe shock before the pain came.

Even if they could have got to him, the station officials would not have dared to touch Hoyle and it was presumed anyway that he was dead, trapped beneath the wheels of the train and probably mangled very badly. One of the more adventurous porters scrambled down beneath the train using the nearest break in carriages as an access point. He carried an emergency lamp and with it he could see Hoyle's body some three metres further on under the train. He inched forward and saw the compressed limbs and promptly vomited up his lunchtime steak-and-kidney pie.

Retreating rapidly back the way he had come, he surfaced with a face the colour of milky coffee and shouted his news. 'Gor blimey, his legs is gone I think, but the poor bugger could be alive. He's below the bloody feeder in't ee.'

Meanwhile, Jenni Theron had not remained to witness the excitement. She was ushered out with the rest and was one of the first to reach surface level where she managed to catch a taxi right outside the station entrance.

After about eight minutes a troop of four white-coated medics hurried onto the platform and pushed their way through the bustling officials who were doing nothing. They took the same route as the porter and carried powerful quartz iodine hand lamps as they scrambled towards Hoyle's slumped body. They found that incredibly he was still breathing in shallow gasps and losing little blood so that only a small puddle had formed beneath each damaged limb, to soak into the rusty brown shale. As the doctors made their first exploratory moves, Hoyle's eyes opened and his teeth drew back in a grimace of agony.

From his position below the feeder rail Hoyle was lying half on his back and could see a thin gap of light between the base of the carriage and the station. He could make out a face on a poster and knew it to be Jane's, the famous poster of her in the white silk underwear. His clarity increased suddenly until, with the almost ringing perception that exists with severe shock, the pain and reality came in great bursting, monstrous waves like crude unorchestrated sound.

Hoyle realised without doubt that he had been very badly hurt and he tried to move his arms and legs to reassure himself that he was not too critically injured. The resulting pain was so intense that he could not seem to draw sufficient breath for a few seconds and gasped as a child will prior to crying, in great shuddering sighs. When the instinctive scream came it was a terrible animal noise which rent the still air of the filthy tunnel as if it were torn from the very depths of his being.

A shocked silence descended on the station and as the scream renewed itself and changed to a dreadful penetrating bellow, those on the platform fell back, their horror now hushed and absolute. In seconds, one of the four young casualty housemen from the nearby St Mary's Hospital in Kensington, quickly thrust the hypodermic into an exposed area of forearm and squeezed off the 20mg of Omnopon.

The vast crushing weight of the train had effectively pinched off the blood vessels in the virtually severed limbs, but the cloth of Hoyle's Austin Reed worsted suit had merely been compressed rather than cut through so that the damaged arm and leg had not become totally detached. In fact they had become slightly elongated by the hundreds of tons of pressure directed through the carriage wheels and the final grinding by the inner flange. Abstractedly the young doctor thought that they resembled those of a scarecrow.

The doctors folded the leg and arm as carefully as possible and signalled for the waiting ambulance men to assist in sliding Hoyle carefully along under the carriage. A narrow canvas stretcher was sent down and eventually they managed to manhandle the limp body onto it and inched it along to the gap between the coaches where they had climbed down. Once on the platform Hoyle was transferred to a larger stretcher and the officials pressed forward in amazement to view the apparently undamaged body. With the dreadful screaming having stopped they had regained their curiosity and watched, marvelling to each other, as Hoyle was whisked away looking almost peaceful and covered in red blankets. The doctors had not even bothered to place dressings over the terrible blood-less wounds.

Jenni Theron had not returned to the embassy in Trafalgar Square but had headed for her temporary flat off the Bayswater Road where a ready-packed suitcase had been waiting for a week. The cab had crawled across the bottle-neck of Hyde Park and she had tremblingly lit a cigarette and tried to read the *Standard* that she had bought. Unfortunately the cabbie was a chatty type and he whittered on about boxing, the weather and the rising price of petrol. 'Course, it's different in Australia I suppose where you come from – eh Miss?' he chattered. Jenni mumbled a few words thinking how many times she had been mistaken for an Australian. As far as she was concerned, all these bloody *rooineks* could keep on thinking that she was an Australian because it assisted in her cover. For hers was a much more controversial nationality and therefore she never contradicted casual acquaintances who made the error.

Ninety-three minutes later she had checked in her baggage at Heathrow for the British Airways flight to Amsterdam where she would connect with the onward KLM flight to Johannesburg at 23.45 hours. Her tickets were first class and had been bought two weeks ago when the plan to kill Hoyle had been finalised. There was no problem getting a seat in the TriStar and by 9.30 she was sitting comfortably in the first-class lounge at Schiphol sipping her second complimentary gin and tonic and gently rebuffing a middle-age American who was blatantly chatting her up. The KLM flight was called just after eleven o'clock and Jenni Theron settled into the big wide seat in the half-full first-class section of the DC10. The big jet whispered off through the night sky accelerating to its cruising speed of 850kph at a height of 33,000ft. After dinner she settled easily into sleep and woke for breakfast the next morning two hours out of Nairobi feeling completely refreshed and marvellously happy to be going home again.

In contrast, Hoyle awoke to a soft yellow light and hushed respectful voices muttering out of earshot. His left leg hurt dreadfully and he tried to turn in the bed to lessen the intense tingling ache from below his kneecap. As if in a dream he found that he was held rigidly by tight blankets and that somehow his right arm seemed to be trapped below him so that it had a peculiar dead, pins and needles feeling to it. I'm dreaming, he thought vaguely, and drifted off again into a drugged exhausted sleep.

When he awoke again the light was different. It was still yellow but with a hint of grey and he knew that it must be early in the morning just after dawn because he often woke up at this time after his increasingly frequent boozy evenings and would stagger into the toilet to relieve his bladder. Again he tried to move and then he knew that it couldn't happen twice, couldn't be a bad dream. Without warning, the fear hit him as it does when the mind is vulnerable after deep sleep. It reminded him of those boyish fears when he constantly dreamed that his mother or father was dead, a sort of shocking disbelief upon waking which always proved to be marvellously vindicated.

This time there was no such warming realisation and he knew with a cold, heart-wrenching certainty that he was badly hurt, even mutilated. And then the terrifying scene came back to him and he remembered pitching out over the edge of the platform, hearing the rumble of the approaching train, then the nightmare as it had thundered over him and the sudden strange release so that he was able to slump down underneath that fatal electric rail.

In mounting conviction that he had suffered some frightening damage, he tried to move his arm and leg and felt the bandaged stumps and then he knew that they were gone and he shouted his despair so that the nurse outside who heard the muffled croak came running to bend over him speaking solicitously. 'Now Mr Hoyle, take it easy, there's a lamb, take it easy, dear.' Hoyle listened to the inane words and he felt the rage building up inside him, felt it bubbling through the pain and the stark realisation that now he was a cripple. 'Take it easy,' he hissed although he tried to shout it. 'Take it easy, are you fucking mad woman!'

He ranted and raved until the doctors arrived and then began to ramble on about getting the police. Initially they took no notice and gave him a sedative but he continued in whispered menacing tones repeatedly asserting that he had been pushed off the platform.

'You stupid bastard,' he said to the young intern. 'I was pushed off the fucking platform, can't you understand that, are you too bloody stupid to follow what I'm saying?'

Until this moment the possibility of attempted murder had not occurred to anyone at the hospital although a sergeant from West End Central had phoned a few times to ask if Hoyle had regained consciousness. After the outburst from the patient they decided to call him but, by the time he arrived, Hoyle had relapsed into shocked slumber.

The news had reached Jane as she was taking the bottle of Asti Spumante from the refrigerator in their small kitchen; it was intended for dinner and was nicely chilled. She took the call on the wall telephone in the kitchen and on hearing the news, dropped the bottle so that it shattered and frothed in a pale golden puddle over the Italian tile floor.

She had taken the Rover and hurtled through the quiet evening crescents of Holland Park, down Queensway and onto the Bayswater Road. Twenty minutes after leaving home she was sobbing brokenly at her husband's bedside. Hoyle had been sedated again after he had been awoken for his brief painful talk with the policeman and Jane sat holding his one limp hand, great tears running down her flawless chocolate-coloured cheeks.

Somehow she knew that nothing would ever be the same again, that this terrible happening would change her husband and therefore her relationship with him. The dread she felt was greater than the sorrow at his frightening injuries because her African mind could accept mutilation, having been exposed to crude violence since childhood.

The police had no chance of being able to interview any of the crowd who had been on the platform at South Kensington without the invaluable aid of the media. Independent Television News and BBC Television both ran requests for anyone who had witnessed the accident to contact Inspector Dawson at New Scotland Yard. Hoyle himself had given the police a good description of the woman who he alleged had pushed him and who he insisted was South African. A couple of people seemed to remember seeing a dark-haired woman near to the edge of the platform just before Hoyle fell but there was no concrete evidence from the TV news requests. It was when Dawson checked up on Hoyle's background and the AFRA connection that it all began to make sense and it was at this stage that he decided to treat the case as attempted murder.

Only six people at South Africa house had advance knowledge of the plan to liquidate Hoyle; the seventh was Jenni Theron and she was safely home in Pretoria when the Scotland Yard inspector made his first tentative enquiry through diplomatic channels in the Foreign

Office. After the old Jeremy Thorpe scandals involving South Africa, and various recent statements by black African embassies and consulates in London that Pretoria's government agents were 'running rife in the UK' the police were rather wary about embroiling themselves diplomatically. The Eschel Rhoodie affaire and the resulting exposé which had revealed that South Africa had planned to buy a British newspaper had not improved the delicacy of the situation.

Embassy staff have diplomatic immunity and cannot be forced to account for their actions. Needless to say, all the staff at South Africa House – including Ambassador Booysens – offered cast-iron alibis without being asked. There was of course, no record of Jenni Theron at the embassy and the South Africans denied that any woman of her description had ever worked there.

In an interview with the press at South Africa House, Ambassador Booysen described Hoyle's accusations as 'the ridiculous rantings of a twisted mind'. Booysens was popular with the diplomatic press corps in London because of his pleasant friendly manner to journalists who all too often were ignored or openly hated by other embassy staffers in the city. After the conference there was cold Cape Riesling and delicious crayfish canapés and everybody had left in a happy state of mind, more or less agreeing with the urbane Booysens that Hoyle was a ranting liberal who had stupidly fallen in front of a tube train and decided to try and capitalise on it.

Two days later at AFRA headquarters, just across the crescent from where Hoyle had had his violent encounter with the enemy, the AFRA executive met in the boardroom to plan their revenge. So far, since inauguration, they had been unable to make any overt moves against the hated but powerful regime in Pretoria but after this blatantly militant attack on the founder of AFRA it had been unanimously decided to plan a retaliation against South Africa. A powerful gesture was required and it had to be targeted at a public figure; the final target and the method were details that had to be ironed out.

Having no military wing themselves, despite their warlike

title, AFRA would need to contract the service of some sympathetic organisation that was both well equipped and experienced in such matters as terrorism and assassination. With a current cash reserve of close to half a million pounds they could now talk from a certain amount of strength and once the plan was divulged to selected sympathisers in London, the Middle East, and the United States, further funds were expected to flow in.

Chairing the meeting was Hoyle's deputy, a young white ex-Rhodesian named Peter Anderson, who banged the table sharply with the flat of his hand to bring the meeting to order. All eight members of the executive were present and four of them were black; Anderson and the absent Hoyle made up the total of ten. Jane Zomba was present in her own capacity as one of the ten members.

'There's no point in even thinking about using blacks,' said Anderson quietly. 'The South African Security Police are just too bloody good and they've got too many informers, a black group would never make it past the border, without being noticed by one of them.'

'What about Germans?' said Hugh Francis, a young barrister who was highly sympathetic to the AFRA cause and had been on the executive for only three months. Anderson nodded thoughtfully.

'That's not a bad idea Hugh.' He paused as a scheme began to gel in his mind. 'Wait a minute, what about a combined group of Germans and coloureds, the Germans to do the synchronisation and training and the coloureds plus perhaps a couple of Krauts to do the final run in and attack? There's some good coloured guys in Namibia now, ex-UMSA apparently, a contact in Cape Town reckons they were responsible for that Hout Bay thing and the attack on the bus last month. Those guys are real pros, they've been at it for ages and now SWAPO have given them a new lease of life.'

All eight members began to discuss the idea with enthusiasm and as their thoughts crystallised, the atmosphere of excitement grew. They were highly intelligent

142

people between the ages of twenty-two and thirty-four; Jane was the single exception and she listened abstractedly, as a child does to adults, not understanding much of what was said.

Anderson thumped the table again and held up his hand for silence. 'OK then, that's the broad base, people. Now we have to make contact with a German group – obviously Baader-Meinhof are now out of the picture.' He paused and there was a titter of laughter. 'Then there's the UMSA men in Windhoek to get hold of. I think the next meeting should be in one week's time so leave your diaries open, in the meantime let's see if we can get some answers; it's all up to you Russell,' he added, looking directly at the young Nigerian economics student who worked three evenings a week as a relief telephone operator on the European section of the West London telephone exchange.

Russell made calls all over the world with total impunity and the official capacity of his position as an operator, enabled him to contact virtually anyone, anywhere with absolute safety. Now he nodded confidently. 'You give me the leads Peter and I'll get hold of the right people,' he said quietly.

Anderson smiled and nodded thinking that now they were really getting somewhere. The cover was perfect and none of the calls could be traced back to AFRA by any over-zealous Special Branch man; he accepted that the AFRA phones were tapped now and this made Russell's services even more valuable. He thumped the table again.

'Alright everybody, I'm closing the meeting now because I'm going to see the boss in hospital.' Everyone became serious and Anderson continued in a soft almost whispering voice. 'I'll give him all your love of course.' They all nodded vigorously. 'And tell him how we are progressing.' He smiled again thinly and added, 'No doubt Douglas will have a few suggestions of his own.'

Leftish newspapers in London, like the *Guardian* and the *Daily Worker* interviewed Hoyle in his modest

143

£140 a day room at the London Clinic and devoted considerable space to his statement that a South African woman agent was responsible for his attempted murder and the subsequent mutilation of his two limbs. 'SA terror squads active in London,' screamed the *Guardian* head-line.

In Pretoria there was considerable disappointment at the failure of Jenni Theron's attempt but Jenni herself felt glad in a way that she had not killed the renegade South African although as AFRA boss he was a sworn and hated enemy of her country. Another part of her wished him dead with an intensity matched only by her colleagues in the Department of National Security. The youthful deputy director summed up the feelings of his department when he remarked to his personal assistant on Hoyle's survival, 'At least the bastard won't be able to get his leg over that kaffir wife of his so easily.' He laughed, a harsh unpleasant sound. 'Maybe he'll use the bloody stump instead.'

Hoyle's amputations had been carried out by a young West Indian intern at the Kensington hospital. The doctor had followed the prescribed method and after neatly cutting away the virtually severed sections of limb had carefully removed every tiny splinter of bone in the muscle and sinew which surrounded the wounds. The left leg had been crushed 8cm below the knee but the arm damage had involved only the lower forearm and hand. Hoyle therefore had a neatly sewn flap of skin over the area of his upper wrist on the left arm and being right handed was thus able to write as before. The clinic brought in a Harley Street orthopaedic surgeon who examined the job done by the young West Indian and pronounced it faultless and Hoyle had AFRA send the black doctor a case of Glenfiddich.

During his three-week stay in the clinic, Hoyle spent a lot of time writing to friends around the world, letting them know that he was still in business and that further financial aid would be most welcome. He knew that in his present condition they would be unlikely to refuse him and he also relished the fact that he had attractive handwriting which he knew would be well received by business men who read typewritten screeds all day long. His medium-blue ink looked particularly good on the white paper with the dark red AFRA letterhead and the gold Parker flowed across the pages with an ease which gave him great personal satisfaction.

Every morning Mary came to collect his mail bringing news of the office and stayed to take dictation for Anderson's daily instructions. She also brought his personal mail which was mostly letters from well-wishers and admirers and would stay until Jane came to cluck and coo over him like a child, her huge black eyes full of genuine love and concern. She always brought a half bottle of chilled Spumante which they would drink together with Hoyle's breakfast orange juice.

There had been various discussions with Anderson and, although he was still weak from the damage done to his body and the resultant shock, Hoyle threw himself wholeheartedly into the plan of revenge. Jane ransacked his lockers in the flat and found his old university notes from Johannesburg and the summaries of his first political debates which had led him on the path to becoming a champion of the oppressed in his home country. Hoyle felt the need to research the coming operation carefully and dredge up every piece of useful information about the country of his birth.

It was in a cutting from an old *Panorama*, the South African government-sponsored Department of Information magazine, of May 1972 that he noticed the piece on the opening of parliament in Cape Town; usually on a Friday in the second part of January. Instinctively, he looked at his watch and noted that the date was 6 July; midsummer in England although you wouldn't think it today, he mused as he looked out at the steady downpour slanting down from the cold grey sky outside the window. In South Africa it was almost mid-winter and Parliament reconvened after the summer recess at Christmas. There was just over six months to prepare for some act which would shatter White South Africa's arrogant complacency. As the idea took shape in his mind, Hoyle smiled and the nagging aches in his amputated leg and wrist seemed to ease.

'The bastards,' he breathed. 'I'll knock the racist swine off their perch.'

Hoyle's opinion of the average white South African was of course biased. But basically the true picture shows the nation to be convinced of its self-sufficiency based on a vast reserve of strategic minerals and the often escalating gold prices. It is a fact that with the opinion of virtually the entire world walled up against it, white South Africa's patriotic fervour was probably only comparable to that of the whites who still remained in the newly-named northern neighbouring state of Zimbabwe, but there it was being fast dispelled in a general exodus down south.

Gerrit de Kock's analysis of white South African character, as being vocally sympathetic towards so-called oppressed groups whilst being tolerant if not secretly supportive of government high-handed militaristic tactics, was more accurate and revealed more of the truth of the average South African's mentality. The situation is however, always precarious, being based on a middle-of-the-road toleration by both black and white and limited government action to keep a workable balance. Any weight in either direction will incline the scales towards urban unrest and in a country with a workforce comprised mainly of blacks and coloureds, the jeopardy to the economy is obvious.

Originally Hoyle was searching for just such a catalyst to start a reactionary swing in both whites and blacks, the former being frightened into leaving the country and the latter into uprising against the State. Later his ideas were to be modified and embroidered by the considerable inventive brainpower of the AFRA executive, and the tenacity of the terrorists they sub-contracted. The consequences for South Africa were to be potentially horrendous.

CHAPTER 12

In Berlin it was raining hard when Tina and Manfred left Nollendorfplatz where again they had sat talking and drinking long brandy and cokes, entranced with each other's company. They left the U Bahn at Charlottenburg and hurried through the drizzle-slick streets towards the dark and gloomy apartment house which Manfred had known as home for more than three years. Willi had told Tina that he wouldn't be back at the hotel until around seven o'clock that evening and it was now only just after 3.30. In any event, she had mentioned the fact that she would be going out to the sauna and then to the shops on the Kurferstendam. She'd further covered herself by casually remarking that she probably wouldn't be back until sevenish, maybe even later. Willi had muttered something, kissed her and left before eight that morning. He was always in such a rush.

Tina had wondered about her attraction to Manfred Meyer. She was drawn to him irrevocably by some strange and almost frightening chemistry. It wasn't that he was good looking, or even attractive in conventional terms, but there was really something there which grabbed her; he fascinated her and his mind was quite wonderful. She glanced sideways at him as they jogged hand in hand through the dingy streets. Feeling her examination he looked back and then his face lit up with that amazing boyish intensity as if he, and he alone, could solve the problems he so often discussed with her. It wasn't self-righteousness but a sort of burning, joyful desperation making him seem like a modern-day Peter Pan. Suddenly he stopped and took her face in his hands.

'You're beautiful Tina, do you know quite how beautiful you are?'

Tina smiled and moved up close to him smelling the Gauloise odour on his breath and the faint man smell emanating from his wet clothes. They kissed briefly, there in the grey dampness of the old city street which had seen so much death and despair and perhaps a little joy in the days since Berlin had been divided by the victors who had succeeded in destroying its heart. The young couple broke apart as suddenly as they had embraced and hurried on to Manfred's apartment, the unstated fact that they would soon share his bed together spurring them on.

Forty minutes later, Tina Heim and Manfred Meyer had made love for the first time and were lying in each other's arms in the lethargic ecstasy of spent passion. Manfred's bed was narrow and not too clean, Tina thought, but it didn't matter because it was his smell and she sniffed now, inhaling the light musty odour which rose from his damp body. It wasn't unpleasant. She snuggled in the crook of his shoulder and ran her hand down his chest. He was very pale, even a bit sallow, as though he had never been in the sun and there was virtually no chest hair on him. But his body was firm and quite muscular and now her hand strayed downwards over his flat belly until she felt him limp and spent and still sticky with their juices.

Even in this post-coital state he was surprisingly big and she grasped him feeling him begin to thicken immediately. She slid down under the sheets and began to trail her tongue down over his chest and stomach. Now, very quickly he was fully erect again and her lips moved softly, brushing over the bulbous tip of him. Even there he smelled good and now she could taste herself on him, the slight acidity tingling on her tongue.

Manfred began to move his hips and writhe as she worked her tongue and lips around him. My God, thought

148

Tina, he was wonderfully big and her mouth was full of
him as she worked into a rhythm, becoming aroused
herself. His hand found her from behind and caressed her
wetness softly and then suddenly he stiffened and pulled
her head away from him and looked into her eyes. He
kissed her gently and longingly and then rolled her over
onto her stomach moving over her to lie against her
buttocks. Slowly she felt him enter her, his length sliding
into her until she felt it pushing against the top of her
cervix. He moved gently still and his hand slid under her
stomach massaging her from the front. Magically it went
on and on slowly, building rhythm and depth, and then
they were totally together and his thrusts became harder
so that she cried in pain and pleasure.

They made love three times that first afternoon and
then got up to sit in the old kitchen. It was that time
between late afternoon and early evening but the sky was
a uniform grey and the rain dripped soundlessly off the
huge pear tree in the garden. Manfred began to talk again
about South Africa and the recent raids that the South
African army had made into Namibia; so-called hot
pursuit raids he said and laughed harshly. Tina felt herself
becoming infected again by his words and remembered
now how Gerrit had felt about these things, how he'd
burned with the same sense of purpose as Manfred. She'd
had a letter from him a few weeks back and he had said
that he was in Windhoek running the Metricor accounts
office there. She thought of Gerrit and his dry matter of
fact manner, of the superb brain. If he said he was
running the office in South West then he very probably
was. She thought of how Gerrit and Manfred would get on
together, how much they would have in common, how
they were both characterised by that same sense of
purpose to right wrongs and improve the lot of the
oppressed.

Listening to Manfred she suddenly wondered about
Gerrit, needing him with his basic black and white
mentality. She remembered his intensity and how he had

looked after her and to a much larger extent, Koos. He had tried to guide her life as he saw best when they were younger and then it had all fallen apart when she had found him that afternoon in the bathroom, playing with himself. Amazingly, now she missed him with an almost painful longing and felt that she must see him. She would write to Gerrit, send him money, in fact book his flight for him and bring him to Germany.

Thinking ahead Tina imagined Gerrit meeting Manfred, wonderful sensitive Manfred. Either in Dusseldorf or Berlin, or wherever, it didn't matter because Manfred always seemed to get as much time off as he needed. Somehow she had become infected with a sense of great things to come, a purpose and destination in life. Gerrit and Manfred would be a part of it. What of Willi? she thought trying to be direct and objective. She would keep him happy because really she loved him in a way; arguing with herself she reasoned that it was quite possible to be in love with two or even more men at the same time. Willi was responsible for her salvation and success in life and she did love him and would take care never to hurt him. Smiling to herself she thought that Manfred would probably quite like old Willi and vice versa. Everyone liked Willi, she'd never met a single person who didn't. As far as Horst was concerned she'd knock that on the head; he had been nothing more than a passing fancy, not a real man like Manfred or even Willi.

Happily she voiced her thoughts aloud, breaking into Manfred's intense monologue. 'You're going to meet my brother, Manfred. His name's Gerrit and he's quite brilliant. I think you're going to like him.' Manfred looked at her questioningly and suddenly she remembered the time, looking at her watch guiltily. 'My God, I must go, I'm going to be horribly late.'

Miserably, Manfred watched Tina leap to her feet. She had already showered and quickly she busied herself with hair and make-up. Sorrowfully he looked at the slender body that had been his only an hour ago. 'When can I see you, Tina, when can we two be·together again?'

Tina bent forward and kissed him tenderly but briefly. 'The next time I'm here of course,' she said brightly. 'Or perhaps in Dusseldorf. I've got your office number and I'll call you when I know Gerrit's time of arrival. You've got to meet him darling, don't worry, it won't be long.' Kissing him again she flew out of the kitchen door and he heard her fast, light steps and then the crash of the front door. Feeling a sense of great loss, he ran to the door and opened it but she was already a hundred metres away running in the direction of the U Bahn station.

Manfred returned to the now dark kitchen and sat down, pouring himself a glass of the cheap Algerian Burgundy from the old earthenware jug. The wine was cold and harsh but he swilled half the glass down in one gulp. The musty room still smelled of her perfume and he ran his hand across his lips still tasting her on his fingers. The girl was inside him and there had never been anything like it before because it had been chemistry and irrevocable, everlasting. His head slumped onto his arms and he seemed to curl up into himself on the old bentwood kitchen mumbling to himself almost despairingly, '*Tina, mein Tina.*'

Tina wrote to Gerrit two weeks later from Dusseldorf and he received the letter one bright morning in Windhoek. Seated high in his office above Kaiser Strasse in the city centre, Gerrit looked out of the tinted glass windows of the twenty-storey building which had been recently completed and into which Metricor had moved only a month previously. Things were going very well in Windhoek and he'd been there for over seven months and was really quite settled. Basically, he had the financial control of the company completely taped and already all but the most vital decisions were left to him so that Rothman the managing director and Schwartz the Jewish financial director let him handle just about everything which constituted the day-to-day running of the company.

It had been Gerrit who had fired some twenty per cent of the sales force and changed their gas-guzzling Cortina

V6s for Volkswagen Golfs. He'd also cut down the product range quite drastically, and elminated items which were slow sellers. Another Gerrit proposal, now in force, had been to formulate a new sales incentive scheme which gave the representatives and country agents more money in their pockets if they sold the lines he wanted them to. At first they'd been hesitant and some were blatantly resistant but he'd chaired a meeting and convinced them with his quiet but powerful arguments. Now everyone thought he was bloody marvellous and the directives between Cape Town and Windhoek referred to him as a heavyweight or wonderboy. So capable was Gerrit that Rothman and Schwartz found time to play golf for two afternoons every week in addition to the occasional hunting trip on Rothman's family farm near Swakopmund.

Now, reading Tina's letter for the second time, Gerrit considered that it was more than time he took a few weeks off. He hadn't had a day away from the office for almost seven months and his social life was limited in this stolid, strangely attractive changing city. He'd taken a furnished apartment in a vast new block which was not unlike Kaiserhof where Metricor's offices took up an entire floor. The flat was as anonymous as a rabbit warren but the company paid the rent with the result that Gerrit now had more money to spend than in Cape Town. In addition, he had received a 20 per cent salary increase and the rand went further in Windhoek than it did in South Africa. He had plenty of money, more than he would ever want to spend in this city, and the R8200 he had invested in gold shares had trebelled in nine months so that now they were worth more than R25,000. Then there was the R5000 he had on fixed deposit with Barclay's downstairs in the Kaiserhof lobby and more than R1500 in his current account. It therefore amused him that Tina had suggested sending him a ticket and also that she had made no mention of the R3000 plus he had invested for her; she'd be surprised to learn that this had now accumulated to almost R10,000.

Gerrit noticed Heim Import-Export's telex number in

Dusseldorf and walked across his office to his secretary's small adjoining cubicle which also contained the telex machine. Mrs van Vuuren was given the 41 number for West Germany and Heim's number which would follow Metricor's own 56 prefix and number. He dictated and Mrs van Vuuren bent industriously to her notebook.

'Personal for Tina Heim from Gerrit de Kock, Metricor, Windhoek. Received your letter, will arrive Frankfurt at month's end. Final times and details later. Regards Gerrit.' Mrs van Vuuren typed the message onto tape and initiated the identifications. The machine typed furiously. Heim's office finally typed 'received' in English and Gerrit smiled to himself feeling the first excitement. He hadn't even considered Rothman and Schwartz and now Mrs van Vuuren's well-plucked eyebrows widened questioningly. Gerrit smiled even wider.

'Well Wilma, I think that the hunting and golf trips will have to be curtailed for a few weeks,' he laughed softly and the older woman smiled back.

'You must enjoy yourself Mr de Kock, heaven knows you've worked hard enough these last months for those two and the company.'

Gerrit left a memo on Rothman's desk that evening advising him that he, Gerrit, would be on vacation from the end of August for three weeks. He then left the office and headed for the Kalahari Sands Hotel and a celebration drink.

All of Windhoek was now officially multi-racial although there were still the magic 'Right of admission reserved' signs above the entrance doors of most establishments. Some all-white enclaves still remained and although blacks and coloureds were officially allowed into them, they never went because some of these venues were frequented by poor whites and thugs. The Kalahari Sands was no problem though, being a typical contemporary hotel in the Hilton or Western International mould. Gerrit parked his own company Golf in the vast, half-empty forecourt and grabbed his jacket from the hanger above the rear seat. That was the only trouble with the Golf, he thought, an otherwise perfect piece of German, small-car engineering was spoiled by poor ventilation and air-flow. He felt the cold air in the foyer touch his damp back and shivered, the Golf would be a bloody stifling little sweat box for eight months of the year.

In the cocktail bar, a few flashily dressed black and coloured women hung on the words and arms of three thickset German businessmen who looked pink and sweaty even in the air-conditioned bar. Both the women and the men were speaking German which was the second unofficial language of the new Namibia and a throwback from the days of Imperial Germany and its far flung colonies. Gerrit ordered a vodka and appetiser, a drink he had come to relish, and took it in a tall glass with four or five ice cubes. He sat sipping the drink feeling the perspiration dart out momentarily on his face and under his arms as the icy liquid hit his stomach.

Sitting quietly in the bar, Gerrit watched the bubbles meandering upwards in a never-ending stream which gracefully circumvented the ice cubes in his second drink. He was relaxed and feeling quite warm towards the world when he saw Gail Wilson walk into the narrow room with a tall, blond, middle-aged man who had unmistakable bearing and no sign of the boorish manner of the average Afrikaaner or *Sudwester*. Heart pounding suddenly, Gerrit turned away towards the wall and lifted the drink to shield his face. He glanced briefly in Gail's direction but she hadn't seen him and was smiling up into the big man's eyes.

Now there were about five people between them and thankfully the bar was filling up. A rash of conflicting thoughts passed through Gerrit's mind as he sat trying to look inconspicuous. Christ, the laws of coincidence were more than frightening but this was the first time that such an outside chance had ever caught him out. When he'd first arrived in Windhoek, Gail had written to him every week but he'd resisted replying. He'd learned from her letters that she'd left Metricor after a confrontation with Marais but still had his Audi. She'd asked what she should do with it eventually because as the letters became more and more desperate she advised him that she was going to leave the country and did he want the car back at the reduced price she had paid him? Still Gerrit had refused to reply and then the letters had become pleading and he'd been sickened by them so that she had fallen in his estimation and the respect he'd had for her had disappeared. Eventually, he couldn't understand why she'd meant so much to him and finally he'd shut her out of his mind and sent back the last few letters unopened. She'd written one last bitter note with 'Please open' typed on it, saying that she was going back to England and that she was greatly hurt by his attitude, some other banalities about the feelings she had had for him, now dead etcetera, etcetera, and that had been all.

In fact Gail had been on the point of leaving South Africa and had been considering buying her air ticket the day after she met Piet van Os. Since Gerrit had left she had been out very little, preferring the seclusion of the little Tamboerskloof cottage and evenings spent listening to music. Sometimes she would cook herself a good dinner and then sit and read until she felt tired. Often she thought of Gerrit and the few precious nights they had spent together in her bed, occasionally she would drink too much and then become depressed and cry herself to sleep.

After the fiasco at Metricor, which came to a head with Marais' firing her, she'd become a temporary with Manpower, an employment exchange in the city, and had been lucky with only three job changes in virtually six months of continuous employment. She'd become quite involved with Yoga and enjoyed the twice weekly sessions and the squash every Friday evening, but basically she knew that she was vegetating. She'd met a few men but there had been nothing and after the lack of replies from Gerrit she'd decided to pack it all in and try again in another country. She'd go back to the UK first of course and see the family, but, basically that would be just a staging post to somewhere else, maybe Australia or the United States.

She'd met van Os almost totally by accident because actually he lived in London and had a flat in Amsterdam where he spent quite a bit of time. He'd been in Southern Africa with a UK trade mission which was travelling right through the Republic and South-West Africa. Gail had met him at the Mount Nelson where she'd decided to stop by for a drink after squash. This was totally out of character for her but she loved Cape Town and particularly this old and beautiful hotel with its colonial splendour of a past era. With hair still damp from the sauna and many nostalgic thoughts she sat in a corner of the Lady Hamilton cocktail bar, wearing a simple cotton shift, sipping an Amstel lager which tasted, as it always did, incredibly wonderful, after violent excercise.

She noticed the big man staring at her and normally she detested this sort of thing from the grossly uncool and gauche Afrikaaners. He could have been Afrikaans or German because he was stockily built and rather serious looking, but there was no mistaking the genuine interest in his eyes. She had thought that he did not show obvious lust for her and so on impulse she returned his fixed stare with a frank and open glance and a half smile. This was all the encouragement that had been needed and the big man walked over and introduced himself and she noted immediately that he had presence, even charisma. His face was slightly ruddy and his hair dark blond and well cared for and he smelled good, a sort of soapy, tobacco odour and she noted his slim gold watch and the cut of his elegant grey suit.

They had talked easily and with immediate liking for each other and his voice had been cultured and vaguely familiar after the years in South Africa but then he told her that he was Dutch, not Afrikaans and the slightly guttural accent had been explained. He'd told her about the trade mission and talked of his job as the vice presi-

156

dent in charge of exports for a world-wide Amsterdam-based electronics company.

It had been an obvious pick-up, but she'd gone along with the suggestion of dinner in the grillroom and they'd had coffee and brandy and just talked and talked. He'd told her of his divorce and the two children at school in London. Of his ex-wife, an American, and how he'd found her in bed with an Italian waiter when he'd returned unexpectedly to the Amsterdam apartment one afternoon over two years ago. She had seen the hurt still there in his eyes, wonderful expressive brown eyes, and then she'd begun to recognise his strength and completeness. Yet, he had a definite vulnerability which was not far below the surface, it was there in the boyish smiles and an occasional haunted look.

He pressed her to stay and have drinks in the lounge but she resisted and had left at 11.30 with a promise to have dinner the next evening. During the drive home in the Audi, she experienced some unfamiliar warm feelings and realised that these were not merely as a result of the wine and brandy she had drunk, it was more a sort of caring which was new to her and quietly exciting.

The next night they had met again, almost like old friends, and this time she'd dressed for dinner and sparkled with that inner warmth and health that characterised the English Rose type. They'd gone to a small French restaurant in Wynberg because he had organised a Mercedes from a colleague; they'd eaten wonderfully and drunk splendid wines and when they got back to the hotel it had seemed natural to go with him to his room.

After another brandy and a coffee they had made love in the big yellowwood Cape Dutch bed which had smelled of his soap and tobacco Cologne. For Gail, who had not been with a man for many months, it had been a pleasing if not totally fulfilling experience but Piet van Os had obviously enjoyed her and almost revelled in her body, touching her face and breasts with a genuine sense of wonder, as if marvelling at his good fortune. She'd left at two in the morning, leaving him asleep, stealing out with her shoes in her hand like a young girl on her first illicit affair. From then on he had hardly let a day go by without phoning her three or four times and before they'd known each other one week had asked her to marry him. For many reasons, some of which she could not quite explain to herself, she had felt convinced of the rightness of her and Piet van Os and so she had agreed and he had been so overcome she thought he was going to cry.

The trip to South-West Africa, now known to most South Africans as Namibia, had been on the cards for van Os as part of his Southern African tour and it had seemed quite natural for her to accompany him. She'd given in her notice to Manpower and they left Cape Town for Windhoek on a beautiful late summer morning. Gail had felt content and almost completely happy, feeling closer everyday to Piet van Os. As the Boeing 737 had banked high over Table Bay and she looked down on the beautiful city sunlit and softened by a light haze, there was one intense and penetrating thought of Gerrit de Kock but she dismissed it swiftly; the chances of running into him during three days in Windhoek were, to say the least, remote.

The Kalahari Sands Hotel was comfortable and quite modern and Windhoek fascinating with its German names on shopfronts and street signs. Piet spoke German fluently and took pleasure in showing it off to Gail and they'd had two wonderful days wandering around the city because Piet seemed to get his work done between eight and twelve noon so from lunch onwards they were able to indulge themselves and spend the afternoons together. To Gail, her new life was all quite incredible and they were to leave for London together in three days' time and even now the shipping company in Cape Town were packing her few personal belongings and she'd sold the Audi. She was going back to England, her own country, as the mistress of a three storey townhouse in Chelsea with a rich and very presentable husband who adored her. She was realistic enough to know that the sex side was a bit lacking but with every chance it would improve; in the meantime she was more content than she had ever been and really one couldn't have everything.

Gail listened to Piet speaking his pleasant sounding German to the middle-aged couple who sat with them in the bar; the man was Fritz von Kleist the local agent for Piet's company in Namibia. His wife Gelda was sweet enough but Gail had little in common with her and had given up attempts at conversation. She glanced idly around the bar feeling secure and a little merry from the two vodka and limes she had drunk quite quickly; it was then that she noticed Gerrit de Kock sitting over in the corner. Almost immediately she felt a flush creep up her cheeks and her neck tingled. Piet happened to glance at her and noticed her complexion change instantly.

'Gail darling, are you alright? he whispered urgently and she nodded quickly, smiling tremulously.

'Something I ate at lunchtime darling, perhaps that crayfish,' she muttered. 'God I feel sort of sick and hot and cold all at the same time.'

Gelda von Kleist nodded knowingly as if sharing in a female conspiracy. Gail headed for the ladies' toilet and passed very close to Gerrit, her face still burning; out of the corner of her eye she saw him casually get off his stool and follow her. In the lobby she stopped indecisively and then turned blindly around a corner and followed some steps down to the basement arcade. She felt the presence of Gerrit following closely behind her and then his hand on her shoulder. She stopped and her bare flesh trembled as if with a mild electric shock as he gripped her gently.

She turned and faced him, determined to take the offensive but all she could say was, 'Oh God Gerrit, why did I have to meet you here, why didn't you write back to me?' Gerrit looked at the well-remembered face with the fine blond hair, now swept up into an elegant chignon. He noted the chic black cocktail dress and the way that the thin straps showed off her tanned shoulders and the valley between those wonderful breasts. He lifted his eyes to hers and saw the moisture brimming there and recognised the hurt he had inflicted.

'Gail,' he breathed, 'you look so wonderful, I have to see you, to talk, there's so much to say, when can we meet?'

She shook her head blindly. 'I can't Gerrit, I can't, it's impossible because I'm getting married to that man in there, in the bar, that man. I'm here with Piet van Os. Anyway, we're leaving tomorrow.' She stood breathless, mouth slightly open, shaking her head ever so slightly as if to ward off the feelings that swept through her.

Gerrit's eyes hardened and he stepped back, his hand dropping from her shoulder.

'I see,' he said brusquely. 'You've sold yourself to a rich Dutchman eh, well that was what I thought would happen with you, it's exactly what I knew in fact.' He softened suddenly as he saw the tears spring into her eyes. 'Well, Gail, enjoy your life.' He looked down, unable to meet her stare but not before she saw the soft gleam of moisture in the depths of his eyes. 'If only,' he began and then stepped forward suddenly and kissed her hard on the mouth. She resisted for an instant, thinking of the people who could be watching them but over his shoulder she could see only a dark wall and a curtained doorway and she melted against him. But then he broke away and stepped back again to turn without another word. He walked around the corner and was gone.

Gail stood, blinking back the tears and shuddering with reaction. Making a great effort she straightened her shoulders and followed Gerrit towards the lobby. There was no sign of him and she knew he had gone; then she saw the door for the ladies' room and rushed through it seconds before Gelda von Kleist came out of the bar, a look of concern on her well-groomed face.

That night Gerrit got completely drunk for the second time in his life. If anything he was in a worse condition than the night of his mother's funeral. He'd found a bottle

160

of vodka and four appetisers in the kitchen and after the
fruit juice was finished, he had just drunk the spirit,
pouring it down neat like water. Collapsing on the sofa in
his compact lounge area he'd woken around three in the
morning and vomited into the toilet before staggering into
his bed.

Next morning he arrived at the office at 10.30 wearing
dark glasses and pleading a migraine headache.

Rothman laughed callously. 'Oh Gerrit, dear boy, don't
worry, I've had migraines too, I always find them
somewhere around the bottom of a whisky bottle.'

Gerrit had ignored him and walked off to his office
where Mrs van Vuuren made him several black coffees.
Rothman sensed that this would not be the best time to
bring up the subject of de Kock's self-authorised leave and
shook his head as he took refuge in Schwartz' company.

'Well well,' he said gloatingly, 'there you go, it just
proves that all *skollies* are the same down deep. I'd never
have thought though that old Gerrit was a piss-cat, but this
morning he looked so pale he's practically white.' He
laughed raucously and slapped Schwartz on the back.
'You can say what you like Issy, there's nobody like the
coloureds when it comes to booze, they can drink us all
under the table. Christ you should have seen the bastard,
he must have had a real skinful.'

Gail and her husband to be, left Windhoek for Johannesburg and their onward connection on KLM to Schiphol,
Amsterdam. The flight left just before lunch and Piet van
Os wondered at his beautiful fiancée's strange behaviour
of the night before when she had proceeded to get quite
drunk in the bar at the Kalahari Sands and then seduced
him in the most marvellous way, almost with a kind of
desperation. He had never experienced anything like the
sensations that she had given him with her tongue, hands
and body, and he'd realised that he was to marry a woman
who was no stranger to men. As far as that was concerned,
Piet had found the fact oddly stimulating and he'd reacted
like a wild animal himself so that she had cried out in her

climax and gripped him wildly. Now she sat beside him in the first class seat, demure and relaxed and feeling his glance she turned to him and smiled and gripped his hand. 'Darling Piet,' she said, 'you are a most marvellous man.'

Two weeks later at 8.10 in the evening, Gerrit's SAA 747 SP was scheduled to take off from Windhoek en route to Frankfurt. The two weeks had passed quickly and at first he'd been troubled by thoughts of Gail and, with the newly discovered possessiveness in his psyche, he conjured up erotic pictures of her and the big man he remembered from the bar in the Kalahari Sands.

Try as he might to suppress them, the images had persisted and his nights had been restless and at times, desperately unhappy. He continued to drink more than he was used to and his work suffered so that in the final week prior to his departure he'd had to work until after eight each evening in order to catch up on the backlog.

At last Gerrit waited at Windhoek's compact and modern airport as the strangely fat South African Airways 747 SP landed and disgorged a few passengers from Johannesburg before it was to speed swiftly out around the bulge of Africa to far-off Europe and its destination in Germany. Fortified by a couple of double vodkas and appetisers in the crowded bar, Gerrit felt the stirring pangs of excitement at this, his first trip out of Africa. He wore corduroy slacks and his soft suede zipper jacket over a fine cashmere polo neck sweater; and carried one suitcase and a new tan leather flight bag. Looking at this outwardly calm and well-dressed coloured, a fellow passenger would have considered him a seasoned traveller which was exactly the impression that Gerrit wanted to give.

CHAPTER 13

Lucas Lundonze, Nicholas Mohapi and twenty-three others had been active in Okavango territory for five months but were now in Eastern Caprivi close to the northernmost point of the Caprivi strip and the big South African military base at Katima Mulilo. Since Zimbabwean independence, and the shot in the arm that Robert Mugabe's victory had given African Nationalists, the South Africans had realised even more that they had a very real low-intensity war on their hands. But, thought Lucas, the bastards were more than well prepared for operations, even here in the heat of the Caprivi where the fast-flowing Zambesi formed the natural northern border of Namibia. On the other side was Zambia where the bloody South Africans did most of their patrolling because, to that old man Kaunda, this was better than having to suffer air attacks on SWAPO bases within his country. On demands from Pretoria, Kaunda had actually pulled his troops back more than twenty kilometres from the wire to give the South Africans free access to areas from which SWAPO staged raids across the border.

It was late afternoon on a typical showery Caprivi day and the sky had that characteristic duck-egg blue colour interspersed with puffs of grey white cloud. Lucas rode an old Raleigh bicycle along the road from M'pacha, the airbase, to Katima Mulilo. The ride was easy because the well-surfaced black top had only just been completed to give the army units swift access from one point to the other. At M'pacha, the South Africans had their forward air supply base and a strike force of Impala jets and Alouette helicopters equipped with the murderous 50 calibre Browning machine guns. The Caprivi was populated almost entirely by Caprivian Africans and a smattering of Bushmen and of course, a mixture of both of these. Otherwise, it was all South African military personnel.

For whites, apart from scattered determined farmers, the only place to live in the Caprivi was Katima Mulilo, the small featureless riverside town grown fat with military expansion and effectively re-inforced with bomb shelters. Katima was the fortress of the Caprivi and thus it was near here that Lucas had planned his strike to have maximum effect on the local population and the morale of the military. Now, cycling along the broad black ribbon of tarmac and dressed in a bright orange shirt and tattered denim jeans, he was passed by various army vehicles including Hippo armoured personnel carriers and the smaller Buffel which was classified because of its mine-proof design. Of course Lucas had worked out the Buffel's weak point and they'd studied the photographs that one of his friends in the M'pacha service base had provided. The photographs and his report had been forwarded to Lusaka months ago.

A section of young South African soldiers in their neat earth-brown uniforms stared haughtily out of a Hippo as the high-sided vehicle passed Lucas. Some of them laughed and he caught snatches of their guttural Afrikaans tongue. They were very confident these young racists, thought Lucas as the sweat trickled down his ribs from the humidity of a recent rain and the now vicious sun. By the end of the week, all being well, they would perhaps change their tune a little.

He had heard from headmen in kraals further west in the Caprivi that lately there had been a few isolated incidents from across the river by the odd drunk Zambian army units or some equally uncontrollable SWAPO groups. He knew that many of his compatriots had IQs in the lower forties and when given an automatic weapon like an AK47, they reacted like dangerous children. The standard was unfortunately not as it should be and some of the best men had been wiped out during the South African strikes across the border in the latter part of the previous year. River traffic had been banned by the South African military only last week because some black South African soldiers had come under fire near their observation post. Of course, the attackers had done little more than bring the wrath of the South African artillery down upon them and had been decimated by all accounts; it was just another typical waste of men and effort and, above all, it had a negative effect on the morale of his SWAPO volunteers.

SAP eight batallion were operating out of the police station at Katima Mulilo and the heat and humidity of this inhospitable arsehole of the Caprivi could not have been imagined by the young constables who sweated and swore, ate tasteless food and dreamed always of 'The States' a term, which together with 'Gooks' had been borrowed by the South Africans from the Vietnam war, but here of course it referred to South Africa and home. Mostly everyday a lumbering C130 Hercules dropped in low over the scrub surrounding the base at M'pacha where the SAP regularly went to pick up supplies. You always knew when it was arriving because an Alouette gunship would take off and clatter away to check the bush on either side of the runway and shadow the Hercules on its final approach to dissuade any insurgent who might like to have a go at the cumbersome transport plane. So far it hadn't happened but the officer commanding Sector 70 reasoned quite correctly that a first time would be catastrophic for morale.

The Hercules symbolised the link between the mainly boring drudgery in this part of the Operational Area and the luxury of 'The States' where there were such things as steakhouses, cold beers, *braaivleis* parties and of course girls, without doubt the most sorely missed commodity. Getting mail from home was almost unbearable because lately the women had taken to dousing their letters with perfume or even spraying them with 'personal deodorants' the effects of which on the olfactory senses of the young policemen and soldiers was close to agonising.

The SAP at Katima Mulilo had little to do with the vast army base and its two forward commands at Golf and Wenela each housing radio, artillery and operations respectively. The decrepit police station formed their headquarters for the area and they were also responsible for the domestic policing of this sleepy little town on the edge of the Zambesi where most of the few thousand residents had some connection with the army. Many of the private residences had sand-bagged bomb shelters in their front gardens but Katima hadn't been mortared for almost a year although, almost every night, one heard shots going off on one side of the river or the other.

Reilly sat in the back of the charge office thinking about life in this bleeding awful place which sooner or later was bound to get blasted again by the terries. Just the other day a five minute fire-fight had taken place when some coons from across the river had taken a few shots at some of the army's kaffir troops who were sunbathing on the side of the river near their OP. He couldn't imagine what they were trying to gain by exposure to the old currant bun because these Caprivians were as black as any other coon as far as he could see. Of course, the white officer in charge of the river OP had called up Wenela and they'd zeroed in the 140s from Golf and a four-shot salvo had blown the kaffirs to hell and gone. That had been that; it had provided them all with a talking point in the mess for a day or two but it didn't help the boredom for very long.

The section's boredom was lifted abruptly when they were ordered out of base to occupy one of the SAP's river OPs. Together with a regular lieutenant and an Ovambo tracker they were to travel thirty-five kilometres downriver to the OP set back in the forest only twenty metres up from the bank of the Zambesi. The first part of the trip would be by Buffel but then they'd have to walk twenty or so kilometres through tropical bush to the position on the river where they were to remain for thirteen days before being relieved. Naturally, they were not allowed to walk along the river bank where there was a pleasant and well-defined game trail, because the gooks would see them and then have the final location of the OP. That was the reasoning at HQ but Reilly reckoned that the gooks knew where the OP was anyway because occasionally boats would call there, so to him it all seemed a waste of time.

They left Katima Mulilo at seven in the morning after a meagre breakfast, and it was pouring with rain when they loaded up the Buffels with the gear necessary for a two week stint in the bush. In contrast to SWAPO, who lived off Zambian Army handouts and the hospitality of local villages and kraals, the South African forces had to take everything with them and as virtually all patrols were on foot, these supplies and equipment had to be carried in back-packs and webbing. The ration packs or 'Rat-packs' as they were known, contained one small tin of corned beef, one packet of dry biscuits, tea, coffee, a vitamin drink and soap powder for each day out of base. In addition, the policeman or trooper carried his R1 rifle with four spare magazines of twenty rounds, two hand grenades, a mortar bomb and only a two day supply of water because in this region the frequent tropical downpours negated the need for water rationing.

By order of the officer commanding the sector, all personnel had to be belted into vehicles when travelling on sand roads and the parachute-type lap and shoulder harnesses were securely fastened and tightened before the two Buffels carrying the ten men and their drivers turned off the tarmac just half a kilometre out of town. The vehicles had no roofs and the rain poured down in slanting grey sheets turning the hard backed, ungraded dirt road into a treacherous miniature river where potholes could cause the Buffel to sink over its wheelarches. Crouched beneath their rubberised groundsheets, all the section had their rifles cocked and on safety and Le Roux and Reilly sat opposite each other staring moodily out at the grey-green bush which swept past on either side of the bumpy track as the Buffel churned along in second gear at about 30kph.

Eight kilometres out of Katima the dense bush opened up into dead flat scrubby country and on the straight stretches the Buffel was able to get up to 45kph as it lurched and splashed through the deeper puddles throwing great columns of muddy water high into the air. Still the rain hammered down and, although it wasn't cold by any means, Reilly considered it fucking uncomfortable sitting belted into this bouncing tin box, clutching a slippery rifle with water running steadily down your neck and soaking into the arse of your trousers; the bloody poncho-type groundsheets were next to useless in this sort of rain.

The Buffel gave a particularly violent lurch dipped its front end and slithered drunkenly to a halt throwing the men against each other so that Van der Merwe almost brained Le Roux with the barrel of his R1. Reilly jerked suddenly awake from his miserable reverie and craned his neck to look ahead over the high cab of the Buffel and there he could see the huge hole in the track. The lieutenant was shouting, 'Take up defensive positions, just like you've been taught, quickly now, quickly.' Reilly lunged across the narrow width of the Buffel and placed his rifle in the slot opposite him whilst Le Roux did the same on his side. Now each small vehicle bristled with four barrels, two to each side, and in Reilly's leading vehicle the lieutenant rode shotgun shouting into the slit behind the driver's enclosed cab, his HMK submachine gun held forward and ready.

'Slowly,' he ordered the driver and the Buffel crept forward to within five metres of the crater in the road and stopped with the engine still running. 'Keep your fucking heads down!' screamed the lieutenant unnecessarily and despite himself Reilly had to smile as he glanced across at Van der Merwe practically prostrate on the floor of the Buffel, one hand holding his rifle and the other over his head. The sight of old Van got through to Reilly and he recalled instantly the terror of the attack near Oshakati and suddenly the adrenalin spurted into his system and his heart began to beat wildly.

'OK, defensive positions on the roadside, at the fucking double, let's go!' roared the lieutenant and in pre-arranged order the section vaulted over the sides of the high-waisted personnel carriers and dropped into the quagmire of the roadside, flattening out with rifles pointing at the screed of bush some hundred metres from the road.

After what seemed an age the lieutenant rose and cautiously approached the crater which had totally obliterated the surface of the dirt track and was already filling up with water at its bottom-most point of some four feet. Even with the rain, the lieutenant could see that the hole had been freshly made and the section clearly heard his exclamation in the still air, even above the clatter of the Buffel engines. 'Sweet Jesus Christ!' he said.

For a while Reilly watched over his shoulder as the lieutenant just stared down into the hole and then he spoke briskly. 'Alright, I think the bastards must be long gone by now, spread out along the road, two to each side, front and rear of the hole, now move it and look for any signs of life or pieces, whatever.'

The section spread out swiftly and Reilly moved stealthily along the roadside with Le Roux opposite him. He held his finger on the trigger of the wet R1 and the adrenalin still caused every sense to be heightened so that his eyes seemed able to cover the immediate low bushes and grass in front of him and the line of scrub in the distance from where he knew any attack would originate. They were about seventy metres from the hole when Le Roux spotted

169

the piece of dirty white painted metal sheet. He called to Reilly and together they looked down at the thing lying in the spiky blue-green grass. It had a rusty sign bearing the legend T O Y O T A and even though it had been partially washed by rain, there was no mistaking the red stickiness adhering to it.

As Reilly felt the bile rise in his throat, there were several shouts of discovery made by other members of the section and a terrible gasp of disbelief. It was the lieutenant who pieced together what must have happened, but it was Van der Merwe who found the girl.

She was lying in the grass about forty metres from the hole, a young teenage Ovambo with big brown eyes like a Springbok doe. She was barely alive and terribly shocked and her right arm and leg had been blown off at the shoulder and thigh. In addition to these grievous wounds, she had horrible gashes in her neck and side in which the blood was congealing in big jelly-like clots. This was probably due to the severe blood loss from the missing limbs which had already been washed into the sodden ground by the still-drenching rain. The lieutenant placed field dressings over the neck and side wounds, and Uys, the medic, bound others over the splintered thin white stumps of bone that protruded grotesquely from the tattered cotton dress and grubby knickers. The girl never murmured as this crude and useless first aid was administered but when the lieutenant supported her head and trickled a little water into her mouth from the canteen, she showed signs of recognition and the Ovambo tracker was ready, bending over her, speaking softly yet urgently and with great compassion.

There had been thirteen people in the battered Toyota Hi-Ace, all local villagers of whom eight had been women and young children. The girl whispered on, seeming to realise the importance of her story and the Ovambo translated quickly for the lieutenant. The old panel van had struck the mines, the lieutenant reckoned at least three piled on top of each other, and the resulting explosion, delayed about a second, had detonated under the centre section of the Hi-Ace blowing the vehicle and its occupants into very small pieces. There was little to show that twelve lives had ceased to exist, except for a few glistening red splotches strewn here and there and had it been dusty, instead of raining, even these would not have been visible.

The rear axle and wheels of the panel van were located a full seventy metres from the crater and the front wheels and engine block were discovered twenty-five metres in the opposite direction. It was a case of overkill in the extreme and the lieutenant reasoned that the charge had not been intended for so light a vehicle as the Toyota; he had a more than sneaking suspicion that the Buffels had been the intended targets. Although the section searched for a further half an hour, no other pieces of human flesh were found other than a severed foot and ankle, still wearing a filthy baseball boot.

To the young men who stared down at the maimed and dying girl, it was incredible that twelve living souls had just disappeared on this muddy stretch of road in the middle of nowhere. The girl had said that she was riding in the cab with the driver which had probably explained her escape, because the lieutenant thought that she may have been partly protected by the mass of people packed up against the cab with their related belongings. There were tears in many eyes and Van der Merwe was not the only one who had brought up his breakfast and Reilly swallowed trying to suppress the retching which threatened involuntarily. There was little else that could be done for the girl and after a few minutes her mouth started to sag and her eyes dimmed from those great wounded brown depths which reminded Le Roux of the first Springbok he had shot as a teenager. As life left the slim brown body, the lieutenant bent down and gently closed the eyes before removing his camouflage cap. They all followed suit and it was Van der Merwe, who, without being asked, muttered a short prayer. As the rain continued to angle down out of the dismal mid-morning sky, the lieutenant detailed Cohen and Van der Merwe to bury the body, and the spades from the Buffels made easy work of the rain-softened clay.

Soon the digging was done and then the Buffels slowly negotiated the hole in the road and they all loaded up, the lieutenant talking on the radio in the cab of the first vehicle. Reilly felt as though something had died inside him and he was not alone in this because they all felt it and nobody said a word as the two little personnel carriers jerked off into the sodden grey light of midday.

About thirty minutes later, the section was dropped at a fork in the road some eighteen kilometres from their destination. Each man loaded himself up carefully with his equipment, first rolling up the groundsheet and carefully securing webbing, rat-pack and sleeping bag. A few jokes were attempted to try to lighten the terrible atmosphere brought on by the tragedy back on the road but the mood sank again as the two Buffels turned around and clanked off back towards Katima, their high exhausts steaming in the dank air.

The long march to the OP was uneventful. Within the first five minutes everyone was soaked and the bush thickened as they got closer to the river so that the overhanging branches deposited showers of water as the section brushed against them. The game trails were narrow and ill-defined in parts and the lieutenant cursed silently to himself as he followed the slim figure of the Ovambo tracker who flitted through the tropical foliage like a wraith. He couldn't get the destruction of the Toyota out of his mind and a picture of the dying girl was etched permanently in his memory traces.

'The murdering black fuckers,' he said aloud so that the tracker turned his head questioningly and halted his easy stride. 'Don't worry Johnny,' said the lieutenant lightly, smiling, despite his grim mood. 'I'm just talking to myself as usual.'

Early that evening Lieutenant Bester lay in the damp

depression in the ground that he had made for himself. He stared up at the rubberised groundsheet that he had rigged as a shelter and considered himself reasonably comfortable and dry-to-damp rather than damp-to-dry. Each man was issued with one groundsheet which he could either rig over himself or lie on, but the lieutenant had managed to pilfer another one from the quartermaster back in Katima so now he had the best of both worlds with a waterproof layer above and below him. The sleeping bags were supposed to be waterproof but obviously the brilliant brains that had designed them had never tested them out in the Caprivi; the lieutenant considered them next to useless in these conditions.

They had occupied the OP, relieving another section who had been on the river for fourteen days and who had greeted them like saviours. It was the first time Bester had been this far down the Zambesi and looking at the facilities in the OP, or the lack of them, he could imagine the longing that would develop for the relative luxury of Katima.

He'd set up the fire-line for one of the MAGs and sighted the mortars to the rear in case of a surprise attack from that direction. A lookout was posted in the huge gnarled Mopani tree that overhung the river and with his glasses, this man could scan one hundred metres in either direction and clearly see the opposite bank which was only about sixty metres away at this point. The lieutenant thus felt reasonably secure and now lay with his sleeping bag pulled over him loosely, fondling himself gently and cursing fucking Sam Nujoma and his SWAPO monkeys for keeping him in this stinking wet jungle.

Thank Christ, in two weeks he had an R and R and was going back to The States, back to Jo'burg and civilisation. Little Isobelle his fiancée would be waiting; it had been ten weeks since he'd seen her, slept with her, screwed her and savoured the satin smoothness of those tanned thighs and incredible firm white buttocks. These thoughts almost drove him to masturbation but he resisted the temptation and instead tried to concentrate on the occasional heavy drops of moisture falling from the enveloping trees onto his shelter. He began to count them and tried to estimate the intervals between them and how many drops were falling per minute. Idly, he considered that some were louder than others because they were either further away or not as heavy. The permutations seemed endless and as he listened to the rhythmic thuds in the increasing gloom, he began to drift into sleep.

Lucas, Nicholas and three others had planted the mines on the road in the hopes that the Buffels bringing the relief section to the riverside OP would detonate them. The Buffel was a sturdy vehicle that had angled upswept sides designed to deflect the shrapnel from the mine but Lucas had carefully stacked the three British AP sixes that had come to them via sympathetic friends in Zambia. He'd placed the so-called 'cheese' P4 plastic between the first and second and the resulting bang would be quite sufficient to blow the first Buffel to pieces and probably kill a few of the occupants of the second with shrapnel and concussion. Depending on the damage to the second carrier, the five Africans planned to finish off the survivors with automatic fire.

They'd done the job the night before and Lucas had been glad of the rain because it kept the locals in their huts and thus off the road. But it had all gone awry and the old fool with the Toyota who operated his makeshift and totally illegal bus service had come doddering along and detonated the mines, those beautifully rigged mines that were designed for the racist army vehicle. They had seen the whole thing of course, from their position 150 metres away in the bush, far too far away to warn the old idiot. Well, he wouldn't make any more of those embarrassing and costly errors because the Toyota had literally ceased to exist and small pieces had in fact dropped on them, even at the considerable distance away at which they were lying.

After this disaster there had been little point in endangering themselves by waiting around for the SAP Buffels to arrive and discover the remains of the Toyota. Lucas reasoned that the police could not have been far behind the doomed panel van and so they had moved out to a position two kilometres away on the river. Here, he and Nicholas had decided to adopt the contingency plan of a strike from the land side on the police OP.

The Africans had moved easily through the thick bush using game trails and little used tracks which had been reconnoitred with the help of friendly locals. By nightfall they had moved up to within a kilometre of the OP on the South-West African side of the river and Lucas settled them and let them eat their cold porridge and meat scraps salvaged from the kraal where they had slept last night. At about 10.30 they would have a weapons check and then at around eleven they would make the strike. Months ago Nicholas had established, via his intelligence network in Windhoek and Lusaka, that this was a police OP and that the SAP, although often courageous, had little of the military expertise that the South African Army could boast. This meant that enemy follow-up operations were less risky and that in hitting this target, as he had at Oshakati more than four months earlier, he would have a much greater chance of success than in taking on the army. In two weeks time there was to be another meeting back in Windhoek. He had heard from sources at headquarters in Lusaka that something big was on the go and so this was to be his last operation for a while. Therefore the necessity to succeed tonight was of paramount importance if he Lucas, together with Nicholas, were to warrant inclusion in the big plan in some sort of major role.

Cohen was on guard in the camp and sat about three metres away from the primed 60mm mortars, both of which were pointing vaguely at the thick bush which formed a wall of blackness only ten metres from his position. With the onset of darkness, Le Roux was no longer ensconced in the tree and Van der Merwe had replaced him on the bank to watch the approach to the OP from the river side. Very much aware of his responsibility, on this his first bush duty outside headquarters base, Cohen sat outwardly calm, yet with an adrenalin-charged body, ears pricking to every sound in the enveloping and still-dripping blackness.

Looking out at the near edge of the bush, he reasoned that nobody could possibly come that close without being detected. The dense vegetation couldn't be more than thirty feet away, he thought, but if someone was to manage to get that close they could really blast the camp alright. Even though the bivouac areas were lower down towards the river, grenades or mortars at that range would be fatal.

Lucas, Nicholas and the three others did not have a mortar between them but each was equipped with his own AK 47 and two fragmentation grenades of Chinese manufacture. In addition they had one RPD machine gun and Lucas really liked this weapon because of its accuracy and superb rate of fire. Their home base was far to the west in Angola, so he had left his much loved RPG 7 in a kraal some fifty kilometres south of Oshakati where it lay safe and dry under the headman's pile of mielie husks which were being stored for winter fuel during the cold desert-like nights in Ovamboland. As the rain began to slacken, the noises of the bush began in earnest and Lucas cursed because he needed this assistance that nature could offer him, the drumming rain and dripping trees would have covered his approach to within metres of the South Africans' camp.

Now the night insects, the many beetles and crickets of the bush, would start their raucous cacophony. The trouble was, these insects had unbelievable hearing and

176

felt every vibration and sound that might warn of the approach of a likely predator so that they stopped their screeching and chirruping at the slightest noise, tiny sounds in fact that were inaudible to the human ear. This sudden abatement of the bush's night-time background music would be horribly noticeable to anyone on watch and Lucas grimaced into the damp night, hoping that the young South African policemen would be as stupid as usual and unaware, up to the last possible moment, of his group's approach.

Lucas was an Ovambo of noble blood, being the son of a village chief and descended from a long line of Ovambo aristocracy. He had been educated near Grootfontein in a mission school and had shown great promise at an early age and managed to attract much attention from his teachers, being a bright, happy, good-looking boy who was always willing to learn. Later, at High School in Windhoek he had learned fluent English and German and a good understanding of Afrikaans although even at that age, like most South-West African blacks, he detested this bastard form of Dutch, seeing it as a symbol of white supremacy. These days he rarely spoke his own language, preferring English which was a language he favoured and had perfected so that he spoke it with hardly a trace of the slightly singsong thickness of the African. He recalled his early expertise in English and the way his teacher had always asked him to pronounce difficult words in front of the class. Those had been good days in Windhoek where they had been well looked after and cared for in the hostels so that he'd grown fit in both body and mind.

They'd tried to get him into the army, to be trained as an interpreter in the intelligence section, but he hadn't been interested and had resisted the advances of the recruiting officer with his winning smile and glib tongue. Like most matriculated black students, he had favoured the obviously more affluent future in commerce and it had been during the first short year that he'd begun to learn about politics, racialism and injustice. It was at this time that he began to hate the whites who had educated him and brought him so far from the dusty kraal where he was born.

With another young man of Basotho blood, named Nicholas Mohapi, he had resigned from the *Deutsches Bank von Süd Afrika* and slipped out of the territory to make the pilgrimage north to Lusaka and the early indoctrination with the embryonic South-West African People Organisation headed up by a bearded and stocky young man called Sam Nujoma. In those days, in the early seventies, there had been so many wonderful windfall victories for Black Nationalism when Angola and Mozambique had fallen to the liberators. There had been brave utterances and warlike slogans about driving the South African racists out of South-West Africa and into the sea off the Cape. But Lucas remembered his first operation when he was just nineteen and how they'd been discovered inside Ovamboland in their stupid leopard-spotted green camouflage fatigues that had seemed so military and effective in the training camps.

The uniforms had been donated to SWAPO by North Vietnam where these colours were probably excellent in the tropical bush conditions of that country. Unfortunately, in the dusty scrubland of Ovamboland they could be seen hundreds of metres away and Lucas recalled with a tremor that first contact with South African forces. Unfortunately for his untried group, the enemy had been a unit of regular troops, well-equipped and confident and his terror had been very real when he had watched some fifty or so of these professional killers advancing towards him in disciplined skirmish lines, their brown uniforms making them almost invisible in the bone-dry terrain.

As a man, Lucas's group had turned tail and run without attempting to fight and the chase had been long and hard and five of his comrades had been killed when the South Africans called up two Alouette helicopters which had strafed them with the terrifying 50 calibre machine guns. Thankfully the discovery had come close to nightfall but had it not been for this they would all have been killed, he was quite certain of that.

This disastrous rout had proved terribly damaging for morale and it had been more than six months before the survivors of their thirty-two-man platoon had ventured across the border again, this time from Angola which had become a regular staging area. They'd started off with a little mine-laying using pure guerilla tactics, living as and looking like locals. There had been some successes and emboldened by these they had attacked a farm near the Ruacana Falls only five kilometres over the border. This strike had been very good for morale and had turned out to be quite a bloodbath, involving the farmer and his wife, two children and three dogs. They'd managed to catch the farmer close to evening when he was out checking his fence posts only about a kilometre from the farmhouse and had ambushed him in his Landrover which they'd set on fire. This had been a foolhardy move because the wife had seen smoke and must have tried to call up her husband on the shortwave radio; Lucas spotted the long aerial too late, just as Nicholas had holed the petrol tank and hurled a clod of burning grass at the riddled vehicle.

Sure enough, the wife had been waiting when they moved on to the farmhouse and Lucas had known that they would have to be fast and sure because she would have very likely called up the police in Ruacana on her radio. The fat white bitch had fought well with an FN rifle and a shotgun and Nicholas had been hit with a few pellets in the shoulder and poor Wilson killed with a shot in the head before Lucas had managed to put an RPG 7 rocket through the lounge windows. The blast had taken out the two children and a couple of growling dogs but the wife had been covered in blood, yet still alive and bringing up the FN, when they'd burst in. Lucas had leapt on her and tried to cut her head off with the bayonet of his AK in a rage that he had never experienced before. Then they'd fired the house and run for the border and there had been no pursuit because the rain had come and covered their tracks. Ever since then, Lucas had relished the rain when they'd been inside South-West African territory and tonight he had hoped for nature to help him; for the rain to maintain itself in a sound-damping deluge.

As he crouched now, slowly drying out in the humid tropical night, he felt a prickle of unaccustomed apprehension and that butterfly fluttering in his stomach. With a suddenly dry mouth, he whispered to his comrades, trying desperately to quell the faltering note in his voice.

'Nicholas, check the RPD and the rest of you check your magazines, we're moving in four minutes.' As the metallic clatter of the firearms began, the insects in the surrounding forest stopped their sounds abruptly. All five men noticed the change and the sudden awful silence; swallowing nervously, Lucas glanced at his watch, it was almost 10.30 and in just half an hour they would make the strike.

His reminiscences in those few minutes had recalled the deaths of most of his old comrades in the two South African raids into Angola during late 1978. The SWAPO recruits had been happily entrenched in their 'Vietnam' and 'Moscow' camps for more than two years and the defensive precautions had been better than anywhere else in the sub-continent outside of South Africa itself and what was then Rhodesia. The camps had been well inside Angola, hundreds of kilometres in fact, but the South Africans had come early one morning in their obsolete Canberras, dropping anti-personnel bombs and blasting the area, keeping everyone's heads down. But only a few had been killed because of the superb and very deep trench system that they'd built up. In the ensuing panic however the South Africans had landed with their black minion paratroopers, despite the fire from the surviving anti-aircraft guns. Their professionalism and determined attack had routed the gunners who could not have been dislodged had they maintained their positions in the trenches.

Many had been killed that day and Lucas and Nicholas had somehow endeavoured to flee northwards with a few others. The camps had been overrun by the South Africans who fortunately had been satisfied with destroying the buildings, gun emplacements and the huge arsenal of arms and ammunition, a good proportion of which they'd captured and taken away in their big helicopters. The slaughter had been terrible and although Lucas and Nicholas had never learned of the exact numbers, they suspected that well over a thousand of their comrades had died on the morning of that awful day.

Now, as he made his way carefully towards the enemy OP, Lucas's fears left him to be replaced with a resolve to kill that always seemed to develop before action. He tightened his grip on the AK and slowed to glance over his shoulder in the black warmth of the damp forest. Nicholas's teeth flashed briefly in a smile just at his right shoulder and Lucas grinned in response, for a split-second, before he turned back towards the game trail that led in the direction of the river bank and the police OP.

Johnny, the Ovambo tracker lay close to Cohen's feet beside the stack of 60mm mortar bombs, his eyes closed and only the ground sheet covering his slight body. In sleep, he was still partially awake and his nostrils fascinated Cohen because they quivered like an animals as he breathed. As he watched, Cohen could swear that the black's ears twitched too, although it was very difficult to see clearly in the gloom. Van der Merwe had a small fire going lower down the bank, carefully screened from the river by thick bushes and reeds. Occasionally the fire would flame fitfully in tiny flickers of light and these would illuminate the features of the sleeping black.

As Cohen idly watched, relaxing now after almost two hours on sentry duty and due for imminent relief by Reilly, he noted the black's eyes suddenly open at the same time as something changed subtly in the night sounds from the wall of jungle in front of him. Gradually, the insect noises built up again but the Ovambo was slithering like a cat towards the mortars and Cohen's hackles began to rise at the back of his neck in a horrible prickling sensation. Subconsciously, his finger pushed forward on the safety catch of the R1 rifle moving the selector through single shot to automatic fire. Silently he sank down as the tracker reached the first mortar and, using his elbows, he too slithered forward on all fours.

Van der Merwe, dozing by the fire, failed to see Cohen's movement but Reilly, who at that moment had rolled from under his groundsheet where he had unsuccessfully been trying to doze off, saw the direction of Cohen's crawl and realised with absolute and terrible instinct that something was very wrong. Continuing his slithering roll he reached the sleeping Bester just as the thunk of the first mortar caused the lieutenant to bolt upright into a sitting position. The crash of the shot was the next thing they both heard and then everyone was moving and the lieutenant was mouthing obscenities and shouting in a strange half-whisper.

The pre-emptive action of Cohen and Johnny the tracker had caught Lucas and his men completely by surprise. They had advanced to a position some one hundred metres from the target and were about to remove the pins from their first five grenades when the tell-tale thunk of the mortar sounded, so close as to be almost in front of them. In the few seconds before the bomb landed Lucas screamed, 'Down flat!' and still clutching the grenades to their chests the five blacks buried their faces in the damp humus of the forest floor.

Lucas had been about to set up the RPD and was carrying it with the bi-pod legs extended so that now it was ready for use and as he dropped to the ground he began to squeeze the trigger without sighting the weapon. Purely by luck, Cohen's first three shots bracketed Lucas's position almost perfectly and within thirty seconds the lieutenant had the second mortar in operation, with Reilly assisting and dropping the compact fragmentation bombs into the tube exactly as the training manual prescribed.

The effect of the mortar rounds in the thick foliage, interspersed with sturdy saplings, was limited, but Bester instructed them to alter trajectory by five degrees on either side of the original setting for one hundred metres. In this way he hoped to catch the attackers as they moved from one position to another rather like a destroyer hunting a submarine with depth charges.

In just over two minutes the SAP section got off around two dozen mortar bombs drawing only one burst of machine gun fire in return, which raked the tops of the trees twenty feet above their heads to arch out across the river into Zambia. Lucas's men were severely panicked by the severity of the barrage and Cohen's fourth shot had landed only metres in front of Lucas but slightly over to the right. The concussion was deafening but most of the blast and shrapnel was absorbed by the dense bush, except for a pocket comb shaped sliver of casing which, spinning through the air at more than two thousand feet per second, caught Simon Sbukwe on the dome of his bent head slicing through hair, skull and brain like a hot wire through butter. The terrified crouching black felt only a light tap on his head and ceased to exist in one blinding white millisecond.

Lucas was desperately considering a move when the lieutenant's first mortar exploded virtually in front of him where he crouched behind a stout mopani trunk. The explosion upended the RPD, blasting it out of the black's slippery hand so that it crashed away to the left and behind him. As the gun whipped up, the trigger guard almost severed the first joint of Lucas's index finger which was pressing the trigger. In agony, Lucas tried to rally his men.

'Nicholas with me to the left, the rest break to the right!' he screamed in Ovambo, 'and fire, just fire at the bastard sons of dogs!' Hefting his AK in his left hand and retrieving the RPD in the right, he broke from his position and ran diagonally left, hearing Nicholas crashing along behind him.

So far, neither side had seen each other and the fire-fight had lasted barely three minutes. Dimly, in the heat of the action, Bester heard the shouted command in Ovambo from the bush and looked questioningly at the black tracker who pointed right and left of their position.

'Cover the flanks!' Bester screamed. 'Van der Merwe, covering fire with the MAG, swing it round onto the right flank for fuck's sake, quickly man!' He glanced at the two mortar bombs which were left from the pile of thirty-six that had been stacked under the camouflage tarpaulin.

'Mortars cease firing. Now all of you ready with rifle grenades. Change your gas settings and eject your first rounds, now.'

Hearts thumping wildly and hands clammy with sweat, the section complied, twisting the circular valve on the end of the R1's breech after pulling the cocking handle to eject the first round from the chamber of their rifles.

'OK blanks in,' yelled the lieutenant, 'and now, on with the grenade launchers, quickly you bastards, quickly.'

Cohen, like the rest of the section, had practised this manoeuvre so many times and felt for the launcher and one of the two rifle grenades, which were carried in his right hand bush jacket pocket. Van der Merwe had neither his grenade launcher nor the required projectiles, so he crouched behind the MAG in abject terror, smelling himself because again he had soiled his trousers in the first few seconds of the action.

'Short bursts to the right from forty-five to sixty degrees, Albertus!' shouted the lieutenant and in his terrified daze, van der Merwe reacted automatically, pressing the trigger for a second at a time and moving the weapon in a shallow arc from right to left, all the time keeping it on his right flank. The trajectory was flat, about waist high, and the bushes and small trees were whipped and shredded by the 7.62mm bullets which cut neat swathes through them.

'The rest of you, ready now!' shouted Bester. 'Rifle grenades at forty-five degrees to the body fire to your front, now,' and there were six hollow bangs as the ineffectual little bombs were lobbed into the air from their canister-like launchers, propelled by the blank cartridges.

The machine gun fire and the grenades found only one target in the blackness of the forest night and both Lucas and Nicholas froze as they heard the horrible shriek on their right which bubbled off into silence. It could have been Simon, Johnson or Robert and Lucas's rage built up within him, killing both the pain from his mutilated finger and the fear of the mortars so that he was able to pull the AK's trigger with the second joint of his right index finger, oblivious of the metal juddering against his exposed nerve endings and the MAG bullets scything through the bush on his left and dangerously close.

Nicholas followed suit and in the gloom he caught the briefest glimpse of a tiny flickering light in the direction of the river. Instinctively, he rose to his knees and sighted quickly, snap-shooting and firing in quick bursts, expending the entire AK magazine of thirty shots in a matter of seconds before rolling and squirming away to a position five metres further left and closer to the enemy flank. He fired again – this time conserving his ammunition – from the new magazine, in fast single shots and was aware of Lucas, still firing on his right, and someone else returning fire from way over on the opposite flank.

Four shots from Nicholas's first magazine caught van der Merwe in the upper stomach and chest, hammering him flat on his back in the mud halfway down the river bank, and leaving the MAG slewed over on its tripod and pointing skywards. Van der Merwe had felt only a series of hard blows like a combination of fast punches and then he was on his back, looking up at the inky blackness of the sky which could just be seen through the umbrella of branches above him. Feeling absolutely lucid and very aware of every noise, he was sure he could hear the rustling of leaves and could even see a few tiny stars which were momentarily blotted out as the foliage was wafted about gently in the night breeze.

Van der Merwe felt a strange tightness in his chest and ribs and a rising warmth which seemed to fill his chest cavity from within. It was at once odd and yet not unpleasant. With increasing clarity, he realised that he had been wounded in some way and tried to check his injuries. He tried to sit up and, finding this impossible, attempted to roll over onto his knees but again found that he couldn't move. It seemed like a nightmare and he remembered fragments of his childhood when he had dreamed that he was trapped with some fearsome beast advancing towards him. On those occasions he had always awoken, bathed in sweat, often with an arm trapped beneath his body and numb with restricted blood circulation. The dream, in such cases, was the brain's method of advising the body that something was wrong; but now he was fully awake and still he could not move. He tried to shout but his mouth felt woolly and he knew that he wasn't making any noise, was unable to speak and then the odd rushing noise began in his ears. It sounded like a waterfall, and, dimly now, he wondered if the river was flooding. Then the blackness started, seeming to loom up from the river like an inexorable marsh mist, and he found himself suffocating but still he could not move, could not fight it.

Limply and without fear, he realised that he was going under but there was nothing really that could be done and he accepted that he would have to let it happen to him, have to just relax and not fight it. He died with a brief gurgle of sound as the blood filled his lungs and forced out the remaining life-giving air.

The lieutenant got to van der Merwe within thirty seconds of his being hit but he was already dead, the blood thick in his open mouth and his eyes staring upwards into the trees. He closed the dead boy's eyes and smelled the dreadful animal odour of him and then the black rage rose in him so that he righted the MAG and checked the belt feed in an instant. It was all OK and he squeezed the trigger at the black wall of bush, swearing and cursing under his breath and trying to search out his attackers with the vicious bursts of steel-jacketed bullets.

The others were all behaving reasonably well and firing from the prone position in disciplined and restrained single shots. Cohen tried to watch for the flashes from the AKs but it was almost impossible in the thick, almost solid, darkness of the forest. He thought he caught a glimpse on the left flank and sighted quickly, firing four quick shots and then after a pause, another couple. There was no answering fire.

The lieutenant was on the MAG now, keeping the frigging *mamsa*'s heads down and presumably something had happened to old Van. Cohen was pleased to find that, again, he felt no real fear other than a sort of heightened awareness of his own vulnerability with all the bullets flying about. There was a controlled excitement that he almost relished and he continued to press the trigger and change magazines like a well-oiled machine; almost like part of the gun, he told himself. Quite suddenly the lieutenant gave the order to stop firing and the deep bangs of the R1s tailed off so that a shocked and almost tangible silence returned to the bush. But the insects did not begin their racket for some minutes.

Lucas and Nicholas had pulled back and were now heading for the rendezvous point at the junction of two major game trails about a kilometre inland from their attack point. It was very black and difficult to see, even a metre in front, so that they stumbled along cursing with Nicholas crying from time to time like a baby in quiet racking sobs. They waited for Simon, Johnson and Robert for forty-five minutes, fingers on triggers and ears pricking for any sound of pursuit. But there was nothing and Lucas knew now that they would not come.

Somehow, by great ill luck, they had failed to surprise the white men and now they were just two with the other three dead or unable to move. Those long-standing and much-loved comrades had been pointlessly wasted in a

187

fruitless attack against the hated whites. Lucas began to doubt his decision to use the contingency plan and the added mistake of staying and fighting rather than just throwing the grenades, firing one burst and running as was the prescribed tactic.

'I shall avenge them Nicholas,' he said gravely pulling the sobbing young Basotho towards him. 'We will kill many of them for those three lives.'

After they had buried the remaining grenades, the two AK rifles and the RPD a short distance from the fork in the trail, Lucas took special note of the landmarks and memorised the spot carefully. Then, sweating and silent in their despair, they set off on the roundabout route, back towards the kraal twenty kilometres west, parallel with the river bank. It was a hard march, but once there they would be sheltered and fed by the headman and his wives.

Once more they had become ordinary-looking Africans, dressed in nondescript clothes and carrying no identity documents. Tatty and unkempt, and noticeably unwashed, they made the trip without problems and eight hours later at daybreak, when a South African army patrol checked out the kraal, they were casually rejected as just another couple of down-at-heel bush kaffirs. Lucas and Nicholas smiled at one another as the earnest-looking young soldiers drove off in their armoured vehicles; once again they had affected the stupid sullen expressions which had exasperated white men since Africa was first colonised and still did the trick as it always would.

With the cessation of gunfire, Bester had made radio contact with the army HQ at Wenela, which was closest and most properly equipped to deal with a follow-up operation. He sent Reilly and Cohen forward to look for bodies or discarded weapons and almost immediately Cohen found the terrie he had shot at. The young African was still alive having taken a bullet through the shoulder a few centimetres above his left nipple.

Reilly discovered the body of Simon whose skull gaped obscenely in the light of his torch, glistening wetly and showing a pink-spotted greyish portion in the region that was totally missing. The sight caused Reilly to vomit, retching up his dry biscuit and corned meat so that he stood, still gazing at the body, quivering slackly with reaction. Cohen in turn found Robert who was the unfortunate who had been caught by the rifle grenades, one of which had blasted away much of his right upper torso and shoulder. The grenade must have landed almost on top of him because the black had obviously tried to pick it up and toss it away. Most of his right hand was gone as well.

The two young policemen collected the weapons but did not touch the dead bodies or the grenades which could easily have been booby-trapped; SWAPO had been known to place primed grenades under the clothing of dead comrades in the style of the North Vietnamese. The survivor, who had refused to talk, was half-carried, grimacing with pain, to the OP where Bester smiled wolfishly and expressed delight at seeing him.

Van der Merwe had been wrapped in two groundsheets and Wenela had radioed through that an army river launch was coming down from Katima Mulilo and to hell with revealing the position of the OP which would have to be moved now anyway. As he looked from the tarpaulin-wrapped body to the arrogant-looking prisoner, Bester felt a murderous rage building again and realised that he was very hyped-up with reaction.

They set the black down with his back against a small tree and tied his hands behind the trunk. Bester approached him.

'You black fucker!' he bawled, his mouth only centimetres from the African's face. 'How many of you cocksuckers were there, how many eh? You sod!' Enraged by the lack of reaction and apparent absence of fear showing in the impassive black face, Bester smashed the prisoner in the mouth with his fist whilst the section looked on fascinated. This was their first glimpse of the enemy and they felt the initial stirring of an almost sexual blood lust growing within them with the realisation that this man was dispensable, that they could kill or at least torture him with impunity.

Johnson's head slammed back against the tree trunk and he tasted blood as his front teeth tore through his bottom lip. His resolve began to weaken when he saw the hatred on the face of the big white officer. It became clear to him that now, or later, he would die and that quite possibly this South African policeman would kill him – perhaps in only seconds. Despite himself, the fear came in waves and suddenly he began to speak, his voice hissing tremblingly through the mashed lips.

By the time the boat arrived, Johnson was barely conscious and Bester had got quite a bit of information out of him as to how many were in the attacking group and what their armaments had been. But as the black was manhandled roughly into the ski-boat Bester watched Reilly and Cohen pick up Van der Merwe's body with a gentle reverence that touched him. What use was the information that the black had eventually given him to poor Albertus? Already the other two surviving terries would be far gone and the prisoner had almost passed out without divulging the rendezvous point or eventual destination. He'd just kept saying, 'No boss, I don't know, boss,' and Bester had been so incensed that he'd hit the fucker too hard so that in the end he'd become irrational and talked pure crap.

By the time the army boys had pulled out the bastard's fingernails at Katima, it would be far too late. The black bastards would always lie anyway and this one could put them onto any of a dozen villages and kraals in the area. For sure the two swines would have gone to ground somewhere, they wouldn't risk walking about with the army out looking for them but it was like searching for a couple of needles in a gigantic haystack and they'd just have to raid every bloody village in a huge operation that would cost the taxpayers back home thousands. Furthermore, it intimidated the locals and made them hate the Army even more and it would all be to no avail because they might as well stay in the barracks and piss the money against the wall in the Mess.

CHAPTER 14

When the South African Airways 747 landed at Frankfurt am Main it was 8.12 in the morning local time and Gerrit looked out of the porthole for his first view of Germany and Europe. It was a blustery yet sunny spring morning and he felt his stomach tighten with excitement despite the resolve to remain cool and unimpressed as far as possible towards what he knew would be quite fascinating. But now he could do little to squash the worms of pleasurable tension that squirmed in his stomach at the prospects of new sights, ideas and cultures.

The stewardess smiled at him as she took the public address handset from the bulkhead two rows in front and sat down to make her ritual announcement in Afrikaans, English and German. Gerrit looked at her closely, seeing that she was obviously South African and yet she had smiled at him with great warmth and even interest in her eyes. Suddenly he felt as if a great and oppressive weight had been lifted from his shoulders because here he was, a fully fledged member of the human race, the same as everyone else, rather than a sort of tolerated embarrassment which was often the case back home in South Africa.

This realisation buoyed his spirits to new heights so that he smiled back openly at the pretty girl whose face and body reminded him of Gail Wilson. Briefly, Gail flashed across his memory and he wondered where she was now and how she was making out with her rich Dutchman, what sort of a life she would have, how many children.

192

The thoughts brought back painful memories and he drove them away, snapping out of his reverie as the big Boeing rocked gently to a halt. Service vehicles immediately rushed forward and darted alongside the now clumsy earthbound monster that had carried him 12,000 kilometres across the world in a little more than as many hours.

As the aircraft's engines whined gently to a final clattering stop, there was a volley of lock-snapping as the 257 passengers unfastened their seat belts and leapt to their feet, stretching dramatically and smiling at one another as they congratulated themselves on having made it once again, back to earth and safety. There was much rummaging and searching in the overhead baggage lockers and loud goodbyes in various languages as the intrepid flyers of a few hours ago now became ordinary husbands, wives and lovers and lost the glamour that they had shared whilst locked in close proximity, travelling at almost 900kph at 40,000 feet above their fellow humans below.

Sensibly Gerrit remained seated whilst all this urgent necessity to leave the now grounded aircraft swept on around him. He sat quietly, indifferent to the clamour although inwardly his heartbeat had increased markedly and a light prickle of sweat sprang beneath his armpits. The stewardess watched him as she waited by the door for the finger gangway to be connected from the terminal building. She had watched the young coloured all night and noted that he acted very nicely, taking great pains to do everything just right.

Despite this performance however, she had known that this was his first time out of South Africa, his first international trip anyway, that was for sure. She could always tell by the way a passenger's eyes would search out everything that was happening in the cabin as if they, the eyes alone, were hungry for information, like live things on their own, desperate for experience and knowledge. She'd watched him with his dinner last night and the breakfast this morning and she'd seen how he was unfamiliar with airline meals and their packaging, how he'd looked fixedly out of the window on takeoff and landing. But he was quite a confident number this one, she mused, and not bad looking, a bit like Richard Jon Smith the coloured pop singer back home. As he finally stood up and began to lift down his baggage and slip into the suede jacket, she watched his slim athletic body stretch and noted the narrow waist and hips. I wonder what it would be like, she thought. Of course, she'd never tried with a black or coloured, but some of the girls had and now she wondered. The thoughts surprised her and as he glanced at her she blushed slightly and covered her embarrassment with another quick smile.

Gerrit handed his new South African passport to the bored-looking young official who merely glanced at it, checked the visa and stamped it lightly, nodding him through to the baggage-collection area. He found his single suitcase on the moving conveyor belt and was for the first time impressed with the efficiency of this airport and of this country, Germany. Loading the case and his briefcase onto a trolley, he strode through the green route in the customs hall without a sideways glance at the uniformed officers who waited in groups, like birds of prey. Broodingly, they eyed the passengers, waiting to swoop on would-be smugglers of ivory, game skins and the much sought-after cannabis; the weed which had a street value in Germany of around one hundred times the purchase price in Durban or Swazilands African kraals.

He saw Tina as he walked through the door, pushing his trolley in front of him and scanning the waiting faces. She stood out like a bright flower in a sea of drab grass. She recognised him in almost the same instant and flew at him, all brown arms and long legs and smelling of the wonderful orangy fragrance from Christian Dior that he remembered Willi had first bought her in Cape Town when she had started going with him. It had been almost two years since he had seen his sister and he felt real emotion as he watched her blinking back the tears in those wonderful

194

eyes. She held him at arm's length and stared at him, her face smilingly alive and vibrant and more beautiful than he ever remembered. People watching them smiled too, the women trying not to stare at the slender, casually elegant coloured man and the men making no effort to conceal their interest, hungrily devouring the stunning looking girl with their eyes.

Tina was dressed in an ivory silk blouse and rich dark brown velvet skirt of slender pencil design. She carried a soft leather shoulder bag in chocolate brown and a thin leather belt was matched to shoes of the same colour whilst her stockings were natural, leaving her long brown legs apparently almost unclothed. She delved into the handbag and produced a large bunch of keys and spoke breathlessly, her eyes shining.

'Come on, Gerrit, I've got the car right outside. Oh God, but it's good to see you. You look so fantastic and so smart.' She looked at him again, hands on hips and her pelvis thrust forward, with legs a little apart so that her slim waist and tight buttocks were accentuated causing the voyeuristic attentions of the male watchers to escalate even more. 'But you haven't changed little brother,' she laughed. 'My God, but it's good to see you. I didn't realise how much I'd missed you until you walked through that door.'

Arm in arm, they left the crowded arrival hall and already Gerrit was struck by the wealth of Germany and the number of people everywhere. Most of them looked well-to-do and outside the huge hall there were Porsches, BMWs and Mercedes lined up with a few uniformed chauffeurs standing attentively, awaiting their employers like stormtroopers on parade. Nobody loves uniforms more than the Germans, thought Gerrit as he watched them click into action holding doors open and springing about to open luggage trunks. Still pushing his trolley, Gerrit followed Tina who stopped suddenly beside a silver BMW 635 coupé which was parked illegally in the tow-away zone. His eyes widened as he looked inside the

195

impressive interior and as they loaded the luggage into the carpeted boot, Tina glanced sideways at her brother, her mouth wide with laughter although there was pride in her huge brown eyes as she giggled, 'Not bad for a little *skollie* lass from Elsies River, eh little brother? This is Willi's actually, but at home when he's in town he uses my Scirrocco and I just love to drive this machine; I drove it down from Dusseldorf yesterday in under an hour and a half.'

As Tina started the engine from the left hand seat, a buzzer sounded and a red warning light flashed on the instrument panel. 'Fasten your seat belt, Gerrit, we're going on a little drive down to Nuremberg for the weekend. Willi has clients to see in Frankfurt so you won't see him until Monday. He's working so hard the poor baby but making a fortune, an absolute fortune. But there's someone else I want you to meet in Nuremberg who's coming down from Berlin especially. I think you're going to like him, his name's Manfred Meyer.'

With a skill Gerrit would never have imagined his sister possessed, Tina manoeuvred the elegant coupé out of the airport concourse and onto the main autobahn south towards Bavaria. In minutes the BMW was in the fast lane moving at over 220kph, in convoy with a Mercedes 600 and a Porsche 911 SC, all of which seemed to be travelling bumper to bumper.

Unused to driving at such speeds, after the 90kph limit in South Africa, and somewhat disorientated by driving on the right hand side of a motorway, Gerrit found it difficult to hold a conversation with Tina who kept up a constant barrage of chatter whilst listening to a Billy Joel tape on the car stereo. The system seemed to have speakers everywhere and Tina said Willi had fitted a booster which developed almost 100 watts of music sound. Gerrit thought that it was like sitting in the middle of a discotheque.

The BMW's three and a half litre fuel injection engine pushed the big coupé along without effort and, allowing for the occasional traffic jam and some slow moving heavy traffic around Wurtzburg, they managed to average 150kph on the 238km journey reaching the ancient Bavarian city at just after eleven o'clock. Tina took the Nuremberg central exit off the autobahn which would snake on through the beautiful countryside, all the way down to the Austrian border near Salzburg. Soon they were driving through the narrow streets of the quaint old town to arrive at the Prinz Regent Hotel before midday.

As soon as they had unloaded the car and carried the cases into the cosy lobby, Tina called the front office manager and asked if a Herr Meyer had arrived.

'*Nein, Frau Heim,*' was the suave reply and Gerrit made a mental note that this immaculate and very typical looking Aryan seemed to know his charismatic sister.

As he watched, the aristocratic young German stared at Tina longingly, a small tight smile exposing his perfect teeth; but his poise did not slip as she caught his glance and smiled back with a slightly reproving grin. Tina had booked adjoining rooms on the eighth floor and Gerrit unpacked, feeling a little light-headed from jet lag and the speed of their journey from the airport. But Tina only allowed him a few minutes to bathe and unpack before she was hammering on the door again and dragging him down to the old *Kaffeehaus* close to the hotel.

Gerrit was no stranger to German food, after almost fifteen months in Windhoek, the capital of what was once *Deutsche Sud Wes Africa,* and he had picked up a little of the language which, added to his fluency in Afrikaans, enabled him to follow a basic conversation. Tina seemed to be speaking German fluently and Gerrit remarked on her expertise.

'Thank you my dear brother, I am indeed complimented,' she said in superb English. 'My darling Willi sent me to lessons in Dusseldorf for six months and then to an English elocution teacher who helped me to get rid of the Capey twang. I spent a bit of time at the Berlitz too and now I'm almost fluent but my accent is still a bit thick in

German and sometimes I get mixed up and actually throw in an Afrikaans word or two which baffles the poor Krauts completely.' She laughed wickedly and again Gerrit marvelled at her beauty.

She had changed in a subtle way, becoming obviously more poised and infinitely more well-groomed, Gerrit remembered that Tina had always had a good eye for clothes, and even in her teenage years, when there was little money, she had been able to match her few dresses and accessories perfectly. Furthermore, she'd always been very hygiene-conscious and had monopolised the tiny bathroom when they'd moved to the new house in Goodwood so that Koos and Gerrit had to queue outside in the mornings and often do without hot water because Tina had used it all before them. Gerrit remembered the way that she had managed to get up, even on cold wet winter mornings, and bath and wash her hair before going to school. Their mother had helped her a lot of course, was supportive of her high-handed attitude with the toilet facilities, petting her and always telling the beautiful young girl how proud she was of her.

Now, with an allowance from Willi of DM3000 every month for clothes and her own personal expenses, Tina was able to indulge most of her whims and affected a casually elegant look reminiscent of a *Vogue* model, yet with far more vivaciousness and sparkle. Gerrit appraised her objectively and thought her to be one of the most attractive women he had ever seen with an air about her that was totally unique and very alluring.

'How is little Koos, Gerrit?' Tina asked without warning, her face animated and full of memories of her poverty-stricken, yet basically happy childhood. 'It's about a year since I heard from him.'

Gerrit replied seriously. 'The last I heard, he was still at the Ford garage in Goodwood, still in the workshops as he always has been since he left school. To tell you the truth, Tina, I think he'll stay there, just like Dad did. He's basically not interested in changing his life. As long as he

198

has a few rands in his pocket and that bloody motorbike, he's happy.'

Tina looked wistful for a moment and then her face took on a blank, faraway look as she became lost in memories of her juvenile years, recalling all the good times of hot summer days when the three of them would be turned out of the house to play in the dirt, literally from dawn to dusk.

Koos had always been the baby and Gerrit had had little time for him, so that Tina had inevitably been there to protect him and comfort him when he'd fallen foul of his older brother or injured himself playing in the derelict houses and dirty streets of Elsies River. Recently those same children, less than one generation later, had begun to rebel against the appalling conditions in which they were forced to live, purely because of the colour of their skin. The unequal system of schooling in South Africa meant that some four times more government money was spent on each white child in comparison to a black or coloured equivalent and so there had been stonings and fire-bombings of schools and Education Department property. It had started with the boycotting of classes and predictably, the bloody stupid South African police had overreacted, sending paramilitary riot police into the troubled areas to solve the problem of a few kids staying away from school. Some children had been shot and a large number detained without trial.

In Germany, there had been quite a bit of press coverage about these schoolchildren protesting against the system in which they were repressed and segregated on a purely racial basis. Tina had been able to buy quite a few publications which were outlawed in South Africa and these included a new monthly magazine called *Confront* which emanated from London and was published by a new group calling itself the Azanian Freedom Revolutionary Army or AFRA for short. This organisation seemed to be quite successful and well funded and she had bought quite a few copies of the magazine to show to Manfred and, of course, Gerrit. Some of the material was quite sickening and sometimes, she found it difficult to believe that she had lived that way, had been a victim of that repressive and fascist neo-colonialism.

Tina's dream was broken by Gerrit's voice. 'Tina, Tina, you're in a dream just like you used to be when you were a child.' Gerrit laughed at his beautiful sister as she flinched suddenly, as if struck and jerked out of her trancelike state. In an instant, she was once more poised and assured and smilingly she turned to her brother as if seeing him anew.

'Sorry, Gerrit,' she said grinning disarmingly. 'It's true, I was miles away, back in our childhood, in the Cape.' With equal suddenness her face changed again and she became serious. 'There are so many things we have to talk about Gerrit, so much for us to do, don't you think?'

With almost telepathic contact, Gerrit knew instinctively that Tina was talking about South Africa and some sort of action against the country of their birth. The thought excited him because it crystallised the strange uneasy thoughts he had been feeling since the Hout Bay riots and yet it frightened him because he could not see what they alone could do against such a mighty adversary whose military strength could only be vaguely estimated by the West.

Yet now he could see inside Tina's head and the revelations were astounding, so much so, that he looked around furtively as if guilty of complicity in acts against the State. The realisation that he was safe here in West Germany and far from the oppression, glowed in his consciousness bringing a feeling of lightness and release.

As if she too could read his thoughts Tina said, 'We'll do it Gerrit,' and her voice was soft, her huge eyes moist. 'But first we must eat. *Bitte Fraulein die karte,*' she called and turning to Gerrit, smiled again with that incredible mouth so that her perfect teeth shone white against the red lips. 'Have you ever tasted *Nuremberger bratwurste?*' she asked, her head on one side like a little girl.

After the early lunch, they walked in the Old Town and the sun shone in the narrow streets where ancient oaks and maples were resplendent in their spring leaf. There was so much for Gerrit to assimilate, so much to see and experience and Tina shared his wonder because she too was still discovering Germany and Europe and had only been to Nuremberg once before with Willi en route to Munich. The two of them felt a mutual closeness which had never existed before and their animated chatter in English, and sometimes Afrikaans, caused those who watched them to smile and stare curiously.

As he walked with his sister in the spring sunshine of that late afternoon, Gerrit was filled with a sense of completeness and purpose and a genuine delight in the company of Tina. She too seemed to relish being with him and clung to his arm like a lover so that, almost incestuously, he wondered what it would be like to have such a woman, to possess her for oneself. Surely she would be more than a handful, because she was wilful and selfish in some ways. But she was unique, she was Tina and his sister and had suddenly become very important to him. He could not remember ever feeling so happy.

There was an immediate mutual identification between Manfred Meyer and Gerrit de Kock. They met that evening, in the small bar at the Prinz Regent, and it was only minutes before they were talking about Cape Town and the incredible beauty of the southernmost tip of Africa. Tina found it difficult to break into the intense conversation, so fine was the level of understanding between the two men, but listening to them she felt almost physical pain in her longing for the Cape and even had fond memories of her home in the coloured township close to Goodwood. Tears sprang behind her eyelids as she recalled the warmth and understanding that her mother had always provided and how she, Tina, had left her without even a goodbye. Left her to become increasingly old and infirm and eventually to die in filth and agony, alone and unwanted by the children she sacrificed so much for in her often bitter years of married life.

Unaware of his sister's morbidity, Gerrit found the young German extremely intelligent, if a little radical. Undoubtedly, he had a brilliant mind with a lawyer's ability to quote figures and relevant detail verbatim. Now he was quoting facts that even Gerrit was unaware of.

'Do you know how many coloureds have fled South Africa in the past decade?' Manfred asked earnestly. Gerrit shook his head and the young lawyer continued, 'Well, the question is highly controversial and the government say little about it. Actually, reliable sources tell me that the figure is in excess of ten thousand, most of these being professional or technically trained people who were well enough established in South Africa to be able to take the considerable step of travelling halfway around the globe to put down new roots elsewhere.

'Obviously Gerrit, these people will never return and some of them leave on exit permits in any event which prevents them from ever again seeing the country of their birth. The loss to South Africa is considerable and the shortfall is especially serious when one considers that those who have left come from the upper echelons of coloured society. In other words, those who would have taken the social and political lead in a community which is sadly already short of guidance from within its own ranks.'

Manfred's use of English was fluent and his articulate and engaging manner held Gerrit captive as he continued. 'Even if the Botha government reversed its policies tomorrow, the damage has been done. By that I mean that the emigrants have made new lives for themselves, they've started again from scratch and they're hardly likely to come back and begin the whole process over again. I have read recently,' Manfred went on, 'that the exodus is beginning to cause some alarm in official circles. As far back as 1968 the government were trying to stem the flow by instigating fees known as "Repatriation Costs" which, even at that time, was a deposit of R300 per adult and

R150 per child. This had to be paid before any passports were issued!'

Gerrit too had heard of other hurdles used by the government to try and prevent coloured emigration from South Africa and quoted them to Manfred, his voice becoming intense with emotion as he spoke softly. 'Did you know Manfred, that in the late sixties it was Canada that offered shelter and great job opportunities to my people?' Without thinking he had reverted to the expression he had last voiced aloud to Gail in Cape Town. 'The Canadians were so impressed with the calibre of immigrant they were getting that they approached the South African government to set up an immigration mission in the country to deal with a backlog of coloured would-be immigrants to their country. Of course the bloody bastard Boers refused and eventually rushed through a bill suspending all emigration of coloured people to Canada until further notice.

'In the early seventies, the brain drain of coloured people began to switch to Australia as Canada was now out of the question,' Gerrit continued. Tina watched him speaking in that intense and very impressive manner that had always made her listen when he had advised her on the initial and hurtful decisions of her teenage years. He was actually just like Manfred in his way – a darker coloured version – and the two of them seemed to be getting on incredibly well. She was glad because she loved them both and had developed a feeling of warmth for her brother that she had not believed could ever have been there, below the surface, suppressed in her idle and self-centred existence. She admitted to herself that it had been so, but now there would be a purpose, a goal to aim for and what was more it was right, so right that it filled her with a sense of well-being and satisfaction that no man had ever been able to give her.

'Those who left for Australia,' said Gerrit, 'included teachers, doctors and skilled artisans, in fact, a Cape Town travel agent, who is a reliable source, termed the exodus "The cream of the coloured community". Of course there was a severe risk to the remaining coloureds that they could be left intellectually bankrupt by this drain of talent but what did the government do? Nothing as usual. Absolutely nothing, they just carried on with their Job Reservation and Group Areas Act and turned a blind eye.'

Manfred nodded and then shook his head as if in desperation. 'Christ almighty,' he said in a very English way, 'let's have another drink, the subject is so depressing it makes me thirsty.' They had been drinking steadily now for almost two hours and Gerrit was trying vodka and lime juice in place of his usual appletiser mixer which was unobtainable. If anything the sharp taste of the limes masked the neutural spirit even more than the apple drink did and he realised suddenly that he had better take it easy and shook his head when Manfred pointed towards his empty glass.

'Just a soda and ice or I'll be under the table,' Gerrit said and Tina watched him and smiled; still the sensible Gerrit, she thought, he never really lets himself go.

They continued the discussion at dinner in the small and comfortable dining room and Tina urged Gerrit to try some of the Rhine Riesling that Manfred had ordered. Now it was Manfred holding the conversation again and Gerrit marvelled at his knowledge of South African affairs and the depth of his understanding of the problems of the blacks and coloureds.

'Just recently,' Manfred said urgently, 'two and a half million South Africans have been left without any political forum whatsoever. The Nationalists who run your country are so blind that they seem totally unable to come to grips with the aspirations of the brown Afrikaaner who claims to be the "only true South Africans" who speaks the same terrible bloody language and who worships the same God. Many of them, like Tina and you Gerrit, bear the same names as leading government officers yet you're not accepted because your skin is just a slightly darker shade of pale; in Tina's case it's not even noticeable!' In an impassioned voice he went on.

'First they tried the laughable Coloured Persons Representative Council, which of course was only a partly elected body. Then, when that failed they moved on to an entirely government-nominated council of Nationalist yes men. Naturally enough, the coloured people wanted no part of this bunch of political puppets and so now, that dream too has joined the others on the government scrap heap. So the coloureds are in limbo once more, which is where they have always been and will always be as long as apartheid lives.'

Manfred glanced down to his plate, after quickly selecting a piece of boiled pork, he added a piece of potato dumpling and a forkful of red cabbage and thrust the lot into his mouth. The faces of the two seated opposite him were rapt with concentration, at the effect of his words, and he felt a great warmth and tenderness for them, this beautiful girl and her highly intelligent brother. Their trust in him was immense and he knew that somehow their destinies were interlinked with his, that the road would be hard and long, but worthwhile.

'It's a sad and tawdry history,' he continued, feeling pleased to have discovered that little used word in his memory traces. 'The South African government's record is one of shabby cruelty which cannot be excused by any thinking person. The political tragedy of your people owes nothing to separate development, that grand design, but it owes everything to obvious colour prejudice, fear and discrimination of the worst kind.

'In fact you know,' he went on softly, as he considered his own words and the basic message that they outlined, 'you people are the Achilles Heel of apartheid because the South African government's treatment of the coloureds has exposed the dreadful weaknesses of their so-called separate development ideals. You, and those like you, are a reminder to them and the world that all the smooth talking and boom economy notwithstanding, apartheid is not based on a division of power, but the retaining of all power in the hands of the whites.'

By now, all three of them were incensed with the idea of improving the lot of the coloureds and blacks in South Africa. Somehow, the coloured case seemed a more worthy one. Were Tina and Gerrit not coloureds, were they themselves not typical examples of the suppressed brilliance of their race? It all came back to the same old answer, if it wasn't for the whites who had come to the Cape three centuries earlier, there wouldn't be any coloureds. Now, in this decade of progress and in a country which undoubtedly was making great strides economically and technically, they were being held back just because of ancient prejudice and a skin colour which did not conform to the 'European' specifications of the government.

Yet, both Tina and Gerrit knew in their hearts that the battle had to be a terrifyingly difficult one. Many had tried, like Adam Small the coloured playwright and countless poets and actors. Their voices had not even been heard let alone noticed and even recently, after all the injustices, the remaining independent coloured leaders had very generously offered to engage in dialogue with the Botha government, in fact with Botha himself. But, still the Nationalists would try and sidetrack the issue, would resist giving full citizenship and voting rights to a group of people who were of their own blood.

They finished off an excellent meal with Cognacs and coffees and Manfred smoked endless French cigarettes as he continued his amazingly accurate monologue. By now, Gerrit was feeling tired and had trouble keeping his eyes open. He had seen the odd glance that passed between his sister and Manfred but the obvious conclusion he drew from their liking for each other did not trouble him. That part of her life was her own, he thought sleepily and she had always chosen the right course and handled her men wisely. As far as he was concerned, Manfred Meyer was an attractive man and one to be reckoned with and if Tina shared her bed with him that was perfectly natural. Gerrit thought that had he been a woman he would have very likely done the same.

Later, when Gerrit had gone to his room, Manfred and Tina had made love slowly and lovingly in the old oak trestle bed. They lay side by side under the light feather duvet and Tina slept the tranquil sleep of a child, her mouth partly open and her breathing soft and regular. Manfred lay awake smoking yet another Gitane and thinking, scheming, wrestling with the problem of what to do and how to combine his talents and knowledge with AFRA. He had written to them after the first issue of *Confront* reached the bookshops in Berlin so that when Tina had showed him the copies she had brought he had laughed quietly and told her that he had seen them all, had written to Douglas Hoyle and was waiting for a reply. With any luck, that reply would arrive soon because someone called Russell had telephoned him at his flat saying that his letter was most fortuitous and that Mr Hoyle would be in contact very soon. Apparently Hoyle had only been back in his office for three weeks after the injuries he suffered in the attack by the South African agent. Manfred was quite sure that his account was accurate and the piece that *Confront* had published was the truth. It was just like them to try it in that way and Manfred was sure they had such agents all over Europe and the States. There were probably even some of them right here in Nuremberg.

As he lay smoking and pondering the various courses of action that came to mind, he thought again of South Africa and his own time there in the Cape with the wonderful little Malay girl called Wendy. It was all such a bloody shame really because the place was an incredible country with everything going for it, except the sodding government policy and their power hungry attitude to 'other races'. Well, their modus operandi was costing them dearly, that was for sure, because even now the border struggle in South-West Africa would be using up in the region of R1,500,000 a day; almost DM3.5 million.

The way it was looking recently, the UN settlement plan for the territory was again in the balance with South Africa taking their time, as usual, over replying to the Western Five's latest schemes. The relative success of Mugabe's crowd in Zimbabwe must be forcing the South Africans to do something concrete soon because the whites left in Namibia were said to be pressurising Pretoria for a workable plan. Even some sources within South Africa itself, for instance the opposition Progressive Federal Party, saw Sam Nujoma's coming to power as a probability rather than a possibility.

Up north, of course, on the border, the army were still conducting their happy little sightseeing tours for the world's press and anyone else who would like to visit. Manfred had read in *Confront* that the bastards regarded the recent dry period as the 'good culling' season, referring to the kill rate against the SWAPO insurgents of Nujoma. They loved to reel off figures and undoubtedly they were right on top at the moment, especially after the raids into Angola where many of the dead had been mere boys between the ages of fourteen and eighteen.

But now the forces were increasing against the South Africans. There was the People's Liberation Army of Namibia, SWAPO's military wing – PLAN, as it was called – and the new Caprivi African National Union which was a breakaway offshoot of SWAPO. Soon, the whites would have a real war on their hands and even if there were serious losses Nujoma and the rest could make up their numbers from the half million or so Cuanhama Ovambos who lived on the Angolan side of the border. Some of these were related to those who lived on the South-West African side and even though the South African Army produced excellent propaganda to dissuade the locals from joining the SWAPO ranks, the well was literally bottomless and the youngsters increasingly keen.

Although the kill rates were very much in the South African favour, virtually all their own losses were young white soldiers so pro-rata-wise the balance was not necessarily on the white man's side. In *Confront* Manfred had read of a weakening of morale among the young troopies up on that hostile frontier. When there is any uncertainty about the cause, the whole issue becomes much tougher and no doubt, there must be an inevitable sense of withdrawal amongst the smarter South African national servicemen, he thought. The contrast was shown recently in issue two of *Confront* when somehow Hoyle's correspondents had interviewed a group of young South African soldiers who had told of the war and expressed opinions which ranged from 'It's all a sodding waste of time' to 'I suppose, in the end, the kaffirs will be running the place anyway'.

Of course, the contrast for the poor little spoiled white bastards must be terrible, thought Manfred as he lay in the warm bed beside the beautiful coloured girl that he had come to love, even worship in some ways. On the one hand, the young middle-class South African was ensconced in luxury in a booming country where he was protected from birth and spoiled rotten, living a life which few children in the world could hope to equal. As teenagers, such youths were bought motor cars as soon as they could drive, could order their household servants around, could swipe alcohol from their parents' liquor cabinets with reasonable impunity.

Suddenly, at the age of seventeen, it was out of the nest and into the bush where they were expected to be able to withstand the terrible conditions and kill terrorists. Naturally enough, there was a pretty good training session first and most South African teenagers were healthy and very much outdoor orientated, but it was the contrast between the virtually perfect suburban life and the hardship of army life in the operational area which took its toll of the conscripts. There had been cases, which Hoyle had also reported, of the green troopies being put through such hard training that they developed serious exhaustion and heatstroke. Hoyle had published figures and had included doctors' reports, together with propaganda rubbish from the South African army, which directly contradicted the medical evidence.

Confront had even managed photographs of the towns up on the border, places like Katima Mulilo, Oshikati and Rundu where the miniscule white population was totally reliant on the South African presence and where ninety per cent worked for the government, the police or the army. Hoyle's journal had shown graphically, that without the army these hamlets – they were nothing else – would become black overnight which emphasised and illustrated glaringly the illusory 'whiteness' of this mineral-rich territory.

As Manfred's hyperactive brain eventually subsided into sleep, Gerrit, in the room next door, was dreaming a dream which may have resulted from the wine and vodka he had drunk, yet which had its origin in the thoughts and conclusions buried in his memory traces. He was back in Cape Town, walking in Adderley Street, the main shopping mall, and it was a fine summer's day, the sky clear and incredibly blue. Against this azure backdrop, seagulls wheeled and planed as he looked down towards the harbour and vast open foreshore office complex. In the upmarket shopping area of Adderley Street, the people walked slowly, browsing idly past the many shop windows and talking together happily. They were of all races and Gerrit saw young girls, both white and coloured and a few black, who were pretty and who smiled at him making him feel respectable, even content.

Quite suddenly the noise came and with it a realisation that the calm tranquillity of this scene was to be shattered. Against the blue sky, there appeared aircraft coming in from the north over the massive flat-topped mountain that guards the city, Mother Mountain they called it and Gerrit had always loved it. The aircraft droned slowly towards him, ponderous single-engined high-wing monoplanes of the type used by private flying clubs and for artillery spotting. It was soon obvious that one plane was being pursued and harried by the others and he noted that this single aircraft was painted a faded olive green and that the remaining machines were a dull brown colour. The realisation came that these were the attackers and that the green plane was an enemy of the State; in that case the dozen or so brown planes could have been regarded as defenders, Gerrit thought abstractedly.

The shoppers stopped in their tracks and gazed up at this unreal aerial ballet which seemed far removed from reality so that Gerrit, even as he dreamed, thought that he was dreaming, knew that this could not be serious. But even though the aircraft were high above the city, it was easy to see them now that they had drifted south of the great mountain with its tablecloth of white, fluffy cloud. Then it all became very real because despite the distance, the onlookers could all hear the sound of gunfire, heavy automatic weapons Gerrit thought, and the excitement rose in him as he watched.

Against the endless blue backdrop, a tiny tongue of orange flame blossomed from the nose of the olive painted aircraft and it turned towards the city centre, losing height now as the brown machines worried it, still firing the thick-barrelled guns which protruded from their cockpit windows. It was obvious to the onlookers that the enemy machine was doomed but when it slowly rolled onto its back there was an audible gasp from many of them and Gerrit realised that it had suddenly become silent because the State defenders wheeled away and stopped firing and circled, watching the deathplunge of their victim.

The midday serenity was now broken because death was imminent for those in the enemy plane. Everything seemed to be taking ages and Gerrit could imagine the terror inside the tiny cabin as the occupants were flung about, smashing into each other in the confined space. It seemed that he could hear the screaming, almost as if he too were inside the cabin – and yet that was impossible because now he began to run towards the place where the machine must crash.

End over end like a falling leaf the plane spun earthwards deceptively slowly, Gerrit thought as he ran. It trailed a long column of oily smoke which was flecked with orange and red and it was going to hit at the south end of Adderley Street where the great open square of the foreshore seemed to beckon like a ready-made graveyard. Many people were running with him and he glanced from side to side noting that they all seemed to have become blacks or coloureds. The whites had disappeared and the day seemed to have lost some of its beauty with their going.

Like a rabid pack of dogs, the mob ran onwards and then the burning aircraft struck with a loud slow explosion of sound and burst apart like a paper bag, shattering itself over the concrete. Strangely, there was no fire now but as Gerrit drew closer he could see the blood, rivers of it flowing across the light grey paving stones and he knew that nobody could have survived the crash.

Then he saw the bodies. They had been blasted out of the wreckage and lay in attitudes of grotesque abandon, limbs outstretched and clothing ripped. Gerrit saw that there was nothing anybody could do because their wounds were grievous, horrific in fact, and as the other leading onlookers drew back in revulsion he went still closer, fascinated by the injuries, peering down from right above the ravaged corpses. One man had a fearsome skull injury which had removed most of his face on one side so that an eye dangled loosely on the optic nerve, congealing against the warm pavement. A second victim had been gutted and lay amongst his own intestines which were strewn about, glistening wetly in the sunlight. Ghoulishly, Gerrit bent even closer, oblivious of the fact that he was suddenly alone.

Then he became conscious of the sirens and shouting and, looking over his shoulder, he saw the camouflaged personnel carriers spilling riot-police armed with automatic weapons and long black batons. The crowd was running, shouting and wailing and streaming towards him again so he crouched down, shielded amongst the bodies of the four dead men, like a hunter taking refuge in the rocks during a buffalo stampede. The police ran in, wielding their batons and smashing heads, striking men, women and children so that the pavements in the square became littered with more bodies. Then they opened up with shotguns and Gerrit saw a crimson flower bloom on the white blouse of a young black girl who fell screaming and terrified only metres from his position.

Still he crouched over the bodies watching the carnage and then the long street was suddenly empty and the sky darkened as a cold wind blew in from the sea. He looked around him and saw the policemen approaching from all sides to encircle him, saw the sub-machine guns at the ready and the faces anonymous behind the black rubber gas masks, and even in his mounting terror he wondered why they wore these because there had been no gas grenades fired. He stood up now, as they surrounded him, and edged away from the dead terrorists and the wreckage of their aircraft. He knew that they were terrorists and wondered why he hadn't realised it before. Enemies of the State, he thought, realising quite positively that the police thought that he was one of them, part of their movement; although it was quite impossible because realistically speaking nobody could have survived the crash. 'I was just passing in the street,' he said pointlessly and the policeman ignored him but moved aside to let an officer come forward.

The man was young and blond and wore no gas mask. His camouflage uniform collar bore the crossed swords and crowns of a colonel and he was very handsome, even beautiful. Gerrit felt his gaze which was cool and appraising but the eyes were light blue like chips of ice and seemed fanatically bright. Then he lifted his ugly black machine pistol and smiled, speaking through his teeth in a voice soft, yet full of authority. Gerrit heard the words and noted that the diction was perfect and the accent almost Oxford English. 'I'm going to shoot you now, you filthy murdering bastard,' the officer said.

213

Sweat burst out under Gerrit's armpits and beaded his brow. He opened his mouth again to protest but he could see the finger tightening on the trigger and he knew it was hopeless, knew that he had only seconds to live. The other policemen, all masked and their expressions unreadable, looked on in silence as the officer's finger pulled the trigger. Gerrit gasped and perspiration flooded down his body in a stream but still, miraculously, he lived and the young blond colonel spoke almost apologetically. 'Oh, so sorry,' he said pulling back the slide on the breech of his weapon 'I forgot to cock it.' He pointed the gun at Gerrit's face and the black hole at the barrel end seemed to grow in size as the clean white finger tightened once again on the trigger.

He awoke sweating and gasping for breath under the unaccustomed bulk of the feather duvet and turned frantically over onto his back, totally disorientated, wondering in desperation where he was. Like a marvellous breath of cool air, realisation struck him and he swallowed nervously, smiling into the dark knowing he was alive, that it was all just a dream, a terrible nightmare. His mouth was dry and foul from the drinking and yet he lay, heart pounding and waited, listening, relishing his life, his aliveness, the way that he had cheated that counterfeit death.

The old hotel was silent and he knew it must be very late, probably three or four o'clock in the morning when everybody slept the sleep of the dead and the human body was, in life, at its closest point to death. Gerrit got up and groped his way groggily through to the bathroom where he drank two glasses of water. His mind was still full of the dream and somehow it held a message for him; symbolically there was something there that he knew he should take note of.

As he analysed the events that had taken place in his home town, in the dream, he saw a contradiction between supposed safety, a sort of false security, and the authorities that he was likely to come up against. They were represented by the blond white officer who was the oppressor, dealing out totalitarian authority and even death to all who opposed his regime. The destruction of the single enemy aircraft, overwhelmed hopelessly by the government forces, represented their own puny force in comparison to those of the white State; yet even in the tremulous reaction from the aftermath of the nightmare, he felt no real terror at what the future might hold. He felt that he knew the risks he would be taking and saw the dream as merely a warning directed by his psyche in order to emphasise the magnitude of the task and the might of the enemy they were to pit their effort against.

Perhaps the fact that the battle had begun in the air and come down to earth, so to speak, represented the pointlessness of wild dreams and the reliance on untried local assistance. There were many questions that the dream had posed but the main ones seemed clear to him and now he was eventually able to relax and return to the damp bed, shaking out the rumpled duvet and turning it over onto the cooler side. He fell quickly into a dreamless sleep and dropped into the depths of total unconsciousness so that when Tina called him up at eight in the morning, he felt rested and ready for the day.

When he pulled back the drapes and looked out on the old town in its early summer trappings, he almost shouted with joy and well-being. The night was gone and though the dark thoughts were still there in his mind, he thrust them aside and went out to meet the brightness and light knowing that he was to see new things, experience fresh sensations. His heart was light with confidence as he hurried down to breakfast.

Gerrit did not mention the dream to either Tina or Manfred. Both of them seemed quiet and a little hungover and Gerrit had more than a sneaking suspicion that they had slept little during the night. In this regard he was absolutely correct because Tina had woken Manfred at around the time that he, Gerrit, had finally fallen asleep.

It was the first time that they had slept together all night

215

through, and Tina was not about to waste the opportunity. She woke Manfred by trailing her tongue down his stomach until she reached the soft springy hairs in his groin and then she took him in her mouth and gently caressed him with her tongue. This time, it took a while before her lover responded but eventually he murmured small gasps of pleasure and rolled over. They had slept little after that and she felt cat-like and sated this morning.

Breakfast proved to be a welcome meal for all of them and after fruit juice, cold meats and filter coffee a miraculous regeneration had taken place. Gerrit felt ready for anything, but he had started off somewhat better than the other two.

'Why is it,' he said lightly, 'that food like this always tastes better in the country of origin?'

Tina smiled and nodded. 'You're right little brother. Willi used to buy this sort of thing from the German delicatessen in Seapoint, back home, but it never tasted like it does here, even though some of it was imported from Germany. Willi always loved his *bundnerfleisch* and *kalbsleberwurst* and that black bread like slabs of concrete.'

Gerrit noted that Manfred scowled at the mention of Willi Heim's name but Tina ignored the expression if she had seen it at all. She chattered on happily. 'Today we'll go down to Salzburg in the car. It's only an hour or so's drive and you'll just love it Gerrit, and then tomorrow we'll go back up to Dusseldorf after lunch. Willi is dying to see you, you know.' Abruptly she glanced at the morose Manfred and laughed, jumping up suddenly and patting him on the head like a child. She glanced at her watch. 'If you two will excuse me for a moment,' she said guilelessly, 'I must go upstairs and phone my husband. You just have a nice chat whilst I'm gone, won't be a minute.'

As the lithe coloured girl strode through the dining room, there were more than one pair of eyes following her and Manfred noted the observations and recalled the night and what they had done together on the old feather

216

mattress. Gerrit saw his expression and looked hard at him and Manfred smiled back a little guiltily.

'Quite a woman your sister,' he said with feeling. 'Quite a woman.'

CHAPTER 15

Hendrik Vosloo was still a major in the South African police but Johann Mostert's star was rising and he had recently become a colonel. The promotion had only come through three weeks ago and he was still getting used to being saluted by majors and captains who had never seemed to bother before. Of course, old Hendrik was a mate and with him rank didn't seem to matter except if there happened to be any top brass around. Since the Hout Bay riots the two men had become firm friends, although they were totally different types, Vosloo being older and more staid in his approach to life and duty while Mostert was trim, athletic and ambitious.

Hendrik will probably retire a major, thought Mostert as the two men sat together in the spring sunshine. They were both off duty and located in the north stand at Newlands rugby ground watching Northern Transvaal play Western Province in the Currie Cup semi-final and so far the game had been good hard-running rugby. At half time the two men had consumed two hot dogs each, washed down with Coca Colas which Vosloo had laced, quite illegally, with brandy carried in a hip flask. Now the young, blond, Northern's captain tried for a drop goal at extreme range and succeeded, drawing universal applause from both groups of supporters. It was a wonderful shot, Mostert had to admit.

The afternoon was warm with the onset of summer evident in the balmy air, and it had been a truly glorious

Cape day, like those Mostert remembered from his childhood. Then they had played, he and his friends often with coloured kids, all of them barefoot and ragged like a bunch of urchins, and in the evening when it was time for bed the old coloured maid-cum-nannie had scrubbed them pink in the zinc bathtub. They'd slept the sleep of all healthy children and gone out like lights until the morning when the whole wonderful experience of each new day had started again.

After the game, he and Hendrik would go to the Forresters Arms, down the road in Newlands, and have a couple more in the vast bar and maybe a game of darts, although that was doubtful because the place would be packed. Mostert mused over his life and that of his family, as he sat there in the early evening in the closing moments of the game. It was as good as won by Province, despite the efforts of young De Klerk, the Northern's skipper, and his pack known as the 'Blue Bulls'.

Mostert was overcome with the beauty of the Cape evening and became detached from the action beneath him on the bright emerald turf. It was still a wonderful country in which to bring up kids, he thought, even though so much had changed and was still changing, in fact, would have to change. Even old PW the prime minister said that. God, how he loved the Cape and this country, *Suid Afrika,* his country and his whole world. He'd never been out of it except to go to the border and what had been Rhodesia and now that country was no place for white men. It was all screwed up, they'd even pulled old Rhodes' statue down and the munts had spat on it. And Jameson Avenue had been renamed Samora Machel Boulevard or some such crap.

As far as Mostert was concerned, this was still the finest country in the world and it was all his, because he was an Afrikaaner part of the white tribe of Africa and there was no place else for him and his kind to go. Nobody else spoke his language, lived in his style and would respect his beliefs. Such patriotic feelings were not common to

219

Mostert but he experienced a real throat-tightening sensation which welled up in him, almost like a joyous shout bursting to get out. Yet he realised that it was etched with desperation, was nervously borne like a kiss to an old sweetheart on her wedding day.

Mentally, he shook himself, suppressing the feelings which swept him and glanced at old Hendrik who sat hunched over, eyes darting after the ball and the tiny figures playing out their ritual drama on the green stage below. How we love our rugby in this country, thought Mostert, smiling to himself. It was almost a South African sickness, a game followed fanatically by English and Afrikaaners alike. Now, with the country ostracised by the rest of the world because of bloody politics, there was little or no chance to play international teams, and so these inter-provincial games had become all-important to the frenzied supporters.

Of course, it was different with the bloody boxing and recently, there had been all manner of contenders coming over for the world title bouts which seemed to be stretching out ad infinitum. South Africa's White Hope, the young man from Boksburg up in the Transvaal, had made nearly a million and even the black Americans were quite happy to come over and fight a few rounds for two million dollars or so. It was all money, boxing, sport didn't come into it any more because the purses were so big and this meant that politics was kept out of it too. Mostert reckoned that the matchmakers and promoters had the politicians, or at least the political agitators, in their pockets. Something like 'Please accept this one hundred thousand rand towards your average black consciousness movement and let us have our fight without any demonstrations.' Nothing talked like money.

An almighty roar brought Mostert from his dreamy state and he focused on the game again, only to see that the final whistle had blown and Province had won by seventeen points to twelve. The happiness he should have felt at his home team's win did not reach him and he stared moodily at the hundreds of supporters flooding onto the pitch to surround their idols. It was all just too sweet and idyllic, too wonderful to be true this way of life, he thought. Just like the economy which, as a result of gold stabilising at around $600 American per ounce, had taken off like a kaffir with Concord up his arse. The Boom was booming and currently South Africa's economy was the most buoyant in the world so that everyone had more and spent more. But it didn't stop there because it brushed off on the kaffirs as well and, as a result, there had been more strikes, more unrest, more racial tension because they too wanted their share of the cake. The same share as the white man whom they outnumbered by almost five to one if one counted the coloureds too.

I'm a prophet of doom, thought Mostert as once again he returned to reality with Hendrik nudging him in the ribs.

'Balls to it all, Johann,' he said. 'You must be getting old son. I know you're a bloody colonel now but that doesn't mean that you can drop off at the bloody rugby man. Jesus, you are bloody unbelievable.'

Vosloo continued along this theme as he drove his Chevrolet 2800 along the packed roads to the Forresters Arms. It took more than twenty minutes to cover four kilometres and would have been far quicker to walk, Mostert thought. When they arrived, the bar was four deep with rugby supporters who were sinking pints of Lion and Castle as if they were in the Namib desert rather than suburban Cape Town. Eventually, Mostert was able to order double Oude Meester brandies and Coca Cola and the two policemen stood, pressed together in the huge smoke-filled room, sipping the sweetened spirits and talking about the game together with the other hundred or so occupants of the bar.

Over an hour and a half later, they left the old hostelry and Mostert generously offered to drive the Chevrolet as Vosloo had stumbled over a beer can in the car park and seemed a little the worse for wear. 'I can manage very well, dear Colonel,' was all that Hendrik said and so

Mostert settled warily into the passenger seat watching the road ahead, although there was no real need to because Hendrik could drink a bottle of brandy and still drive well enough.

They headed west towards Bellville where Vosloo lived and passed close to Mostert's home in Rondebosch which would be empty tonight. Lorraine had taken Janine over to her mother in Somerset West and the child loved the smallholding where she could play with the ducks and chickens and ride the old mare that had been there as a foal when Mostert had first begun to court Lorraine fourteen years ago. Tomorrow he would go out for one of those old Cape kitchen Sunday lunches that his mother-in-law cooked. Quite unbelievable her cooking was and the thought made him hungry for the *braaivleis* that would be waiting at Hendriks. *Wors* and steak it would be and very nice too when you were as hungry as he was.

Koos de Kock had been to visit a friend in Grabouw which was over fifty kilometres from the tiny flat near Bellville that he had moved into when Gerrit sold the house. In the eighteen months since they had seen each other Koos had filled out a bit and was pushing weights and doing a bit of karate. His first love however, was the Kowasaki 750E he had recently traded his old bike for. Now he lay low over the tank of the metallic green machine as he sped along the N2 in the righthand westbound lane thinking of Pauline, the little Malay girl he was taking out tonight to the movies. If he didn't move it, he'd be late and, knowing her, she might just go off with some other bastard.

The Kowasaki was travelling at some 60kph over the legal limit of 90kph and the stiff sea breeze buffeted the big machine as the highly tuned engine hummed sweetly at only about two-thirds throttle. Under his new Bell helmet, Koos peered through the tinted visor, hearing very little because of the wind noise. He had yet to buy a fibre-glass faring, like the big BMWs and Hondas had, but the cost was around R500, even with all the discounts he could get with being in the trade. It would just have to wait a few weeks.

Some five kilometres from the Bellville exit ramp, he was flashing along, passing all the silly old arseholes in their Datsuns and Toyotas, when he saw the police trap and the constable flagging him down with the torch. In the dusk, he almost hit the bugger and had had no chance of spotting the rubberised trip wires which had recorded his speed at 158kph. He knew that he was in trouble and visualised a fine of up to R400 which would account for the faring he'd planned to buy next month. He couldn't afford such a loss.

Although his brain told him he was taking stupid risks, he opened up the throttle as he saw the policeman jump back onto the verge in his mirror. He seemed to be speaking into something in his hand and Koos knew that they would have a catcher bike positioned somewhere along the freeway but now he was up to 180kph and passing traffic like it was standing still. At this speed he'd be at the exit in a couple of minutes and with any luck he'd lose the pigs and be safe home in Bellville by eight o'clock. There was no alternative now, anyway, he had to go for it.

Vosloo approached the Bellville turn-off travelling east at the regulation 90kph. It was dark now, pitch bloody black in fact, and a light rain was spotting the windscreen causing him to switch on the wipers and swear immediately at the streaky marks they made. 'Just look at the weekend wankers,' he muttered to himself and Mostert smiled. The freeway was busy with slow-moving Saturday-night traffic coming home from the city and the beach and he thought happily of the short distance they had to travel now and hoped that the rain wouldn't continue and ruin the plans for Hendrik's *braai*.

He saw the single light coming at them at unbelievable speed from nowhere but Hendrik had seen it too and was braking as much as he dared in the greasy conditions. Still

Mostert shouted the warning and then the screen was filled with light and he threw up his arms thinking that this was a very stupid way to die but that he had no control over it anyway. Miraculously the light seemed to pass low over them with a roar like an aircraft and then there was a ghastly crash from just behind and a screaming started, shrill and terrible. Vosloo managed to pull over through the other stunned motorists and reach the nearside verge, switching on his emergency flashers as Mostert leapt out and ran back along the grass.

Koos had seen the single light coming up far behind him and recognised it as a police pursuit, probably one of those old cooking Hondas or Suzukis they used but it seemed to be going alright. The light wasn't gaining but already he had to make the decision as to whether to take the Bellville turn-off and at a speed of over 190kph he was past it before he managed to decide. In any case, the cop would probably have caught him in the suburban traffic so it was better to stay on the highway and make a race of it, carry on towards the city and try and outrun the pig behind him.

Those police bikes could never catch him with the lead he had, he was sure of that, and he glanced down at the speedometer as he opened the throttle fractionally wider. The wind was fantastic and he revelled in the feeling of speed, the needle read just under 200kph and he glanced up again quickly, realising suddenly that he was going very fast in heavy traffic conditions.

As he looked up, after only that fraction of a second, the road was suddenly blocked with a huge slow-moving shape and he screamed in silence under the helmet, knowing instinctively that he was fatally committed, yelling in desperation for the life that he knew he was going to lose. Hopelessly he tried to get by on the outside of the huge empty trailer which had pulled out without warning to pass a car transporter in the middle lane. The Kowasaki's front wheel struck the coping of the centre verge and the machine veered right and took off, flashing up the grass and through the thin anti-glare fence. Koos felt metal tear through his jeans and the sudden smarting as his right leg was laid open from knee to thigh, and then he was flying and there were headlights underneath him and others just behind them. The revs hit 9,000 and the motorcycle screamed under him and he saw the back of the illuminated ninety kilometre an hour sign on the opposite side of the freeway. Then slowly, he was coming down and it all seemed to take so long, was so slow and drawn out until the last second and the Kowasaki struck the bridge buttress and something hit him on the head and he stopped thinking.

The motorcycle flew through the air at around 180kph and reached a height of some six feet, skimming over Vosloo's Chevrolet and a Ford Cortina in the inside lane, before slamming into the bridge carrying the Muizenberg road over the freeway. The machine struck the reinforced concrete pillar at about a metre above ground level and shattered itself instantly, hurling Koos head-first into the vertical wall. His Bell helmet burst open like a peanut shell and his head and shoulders drove against the buttress, telescoping down into his trunk and shortening his body by ten centimetres. Such was the force and forward velocity, that Koos hung there for a second before sliding slowly down the pillar leaving a dark stain on the dirty grey concrete.

It was the woman passenger in the Volkswagen Passat who got the first view of the mangled body because her husband had stopped the car right alongside the remains and leaned across to shine a torch on the awful mess. Koos was barely recognisable as human and he had slumped back into the gutter, trunk upwards. Virtually every bone in his body had been shattered by the impact and the head had gone totally, becoming a white spattered bloody mess, truncated into the broken shoulders and upper chest. Both arms were broken and thrust limply out from the corpse and one of the handlebars of the Kowasaki had turned on impact and was embedded in the lower stomach, as were various other pieces of metal from the frame.

The woman, who was to remember the sight for the rest of her life, began to scream so hysterically that her husband had to slap her hard across the head. But first he turned off the torch. Mostert reached the mess that had been the motorcyclist and, by now, there were other cars stopping and he grabbed a torch from an approaching onlooker. 'I'm a police officer,' he said brusquely and bent beside the corpse trying to lay it onto its back with great, though unnecessary gentleness.

Feeling over the blood-soaked leather jacket he found the inside pocket and the stained wallet containing ten rands, driving licence and identity document. Vosloo pounded up alongside and together they examined the sticky papers; in the background a man was retching drily and others came to peer ghoulishly at the remains. There was a folded piece of dirty card sellotaped to the back cover of the licence which said that in the event of an accident, communication should be made with either one of two relatives: Mr Gerrit de Kock of 1157, Protea Apartments, Wilhelmina Street, Windhoek, SWA, or Mrs Tina Heim, c/o Heim Import Export, Box 47893, Dusseldorf 71449, West Germany. The licence was issued in the name of Koos de Kock of 14 Parow Gardens, 91a Bok St., Bellville Cape.

Vosloo sucked in his breath as he read the names and then let it out, whistling softly. 'I've got a docket on this lot, this Koos was the stupid one but Gerrit and Tina are a very bright pair, especially Gerrit. So now she's living in Germany, must have married that Willi Heim she was staying with in Seapoint. And I see that Gerrit is in South West now, in Windhoek, eh. Last I heard he was with Metricor in Parow, at least he was at the time that his sister was messing about with the Kraut. *Ag,* I'd better check with Metricor Parow on Monday morning.'

The Saturday in Salzburg had been a magic day and one which each of them would remember. They had visited the

castle with its amazing military museum of the old
Hapsburg Empire and lunched at the *Weiskranz* on *eisbein*
with sauerkraut followed by *Salzburger Knockle* for
dessert. With it they'd had two bottles of a wonderful
Gewürztträminer and the meal had been like the day,
amazing and wonderful and quite unforgettable.

The first intensity of their meeting had worn off and
they had casually bounced theories and ideas off each
other but had come up with no fixed plan as to how to act
against the country they hated so much. They sat with
second cups of coffee and lapsed into silence and then
Manfred spoke, breaking the peaceful after-lunch reverie.

'I have an idea I may be going to London next week,' he
said conspiratorially. 'Is there any chance of you making it
Tina?'

The girl shook her head firmly. 'No my sweet,' she said
quite openly and Gerrit did not react at all. 'I'll be in
Frankfurt all week with Willi, so it's quite out of the
question. But Gerrit, what about taking Gerrit along?'
The idea took shape in her mind and she went on
enthusiastically, 'Oh Manfred, you must take him, he's
never seen London and it would be easy to change his
ticket.' Gerrit looked from one to the other and Manfred
smiled.

'I was planning to ask him to come anyway Tina, I think
I may be going to see the AFRA people and there should
be a letter or telegram waiting when I get back to Berlin.'

On Sunday they dropped Manfred at Frankfurt am
Main, veering off the autobahn for a few minutes, and
Gerrit waited in the car while Tina ran into the departure
hall with him. When she came out she was dry-eyed and
happy and Gerrit marvelled at her adaptability and lack of
emotion. Manfred caught a British Airways shuttle to
Berlin at 17.45 and the Trident was only about one third
full so that he was able to sleep on two seats for most of
the fifty-five minute flight. By seven o'clock he was out of
Templehof and driving his old Volkswagen Beetle through
the light traffic to his flat in Charlottenburg. Twenty

227

minutes later he opened the front door and saw the letter on the mat and almost with a sense of déja vu, he opened it, noting that it was registered and marked 'Priority Mail'. It had been posted in London on Thursday.

The first thing he saw was Douglas Hoyle's name at the base of the page and the dark red AFRA logo at the top. The paper was starchy and elegant and the signature beautifully scripted. Manfred read on:

Dear Mr Meyer,

I was most pleased to receive your letter and hope that my colleague who called you communicated this fact. This letter serves as an official invitation to visit our London offices at your earliest convenience so that we may discuss matters of mutual interest.

Enclosed, you will find signed travellers cheques to cover the cost of your return flight and incidental expenses and we have made arrangements from next Tuesday (18th) at the Hotel Buckingham in West Cromwell Road. I hope that you will be comfortable there and that you can make this date. My colleague will telephone you again to confirm your arrival.

I look forward very much to meeting you.

Yours faithfully,
Douglas Hoyle,
Chairman, Azanian Freedom Revolutionary Army.

Manfred smiled at the page and replaced the letter in the envelope. Gerrit was to call him as arranged on Monday morning and, all being well, he could fly over on the Wednesday direct from Dusseldorf so that Manfred could meet him at Heathrow. Gerrit de Kock would be an added bonus for Douglas Hoyle, living as he did in Windhoek in a sort of no-man's land close to the area of conflict and the enemy. At this stage, Manfred did not know whether any plans had been worked out by the AFRA executive but he had an idea that some sort of action was being contemplated.

Hoyle's publisher's message in the last issue of *Confront*

had hinted at some type of action, some effort against the South Africans which in his words would 'Make the world sit up and take notice.' He had ended with, 'It is time for the talk to end and the action to begin. No longer can free men stand by and condone the oppression of the majority in Azania by a white fascist minority of bigoted racialists. It is time for AFRA to act, the time has come to move.'

What moves Hoyle had planned were not specified but notwithstanding this, the Department of National Security in Pretoria had taken note. They had all the issues of *Confront* and received their copies before they were even posted to subscribers like Manfred Meyer in Berlin. The reason for this was that a young Rhodesian who had lost a leg in the war against Robert Mugabe's ZANLA forces, all to no avail, worked in the binding department at the printers in Wimbledon who produced Hoyle's journal. The Rhodesian's brother was a sergeant in the Special Reconnaisance Group, or Recces as they were called, and spent most of his time in Eastern Caprivi and Ovamboland. The Recces were the South African equivalent of the Rhodesian Army's now disbanded Selous Scouts. Pretoria allocated the one-legged sympathiser £50 every month. Beer money the deputy director called it.

Now, the embassy in London was close to penetrating AFRA itself and the reluctant agent was a stylish young Jewish gynaecologist who had been born in Johannesburg. The doctor had succeeded professionally in London and was very well in with the modelling and TV fraternity; he was getting closer by the week and seemed to have Hoyle in the palm of his hand just recently. Of course, he wouldn't have done it out of pure patriotism because he didn't care about anything except money and his warped little sexual adventures. The deputy director considered the doctor to be little more than a social-climbing weak-willed pervert.

It was through his financial fun and games that David

Mendelsohn had first come to Pretoria's notice. Before leaving South Africa, after graduating from Medical School in Johannesburg, he had contravened currency exchange regulations by buying a platinum share on the Johannesburg Stock Exchange and selling it illegally on the London market. Encouraged by the success of this relatively simple operation, which the Reserve Bank computer in Pretoria had revealed within hours of the sale, he returned to South Africa for a holiday after an absence of six years. It had taken Mendelsohn five years to become a moderate success in London's fashionable world of private medicine but he had made it and had a Porsche, a flat in Belgravia and a bank account in Sloane Street which he looked after very carefully.

Mendelsohn bought sixty-five Krugerrands from a legitimate dealer in Johannesburg with money provided by his father. The older Mendelsohn, who was a successful stockbroker, was desperate to get money out of South Africa and build a capital base elsewhere as a hedge against eventual political upheaval and the possibility of anarchy which could cause him to lose all his assets.

The computer in the Department of the Interior had spat out David Mendelsohn's name, recording him as a wanted person who had re-entered the country, and agents of the Fraud Squad and the Security Police had put a careful watch on him. The operatives had recorded Mendelsohn's purchase of the Krugerrands and reported back to Pretoria to ask for further instructions. It had been fairly obvious to the Security Police that Mendelsohn planned to do something with the gold and it was thought highly probable that he would take the coins out of the country.

At a market price of R385 each at that time, the sixty ounces of gold cost old man Mendelsohn just over R23,000 and he had liquidated all his disposable assets and ready cash in order to buy them. The coins weighed around four kilogrammes in total and Mendelsohn placed them in the bottom of a used-looking aluminium professional camera case, slotting them in underneath the layers of foam liner. Having determined Mendelsohn's return reservation date with British Airways, Pretoria had checked back with the London embassy in Trafalgar Square to establish the young doctor's social connections and lifestyle and how best they could make use of him. It was found that, like many South Africans who find financial success in the US and Europe, Mendelsohn had become a liberal who took out black women with whom he often slept. It was further established that he had engaged in several homosexual relationships with men of mixed race and had lived with a young Nigerian for some months.

The head of the then Bureau of State Security, BOSS, General Hendrik van den Bergh, personally instructed the Security Police to ignore the fact that Mendelsohn obviously planned to smuggle the gold out of the country. So they let him take the coins when he left, and agents in London noted that a safe deposit box in the name of H.O. Mendelsohn was rented at the Sloane Square branch of Barclays and that the necessary withdrawal forms and signatures had been lodged with the deposit. The twenty-two-year-old girl who had made these discoveries was employed at Barclays head office in the city but she came from Pretoria and her name was Johanna Theron, the sister of Jenni.

After the South African Department of Information scandal which brought down the Minister of the Interior, the Minister of Police and eventually the Prime Minister himself, Van den Bergh disappeared from office and BOSS was purged and renamed the Department of National Security, DONS. Meanwhile, Mendelsohn had settled back into London life and his practice gradually became more lucrative so that in 1978 he was able to buy premises in London's fashionable Harley Street. His pre-tax income that year was just over £100,000.

In the shake-up and revamps that followed the demise of Van den Bergh, the Mendelsohn dossier was filed away with many others until the dust settled and clandestine operations could be resumed as normal. The dossier was regarded as an ongoing case and it was Jenni Theron's superior who had dug it up and contemplated using the evidence against Mendelsohn in the light of the recent strengthening of Hoyle's AFRA organisation.

Carefully, and at times painstakingly, the Security Police went back over the intervening years and put together indisputable evidence against Mendelsohn and his father, who had acted for him on the platinum share purchase. Reports were drawn up and further details unearthed and finally an entire breakdown was summarised, copied, bound and delivered to Mendelsohn at his rooms in Harley Street by a messenger from Trafalgar Square. With the incriminating document, was an unsigned and untitled letter stating that Mr Harold Oswald Mendelsohn of 15 Westcliffe Terrace, Johannesburg was under Security Police observation pending charges for contravention of South African exchange control regulations and complicity in gold smuggling. The attached evidence would be used against him, the letter said, and added that the sentence would be a minimum of ten years, possibly fifteen.

Furthermore, the letter continued remorselessly, is Harold Mendelsohn's licence on the Johannesburg Stock Exchange would be withdrawn and he and his wife's passports seized and held by the police. The last statement was to the effect that quite probably the judge might order that Mr Mendelsohn's assets be disposed of in order to pay for the gold 'stolen unlawfully from the Republic of South Africa'. The value of the said gold was almost US$50,000 at current market prices.

The letter bore a footnote which suggested that Mendelsohn should telephone a Mr Van Pittius at a London number to discuss the matter. It further reminded him that should he go to the British press with these documents, the case against his father would proceed immediately.

Mendelsohn's almost too perfect world had been effectively shattered by these terrifying revelations. He had called the number immediately, shaking with reaction, sure it could only be a bad dream, yet knowing that he was awake and that it was all true. Van Pittius had told him smugly that there were certain 'services to his country' which could preclude action against either himself or his father. He urged Mendelsohn to do nothing except await further instructions which would be delivered to Harley Street by messenger.

And so it had started. Mendelsohn had been forced to agree to the South African terms and had begun his social espionage on behalf of a regime he had come to despise. He continued to go to the parties and was seen at trendy wine bars, pubs and clubs in south-west London, as before, maintaining the same affluent lifestyle. Pretoria paid him for his services and, although at first he refused the money he eyed the cheques for £250 which arrived at the end of each month at his home address. For six months he resisted and told Van Pittius that he didn't want his 'dirty money' but the Afrikaaner merely laughed. Eventually, Mendelsohn capitulated and banked the cheques and in doing so felt an almost masochistic pleasure at the awful commitment he had made.

When the first encashment was recorded and telexed to Pretoria, the deputy director smiled and called his superior. 'He's really on the hook now, sir. I think it's time to use him on the AFRA thing,' he said gloatingly, and that night finished a half bottle of Ballantines in lonely celebration.

Van Pittius telephoned on one of those rare and beautiful late spring days in London when people smile at each other for no apparent reason and parts of the city suddenly start to look like Paris. Mendelsohn had not heard from his contact for three months and had merely sent in his weekly reports to the address in Paddington. The call ruined his first coffee of the day and he cursed the hysterectomy he had scheduled for eleven o'clock at the London Clinic. The patient was the matronly wife of the

Nigerian ambassador and the thought of delving around inside her flaccid and diseased uterus caused him to swear horribly. He so surprised his svelte receptionist that she dropped her Royal Doulton coffee cup into its delicate saucer, breaking off the handle.

'Good morning Dr Mendelsohn,' Van Pittius had begun in his atrocious Afrikaans-accented English. Mendelsohn had cringed, hating and fearing the voice. An urgent set of instructions and a cheque would be delivered before lunchtime, Van Pittius had said, and added that Mendelsohn should study them carefully. The contents were vitally important and he must call back and confirm receipt.

The letter was very explicit. The South African government were anxious to gain information on the operation and motives of the Azanian Freedom Revolutionary Army and had particular interest in finance, armaments (should there be any) and tactical planning against South Africa. Personal dossiers on the executive committee were also required. To initiate this sensitive task, Pretoria had arranged a deposit of £15,000 to be credited telegraphically to Mendelsohn's account at Coutts in Sloane Street. £10,000 of this amount was to be forwarded by Mendelsohn to AFRA on one of his own cheques as a legitimate donation to the cause. It was thought that the size of the donation would bring Mendelsohn to the notice of Hoyle who would most certainly write a letter of thanks and perhaps invite the donor around to his offices to be thanked in person.

The remaining £5,000 was Mendelsohn's and had been paid to ensure his understanding of the vital nature of this mission. 'Money is no object,' Pretoria added, and should more be required it would be forwarded at once; Mendelsohn merely had to advise his contact in London. Time was also not that important although progress must be made soon as 'the security of the State may depend on it'. It never failed to amaze Mendelsohn how his paymasters spouted this nationalistic rhetoric. It was almost as if he were presumed to be a dyed-in-the-wool patriot instead of a puppet totally under their control, and hating every minute of it.

Mendelsohn had written a brief note for the personal attention of Douglas Hoyle, and enclosed the cheque. A letter had arrived from Hoyle two weeks later. Would he care to call at the offices in South Kensington? AFRA was very grateful for his generous donation; the writer would like to thank him in person; etc., etc. Hoyle had mentioned in his letter that he understood Mendelsohn was South African by birth, as was he of course. Surely they had much in common, perhaps matters of mutual interest with regard to the future of Azania.

Mendelsohn had paid his visit to Hoyle and as it had been a noon appointment, had been invited to lunch, which he had half expected. He had found Hoyle intense and boyish and very likeable and his host had been equally impressed with the famous young doctor who seemed to have half of London society's female population in the palm of his hand, so to speak. They had lunched with casual elegance at Bill Bentley's in Beauchamp Place and found that they had both studied at the University of the Witwatersrand in Johannesburg and, although Mendelsohn was three years older than Hoyle, there were many mutual recollections of their student years.

Mendelsohn had sympathised professionally with Hoyle's mutilations and had covertly been shown the stump of the left arm to which a mechanical hand was shortly to be fitted. An articulated metal foot had already been attached to the stump of the left leg and Hoyle was able to get about quite easily with one lightweight alloy crutch. It was obvious to Mendelsohn that he had been a very fit man before the attack and that now what he lacked in mobility he made up for with a burning determination for his cause. Hoyle had talked of the inefficiency of the Metropolitan Police in failing to locate his attacker and had been bitter about their apparent doubt that such a woman 'South African assassin' actually existed.

After this first meeting, when Hoyle had done most of the talking, Mendelsohn had met Jane Hoyle and had been invited to dinner twice at the Hoyles' apartment. Just next week he was to go to a gala AFRA function at the Royal Garden Hotel in Kensington; it was to be a fund-raising effort, and, as one of the organisations largest private donors, Mendelsohn was to have a table close to the executive committee's. He was getting closer all the time and had now been accepted by Douglas Hoyle and his followers.

The deputy director of the Department of National Security in Pretoria was more than satisfied with his agent's progress. As he and Jenni Theron shared a lunchtime bottle of Fleur du Cap Riesling in the Grill Room of the city's Burgerspark Hotel, they discussed Mendelsohn and AFRA at length. The recent article in *Confront,* which had featured the interviews with the South African troopers on the border, had antagonised the deputy director greatly.

'There'll be no more of that crap,' he said angrily. 'Both the army and the police have issued directives that any soldier or constable speaking to a journalist without his superior officer's permission, will be court-martialled and or charged under the Official Secrets Act with subversive activity against the State.'

Jenni Theron nodded idly, only half listening. She glanced outside into the sunshine and watched the people strolling by on the wide boulevard. Although it was only two weeks after mid-winter in Pretoria, the midday temperature was mild and the air crisp and clean. She sipped her chilled Riesling and looked out at the lines of large spikey trees that lined each side of the street. At this time of the year they were dead and uninteresting but within three months they would be transformed into one of the most beautiful trees in the world.

Aloud she said, 'Just a few months and the jacarandas will be in bloom.'

The deputy director nodded, imagining the annual wonder of the purplish blue blooms that filled the pavements with a carpet of delicate mauve petals after the late afternoon rains. He snapped his fingers decisively, 'That's what we'll call it – Mendelsohn's infiltration of AFRA, I mean – Jacaranda, Operation Jacaranda.'

From that time on Mendelsohn himself became known as Jacaranda and, as the autumn evenings began to shorten markedly in Europe and lengthen marginally towards summer in the Transvaal, his controller watched his progress towards full acceptance by AFRA. Jacaranda's last report had mentioned that he thought that a seat on the executive was a possibility. The deputy director was very excited by this and could not remember being as enthusiastic about an operation since last year when they'd infiltrated the National Union of Students with that young security policeman posing as an economics student at Wits University. Some of those little pinko bastards were still sitting in Pretoria Central on ninety day renewable sentences. They hadn't seen a trial of course, that would be fatal as far as the press was concerned and he supposed that they'd have to be let out sooner or later. If he had his way they'd sit until they rotted.

Jacaranda never considered feeding his masters false information. They would find out soon enough if he did and he had no doubt of what their reaction would be. He was quite sure that they could have him killed or maimed as easily as they had dear Douglas mutilated. Poor Douglas was now irrevocably injured for life and Mendelsohn was sure that psychologically he would never be the same. In his personal life he was in many ways a very naive man and somewhat effete, even effeminate. Mendelsohn was quite sure he could be pushed over the line without much trouble and was a perfect example of a closet queen. The closest they'd got had been an early evening session in his apartment with a very athletic Jamaican girl who was crazy about having two men at once. Mendelsohn had seen Douglas eyeing him once or twice and of course their bodies had touched when they were giving it to the girl. Hoyle had looked as if he'd like to make the move but couldn't bring himself to do it. For his part, Mendelsohn had been oddly excited by Hoyle's slim body with its missing limbs and the girl had gone crazy about it. He thought there were definite possibilities in that direction and he longed to explore them, to know Douglas Hoyle under normal circumstances. But of course, that was impossible because the present circumstances were far from normal.

CHAPTER 16

The slim Lufthansa Boeing 727 throttled back as it banked gently to follow the course of the Thames which wound through the green fields below like a great grey snake. The cloud was low and quite thick but Gerrit could clearly see the great river and the series of wonderful bridges; so much a part of this city and this country that he had longed to visit since childhood. The rain hammered against the perspex porthole and streaked back into the slipstream whilst the cloud whipped past in feathery streamers giving an indication of the speed of the aircraft as it settled into its final nose-up approach at around 160 knots.

The landing was a copybook effort and the engines howled for a few seconds in reverse thrust and then they were taxiing towards the terminal and Gerrit had his first disconcerting view of London Heathrow. Flight LH 052 from Dusseldorf had landed in the late afternoon of a rainy August day and immediately the all pervading greyness formed an overall first impression of mild shock. In contrast to Dusseldorf airport, which had been clean and immaculately organised in typical Aryan fashion, Heathrow was a sprawling, chaotic menage of dirty-looking termini each of which were dotted with various aircraft seemingly from every corner of the globe.

In a fascination born of disbelief, rather than excitement, Gerrit peered out of the porthole at this grimy gateway to Britain, which somehow looked far worse when compared with the pristine interior of the German aircraft. The negative impression escalated when he left the aircraft and began the long hike down the endless passages to passport control and immigration. Carrying only a briefcase and his flight bag, Gerrit was not overburdened but all around him a mass of harassed, pallid-faced humanity hurried along, partially obscured under children, carrycots, folding prams and a variety of packages. Posters screamed at him 'It is an offence to import Rabies into Britain' whilst others proclaimed 'Britain welcomes the overseas visitor'.

When the never-ending grubby corridors miraculously finished abruptly in the bottleneck which was passport control, Gerrit queued for some fifteen minutes in the section labelled 'Foreign Passports'. Already feeling very alien, he eventually made it through to baggage collection and rescued his single suitcase from the whirling carousel which was presided over by a bored looking black man who spoke with an accent that Gerrit could barely understand. It was all terribly different to what he had imagined.

Then, thank God, Manfred was there, waiting patiently at Terminal 2 arrivals and soon he was pushing the dilapidated trolley towards the car park which seemed to be at least another kilometre distant. Manfred had hired a Ford Fiesta from Hertz and after another ten minutes they were out of the mad Heathrow bustle and heading east along the motorway into central London.

In the car, Gerrit continued to stare out at Britain with a feeling of disbelief. The houses were small and grey and begrimed with the smoke of a million chimneys and the gardens were scrubby patches of unkempt grass, just a few metres square. Occasionally, there were glimpses of alleys between rows of identical houses and here and there children clustered in groups or played in the gutters. Some of these children were black, Gerrit noted. Everything was wet and dismal and totally in contrast to the sunshine and orderliness of the Germany he had left only a couple of hours earlier. Even the motor vehicles were somehow mean and tatty looking and when they passed a factory exit he saw a strange three-wheeled vehicle which looked like a fanciful invalid carriage and swarms of men in capes riding small motorcycles. They looked grotesque, unhappy and self-righteous all at the same time.

Manfred laughed at Gerrit's expression and had to comment on this first shocking appraisal of Britain in the 1980s. 'Not really what you expected eh, Gerrit,' he giggled. 'A bit of a change from old Deutschland isn't it. London is actually a terrible place in the daytime, at least in all but a few areas, but at night it's different. It really can be fun, you'll see.'

Gerrit failed to comment and they spent the forty minutes drive in virtual silence and then the Hotel Buckingham appeared on the right hand side of the impossibly busy West Cromwell Road and Manfred turned left off this main freeway into the West End and managed to park in an area labelled 'resident parking only'. They walked the two blocks back to the small seedy hotel and still the rain came down in a continual downpour which was light and yet so drenching that Gerrit's hair was glistening with droplets when they reached the hotel. He found the place very depressing because he had imagined a hotel with the name Buckingham to be an elegant establishment in the great London tradition. The Kalahari Sands left this place in the shade, he thought as he followed Manfred into the small lobby where a disinterested Pakistani booked him in and handed him his room key.

That night they went to a club which Manfred knew. It was within walking distance of the hotel, being located on the corner of Exhibition Road and West Cromwell Road, and they paid £5 each to get in and then went upstairs to be sandwiched into a small room which served as a bar. They were charged £1.50p for small whiskies which were served by black girls in fishnet stockings and mentally Gerrit began to ponder the cost of life in London. Looking around at the obviously affluent junior jetsetter types, he

241

could not understand where they all found the money to live in this style and as he glanced at them they stared back haughtily as if he were an intruder. In most respects he felt very out of place and although there were a few blacks and Asians in the place, he knew somehow that he didn't belong. And yet he felt that he was now here in London and that they should realise that it was wonderful and exciting for him, and greet him in some way. Instead, he felt completely alienated and miles apart from the happenings around him. These people could just as easily have come from another planet.

The next day everything was different. Manfred had already briefed Hoyle on Gerrit's arrival and the AFRA Chairman was keen to meet the Cape coloured whom Manfred had described as 'having an exceptional mind'. They met at the South Kensington offices just before 12.30 and after a ten minute interlude of pleasantries, where both men weighed each other up, were whisked off to lunch in a black Mercedes 350SE which flew a tiny AFRA pennant from its radio aerial. The venue was a French restaurant in Walton Street and lunch proved to be long and memorable with beautifully balanced dishes and excellent old wines. It was one of the finest meals Gerrit had ever eaten and over coffee and Martell Cordon Bleu, Hoyle quietly began his pitch which was a summary of AFRA's aims and achievements to date. Gerrit listened closely because Hoyle's delivery was intense and spellbinding and Manfred sat slightly to one side, smoking a cigar, a small smile on his thin lips.

Occasionally Hoyle broke into Afrikaans to explain a fine point more precisely although it was quite unnecessary because Gerrit's English was absolutely perfect and his vocabulary extensive. The Afrikaans was pure self-indulgence on Hoyle's part and Gerrit recognised this fact and digested it without further thought except that it seemed stupid to have to translate to Manfred when they both spoke very adequate English.

At 3.30, after much bowing and scraping on the part of

the restaurant owner, they returned to the offices and met Anderson and Francis the young barrister. Mary brought more coffee into the small boardroom which adjoined Hoyle's office and Manfred noticed the Hockneys and a few choice Art Nouveau pieces. He recognised money, success and a certain class which understated the recent power of this organisation. AFRA is here to stay, he thought.

The plan had apparently originated in Hoyle's mind and been modified by Anderson, this fact Hoyle admitted and smiled genuinely across the table at his young deputy. They had decided it was safe to bounce the basic idea off Manfred, and now Gerrit de Kock, as an invaluable man on the spot. The operation was to involve several groups and a nucleus of key personnel, Hoyle explained and added that although its purpose was simple, the execution of the various roles would be very complicated.

Manfred Meyer had already indicated that he was interested in becoming involved, said Hoyle, and his role would be vital in that he must contact a sympathetic group in West Germany and liaise with them on AFRA's behalf. If they were, in turn, agreeable, they would be contracted by AFRA to take a major part in the operation. Entering South Africa as ordinary tourists, they would link up with the UMSA group and two key SWAPO operatives. The target area was to be Cape Town and the target date and the site chosen would, together with the victim, strike a vital blow for the future of Azania.

Gerrit sat unbelieving, trying to assimilate this plan which was of such enormity yet was being discussed here like a casual cocktail rendezvous. Undoubtedly, if successful, the operation would have a truly global effect and would shatter the illusion of South Africa as an unbreachable bastion of white power. Furthermore, depending on the reaction of the so-called European population and with luck on AFRA's side, the country might be thrown into anarchy and chaos. Whilst he dwelled on these incredible thoughts, Gerrit pondered on the fact that

AFRA had accepted him and Manfred so swiftly, and had revealed the bones of an amazing plot against South Africa. Now, they were actually asking his advice on the operation and whether he could be of service locally as a contact to assist with co-ordination in the areas of supply and logistics. Gerrit heard himself agreeing to become a part of the whole thing; he watched himself as if from afar, smiling and shaking hands with Hoyle and Anderson. Inside he felt the recurring fear of the dream and the factors his subconscious had revealed as danger areas. But the will to fight was now born in him and it overruled the uncertainties, driving the dark images away and replacing them with the wonderful golden light of freedom.

It was agreed that AFRA would pay the Germans for their efforts but at the same time it was stressed that Manfred should ensure that they be sympathetic to the cause. There would be no hiring of mercenaries, Hoyle stated categorically. The money would merely be an added bonus; financial assistance for their own struggles against the fascist forces still wielding power in West Germany. Once the operation succeeded, AFRA would admit responsibility for the death and destruction and urge further action in support of the insurgent forces trying to liberate Azania. It could set South Africa back five years, said Hoyle. Could just possibly bring the economy to its knees and would be a shot in the arm for the outlawed movements like the PAC and the ANC, not to mention UMSA which had showed its determination at Hout Bay and in the De Waal Drive bus attack.

Armaments would be a problem, Anderson said, and here he would defer to AFRA's armaments expert Reggie Smith who was absent, but who had worked out a plan of supply via the small independent mountainous kingdom of Lesotho. This country was totally enclosed within the borders of South Africa and all its sea and airfreight normally came through South African ports; namely Cape Town, Durban and Jan Smuts airport, Johannesburg. There were however, fairly relaxed customs restrictions between the borders of Lesotho and South Africa and thus, the problem would be to get the necessary hardware into Lesotho without using the normal ports. Anderson and Reginald Smith, a young black American who had served in Vietnam, had pondered the question at length and worked out how to bypass South Africa by shipping the merchandise to Maputo in Mozambique before flying direct to Maseru, Lesotho by the Mozambique national carrier LAM. Once in Lesotho, the arms would be simply driven over the border by one of various methods but probably concealed within the regular consignments of Lesotho handicrafts which were never searched. The target date was around mid-January and so they had five months to prepare the detailed strategy and execute the plan. They would have to find a sympathetic shipper but that was not envisaged as a problem.

Hoyle stressed that security was of paramount importance. South African agents were everywhere, he said. In London of course, there were many and he grinned ruefully, gesturing towards his own missing limbs. Gerrit seemed to notice them for the first time, so impressed had he been with the powerful character of the man. But the enemy's agents were also in Berlin, Dusseldorf and, naturally enough, seemed to be in plentiful supply in Windhoek where Gerrit was based. They all laughed at this but then Hoyle was serious again and repeated his warnings.

'Only the AFRA executive and you two gentlemen, here present, are aware of the existence of this plan. It is obviously essential that nothing is mentioned outside the walls of these offices,' he said urgently and then smiled, drawing towards him the desk-top calculator which was placed in the centre of the table within easy reach of them all. He stroked the machine fondly and looked up at Manfred, still smiling.

'This is not really a calculator gentlemen,' he said smugly. 'It is, in fact, a scrambling device made in East Germany which reduces human voices to a meaningless burble. I'm not sure how it works but I know that it emits a high-pitched hum which cannot be detected by the human ear but which combines with normal voices and distorts them hopelessly. So, if our friends from Pretoria are somehow listening to this conversation, although our security man checks these offices for bugs every week, they're not going to have a very satisfactory recording.'

The meeting ended at six and Gerrit went away feeling tremendously impressed with Douglas Hoyle and his casual yet effective organisation. Both he and Manfred were inspired by the plan of Hoyle and Anderson and when the Mercedes dropped them back at the Buckingham, they were both in great good humour. Thoughts of the proposed strike against South Africa filled Gerrit's mind as he asked for his key in the reception area which somehow seemed less tatty today. Although the actual target had not been identified, Gerrit felt sure that it would be a group, or a person of great importance and he longed for the further details that Hoyle had promised at their meeting scheduled for the following afternoon.

He saw the message which the Pakistani handed him with the key. It was crudely written and barely legible but it asked Mr de Kock to call his sister Mrs Heim at the Frankfurterhof Hotel in Frankfurt. It was very urgent. Gerrit felt a prickle of alarm and asked the lounging Pakistani to get the number quickly, please. There would be a delay said the receptionist idly. Where would the gentleman be so that he may call them when he had got through to Germany? 'We'll be in the bar,' said Manfred brusquely and the Pakistani nodded and smiled knowingly and Manfred led Gerrit into the small cocktail lounge off the lobby. Both felt a deepening sense of apprehension and Gerrit drank two vodka-and-limes before the call came through.

He took the call in the lobby and Manfred went with him and saw his face grow paler as he listened to Tina. Tears sprang from Gerrit's eyes and coursed down his cheeks and still he hadn't spoken so that Manfred pressed

246

closer, asking what had happened and wanting to speak to Tina himself. Gerrit shook his head and the Pakistani receptionist watched in fascination as he mumbled a few words and replaced the receiver.

'Bad news, sir?' he asked gloatingly but Gerrit ignored him and turned to Manfred.

'It's our little brother, Koos,' he said despairingly. 'He's dead, killed in an accident last Saturday.' Manfred looked at the broken face and saw the raw agony. He put his arm around Gerrit's shoulders and gently pulled him away from the desk and upstairs to his room.

Tina and Gerrit rendezvoused in Frankfurt to connect with an onward South African Airways flight to Johannesburg. Once there, they would take the local airbus to Cape Town and attend the funeral at the Elsies River cemetery. There had been no time for a second meeting with Hoyle because Gerrit's flight to Frankfurt had left London before midday. Gerrit had been filled with a dire urgency to meet his sister and get back home for Koos' funeral. He had called Tina later that evening and instructed her to contact the authorities in Cape Town first thing in the morning and had then telexed Metricor in Windhoek and instructed his secretary to call the Parow head office and request arrangements with a local funeral contractor. Koos was being kept in the morgue at Groote Schuur until funeral facilities had been finalised; the police had told Tina this.

The British Airways Tri-Star landed at Frankfurt am Main at 14.10 local time and Gerrit hurried towards the now familiar arrival hall where he had first landed only six days earlier. Now, it seemed a lifetime ago. Tina was waiting with Willi and both wore black, Tina in a smart wool costume and Willi in a lightweight worsted suit which contrasted vividly with his white blond hair. Gerrit wore his suede jacket and tan corduroy slacks, having no black clothing with him.

The trio had a late lunch at a restaurant within the airport complex and Gerrit and Tina talked of Koos and the tragic manner of his death. Both of them felt guilty, through a sense of negligence, towards the younger brother whose welfare they had partially disregarded in favour of their own advancement in life. Tina cried softly as she recalled childhood scenes and how Koos had always depended on her when their mother had been away at work and Gerrit spoke of the funeral where he and Koos had stood together in the rain and then broken down and got maudlin drunk after the ceremony. Thoughts of the old house and their childhood years brought painful memories and, despite himself, he wiped a tear from his eyes and held Tina's hand across the table whilst Willi Heim looked on helplessly, unable to share their grief yet desperately unhappy for his beautiful wife.

Gerrit spoke quietly and kindly to his sobbing sister yet there was a steeliness and determination in his voice. 'First it was Dad and then Mother and now it's little Koos. There's only the two of us left now Tina, just the two of us, you know what that means?' The girl looked up at him, still beautiful despite the puffy red eyes and smudged mascara. 'Yes Tina,' he said, 'we're the last two de Kocks now, but they will remember us, they'll remember us, that's for sure.'

Willi Heim looked on in puzzlement, not understanding the bond that existed suddenly between the brother and sister. It had never been there before; if anything they had despised each other in the old days. Willi wondered what had happened to change things.

South African Airways Boeing 747, flight SA 253, lifted off smoothly from Frankfurt at 17.30 local time just five minutes behind schedule, a time deficit that would be easy to make up before the first stop in Lisbon. Gerrit and Tina sat in vast and comfortable first-class armchairs sipping from flutes of chilled Cape sparkling wine and nibbling at canapés of crayfish and smoked salmon. Heim Import-Export had surprised Gerrit by paying the excess on his

248

return economy excursion ticket and Willi had cut through Gerrit's protests by saying that by the time his auditors were finished with the account, the German Federal Government would foot the bill. In any case, economy class had been overbooked and they would never have managed reservations.

A few hours later, and now one minute ahead of schedule, the big jet whispered off into a clear night sky from Lisbon and set course for Ilha do Sal, South African Airways' refuelling stop on the bulge of Africa. Despite the grief that had been with them since the telephone conversation of the previous evening, Tina and Gerrit began to enjoy the flight and the cosseting by the cabin staff who hovered around pandering to their every need. Koos was momentarily forgotten as Gerrit summarised the AFRA tactics that had been proposed and talked of the intended liaison with a Berlin-based group dedicated to the destruction of all neo-fascist regimes. He spoke quietly, almost in a whisper, and glanced at his watch as he saw the rapt concentration on Tina's face.

'Even at this very moment, Tina, Manfred will be with Hoyle, working out the fees to be paid and finalising the basics of the German involvement. It's very exciting, very exciting indeed and I'll tell you more when we get home.' Suddenly he wondered why he had said home, referring naturally to Cape Town. But of course it was just that, home and a wonderful home too. It was the system of apartheid that was the evil cancerous brain of the South African State; it would have to be grievously wounded, struck in the nerve centre and eventually destroyed. Only then would it truly be home, Azania, a new and free country for all.

After the telephone call from Tina and the miserable and hurtful evening that had followed, Manfred had made plans to drive Gerrit to Heathrow the next morning. An all-night travel service, which simply linked up with the

ITV air travel advice computer, confirmed a seat on the morning British Airways flight to Frankfurt and then it was a case of making hurried plans. They would liaise via Tina who would contact Manfred in Berlin on her return from Cape Town at the end of the following week.

In turn, Manfred would obviously maintain close links with Hoyle and Anderson and AFRA would arrange a further meeting within two months. The location for this meeting was at this point unknown. Manfred felt a sense of loss when Gerrit's Frankfurt flight was called. The two men had grown close to each other during their few short days together and the acquaintance that had developed would surely blossom into a bond which would continue to strengthen with time. Manfred was very sure of that.

After that evening's meeting at South Kensington, Hoyle invited Manfred, on impulse, to the AFRA gala ball at the Royal Garden; had Gerrit been there, he too would have been invited. Hoyle felt happy and content with the progress of his plans and the inclusion of de Kock and Meyer who had both appeared fortuitously at a time when they were most needed. AFRA's fledgling security department had checked them both out to the best of its ability and Russell had pronounced them clean of all possible involvement with the Pretoria government; Hoyle felt well satisfied with progress to date.

The Nigerian chauffeur guided the Mercedes smoothly through the late-evening traffic and within twenty minutes they arrived at the Holland Park flat where Manfred was kitted out in a borrowed black velvet jacket and matching bow tie. Hoyle showered and changed into a three-piece evening suit of midnight-blue mohair and Jane Hoyle wore a silver lamé trouser suit which clung to her lissome figure like a second skin so that Manfred found it difficult to keep his eyes off her as she moved gracefully around the stark white interior like a dramatic black butterfly. Jane bent to pour Moet et Chandon 1971 Imperial into crystal flutes and Hoyle, who walked into the room in time to catch Manfred's appraisal of his wife's tight buttocks, smiled to himself. He briefly thought of the Asti Spumante, now relegated to the confines of his bedroom; what he sometimes did with Jane and those bottles would make Meyer blush.

The Kensington Room at the Royal Garden Hotel was packed with the so-called glitterati, notable members of London's show-business and fashionable society of which, tonight, some one third were black. As Hoyle, with Jane on his arm, preceded Manfred into the reception his eyes shone with a fanatical light and he manhandled the alloy crutch skilfully as he headed for his place on the top table. On the way, he stopped to exchange greetings with AFRA benefactors and friends and all the way there was a polite smattering of applause which swelled to a crescendo as the Hoyles reached the end of the long room. This recognition pleased the AFRA founder as he joined the rest of his executive committee at the elevated table. Below him sat two of his guests and he saw that already Manfred Meyer and David Mendelsohn were exchanging pleasantries. Mendelsohn had brought along two Haitian models with incredible beaded hairstyles and the girls were twin sisters and dressed in identical clinging white gowns. As Hoyle looked down at Mendelsohn, the young gynaecologist glanced up and smiled slightly, inclining his head towards the models. Hoyle smiled back briefly, Mendelsohn's inference had been unmistakable. It was not lost either on Manfred Meyer who felt a sudden heat rise in his groin as one of the black girls smiled winningly at him.

During the evening, speeches were made by Anderson and Hoyle and there was a short dramatic slide show based on the articles and photographs that had recently appeared in *Confront*. Hoyle had taken great care with the commentary which he had recorded himself and his voice penetrated through the affluent burble in the darkened room like a knife through butter. Silence reigned and the transparencies began with the fortifications at Katima Mulilo and along the Zambesi and the tropical colours flared gaily on the screen, but always there was the deadly brown drab of South African army personnel and their various armoured vehicles. Next came a selection of shots of Soweto, the vast black township outside Johannesburg, where ragged children played in filthy streets. Interspersed with these evocative pictures were newspaper blow-ups in black and white of white policemen firing on students during the 1976 Soweto riots and some pathetic huddled figures blotched with the black smudges of blood.

Hoyle finished up with some stock shots of white palaces in the northern suburbs of Johannesburg and Constantia in Cape Town and cleverly compared these with photographs of the latest unrest in the shanty townships which constituted the coloured areas of the Cape. Lastly there came a shot of coloured youths allegedly shot by police and one amazing colour action picture of a young coloured girl whose white dress was splashed with red across her breasts while one hand clasped a pathetic missile of some sort. The young face was frozen in agony and it was obvious to the viewers that she had been shot; in fact, the photograph had been staged by a black Cape Argus photographer sympathetic to the AFRA cause, but not one of the audience would have believed it. Finally the screen went blank and then a white cross appeared against the black background with the words 'AFRA SAVES BLACK LIVES WITH YOUR HELP' printed underneath.

As the lights came on, Manfred noted quite a few women wiping back tears and as many men with stern, tight-lipped expressions. Hoyle's presentation had been masterly and Manfred caught the eye of the young Jewish doctor David Mendelsohn to whom he had been briefly introduced. Now Mendelsohn smiled back with eyebrows raised in appreciation. 'Quite a show eh,' he said. 'Douglas really knows how to put our case properly. What brings you here Mr Meyer?'

Gerrit dreamed that he was flying in a nameless aircraft

high above the earth's surface. So high that the curvature of the planet was clearly visible and the sky inky blue graduating to ochre at the horizons. He was cushioned in some sort of incredible gravity couch in which he virtually floated and he seemed to be in the cockpit of the aircraft because his vision ranged through 180 degrees. Voices came dimly, as if from a great distance, and then they increased in volume and a hand seemed to be shaking him by his shoulder so that he came awake with a waft of the familiar lemony Dior fragrance. Tina's face smiled down at him and the voice came soft and laughingly into his consciousness. 'Oh, Gerrit, you sleepy little boy. You went out like a light after the movie and missed breakfast because I asked them not to wake you. And now we're landing in a few minutes.'

Gerrit stared out of the window and looked down on the vast yellow mine dumps and sun-baked brown veld. In the distance was the great sprawl of a city, with tall office towers, partially obscured in a light blanket of smog. Below, in the early morning light, were tiny toy houses with glittering jewel-like swimming pools set in postage stamp lawns. Roads criss-crossed the brown landscape and complicated clover-leaf junctions prescribed perfect concrete circles through a land where once elephant, lion and buffalo had roamed in profusion. The seat belt sign flashed on the periphery of his line of vision and the stewardess began her monologue in Afrikaans, English and German. This was Johannesburg, thought Gerrit, the great commercial and industrial powerhouse of white South Africa which to him was as strange as Frankfurt because this would be his first visit.

Their connecting flight to Cape Town would be ninety minutes after touchdown, not long to get an impression of Johannesburg. In fact, this international airport would probably be designed to give a favourable and therefore false impression, Gerrit imagined. Together with the other first-class passengers, he and Tina were shepherded through to passport control by two immaculately groomed ground hostesses. The officer at the booth was young and blond with a straggly moustache and pink, pitted face. He scowled at Gerrit and spoke to him in brusque, slightly patronising Afrikaans trying to bring this *skollie* down to earth again after his first-class passage through the skies. In contrast, Tina was addressed in English and the officer smiled lustfully at her, exposing yellow teeth. He even tried a *'danke schon'* in deference to the dark green West German passport.

Fifteen minutes later they sat in the coffee shop in the domestic arrivals hall and watched the people around them, listening to the unmistakable accents, noting the odd behavioural traits of these white and black South Africans who lived lives far removed from one another within the tenuous framework of this industrial giant of a city. In the background came the omnipotent drone of Afrikaans over the public-address system and the typical and obvious South African advertising for such products as Lucky Strike cigarettes and Castle Lager. Here too was the ludicrous baby-doll clothing of certain Afrikaans women and the unlikely powder blue and mustard safari suits of their men.

African porters in brown overalls, and nameless other blacks with plastic identity cards pinned to their shirts wandered about with eyes vacant, their posture fluid, yet oddly lifeless. Small children, tanned and healthy, embraced returning fathers and occasionally mothers and struggled in embarrassment as they were held aloft in long lasting bearhugs, unfairly exposed to bristly chins and stale tobacco-tainted breath. Gerrit and Tina just sat and watched and, for Tina especially, it was like taking a giant stride back in time. But she knew that in Cape Town it would all be more strangely familiar, like reading an old diary or looking at a photograph of a long-past summer and remembering the very day, the weather and the happiness. Memorics were almost always happy, she thought, because our psyches are inclined to bury most of the hurt and nastiness.

So it was that she felt a new identification with the country of her birth, yet stood apart from it all like an observer from a future era. Indeed, so much had changed for her and momentarily she wondered why she should get involved in trying to change this place, these people; risking her life in what could well prove to be a fruitless and feeble attempt. Then she looked across the concourse and saw the policeman in the olive green uniform of the railways, airports and harbours department. He was ogling her and licking his thin lips in a horribly obscene gesture as his eyes crawled over her body like foul insects. He had lank black hair, shorn high at the back of his neck and around his ears, and the greasy olive yellow skin typical of so many Afrikaaners who had coloured blood. He carried an ugly black machine carbine and an automatic pistol and his eyes roved over her so that she could imagine him undressing her and the way his hands would feel on her body.

She hated him because he reminded her of the white policemen who had abused her during her teenage years and although that seemed a lifetime ago, the hatred flared in her eyes and was very real. The policeman saw it and looked away, unable to meet the huge dark eyes that burned back at him. Tina knew then that she would be able to do it, would be able to kill that very policeman if she could be sure of getting away with it. If she had a gun and the opportunity, there would be no qualms; the realisation surprised and excited her.

Just over twenty-four hours later, the computer operator in the vast underground basement of the Ministry of the Interior in Pretoria, scanned the list of names on the flimsy print-out. The impersonal grey and cream area hummed faintly with the sound of the air conditioning and the occasional rattle of electronic machinery was the only sound that broke the library-like hush. There were thirteen names on the list which was a daily dope-sheet fed through to the Security Police just down the road. It listed persons in whom the police had an interest and who had reappeared within the country's borders. Almost two years previously, Vosloo had reported Tina de Kock as possibly re-entering the country with the name of Mrs Willi Heim or Tina Heim and his deduction had paid dividends. Tina de Kock's name had been routinely listed by Vosloo in 1974 because she had knowingly contravened the Immorality Act.

The operator read off the listing which had recorded the entry of Tina Heim (née De Kock) South African citizen, destination Cape Town. Return ticket destination Frankfurt on SA 250 08/26 at 1600 hours, via Windhoek. Registered Holiday Inn, Bellville, Cape until Tuesday 08/26. The name meant nothing to the operator who routinely passed it on for the courier, dropping the flimsy into a basket marked SAP Security. Gerrit de Kock's name was not on the list, although it had been recorded by immigration and was stored on tape. By the end of the week it would be routinely passed on with thousands of others to the returning residents' section in the Ministry of the Interior.

In his report to Van Pittius that Friday, Mendelsohn listed details of the AFRA fund-raising ball at the Royal Garden Hotel. He had established from Hoyle that the tickets had been £125 per couple and that some 250 guests had attended in total. Mendelsohn reckoned that, discounting the costs and the occasional free guest like himself and Manfred Meyer, AFRA should have netted around £10,000 at least, even allowing for a fairly high figure of £20 per head for the three-course dinner and some very average wine. On top of this would have come the donations which should have poured in after Hoyle's slide show. Mendelsohn summarised this presentation and the effect it had on the audience.

Also listed were references to 'a plan of action' which

would 'set the racists back on their heels' and Mendelsohn had said that there appeared to be much optimism about the future when the wine had flowed freely towards the end of the evening. Two names were listed for Van Pittius to forward on to Pretoria; one: Manfred Meyer, a known left-wing sympathiser and West Berlin-based lawyer; and Gerrit de Kock, not present at the ball, yet somehow involved in recent discussions with Hoyle and Meyer. Mendelsohn also had managed to pick up that De Kock was apparently a very intelligent Cape coloured, now resident in Windhoek and employed as an assistant to the financial director with a large South African-based company.

Van Pittius had been justifiably pleased with this information and the idea of his operative being this close to the AFRA set-up delighted him. The information was coded and telexed to Pretoria and the deputy director saw it as the fruition of his long-held suspicions that AFRA was planning something big. He was almost sure of it now and phoned through to the director's secretary and requested an hour of his superior's time that very afternoon.

CHAPTER 17

Things had not been going well in Cape Town for either Vosloo or Mostert but for the Riot Police colonel in particular, the recent days had seemed like a perpetual bad dream. The cause was the continuing boycott of coloured schools which appeared to have become a permanent fixture in the lives of the short-staffed policemen. There had been long, tense days in Elsies River and Langa and elsewhere in the Cape Flats, from Athlone to Mitchell's Plain on the coast, the unrest simmered and threatened to erupt at the slightest provocation.

By any standards, the Flats were an unpleasant area in which to work and Mostert, to some extent, sympathised with the coloured people who were forced to live there. Blustery and windswept for most of the year, the area had suffered heavy rains towards the end of winter and parts had been flooded quite severely. This worsening in the inhospitable nature of the Flats could well have provided the fuel needed to kindle the fires of unrest that forever burned amongst the coloured community. Mostert almost understood their reasoning, accepting privately that people could only be pushed so far. Had he been coloured, he imagined that he too might have felt that the prospects for the future were bleak enough to warrant the risk of rioting against the authorities.

The problems had begun in Guguletu and Nyanga where students had refused to attend school because of the recent revelations about the relative amounts spent on white, black and coloured schooling. The rioting had begun with the stoning of class windows and graduated to education department buildings and Mostert's Riot Police had been called in, but each man had been briefed to keep a low profile and resist provocation as far as possible. For this reason, weapons had been restricted to sidearms, which were to be kept in holsters at all costs, and there were to be only two shotguns per platoon of thirty-two men. Gas grenades were carried but the main weapon, in the event of outright attack, was to be the riot baton while defence was to be provided by the big black rubber shields.

In the beginning the tactics had worked and the actual clashes had been kept to a minimum and the mobs were easy to break up after mere abuse and a few isolated stones had been hurled at the police. Towards the end of the first week, Mostert had hoped that things were improving but then the little bastards must have realised that they were getting nowhere because they had started to stone trains along the line between Guguletu and Manenberg, smashing windows and terrorising the coloured workers who commuted daily to Cape Town. Things had got progressively worse and cars had been attacked on the airport road near Guguletu and barricades had been thrown up around the perimeter fences in order to stop the mobs reaching the aircraft and airport buildings.

One morning, out by Elsies River, one of his constables had caught a bloody great rock on the cheekbone which had laid open his face from eye-socket to jawbone and the blood had flowed. The mob had sensed victory and moved in, closing with the front ranks of riot police and in the melée there had been two stabbings; another man had been badly slashed with a bicycle chain. They had closed in incredibly fast and there had been no chance to fire the gas grenades and no bloody wind either to disperse the smoke away from the platoons.

Mostert had judged that his two platoons would have been overrun and he had pulled out his Walther P.38 and fired two warning shots into the air but the students had been so incensed that they had ignored the warning and some five hundred screaming kids had attacked his two box formations of sixty-four men with rocks, iron bars and bottles of petrol. There would have been absolutely no chance of survival and the men were falling back when he had given the order to fire one volley only. The four shotguns had opened up and about thirty shots were fired from the pistols in a matter of seconds and the mob had broken in terror and run.

Of the four bodies that had been left lying in the dust, one had been a young girl who'd taken a charge from a twelve bore right in the stomach at close range. She'd writhed there in the dirt, hands clasped over the bubbling hole in the front of her jeans and blood was everywhere and she was screaming like hell. God, how she had screamed – Mostert would never forget it. After the initial shock, the first thing that had occurred to him was that, thank Christ, they had banned the bloody press from the area because a photograph of the girl would have been the bitter end had it got out.

She had died within twelve hours but there had been another fatality: the youth who had stopped a 9mm bullet right in the forehead had the back of his head blown out and was killed instantly. Two students were still in hospital and quite a number of others had been badly peppered with shotgun pellets and the odd flesh wound from a pistol bullet, and had received casualty treatment. Mostert had been amazed that more had not been killed and wounded; they had arrested twenty-seven people when reinforcements arrived. But the cost had been high because one of his men had died in hospital from stab wounds and there were two others who would never look the same again. All in all, it had been a very bad business and the pot still simmered, fuel having been added to the fire by the death of the girl who had been only sixteen. And the kids were still staying away from classes.

Hendrik Vosloo had told Mostert through his Security Police contacts that professional agitators were thought to be at work in the coloured townships and Mostert's own enquiries had confirmed these suspicions. His men had all been briefed to look out for any such suspects and, prior to the press ban, a squad out at Langa had actually caught an English journalist bribing a youth to throw a bottle of petrol at a parked police Landrover. They had caught the sod and the kid had admitted quite openly that the man had offered him twenty rand and shown them the money.

They'd let the kid keep the cash and released him because there was no way they could make an issue out of the incident. The Minister of Police himself had squashed the affair, but they had confiscated the journalist's camera and his press pass and he'd been escorted to D.F. Malan airport by some very unfriendly regulars from the Task Force. These members of the police anti-terrorist squad were really hard bastards and apparently they had scared the pommy so much that he'd peed his pants in the car. Pretoria had got him on the first direct flight out of the country from Cape Town because they didn't want him spouting to any of his mates in Johannesburg and so it had been Buenos Aires for him which was as good a place as any for the little sod. Mostert reckoned that he'd have a fine time explaining the story to his editor because Pretoria had instructed the embassy in London to tell the editor the truth as it happened. With any luck, he'd get the sack, the shit-stirring swine that he was.

The story of the teenage girl's shooting had nonetheless made headlines all over the world, thankfully however without any accompanying photographs which everybody agreed would have been the kiss of death. But the damage had been bad enough and Mostert had been on the mat in front of the brigadier to explain just what had happened. Fortunately, his account had been accepted and he'd been let off the hook.

It was all so bloody unfair though, thought Mostert, the way the international press ganged up on South Africa. He and his fellow officers were becoming increasingly embittered that sundry rioters throughout the world could be shot, clubbed, gassed and mutilated virtually with impunity, while in South Africa, even the arrest of a dissident was guaranteed to make the front pages of the international dailies. Mostert read his *Time* magazine and knew of the hundreds of thousands killed in Cambodia, the thousands executed in Iran and the countless numbers terrorised and mutilated in just about every black state to the north of them.

In Zimbabwe, Mugabe's crowd had only won the election through intimidation and Mostert could not understand that the West, and particularly the British, who had a wealth of experience in such things after their vicious little wars in Malaya and Cyprus, would accept such tactics. There had been a number of ex-Rhodesian policemen coming down to join the force lately. Both they and some of the now disbanded Rhodesian Light Infantry chaps had told him that the army and the airforce were all ready to scribble Mugabe's ZANLA forces right there in their assembly points. There'd been a lot of publicity that had got out about that little plot but somehow, at the time, it had all gone by the board and the army had been told to shake hands with their enemies and that had been that. Overnight it had been goodbye Rhodesia and hello Zimbabwe, simple enough except for the poor sods who had lived there all their lives and had the odd arm or leg blown off fighting for the place.

But Mostert, like most other South Africans employed by the police and armed forces, had become something of a pragmatist, as far as his country was concerned. As the international pariah to beat all others, South Africa had been given a short respite in the furore following the Iran debacle but now, with no light in sight down the dark tunnel which Iran had become in international politics with its so-called religious revolution, South Africa had once again become the favourite target for vitriolic attacks. Threatened boycotts ranged from the supply of oil to the curtailment of air transport and the anti-apartheid movements and ANTISA organisations were again stepping up their activities all over Europe and the United States.

The new crowd in London, AFRA, seemed quite a force to be reckoned with and Mostert had seen their magazine *Confront* which was a professional *Time*-style journal issues of which had been circulated to upper-echelon officers in the police and defence forces. Mostert had been forced to admire the presentation, even though the magazine was filled with all manner of garbage which bore no relationship to the true situation in the country or on its borders.

Although the student problem seemed an ongoing fact of life, there had been no further terrorist activity in the Cape but up north in Pretoria, a bunch of ANC kaffirs had ineffectually tried to clobber a police station in one of the black townships. The most dangerous situations were those involving hostages of which there had only been one so far, thank God, thought Mostert fervently. Recently there had been some very alarming new directives which ordered Task Force and Riot Police units to shoot through hostages, if necessary, in order to liquidate the terrorists who held them. The implication of such action could be quite horrifying, but the Minister of Police himself had stated just the other week, that 'South Africa was at war' and had added 'that sacrifices must be made by everyone to halt the onslaught against the country'. Mostert was not certain that these remarks were to be taken quite so literally.

The sun shone brightly through the window of the office in Seapoint and Major Hendrik Vosloo watched tiny motes of dust captured in a ray of light between the old bottle-green roller blind and the window frame. The light beam fascinated him and he leaned back in his old leather chair and blew a thin plume of smoke towards it from the cigarette he had just lit. It was his seventh of the day and it was only ten o'clock. The backrest of the chair came into contact with the cream gloss-painted wall of the office and settled comfortably into the groove in the plaster which had been made there by Vosloo and his predecessors over the years. Vosloo inhaled and grimaced as the smoke from the toasted tobacco caught in his throat so that he shook his head and looked down distastefully at the overflowing ashtray. 'Bloody coffin nails,' he muttered audibly and took one more drag of the Chesterfield and stubbed it out.

It was already quite warm for the time of year and Vosloo sighed as he glanced down at the docket on his desk and then out at the young leaves which nodded gently on the branches of the plane tree right outside his window. What a day for fishing, he thought, and cursed the name on the brown card cover in front of him. The name was De Kock and on top of the folder was a lengthy sheet of paper which constituted a report from the coroner on the death of Koos de Kock. Shaking off the images of his old ski-boat, moored just over the mountain in Hout Bay, Vosloo grimaced again and began to read the officially stilted prose of the pathologist.

'The subject suffered death,' the doctor had stated clinically, 'through massive fractures of the cranium and severe fracturing and displacement of the spinal column. In addition, the sternum and six ribs were severely fractured and both the heart and lungs were therefore punctured in several places. Further damage was sustained in the abdominal cavity by the impalation of the spleen and liver by foreign bodies driven into the abdomen by the force of the impact. Any one of these injuries would have been fatal to the subject,' the doctor added. A footnote stated that the deceased had been buried in Elsies River coloured cemetery on the day before.

Vosloo opened the docket and placed the coroner's report underneath the pile of other papers, clippings and notations. Koos was not important to him and had now conveniently ceased to exist but had served his purpose in bringing the other two De Kocks back to South Africa, and to his notice. Vosloo was interested in Gerrit de Kock, and to a lesser extent in the girl Tina who had married the German as he had guessed she would. He saw from SAP Security that the two of them had returned to attend the funeral but he might not have seen the connection had he not been right there at the time that Koos was killed not to mention almost killing himself and Johann in the process. As the officer who had put forward Tina de Kock's name because of the immorality business, Vosloo had received the information back after all this time. Computers were wonderful things, he thought.

The sense of déja vu had struck Gerrit heavily as he and Tina stood beside the open hole in the ground and listened to the high, whining voice of the old coloured priest. There were a few assorted relations there too but nobody whom he could call close and they had only come for a drink, he was pretty sure. Well, they'd be disappointed, he thought, savagely, because after the ceremony he and Tina were going straight off back to the hotel. There was no way he was going to hang around in some hovel drinking cheap wine with that lot. He would rather drink with bloody Afrikaaners like Marais than suffer the hypocrisy of those hangers-on.

The last time that Gerrit had stood here in this bleak cemetery, Koos had been at his side and it had been his mother they had lowered into the ground on that rainy afternoon. Now Koos was down there too, beside her in the dirt, and this time it was Tina who threw the first handful of soil. Obliquely, and with an odd foreboding, Gerrit thought who might be next, who would stand here listening to the meaningless prattle of the minister and throw the first handful onto the coffin. It was perhaps odd that he experienced this macabre thought because all around them were the signs of spring greenery, new growth and life and the sun shone strongly out of a cornflower blue sky. For once the wind was still and only a tiny breeze eddied the dust at his feet; it was as if the great unprotected basin of the Cape Flats was holding its breath in disbelief at the wonderful weather.

Gerrit had seen Koos, or what was left of him. The undertaker in Bellville had tried to reassemble the shattered skull, padding it out with polystyrene and attempting to repair the awful rents and gashes. The result was that Koos now resembled some kind of Frankenstein-like monstrosity and bore no resemblance to his former self. Gerrit had found him totally unrecognisable and quite hideous. He had taken only one swift glance and looked away, unaware that this had disappointed the undertaker who had worked long and hard to restructure the face in particular.

Gerrit had not allowed Tina to see the body feeling that, like him, she would be haunted forever by that dreadful visage. After the ceremony they left immediately for the Holiday Inn, Gerrit driving the swift little Volkswagen hard out of the hated cemetery where his mother and now Koos would lie and rot under the dank barren earth. They sat together in the bar and drank and drank and by early evening Tina was hardly able to stand and her mascara had run from eyes red and swollen with silent weeping. Somehow, Gerrit managed to get her to stand up and manhandled her out of the bar and up to her room among knowing mutters and nods from the other patrons of the bar. Once there, he stripped off her black silk dress and removed her shoes, shoving her under the covers of the big double bed. Then he lay down beside her and collapsed into an exhausted sleep.

It was pitch black and very silent when he awoke, frightened and momentarily unsure of his whereabouts. Hands fluttered over his face and then he heard the quiet sobbing and sensed the warmth of her body pressing against the length of his. The air-conditioning was still on and he felt the chill of the room and struggled in beside her under the blankets and drew her to him like a child, hearing her murmur in half-sleep and cuddle up against him. Despite himself, Gerrit became aware of his sister's half-naked body and silken slender legs and was unable to control the stiffening in his groin. His shame and embarrassment reminded him of the time in their youth when she had walked in on him in the toilet and he held his body rigid, daring not to move in case she misunderstood his intentions.

But Tina seemed oblivious and her head was on his shoulder and the scent of her hair in his nostrils and then her hands fluttered down his chest and he knew what was happening, and all his senses screamed at him to stop it, yet he was powerless to resist. She murmured again contentedly and moved closer still to him and his senses raced now, but still he dare not move. And then her hands found him and moved on him and she slid over him and he could not believe it was happening yet found it impossible to speak, let alone move away from her.

With a desperation born of emotional unrest and deep sorrow, they drew from each other in the dark soft bed, and still partly numbed by the liquor, he thought it was all a dream and that he would awake. Instead, he slept and in the morning when he awoke, she was gone and only the smell of her perfume remained on the pillow beside him and then he thought he really had dreamed the whole thing, yet it was all too real and he knew that it must have happened. But he felt no shame, no regrets and dragged himself from the rumpled bed and ran a bath and drank three very large glasses of water. Then he drew the curtains, looking out on the greenery and the blue sky and the hazy purple mountains in the distance.

They sat together for a late breakfast, both still suffering from the intake of alcohol which made their mouths taste woolly and their heads ache a little. Tina wore dark glasses but her eyes were huge and liquid behind them and she smiled at him and talked a little of her mother and brother and having to leave so soon and how she loved Cape Town. After two cups of coffee,

Gerrit looked at his sister and then down at the gold Longines on his wrist.

'It's already 9.15, Mrs Heim, and we're leaving on Tuesday. We've got two days left to see some of this old city of ours so don't let's waste any of it.' Tina smiled and they left the dining room hand in hand and walked outside to the car park and the little red Golf that Metricor had loaned him.

Vosloo's memory searched back through the years to 1974. In front of him was the communication from Pretoria listing the name of Manfred Meyer as being a person known to have AFRA connections. Vosloo had been a captain then and it had been his decision to arrest Meyer and the little Malay girl Wendy Richards who had lived with him quite openly, up in Loader Street on Signal Hill. Of course, these days more and more of it was going on but the official view was to turn a blind eye to it. Pretoria only acted in the most outrageous cases which were deemed detrimental to the well-being of the State. Vosloo approved of this policy because he wasn't particularly bothered about whites and coloureds cohabitating together. It was the blacks that were the real problem although, thank God, there were not too many of them down here in the Cape.

In Pretoria, the Department's computer link to the Ministry of the Interior, had reacted to the name of Manfred Meyer and responded by listing his history as far as it was known to the South African government. The deputy director had not really been that surprised to learn that Meyer had lived and worked in the Republic for almost two years and had been deported back to West Germany in 1974 after proven contravention of the Immorality Act with a coloured female. The arresting officer had been a Captain Vosloo who was still down there in Seapoint, Cape Town, and the deputy director wanted him contacted, wanted a full report on Meyer's habits, general character, reactions when he had been arrested and all that sort of thing. All the bloody computer could tell them was that he had been suspected of having liberal leanings and that he had been deported on 28 October 1974. The deputy director snorted to himself as he read this, the man's liberal tendencies were pretty obvious to him, otherwise he wouldn't have been living with a *skollie* slut.

They would try asking the Germans, of course, but Bonn had been a bit reticent with this sort of information lately and he didn't really expect too much help from them, the square-headed bastards. The Krauts were funny like that anyway. If they had anything on Meyer themselves he reckoned they would consider it a sort of national secret, but he supposed it wouldn't harm to try them. The whole of Europe was becoming a hotbed of anti-apartheid activity these days and all the bullshit and brave words from a bunch of long-haired radicals, most of whom were convicted drug-takers, seemed to rub off on the respective governments. They were fucking hypocrites, those Germans, the director thought. Here they were in South Africa with bloody Siemens, Mercedes Benz, BMW and Volkswagen and countless other industrial companies, and bloody Lufthansa bringing in tons of freight weekly and grosses of those identical looking super-efficient Kraut businessmen. Oh, they were happy to take South African money alright but when it came to helping out with a matter like information on Meyer, the bastards would very likely clam up.

The deputy director pondered the problem of AFRA and De Kock's connection. He was back in the country right now and within minutes he could be picked up and put away for ninety days without trial under the Suppression of Terrorism Act. All that was needed was a good suspicion and they could keep him there indefinitely. Once inside, they could get anything out of him, the deputy director was pretty sure of that, and yet he held back, was loath to act just yet. They would watch De

Kock and his sister whilst they were here in Cape Town for the next few days and then they could go, free as birds. The deputy director smiled mirthlessly to himself. Rather let Jacaranda do the work in London and advise them weekly on what was going on in the AFRA hierarchy and then they'd get the lot in the end when they set foot back inside the country, which he was pretty sure was their intention. They'd be crushed like the verminous wretches they were but first they'd talk and tell the whole story. Inadvertently, the deputy director's right hand had mashed the gold box of Benson & Hedges Special Filter with which he had been toying. He opened the mangled lid and tipped the box, spilling out shreds of tobacco and tatters of white paper. He cursed roundly; the packet had been half full.

The report on Meyer had taken Vosloo a good two hours so far and he had gone back painstakingly through his records and found the old docket on the German. His policeman's mind had little trouble recalling the events of September and October 1974 once he read the pencilled words in his own handwriting. It was the typing that would take the time because he would have to do it himself as the whole matter was highly confidential. He grimaced and looked at the old black Remington which was not the ideal machine on which to submit reports to the computerised and much hallowed halls of power in Pretoria. Especially when destined 'For the express attention of the Deputy Director for National Security'.

But today, even the deputy director would have to wait because it was Friday afternoon and his monthly afternoon off which would make his weekend long and restful with the Saturday he had coming as well. He could finish off the Meyer report over the weekend though, and maybe spend a couple of hours on Sunday with the De Kock file too. In the meantime, Hout Bay beckoned and the six pack of cold Castle lagers and some home-made ham sandwiches that Celeste had made for him; all snug in the trunk of the Chevrolet.

Vosloo had bought his old marine-ply Fairey ski-boat in 1973 and the small craft had given him endless hours of pleasure. At the beginning of this season, he had sold off the old Evinrude motors and bought a new Suzuki twin sixty-five horse power motors which had cost a fortune and which he would be paying for for another twenty-seven months. But the boat was his only indulgence and he loved it. It was the only cxcrcisc hc got.

Sometimes he would take a friend out with him and Johann had joined him quite a few times when they had managed to get weekends off together, like that recent Saturday for the rugby. But fishing was not really Johann's sport, and in any event, Vosloo enjoyed his solitary expeditions and was very much respectful of the sea, never taking any chances and always checking with the harbour master on expected weather conditions. He never went very far out on his own, rarely beyond sight of the shore, and would always be back long before dark, even if the fish were biting like crazy. His wife Celeste tolerated his passion for the sea because she knew he needed it; as far as she was concerned he could have it because she hated going out on the water and had never set foot in the boat.

Five kilometres off Hout Bay was usual for Vosloo on his afternoon outings and here he could catch snoek, cob and small yellowtail if he was lucky. Round in the warm waters of False Bay there were red roman, stumpnose and the butter-tasting rock cod but that was a good cruise of around an hour in average seas and he didn't have the time today. Using his old boat rod and hooks baited with squid, Vosloo had caught three and four kilo cods when they were biting but today he'd just go about four kilometres out and drift with the current. Trying for anything that was biting, because squid was a marvellous general bait, and with six hooks on the line, Vosloo had sometimes caught three varieties of fish with one baiting.

The Indian Ocean officially began at False Bay and the warm water fish could be literally pulled out when they had the taste of the squid. Friends of Vosloo's had caught up to eighty and ninety kilos in a morning and come back with their boats so low in the water that it looked positively dangerous. But to Vosloo, these were the things that dreams were made of because he was not a serious fisherman and enjoyed the sea and the weather as much as the fishing. Most of all, he enjoyed getting away from the dusty old desk in the station and being on his own. He loved to be alone and sometimes wondered whether he would have been happier as a bachelor because he and Celeste lived in a sort of contented state of tolerance with each other and there had been no children.

When the old electric clock in his office read 12.30, he closed the office door and walked over to the steel locker in the corner and changed from his summer uniform of bush jacket and slacks into his old patched corduroys and a faded denim shirt. He put the De Kock docket, and the rough draft of the Meyer report into his battered tan briefcase and rolled up his Sam Browne combination belt with the P 38 Walther pistol. Then he remembered the recent directive about carrying sidearms at all times and removed the pistol from the holster. He dropped the gun into the case with the papers and buckled the straps before picking it up and walking jauntily out of the office.

Acknowledging the jealous mutterings of the two young constables in the charge office, with a mock icy stare and a half smile, the commander of SAP Seapoint left his station via the back door and walked out to the car park. Gerry Mortimer (his sergeant) and the second in command would be in at 12.45 and Vosloo would have time to have his sandwiches and a beer or two down at the harbour. He liked to have a snack before going out and he had to buy the bait down on the harbour anyway.

There was a slight off-shore breeze which whipped white caps onto the waves that glittered in the inky blue Atlantic as he drove along High Level Road heading for the neck between the mountains which wound down into Hout Bay. It was getting on for two years now since the riots in the small coloured fishing community down there past the harbour. God, that had been a night, he thought, remembering the fierce fire-fight that had followed and poor old Jeannie Walker and that reservist Wright who had died so horribly. Today, as he freewheeled down onto the harbour, the little village could not have looked more peaceful in the soft light of this spring early afternoon, this place which was so much a part of what that English sailor had called the fairest Cape in all the world. Vosloo parked the Chevrolet under a big blue gum tree, drank a Castle and munched on one of Celeste's sandwiches in the dappled shade. He felt a little tired and wondered why; perhaps he had not slept as well as usual last night.

Vosloo finished the sandwich and swallowed the last of his beer. As he walked the hundred metres to the fish processing factory's retail trading store, he felt the slight burning sensation in his stomach and tightness in his chest. There was no doubt about it, he was not totally up to scratch. Must go and see old Dr Kloppers he thought absently, not really seriously concerned. He bought two kilos of frozen squid from the store and looked down at the congealed mass of white rubbery substance. He had never eaten the stuff himself and couldn't understand how people were prepared to pay five rand fifty for a plate of calamari in those fancy restaurants in Seapoint and Wynberg. Heaven only knew what they charged for it up-country.

The weather was warm and Vosloo sweated slightly as he lugged the cool-box, tackle bag and the two petrol tanks from the trunk of the Chevrolet. He carried the lot across to the gleaming wooden boat he had fondly named *Marlin*. Although he had yet to catch such a massive sea creature as that ultimate fighting fish, he hoped one day to get his chance and go to Mauritius. Perhaps when he retired, he would go and try a deep sea run in a fast ocean-going cruiser and sit in the fighting chair, watching the outrigger and waiting for the incredible thump as the great fish took the bait. In the meantime, he would trawl happily out of Hout Bay and keep Celeste's deep freeze full while enjoying himself enormously into the bargain.

By the time he had removed the canvas tarpaulin, connected the petrol lines up to the tanks and walked back to the car for the briefcase, which he almost forgot, he was sweating freely and wondering why, because it wasn't all that hot. He cast off the boat and jumped in, floating off about fifty metres from shore and resting in the single swivel chair behind the wheel. Another Castle and a third ham sandwich seemed to do the trick and he felt better and enjoyed the sandwich which was cold and moist from the cool box. Then he made everything shipshape and stowed the box and bags in the little bow locker.

At the first touch of the button the Suzukis fired and Vosloo relished the soft burble of power as he cast off from the little wooden jetty by the harbour. He paid R200 per annum for moorings there, and the nightly watch boy who prevented the theft of engines and boats. The wake made a smooth white arc across the calm deep blue waters of the wide bay and Vosloo looked over his shoulder at the mark of his passing and felt the sea-breeze on his face. He felt much better now and put on his dark glasses against the glare and looked up at the great grey-green bulk of mountains on his left, rising up from the sea in a vast eternal wall. Idly thinking, he gazed at them and wondered what they had seen, what drama they had witnessed over their million-year life span. There were no other boats in sight but he knew by the following morning that all the ski-boat fanatics would be down on the slipway launching their boats from trailers. That was another reason he didn't mind paying for the moorings, he hated dragging the boat around and going through all the trouble of launching it, because it was so heavy and, in any case, there was no bloody room for her at home. These days you couldn't get moorings in Hout Bay at any cost and if he ever gave his up, there would be one hell of a scramble for them.

Ahead was the open Atlantic and now Vosloo could feel the swell. He opened up the motors and *Marlin* rose up gracefully and began to plane, thumping across the rollers

274

with a nice solid rhythm, skimming along steadily at thirty knots. He debated, was tempted to go around the point and head for False Bay but it would be a good three-quarter-hour cruise even at this speed. On top of that, fuel was a terrible price these days and so he decided to stick to his original plan and go straight out for about three kilometres and then watch for signs of fish. Just a nice easy trawl would be the answer or even a drift for snock and kob.

An hour later, the Fairey rolled in the swell, the engines dead and Vosloo was feeling very odd and quite definitely bilious as he baited up the slimy squid. From time to time, he looked towards land and felt a little better as he registered on a solid horizon; the old fisherman's trick which always seemed to work. But he couldn't understand the sick feeling because he'd been ski-boating for about seven years before he got his own boat. Fifteen years on the water and it was a very rare moment when he felt seasick. The shoreline seemed to blur as he watched it and then a big black-backed gull swept low over the boat and he turned to watch it wheel in the sky above him, and suddenly he felt faint.

Slightly worried now, he put the line over the side at the stern and wedged the rod under the port motor and let out line. It was deep here and the sinker went down and down until it stopped it at around one thousand feet, then he sat down heavily in the swivel chair. He sat still, holding the rod and staring out over the stern, trying to focus and wondering what in hell was the matter with him. Finally, he put the rod under his left foot and lay back, trying to relax and take a deep breath which just didn't seem to want to come. He felt thirsty and remembered the water in the polythene bottle in his old haversack and groped backwards into the bow locker with his right hand because his left arm felt a little stiff and seemed to ache dully as if it had been bruised badly. He pulled out the cool-box and briefcase and eventually found the bottle and lifted it out, fiddling uncharacteristically to undo the screw top.

Then he felt the unmistakable knocks transmitted along

275

the thousand foot of line and up the length of the glassfibre rod. They thumped clearly through the sole of his gym shoe and, as always, his heart leapt and he grabbed the rod and struck upwards and slightly to the side making sure that the hooks would hold. He stood up clumsily and began to reel in smoothly and then felt the mighty blow deep in his chest and the huge pain which shot down his left arm. The agony was such that he screamed out in a raucous shout which startled the wheeling gulls and made them shear away.

The clot which had formed in Vosloo's bloodstream almost six months earlier had finally lodged in the coronary artery which supplies the lung and brain with much of their vital blood. Vosloo's love of dairy products, like cream and cheese, and his vast appetite for such fatty meats as pork and lamb had fatally thickened the walls of his arteries and if he had not suffered the massive heart attack he would probably have succumbed to an occlusion within the next few months.

Vosloo's lack of exercise and his sedentary life in the police station had also contributed to the slow circulation of his blood and a tendency towards thickening of the arteries. The clottings formed by his heavy cholesterol intake, his excessive weight of over 212 pounds and a more than average intake of alcohol were all that were required to push his heart into a condition of crisis. He was to be fifty-three years old at his next birthday in December.

Now he gaped up at the intense blue of the sky and momentarily seemed to see everything with extraordinary clarity. The pain was intense so that he seemed to have trouble drawing breath, and his face had paled to a deathly grey. Sweat stood out on his upper lip and forehead and he took two stumbling steps towards the stern and overbalanced, trying to bring up his left arm which seemed somehow to be numb, whilst hurting terribly at the same time. With the blood supply to heart and brain cut off to a virtual trickle, Vosloo reared upwards once more and bent backwards in agony. Then he fell, slumping sideways to wedge in between the two engines, his head and shoulders in the water. With his last breath he took in a great draught of seawater which flooded into his lungs but he failed to taste it or choke because he was already dead.

The extra weight over the stern of the boat was too much and *Marlin* shipped water, slowly at first and then a big roller swept all the way to the bows and she settled by the stern, the weight of the big Suzuki taking her under. Vosloo floated free and rolled on the surface for a few minutes and then the remaining air bubbled from his lungs and he sank, following his boat down into the icy depths of the Atlantic. Into the sea which had always fascinated him and which now had claimed him permanently.

The leather briefcase, containing the De Kock docket and the report on Manfred Meyer floated free of the ski-boat and, buoyed up by trapped air, was tossed about by the swell for almost thirty minutes. Eventually, it became waterlogged and the weight of the Walther pistol carried it below the surface of the blue-grey waves and it turned gently over and over as it sank slowly through 1200 feet of water. Vosloo's boat rod, with the two snoek and the one big kob still on the hooks, was dragged deep by the frantic lashings of the three fish but the weight of the rod and reel eventually exhausted them and they flapped weakly on the bottom. Later they were taken by bigger predators which came inshore to feed in the hour before nightfall. Gulls swooped down to snap at the thawing block of squid which broke up in the increasing swell and finally, when it was all gone, they swept up into the stiffening breeze crying mournfully. They circled for a while and then, as the twilight began to gather, they broke off and winged away to follow a fishing boat into Hout Bay harbour.

In the days that followed, Vosloo's body rolled about on the sandy bottom and was taken by a group of small basking sharks which snapped away at the carcass, causing it to twist around like a log of light wood in the surf. Other smaller fish rummaged among what was left inside the sack of Vosloo's clothes and the larger bony pieces of him were dispersed about on the ocean floor in an area covering several hundred square metres. The sharks worried at the briefcase and eventually it fell apart and the papers inside rotted and disintegrated.

Celeste Vosloo telephoned SAP Seapoint at 6.30 that evening expecting to find that her husband had returned there for some reason. When she heard that he had not been seen since midday, the first pricklings of alarm caused her stomach to flutter and turn over uncomfortably. She asked Sergeant Mortimer if he would check with the harbour master at Hout Bay and call her back.

Mortimer telephoned immediately and was disturbed to hear that the harbour authorities were about to list Vosloo as 'suspected missing'. He jumped into the station's Ford Granada and shouted for Constable de Klerk, telling him to telephone Mrs Vosloo and tell her the bad news. Mortimer headed for Hout Bay in the twilight and glanced out of the window at the calm and friendly Atlantic, glassy and peaceful, on his right as he followed the coast road over the mountain. It was inconceivable that Hendrik could have drowned, he was such a careful sailor. Mortimer bit his nails as he pushed the three litre Granada round the gentle curves fast enough to make the tyres wail in protest.

Navy helicopters from Simonstown were out searching in the dusk when Mortimer arrived but he had the hollow feeling in his stomach that proclaimed Hendrik to be dead, and with those sort of hunches he was never wrong. The search continued from first light the next morning but by lunchtime it was declared that Major Vosloo was 'missing presumed drowned'. Mortimer had given up the vigil and gone home at midnight.

Mostert was appalled by Vosloo's death; more so than he would ever have imagined possible. He and Lorraine spent most of the weekend with Celeste Vosloo, trying to

278

give what comfort they could to the distraught woman. Celeste kept cursing Vosloo's boat, describing it as a bloody dangerous death trap but Mostert knew that some ill must have befallen his friend because Hendrik had been more than capable on the water. And the weather had been perfect, the ocean like a mill pond all weekend. It was odd to think that Hendrik was out there somewhere, maybe five or ten kilometres off shore, and countless fathoms down in the cold silent depths. Mostert shuddered and swallowed his large brandy in one gulp. That one was for Hendrik, he thought bitterly.

For the deputy director, Vosloo's death was untimely and irritating in that it frustrated the progress of what was becoming his pet project. The Security Police in Cape Town attempted to trace other officers who had been around at the time that Meyer was arrested and were instructed to interview them when found. Only two were discovered and both had long since left the force and were of little help. A second cause of aggravation was the fact that the deputy director was trying to put together a profile on Gerrit de Kock without raising the suspicions of the man through his employers in Windhoek or Parrow in the Cape. The staff of SAP Seapoint had reported that Vosloo had been putting together just such a document himself but there was not a trace of it in the station, nor of the docket on his sister Tina.

Sergeant Mortimer and his constables went through all the records and ransacked Vosloo's untidy office to no avail. Mortimer recalled that Hendrik had always taken his old briefcase around with him and as this, and his service pistol, were missing, he deduced that the briefcase had very likely been with his superior when he met with the accident at sea. When these facts were communicated to the deputy director he swore and threw a brass ashtray – that his wife had given him and which he had always hated – across the room. As the ashtray boomed off the plaster wall, leaving a sizeable chip in the cream surface to mark its passing, the deputy director swore aloud and muttered to himself 'Why the hell did the old fart have to take the bloody files fishing with him?'

All they had been able to find on Meyer was the 1974 entry in the occurrences book. He had spent a day and a night at the State's expense and then after hurried arrangements with the German consul, had been deported via Johannesburg on a scheduled Lufthansa flight. That was it, and there was nothing on De Kock at all. As expected, Bonn clammed up and came back with tactful and diplomatic jargon which was a polite way of saying sorry, we're not telling. The deputy director had cursed anew when he read the brief telex and pondered whether he could safely have Meyer watched in Berlin by agents operating out of the Bonn embassy. This operation was becoming very expensive and there had already been a few mutterings from upstairs. But to hell with that, the deputy director was certain of his direction as far as AFRA was concerned and the loss of Vosloo in his stupid boat were just minor irritations in the broader sphere of combatting the enemy. Something was going to happen, he could feel it in his water.

CHAPTER 18

Nicholas Mohapi had died by misadventure, blown to pieces by a faulty fuse on a Russian TM 52 anti-personnel mine. Together with him had been Robinson Llennon, a young Ovambo that Nicholas had been training. Lucas would have been there too had it not been for the fact that he had eaten some rotten meat and been confined to bed by that idle bastard of a doctor who had done the right thing for a change. Now, as Lucas read the few papers that were all that remained of his two comrades' short lives, he shivered, sobbing, thinking of the mangled bodies that they had buried. Nicholas's head had been blasted from his torso and ripped by shrapnel but he had still been recognisable and his face had had a look of surprise, mouth open and eyes wide and staring in disbelief.

First, Lucas read the diary of young Robinson who had been on a few sorties across the border and last year had accounted for a Boer farmer and his wife with a dusk ambush just outside Ushingo. The words were childish and poignant and told of the bitterness of their struggle and the lack of organisation, supplies, ammunition and, most important lately, food. But they reflected accurately the difficulties they had experienced recently and the way that the South Africans had harried them, searching them out wherever they were, often well inside Angola. Even he, Lucas, had begun to despair because the losses had been so severe.

Robinson had written in English in his large juvenile

handwriting: 'Oh how the Boers caught us when their airplanes came. They were so sudden and we had no chance, poor Henry died and many other of my comrades. We were just about to move, to fulfil our plans when they came and seventeen of our comrades died.' On another page Robinson had continued with his tale of woe and Lucas admired his understanding and intelligence; he had had no idea of the young man's knowledge.

'The situation is bad and I think that the enemy receives information about our operations in advance. Our defences are not as they should be and the enemy have far better weapons, also our tactics are not as they should be.' Tears came to Lucas' eyes as he read on:

Generally, our combatants are starving. We eat once a day and often go on combat missions hungry. We cannot be fed by the people in the kraals because of drought and their crops which have been destroyed by the enemy. Some of our combatants have turned into thieves and others have defected because of hunger and because they return from long combat missions and there is nothing to eat.

The result of all this is demoralisation and defections which are becoming more every day. War also plays its part in all of this, but everyone is just human. This week we had only fifteen bags of mealie meal to feed more than fifteen hundred who are already hungry and, apart from the desertions to the enemy, there have been some suicides in the field.

Lucas read on, fascinated by the insight of the young soldier who had been happy and a confident youth on the surface. There had been no inkling of the emotional undercurrents in his character and the bitter, almost pathetic feelings he had about the struggle. But he had kept on fighting and shown great courage and had wanted to learn everything; that was why Nicholas had been going over the mine-fusing procedure with him.

'My friend Christopher killed himself today,' Robinson had written against the date of 11 March. Lucas remembered the date well. 'He put the barrel of the AK in his mouth and pulled the trigger and he left a note saying that it was because of the suffering and that he could no longer continue.' A few weeks further on there was a reference to the South African's psychological warfare on the local population, a factor which was worrying officers like Lucas:

> The enemy-organised UNITA bandits are helping the enemy to drive the people into a sluggish state of obedience and collaboration and the enemy will pay up to R1500 for information. The general situation is tense because the Boers are all round us, inside Angola and across the border in Namibia. All the time the enemy constructs new roads and airfields to mount more operations against us and to prevent the infiltration of our comrades to the south. She conducts secret movements and hides herself from the masses.

The diary ended on a note of desperation:
'Yesterday my old school friend Samuel Kamatundu died when the enemy attacked us using helicopter gunships and commandos, we cannot go on like this.'

Lucas closed Robinson's dog-eared diary and put it away with the few possessions he was sending to the boy's mother. He looked out of the hut window at the arid scrubby bushland, bright and harsh in the sweltering sun of midday. He had been dreading opening the tatty brown envelope which lay on the plastic table in front of him because he knew it was for him, had been written just two short months ago. Nicholas had kept no diary but the letters had been a thing between them both. Nicholas had kept one too from Lucas.

He had found the letter inside the battered tin box in which Nicholas had kept his money, his camera and the letters from his girl Leni. It had been there inside the tatty plastic wallet, a brown dirty envelope, together with the one he had written. He opened the one with his name on and saw that Nicholas had added the words 'Only to be opened if I am killed.' They had exchanged the envelopes in this very room and then laughed to break the seriousness of the occasion and got very drunk on some rough Polish vodka.

My dear brother and comrade Lucas. Now I am dead and our enemy has claimed another young life. But my blood has been spilled for our cause, for our Namibia and I know that whilst you still live, you will carry on the fight. Tell my Mother that I died like a man and please, will you remember me that way my brother Lucas.

Sometimes I was very afraid when we were in the bush fighting the enemy. I hope that you were not ashamed of me, you were such a fine comrade to have and a great strength to me and our other young men.

I have been very afraid lately. Sometimes I have thought that I am to die soon but I suppose that I was lucky to have lived so long. Sure, we have killed a few of the Boer swine you and me. But everybody's luck must run out some day. We talked often of the struggle and the great Soviet Union which one day we were to visit. Now you must go alone dear friend but I know that you will see everything through my eyes too because we were as one my brother.

Tell my Leni that I have never loved another but say that she must forget me now and make a new life for herself, find a new man, perhaps you my brother. She always admired you.

One day we will carry this fight across the borders into Azania into the cities where the Boer racists rule our people by tyranny and by guns. We will kill them there in their homes. Perhaps you will take part in this great event and how I wish that I could be with you.

Lucas was crying now, great splashes of tears running down his cheeks to smudge the black ink and the large round letters. It was as if Nicky were there, watching him in the room.

'Do not cry for me dear brother. Carry on the struggle and kill the oppressors of our people. Save our Motherland and do not mourn me because we will surely meet again one day in heaven because our cause is right.' It was signed, 'Your brother in war, Nicholas.'

The mine had been detonated two days earlier at ten o'clock in the morning at the forward training camp sixty kilometres north west of Rocadas, almost two hundred kilometres inside Angola. Nicholas had been instructing one man at a time and had practised with the mine with three others before Robinson had stepped forward to take his turn. The TM 52 is a plastic-cased general-purpose device which can be used against light-armoured vehicles which it is powerful enough to blow apart, should the detonation occur under the centre section. The one they were using was supposed to have been made safe by a Cuban instructor who had first demonstrated it six months before. He was long gone now and back in Luanda, or maybe even Havana.

What had made this mine explode could now never be determined but Lucas was thankful that the thing had gone off in the specially prepared basin where fusing demonstrations were held. The banks of earth and gumpoles had absorbed all the blast but one of the group had been watching from the bank above the safety level and a piece of shrapnel had torn through his shoulder, almost amputating his left arm.

Robinson had virtually ceased to exist as he had been bending right over the device and they had not found any pieces of him much bigger than a matchbox. Nicholas's body had been partially shielded by the crouching pupil but his head had been clear and this had been cut from his body and flung over a hundred metres away. The rest of the charge had blown his torso and limbs from each other and there had been little left of him to bury either.

Lucas had been in the tent hospital at the time but the wind from the blast had clapped against the side of the canvas shelter like a giant fist and he knew immediately that there had been an accident. He had hurried from the pile of soiled blankets on which he lay, and tottered groggily to the makeshift weapons range to find a metre-wide crater in the ground. There were smoking rags scattered around the hole and one man was screaming and clutching a dangling arm whilst two others were vomiting with reaction. It was some time before he realised that the bloody mess of olive green denim was all that remained of Nicholas.

He had screamed at them and ranted in his anguish but now it had penetrated that he would never see Nicholas again and he read the letter once more and then burned it in the dirt of the hut floor. He dried his eyes and sniffed, wiping the sleeve of his shirt under his running nose. Nothing would ever be the same now that Nicholas was dead. The two of them had been like brothers, had survived South African ambushes, aircraft and gunship attacks and three major raids on their camps by enemy commandos.

In four and a half years in the field, they had together survived forty-three contacts with the enemy and were battle-hardened veterans and more than capable guerilla soldiers. Despite all this experience, Nicky had died uselessly, killed without anger in a terrible, yet thankfully painless accident. Lucas cursed the unknown assembly plant worker in some Russian munitions factory who may have taken his or her eyes off a die-casting machine for a few vital seconds. Perhaps that was the reason, or maybe it was the Cuban captain, that silly adventurer who affected Che Guevara dress and beret and smoked the filthy-smelling cheroots. Maybe he had miswired the mine and it had taken all this time to make some sort of contact. They would never know now.

But Nicholas had been right about the plan to hit the South Africans hard and right in their home base. Lucas had mentioned the brief outline to his old comrade and they had both been excited at the plan and liked the daring procedure which should completely outwit the enemy. It was all going ahead and on the very day that Nicholas had died he had received a communication via Luanda that there was to be a meeting in Maseru, Lesotho in early November. He was to fly there from Mozambique, a place where he had spent two months in 1977 training in plastic explosives and demolition techniques. For once, there was no apparent problem about money and it was all set up, his ticket for Maputo, via Lusaka, would be sent with a complete itinerary. Poor Nicholas was to have accompanied him and Lucas's mouth set in a bitter line and he sat down on the hard wooden chair and put his forehead on the soiled cream plastic top of the table. After a while he sat up and pulled the cheap block of lined notepaper towards him. He would write first to Robinson's mother and then Nicholas's and save Leni to the last.

CHAPTER 19

Gerrit and Tina had enjoyed their two and a half days in what was to them the Mother City. They had visited a few relations in Bellville and the Flats and Gerrit had tidied up the loose ends of Koos' affairs. There had been no money left and the rent was owing for two months on his small bachelor flat and Gerrit had sold the hi-fi and tape deck to pay these arrears. The few other belongings he gave to a young cousin. During their stay he had managed to dispose of the Audi which Gail had left with a friend at Metricor and he had seen Marais who had been solicitous and apparently genuine in his condolences over Koos' death. The unseen Security Police had tailed them everywhere using various different operatives, cars and motorcycles but had nothing of any substance to report to Pretoria. The De Kocks had behaved like holidaymakers.

SA 250 was to leave Johannesburg at 1600 hours for Windhoek where Gerrit was to deplane leaving Tina to carry on to Frankfurt where she would arrive next morning. Two security policemen in plain clothes watched the brother and sister leave D.F. Malan airport Cape Town on the early afternoon airbus to Johannesburg. One of the men, a young swarthy thick-set type dressed in jeans and T-shirt, licked his lips and grinned at his older companion.

'*Ag* Pierre man, she may be a *skollie* that bird but she's the best piece of arse I seen in a long time.'

His colleague, a man married for some years and with

two children and a sizeable mortgage grunted, thinking of his meagre police salary and the crippling expenses which seemed to grow with his two daughters. He shook his head thinking that the coloured girl had looked like money, real money. 'You're a fool young Piet. All you think about is *poes* man, that girl is money man, more than you will see in a lifetime I'd guess. There's more to life than *poes* my boy, I can tell you that.'

The younger man laughed, a short harsh sound of disbelief. He had met his partner's wife on a few occasions and knew her to be a blowsy, raddled old cow. Christ, he wouldn't touch her with a barge pole the sour-faced bitch. But he knew about women, he'd had his fair share for his age and was prepared to bet that they far exceeded poor old Pierre's ration. Life and women he knew about; he could tell Pierre one or two things that would make his hair stand on end. The two men watched in silence as the big white airbus with the orange tail-fin rose steeply into the air and then levelled off and prescribed a graceful turn out towards the coast. The older man Pierre, cursed beneath his breath because in truth he too had lusted aftcr the coloured girl and his groin thickened as he imagined her naked and spread apart for him. He thrust his hand into his trouser pocket and thought of his wife and her greasy hair and pinched mouth, and the way she complained day in and day out.

What had happened to the bubbly blond he had married only thirteen years ago? He didn't feel any older, didn't look that much different to the way he had on his wedding day, but she was a disaster now, fat and unkempt. At the thought of her, his lust subsided and with it the erotic image of the beautiful coloured girl who was up there in the aeroplane, as unreachable to him as she would be on the ground. He caught young Piet grinning at him knowingly and he felt old and jaded suddenly, but he snorted to cover his embarrassment and tried to cover up his inadequacy with bravado.

'What the frig do you young bastards know about

women anyway. You think you've got all the answers you buggers these days, you drive me bloody mad with your smart notions.' He tried to think of some other clever remarks but could not and snarled at his junior in irritation. 'Come on Romeo, let's get back to town.' Piet followed him out demurely enough but Pierre felt the complacent smile burning into his back and fumed inwardly.

The first-class flight to Windhoek was comfortable and they were cosseted and plied with drinks as they had been on the outward journey. Gerrit was sorry to leave the big safe aircraft but he was deeply upset to say goodbye to his sister. Tina kissed him in the transfer hall at Windhoek as they called the onward flight.

'I'll be in touch from Willi's office, darling Gerrit. Thank you for everything my dear, dear brother.' Tina's eyes sparkled with tears and she looked unbelievably beautiful. Was it possible to fall in love with your own sister? Gerrit thought irrationally. 'We'll see each other again very soon, don't worry,' Tina added and there was a catch in her voice.

Once again Gerrit sensed the unaccustomed tears in his eyes and he kissed her brusquely and walked quickly away. He watched the winking tail-lights of the huge Boeing as it taxied out, the cabin lights making a yellow glow against the blackness of the surrounding bush. The engines roared to a crescendo and the huge aircraft gathered speed ponderously and seemed to rise gracefully into the air at a surprisingly low speed. Once airborne, the lights dwindled quickly but Gerrit watched them until they disappeared completely.

After the night, cocooned up there at 35,000 feet, whispering through the hours of darkness, she would be back in Frankfurt. Only two short weeks earlier it had been him on the plane and he remembered the restrained excitement. Now everything had changed and he felt older and wiser. So much had happened and somehow something had gone out of his life with the death of his brother,

290

yet that void had somehow been filled by the love of his sister. Gerrit caught the South African Airways bus into Windhoek and walked the short distance from the terminus to his apartment lugging his suitcase, briefcase and flight bag through the deserted streets. It was warm and peaceful and the city was very quiet in contrast to the busy European centres he had just left, but it was just as he remembered it. Have I really been away? he thought. Is AFRA real, is it a force to be reckoned with and, should we succeed, how will all this change?

Manfred stirred in his sleep and tried to blot out the persistent ring of the telephone. It went on and on and he groped for the light switch and looked at his watch; it was 3.10 in the morning. The call was from Russell in the London telephone exchange and the message was brief and to the point but it succeeded in rousing him into a state of excitement. He lay awake until dawn, thinking of his second trip to London and the meetings with Hoyle and Anderson. Now he had just heard that in the first week in November he would be going to Lesotho, Southern Africa, for a meeting with some key SWAPO and UMSA men. With him would go the two Germans he had been liaising with in Berlin.

One of them was the girl Ursula Hartmann and Manfred's hand strayed to his crotch as her image came to his mind. She was a typical *Deutsche fräulein*, a slender beauty with flaxen hair, wonderful unfathomable blue eyes, and a brain to match. Her political beliefs were frantically anti-establishment and definitely left of centre.

The man was Wolfgang Krug, a dark taciturn little economics graduate whose parents had been born in *Deutsche Süd West Afrika* and who, like Hoyle, had rejected his colonial ancestry. He had despised the white regime that remained in Africa long enough to take militant action against it. Hartmann and Krug were both in their mid-twenties and typical of the post-war middle

291

class German society which sired such contemporaries as Andreas Baader and Ulrike Meinhof. Berlin, in particular, had always been a hot-bed of radical political activity born of the transitionary student population. In the cafés and beerhalls, the jazz clubs in the condemned buildings and the hash-smoking parties in the old warehouse apartments, the language of revolution was discussed by ardent young anarchists many of whom had formidable IQs.

The left-wing backlash that these children of Hitler exhibited could not be altogether unexpected. They had seen their parents' generation reviled after the atrocities of the concentration camps were exposed and the late sixties saw them turn to socialism as an idealistic way to lift the stigma of the Nazis from their generation. Organisations such as the AStA (Allgemeiner Studeten Ausschuss) or General Students Council began quite innocently but their clashes with the police and authority in general resulted in an escalation into total anarchy and the formation of the RAF (Rote Armee Fraktion) or Red Army Faction better known as the Baader-Meinhof terrorist gang.

This was the first group within West Germany which was able to organise an underground urban guerilla movement. At the start of the seventies it made world-wide headlines with forays into suburban banks and running battles in the streets with the West German police. Although the gang members, who were eventually arrested, would always claim to be 'political prisoners' they were branded by the authorities as common criminals and their allegations that they were 'fighting imperialism, capitalist exploitation and obviously, fascism' fell upon deaf ears.

But their war against what they termed 'an imperfect society' gained them more than a little sympathy, even in West Germany itself. Here the rich dilletantes thought it fashionable to be left-wing even whilst they enjoyed the trappings of Europe's highest standard of living and most materialistic society.

The effective end came for the Baader-Meinhof group in June 1972 when Baader and two compatriots were arrested on the first day of the month in Frankfurt. Only a week later, Baader's lover Gudrun Ensslin was tracked down in Hamburg and after a further eight-day hunt Ulrike Meinhof was caught by police in Hanover. At vast expense to the Federal Government, these five languished in a specially constructed prison (cost US$4 million) and enjoyed the attentions of the world's press which built up to a crescendo as the trial started in May 1975. Needless to say other terrorist organisations such as the Palestinian PFLP and PLO agitated mightily on behalf of their German 'cousins'.

International links between terrorist organisations had become par for the course in the early seventies and Black September liaised with Baader–Meinhof and the Japanese Red Army; info-centres were established in major world cities to aid in weapons supplies and logistics.

While Ulrike Meinhof was a respected, if notorious, journalist in West Germany Andrea Baader was a pampered Mummy's boy who had never done an honest day's work in his life. Baader exhibited all the psychopathic characteristics of the sixties youth and the RAF was a means to an end for him; a marvellously legitimate way of committing mayhem and anarchy against a society which had never given him what he wanted. The fact of the matter was that Baader was unfortunately not intelligent enough to succeed in post-war Germany on his own. Ensslin and Meinhof were to be the catalysts for his new lifestyle, eventually his pop-star image and finally his martyrdom.

Within this still catalytic society, Ursula Hartmann had found satisfaction in a just cause to fight. On the surface she had not changed from the affluent-looking young lady she had always been and had never favoured the cause of the great unwashed. Not for her, that cult of the mid-sixties which had changed the face of the world's youth in a snowballing reaction that is still being analysed by psychiatrists today and which will probably be the cause of some fascination to the anthropologists of the future.

Uschi Hartmann affected smartly casual clothes, wore French underwear, drank Remy Martin and Southern Comfort and liked Rive Gauche by Yves Saint Laurent, because on her the perfume evoked an aura of summer wild flowers and aristocratic summer eroticisms. Such lusts that she had she did not restrain and considered herself totally emancipated sexually.

Uschi was very beautiful and had attended excellent schools and, lastly, a finishing academy in Geneva. She spoke English and French fluently yet she despised the parents who had given her all the things she had ever wanted. Her father was managing director of a fair-sized chemical engineering concern in Duisberg near Dusseldorf and the company had thrived in the few good years between Germany's two wars and expanded by leaps and bounds in the new affluence of the seventies. Uschi had an independent income, from shares that had been invested for her by the family, and a sizeable monthly allowance from her father. For her twenty-first birthday she had been given a white Porsche 924 Turbo and had been allowed to choose all the furniture for her apartment from Roche-Bobois. She was spoiled, very bright and highly dangerous.

Wolfgang Krug's background was almost totally opposite to that of Uschi Hartmann's. Born in Bremen in 1954, Krug came from a working-class background and had experienced a childhood which had been filled with hardships and suffering. His parents had hated Germany and constantly referred to the idyllic life they had left in *Süd West Afrika* and his father never let a day pass without cursing the fact that they had left that wonderful sunshine society of ex-patriots. The Germany of the fifties and sixties had offered little to the morose and bigoted Thomas Krug and by 1971 he had eventually become an alcoholic, spending entire evenings in the neighbourhood bars and leaving his shy and inoffensive wife to bring up their neurotic child. But unlike his inadequate parents, Wolfgang had showed great aptitude at school and with a natural command of the spoken word, he would verbally lash his unfortunate mother and ridicule his absent father unmercifully. At the age of seventeen he finally left home after a violent scene in which he had tried to protect his mother from her paralytic husband; it ended when he hit his father with a schnapps bottle and walked out. Two weeks later he had managed to get a Federal government grant and secure a place at the University of Berlin for a degree course in politics and economics. The securing of a place of study in Berlin meant that Krug was exempt from military service.

The fertile and liberal campus existence suited Krug down to the ground and he became a skilled debater and, like most of his fellow students, a radical anti-government activist. Despite his left-wing sympathies however, and the odd battle with riot police, Krug had only been arrested once and on that occasion it had been *en masse* with some two hundred other protestors. He had kept his nose clean, waiting for the big one, and the authorities had no record of him as a political agitator.

Academically Krug was brilliant and had sailed through his degree in three and a half years, almost a year less than average for the course, and seemingly without any strenuous effort. He was the type who had no need to cram and study hard, prior to an examination, and merely read through his lecture notes to bring particular subjects back to mind. His ability was rare indeed and was a combination of a photographic memory and an extremely logical brain which could do mental arithmetic almost as fast as an electronic calculator.

Once qualified, Krug began a post-graduate study in economics but found it to be an anti-climax after the ease with which he had obtained his honours degree. One day, he suddenly decided to reject the idea of further academic years and, instead, ventured out into the marketplace to gain experience in commerce and industry. He worked first as a cost accountant with a small West Berlin-based herbal cosmetic company and then did almost two years of temporary work with an executive employment agency which specialised in cost efficiency and time and motion studies. The bureau had little trouble in placing the well-qualified Krug and he held a variety of posts which ranged from the evaluating of media schedules in an advertising agency to comparative data studies in a computer bureau. Each task proved simple to Krug who did exhaustive personal research in order to master each new challenge, his super-brain coping with the work load in less than a third of the time necessary for a person of average intelligence. Virtually all his temporary employers offered him permanent positions on their staff and he rejected offers of swift advancement and fat end-of-year bonuses.

Eventually he became bored. The ease with which he mastered each new challenge irritated him instead of giving him satisfaction and, like Ursula Hartmann, he searched for a purpose in life, a worthwhile goal to strive for. When an old university friend invited him to attend a meeting of two radical left-wing organisations in the West Berlin suburb of Wedding, he agreed and went along out of curiosity not knowing that he was to find his *raison de être*.

The two loosely aligned movements were the *Deutsche Freiheits Bewegung* and *Die Armee Socialer Gleichheit;* roughly translated as the German Peoples Liberation Movement and the Army for Social Equality. Of the two, the DFB had the most impressive membership and had been in existence longest but the ASG was a fast-rising movement which, it was rumoured, was funded by Middle East money. There was only one oil state that would be sympathetic to such an organisation and Krug correctly deduced that Libya was the ASG paymaster. The two movements had recently formed a tenuous liaison but the leadership struggle within the proposed coalition was threatening to tear it apart. Stress areas were obvious and centred around the age of the DFB boss and the relative youth of the ASG's Helmut Gerber.

It was fortunate for the ASG that Krug witnessed this petty bickering first hand because his inclusion in the movement was to assist it greatly in the years ahead. Within five minutes he had decided his allegiance and when the meeting deteriorated into a slanging match he left, after securing the address of Helmut Gerber. Notwithstanding the small-mindedness of the ASG and DFB hierarchy, Krug had been impressed with the zeal of the ASG leader and the strength with which he had pressed his arguments. The short visit to the meeting had revitalised his revolutionary feelings which had laid dormant since his student days. The following day Krug wrote to Gerber, offering his services to the ASG and suggesting that it remain autonomous.

That was how it all started and after only two months Krug had been placed on the payroll permanently and was put in charge of the organisation's publicity and propaganda machine. It was Krug's job to decide where best to spend the slice of the monthly cheque from Tripoli that was allowed him by Gerber and the two men became firm friends. Krug's inclusion in the ASG operating committee soon paid dividends and it was as a result of his activity that a number of new members were attracted to the movement. One of these was Uschi Hartmann.

In late 1978 the ASG set up a training camp in a portion of the Black Forest some thirty kilometres north-west of Zweisel in Bavaria. The camp was an altogether clandestine set-up close to the Czechoslovakian border where tourists and wild-life enthusiasts seldom wandered. The movement secured a fifteen-year lease on an old hunting lodge, together with fifty acres of rolling woodland, and there were several solid outbuildings and barns: Gerber's first task was to convert some old stables into fairly comfortable barracks for fifty people in which men and women would bunk together. The location was absolutely ideal for the organisation's purpose and here Krug, Hartmann and some one hundred others had learned the mechanics of modern-day revolution. They had worked with the Russian AK 47 and American M 16 assault rifles and become familiar with a variety of hand grenades of Communist Bloc manufacture. Both became adequate pistol shots and Krug showed much promise with a rifle so that he developed into a capable sniper. He used various weapons ranging from the heavy Weatherby 460 hunting rifle to the collapsible French Unique, a .22 calibre weapon which could be fitted with a silencer and was the ideal assassin's tool.

Mostert sat on an uncomfortable wire chair at a round plastic table. He was within one kilometre of his home in Rondesbosch and was eating an ice cream imaginatively described as 'English Toffee' flavour. A few metres away, three coloured youths swarmed over his white Mazda with sponges and rags and suddenly sprang back as if by pre-arrangement, when a fourth switched on a high-pressure hose and blasted the little car with hot water. The Jetsetter car wash was a recent addition to Rondebosch's suburban services and for only three rand one could get a really good interior and exterior clean; with hot jet wax no less.

It was almost one month now since Hendrik Vosloo had failed to return from his afternoon fishing trip. They had not found any trace of him or his boat and Mostert suspected that he must have sunk in very deep water. He personally, had never felt particularly safe out there, so many kilometres away from shore. When Hendrik had decided to give up fishing for the day and headed back he'd always been glad, secretly rejoicing that he'd soon have his feet back on dry land. Often Hendrik had smiled at him and Mostert thought that perhaps the older man was aware of the fear he had for the sea. But dear old Hendrik, he had never said a word, never would have because that just wasn't his way.

Now the Mazda gleamed wetly as the wax rinse was applied and Mostert finished his ice cream and sat back relaxing and enjoying the warm sunshine. Next to him a strapping youth was hosing away at a red Ford Escort in the self-wash bay. Mostert had tried that; it only cost fifty cents but by the time you'd finished you'd just about washed yourself as well. For two rand fifty difference you could let the boys do it and there was no contest, especially when you soaked yourself into the bargain. He'd ruined his best pair of bush suedes and noted wrily that the car-wash boys wore rubber boots. They knew what they were up to.

Of late, there had been no further terrorist activity in his area. Soon it would be Christmas and the hundreds of thousands of Transvaalers and Freestaters would come swarming down to the Cape, descending onto the beaches on the yearly pilgrimage from the concrete jungles and baking mealie fields up north. He'd seen them at Camps Bay and Llandudno wandering about on the white sand like overblown pink lobsters, ogling the tanned Cape Town girls who ignored them as if they belonged to a sub-species. Sometimes, they would dash into the freezing Atlantic and yelp like puppies before scampering out again, and all the while the local beach fraternity would sniff in disgust and turn over to bake their golden bodies just a shade deeper. Mostert had been down on the beach a few times lately with Lorraine and little Janine who loved to scamper about on the water's edge and build sandcastles. Lorraine still looked something in her white bikini and she seemed to keep her tan year round. He'd felt quite proud of her as he always did.

His Riot Police units had been quiet recently and he had been able to do some forward planning and catch up on weeks of paperwork. It seemed almost as if South Africa had been temporarily forgotten in a troubled world of international upheaval and ever-rising oil prices. But Mostert knew that it had to get worse, there was no way that it could get better, nobody could be stupid enough to believe that. Deep within himself, he saw the New Year as being a critical period for the country; the prime minister continued to rant about the total onslaught against the Republic but so far it hadn't come to that. But Mostert believed that it was on the cards. Like his unknown colleague, the deputy director in Pretoria, he felt it in his water.

A few weeks back, Holsworth had arrived at Mostert's headquarters unexpectedly. He'd been on leave from the Operational Area and had apparently settled now in Cape Town just down the road in Wynberg. The two men had met for drinks and Holsworth had told some fascinating tales of the war and SWAPO's latest ploys in intimidating the local Ovambos. They were getting a thrashing lately, there was no doubt about that and Holsworth had been on the recent 'Smokeburst' raid into Angola when they'd cleaned up two more bases and killed over six hundred although the newspapers had published the figure as only eighty. Holsworth had said that there were bodies everywhere and quite a few women and kids too. Unfortunately, some of these camp followers had been killed by mortars in the preliminary softening up and that was why the press hadn't been allowed in and the real facts made known.

CHAPTER 20

In London, Reginald Smith the young Vietnam veteran who styled himself as the AFRA arms advisor, had checked with his opposite number in the ASG and was looking at a shopping list of what the Germans required for the coming operation. AFRA had used the youthful lawyer Hugh Francis as a personal messenger and he had collected the list, making the return trip in one day. Hoyle favoured Francis as an emissary because he was urbane, intelligent and furthermore spoke reasonable German. Hoyle regarded an ability to speak the other party's language as a courtesy in delicate negotiations with foreigners.

The armament requisition had in turn been forwarded to AFRA as a courtesy because the London movement would not even be paying for the weapons. The ASG had their own methods of supply and could obtain weapons and explosives from various sources through any one of six countries. One of these was Mozambique and anything that the black government there did not have would be freighted in from the Eastern Zone; there was absolutely no logistical problem, the Germans had assured them. Reggie studied the list and smiled bleakly to himself. You had to hand it to the Krauts, they were bloody thorough bastards. In perfect English, the ASG had typed up a selection of arms like some sort of requisition for office stationery. Reggie read it with interest.

Item: Kalashnikov AK 47 assault rifle (carbine model –

units four. Item: KL6 fragmentation grenade – units twelve. Item: M 82/7 phosphorus grenade – units twelve. Item: Unique calibre .22 knock-down auto rifle (with silencer and telescopic sight) – units two. Item: One by half kilo sack polystyrene pellets (obtain at target). Item: five litres gasoline (obtain at target). Ammunition for the above arms: six thirty-shot magazines Kalashnikov soft-nose 7.62mm calibre, one hundred rounds .22 calibre long rifle, high-velocity solids.

Quite a party they could have had with that lot, thought Reggie. The polystyrene and petrol would be used to make bath-tub napalm. It was quite simple: all you did was leave the pellets to soak in the petrol overnight and in the morning you were left with a syrupy white slush like weak porridge. This you then decanted into thin glass bottles and used a fuse of a paraffin- or petrol-soaked rag and there you had it – a miniature napalm bomb, the latest development of the old Molotov Cocktail. When the bottle smashed against the target, the syrup splashed everywhere but, unlike petrol, it stuck and didn't evaporate so quickly. But it still burned hot and hard and Reggie had seen what it did in 'Nam, he still had nightmares about it occasionally.

Manfred had contacted the ASG on behalf of AFRA and outlined Hoyle's plan to their operating committee. At the end of his presentation he had offered an amount of £150,000 as a fee for the operation and Gerber had visibly sneered and then laughed abruptly. Slightly non-plussed, Manfred had thought that he may have to go up to Hoyle's limit of £250,000 but Gerber cut short his tentative stumblings in that direction. A quarter of a million pounds was just about one million Deutschemarks and would make one hell of a dent in AFRA's bank balance, Hoyle had said that this would be their absolute maximum.

Very surprisingly, Gerber had refused AFRA's money stating that the ASG had all the funds it needed and that it would always be prepared to fight any just cause in the

302

struggle for social equality and justice for all men and had long awaited an opportunity to assist the oppressed majority in South Africa. For Hoyle, the answer had been like a dream come true and he had immediately sent Francis over to Berlin with an effusive letter of thanks and a draft for DM200,000 which he included as a donation to the ASG funds. Enclosed too was an invitation for Gerber to visit London any time as AFRA's guest but the German had declined in the interim in the interests of security, which was as Hoyle expected. However, the pleasantries had been well received on both sides and AFRA's cheque was accepted by the ASG. The relationship between the two movements was more than cordial and it could be said that everything was going better than hoped – in fact, far better than Hoyle had ever dreamed.

The Porsche was in for service at a garage in Sloane Square and Mendelsohn stood on the almost deserted platform at Baker Street underground station. It was well past the evening rush hour and he had been working in his surgery on some case histories and had not even noticed the time until a patient had telephoned, surprised to find him still in Harley Street at seven o'clock in the evening. On the tunnel wall opposite, in this busy Bakerloo Line station, was a huge black and white poster illustrating a pair of black hands pulling apart some massive chains. Underneath was written the caption 'South African Blacks are breaking the chains of apartheid.' Below this, some sympathiser of South Africa had added a postscript in red aerosol paint 'Kaffirs will break anything.' The graffiti merchant must have taken the considerable risk of crossing the line late at night to write the message, Mendelsohn thought. Despite himself he couldn't help but smile and wondered if Van Pittius had seen it. He smiled even more when he envisaged Hoyle's reaction.

As far as AFRA was concerned, Mendelsohn knew that something big was on the go, and he had an idea that it was scheduled for early in the New Year. He had heard a rumour that Hugh Francis was to go to Africa next week and Hoyle had hinted about a 'turning point in the struggle', 'a new offensive against the enemy' and, perhaps most important, 'the elimination of a leading political figure of the racist State'. There had been something going on with Germany too but they were all keeping very hush-hush about developments and he hadn't been able to get details. Mendelsohn wondered whether perhaps Hoyle did not suspect him of complicity with the South Africans. As he considered this possibility he immediately rejected it. There was absolutely no way that anybody could know; the only ones that did were in the embassy in Trafalgar Square and presumably certain of their masters in Pretoria and surely they weren't talking.

He'd seen quite a bit of Douglas in the past few weeks and they'd managed to have the session with the twin sisters from Haiti. The whole thing had been highly erotic because they'd all got very high on some superb Mexican grass and Moet et Chandon. It had been very confusing to establish which girl was which and he and Douglas had changed places several times and the girls hadn't even seemed to notice. It had all seemed like some weird double-vision dream sequence and the grass had kept them at it for hours, or so it had seemed.

As before, he'd become oddly excited about Douglas's missing limbs and at one stage they'd touched fleetingly and Mendelsohn had felt that incredible electric tingle of awareness and he'd known that it had been mutual. But any further contact had been lost when one of the twins had put him inside her hot, wet mouth and almost swallowed him. Afterwards, however, when he was alone and he'd sobered up a bit, he remembered the moment clearly. Van Pittius had been pressing him for more details and information but Mendelsohn was afraid to ask Hoyle any questions because, since the liaison with the unknown Germans, he'd become very secretive and security-conscious. Mendelsohn just had to sit by, waiting for tit-bits when they were accidentally dropped. But lately they had been few and far between.

Among the many details that Mendelsohn had failed to learn was that AFRA had coined a codename for the operation. It was Ajax. Hoyle was pleased with the name which he had made up from the initials Azanian Joint Action Expedition. He liked the ring of it and deemed it sufficiently military; Gerber had made no comment so presumably he found it acceptable. The final planning for Ajax was to take place in Lesotho in November, as arranged, and rooms had been booked at the Hilton in Maseru under false names. The group would be eight and included Meyer, Hartmann and Krug from Berlin and Anderson and Francis from London. Gerrit de Kock would travel up from Windhoek where he was now back in residence.

Originally, there were to have been the two Africans from SWAPO, Lundonze and Mohapi and the UMSA coloured Ronald van der Walt who was based in Oshakati. Recently however AFRA had heard of Nicholas Mohapi's death and so now the total would be eight but, of these, just six would take part in the actual operation, Anderson and Francis being involved only in the planning stages. The plan itself could still change but both AFRA and the ASG had agreed that the six chosen were all the personnel required together with a local UMSA man in Cape Town.

The Germans had maintained that a certain security risk existed with the use of De Kock who was known in the operational area but Hoyle insisted, stressing that De Kock's inclusion was essential to the plan. There had been a recent letter from Windhoek indicating that the sister Tina, might 'like to visit South Africa again' and Anderson and Hoyle were considering her taking part. If it would improve Gerrit de Kock's performance, they were all for it. The ASG were incredibly security-conscious and had made their influence felt in AFRA by insisting on a tightening up of controls at the London end and no open-line telephone calls or postal correspondence. Now all correspondence was in a special code which involved a pre-determined vocabulary of loosely worded and meaningless pleasantries. Finer details like dates, places and times were all carried from London to Berlin and back by courier. Only Russell conveyed brief messages by telephone because the joint planning committee for Ajax doubted that anyone could tap a British Telecom operators' line.

To get to Lesotho, Anderson and Francis would travel on a scheduled British Airways flight to Harare in Zimbabwe while the three Germans were to make the same trip by Lufthansa from Frankfurt. De Kock would come in from Windhoek via Johannesburg and then all six would fly by LAM to Maputo, in Mozambique, and from there on to Maseru by the same airline. For reasons of security, they would all travel at different times spanning a period of five days and would rendezvous on 14 November in the Hilton Hotel. Hoyle had noted that the 14th was a Friday and that his group would miss the unlucky 13th by one day; he took this as an excellent omen. The UMSA man and Lucas Lundonze were to drive to Lesotho independently from South Africa. The small country was a favourite haven for holidaying South African coloureds and was a totally multiracial state; an island of racial harmony in the vast white republic on which it depended for most of its trade and infra structure.

Lundonze, the SWAPO lieutenant, had experienced no problems in the past in moving around within South Africa. From sources in Luanda and Lusaka he had been supplied with the various pass-books which Africans were required to carry by law in the white state. Failure to produce an up-to-date passbook meant a few nights in prison, a fine of R50–100 and possible deportation to what the authorities might deem the accused's 'country of origin'. This hated law formed the basis of many protestations against the government but Lundonze had taken note of it and was well prepared for any eventuality. In the past few years he had visited Cape Town on three occasions and Port Elizabeth once to attend clandestine meetings of the military wing of the AZAPO movement. AZAPA, the Azanian People's Army, was an offshoot of this parent organisation but had recently been blown and systematically purged by the South African security police. Most of the leading members were now dead or serving life-imprisonment terms and Lucas had heard nothing of them for many months.

Lucas's three pass-books listed him as Basotho, Zulu and Ndebele but he would choose the Zulu one for the trip which described him as a long-distance lorry driver. He spoke this language fluently and understood enough Setsotho and Ndebele to fool the average policeman who might challenge him, but for this trip he would become a Zulu and drive down in the old Volkswagen with which SWAPO had provided him over the border to Upington and then via Kuruman, Kimberley and Bloemfontein to Maseru. The VW would be fitted with Orange Free State licence plates and equipped with the necessary documentation – his pass-book listed him as a resident of Christiana some 100 kilometres north of Kimberley. He would therefore be travelling very much within his own area and there should be absolutely no problem in getting to Lesotho. His name in the Zulu passbook was Abel Mtlanga.

Ronald van der Walt was similarly equipped with papers which were excellent forgeries, provided by Luanda but originating in Moscow. He had not set foot inside South African territory since the De Waal Drive attack in Cape Town but had no qualms about the trip to Maseru; his South African passport showed an issue stamp from Cape Town in 1978 and had various date stamps from Lesotho and Swaziland. His new name was Harris Koopman. Abel Mtlanga, however, would not require a passport as few Africans possessed them in South Africa; his pass-book would be all that was required to allow him entry to Lesotho.

The important ninth man at the Maseru planning

conference would be an Englishman by the name of Simon Charles Drake. Drake had been a resident of the tiny mountainous kingdom of Lesotho for seven years, had made the country his adopted home and had prospered relatively in his chosen profession. Five years previously Drake had been involved in a petty apartheid incident in South Africa when he and a black male friend had travelled down to Cape Town on a motorcycle. Stopping at a Wimpy Bar in the small seaside resort of Knysna on the Wild Coast, the two men had sat on their machine enjoying hamburgers and orange juices outside the seafront restaurant. The Afrikaans proprietor had taken exception, stating that blacks and whites could not use the same facilities and that the carpark was a white area. No signs were in evidence and the quick-tempered Drake had told the man to leave them alone. The words he had chosen were rather insulting.

Within minutes, the local security police had arrived and both men were instructed to get on the motorcycle and follow them to the police station. After lengthy questioning and a thorough search of the motorcycle and their backpacks, the two were released and advised to return immediately to Lesotho. This they failed to do and continued with their holiday as planned, the black going to visit his family in Oudtshoorn near Port Elizabeth, and Drake journeying on to Cape Town. Two weeks later they met up again on the coast road near Wilderness and rode back to Lesotho without further incident or any problems at the border. Three months later, however, when Drake left Lesotho on a planned business trip to South Africa, he was turned back at Jan Smuts airport and refused entry for no apparent reason except that he had been listed as a prohibited immigrant. Letters to Pretoria failed ever to raise a reply and Drake began to hate the powerful white state which surrounded his adopted country.

Although the prohibition order was irritating and had cost him time and money in finding middlemen and wholesalers to handle his merchandise, Drake's business of exporting handmade articles and karakul wool rugs from Lesotho, prospered and he sent regular shipments to retail outlets and redistribution depots all over the Republic of South Africa and exported even larger quantities via Jan Smuts airport, Johannesburg. But he himself had become persona non grata within South Africa and although he could fly out of the country in transit through Johannesburg, he could not set foot over the border which was only three kilometres from the centre of Maseru.

Drake had always been a liberally minded man and the hate simmered within him through the years. He longed for an outlet – some positive yet undetectable way in which he could inflict harm on the autocratic racists to the north, south, east and west of him. Recently, Drake had studied more about racial discrimination in South Africa and become a subscriber to *Confront* which was occasionally available in Lesotho. He had travelled to London on business in late October and telephoned the AFRA offices from his hotel. Francis had met him with Anderson and another natural link had fallen into the Ajax operational chain because Drake was eventually persuaded to secret the arms needed within a consignment of rugs and artifacts bound for Cape Town. His shipments were never searched and he sent large containers twice every month. The Cape Town agent for his regular German market was Heim Import–Export.

The jacarandas were blooming in Pretoria but the luxuriant sight of them failed to fill the deputy director with the customary pleasure. Instead, the spectacular purple blooms, stretching away on the ranks of trees, reminded him of his agent in London and the boring communications that had been forwarded lately from the London embassy. It seemed that Jacaranda was failing to get any closer to the AFRA nerve centre and the reason he had given his controller was that security had been tightened up markedly. This indicated to the deputy director that

309

something was definitely afoot and he cursed in his impotence, considering his options and wondering how he could precipitate some sort of a breakthrough.

The surveillance of Meyer in Berlin had also failed to pay dividends. The young attorney had been observed making several calls to the offices of a minor left-wing organisation known as the ASG. The deputy director had not bothered to determine what these initials stood for but his man in Bonn had assured him that the movement was a tin-pot, bottle-throwing brigade of no consequence. A request for information via the embassy in the German capital had also failed to result in anything concrete. The Germans knew that the ASG existed but disregarded it as a political body and came up with an embellished description matching that of the Bonn operative; there was nothing further to go on. One interesting point was that Meyer had recently gone to London for a very short trip but Bonn had taken too long to let Trafalgar Square know and the London operatives had just missed him at Heathrow. The men watching the AFRA offices had not reported him as visiting there either but the deputy director reasoned that this could have been the only cause of his visit; he had pressed Van Pittius for details but there had been nothing else. The trail had cooled and died and then Meyer was reported as being back in Berlin. Bonn had also reported that the De Kock girl was back with her husband in Dusseldorf and her brother once more ensconced at Metricor in Windhoek where the security police had watched him for a few weeks. The deputy director had eventually called them off too and he cursed the inactivity. So far, it all seemed to be coming to a grinding halt and yet he had a feeling that somewhere, somehow it was all about to begin.

Staring out of the fifth floor office window onto the avenue below, he watched two young girls walking past, their backs arrogantly straight and their breasts jiggling under thin blouses. The recent warm weather had caused a rash of scantily dressed females to appear on the streets and, as he watched, the deputy director felt the heat rise in his groin. Immediately, he thought of Jenni Theron, of the smooth ivory skinned legs and the thick black hair which reached halfway down her back. He pressed the intercom button for his secretary and spoke brusquely.

'Ask Miss Theron to come through before five o'clock, Mrs Hoekstra, and I want no more calls, thank you.' It was already well after 4.30 and Mrs Hoekstra would be leaving at a quarter to five. There was a bottle of Ballantines in the cocktail cabinet and ice and water in the little refrigerator. The deputy director sat back in his chair and lit his thirty-second Benson & Hedges Special Filter of the day. Involuntarily, his left hand strayed between his legs as he waited for Jenni Theron to arrive.

It had started between them quite casually with the odd lunch date and then a dinner at Lombardi, the marvellous Italian restaurant to the north of Pretoria. The same week they'd driven through to Johannesburg to Le Bougain-villea and then he'd asked her back to his flat for coffee. Since the painful divorce from that bitch Marie, the deputy director had led a fairly monastic life, concentrating on his demanding job and the scope for advancement within the newly organised department which now fell under the direct control of the Ministry of Foreign Affairs. He had sold the house in Waterkloof and had bought a condominium in Lynwood which was a starkly decorated bachelor environment untouched by any feminine hand. The apartment had looked rather like an outsized school-boy's bedroom cum den, its walls adorned with photographs from his college days and the years he had spent in the South African Navy. In addition to these unprepossessing mementos, there was an antique gun, a couple of swords and some naval impedementa which included his old cap from the days on the *President Steyn*, South Africa's first modern warship. The deputy director had risen to the rank of captain in his country's fledgling senior service and had enjoyed every moment of his time at sea.

Jenni Theron had found his apartment horrendously

masculine and faintly amusing and had laughed openly at the photographs of her superior in uniform, staring sternly at the camera in a variety of poses. She admired the deputy director, rather than fancied him, but he admittedly had an undeniable male aura about him and indisputable power. She had heard of his meteoric rise in the newly reconstructed department and there was a rumour that he would inherit the position of director before he was forty. He was thought to be quite brilliant and was one of the Eschel Rhoodie protegées who had survived the Department of Information purges. Jenni Theron considered him to be a fair catch and she knew that he liked her; she reasoned that it would be a positive move to sleep with him. When she had stood, that night, making coffee in his tiny kitchen, she had felt his presence behind her and then his body pressed against her and his hands encircled her waist and then slid upwards over her breasts. He had bent to kiss her neck and she had been surprised at the strength of his maleness and her instantaneous response. The coffee had been forgotten and he had subsequently proved to be one of the most considerate lovers she had ever had.

Jenni Theron entered her superior's office at 4.55 and fifteen minutes later, with the building silent and empty, the deputy director entered her on the carpet behind his desk. Afterwards, the two of them sat on the large velvet Chesterfield, sipping their Ballantine and ice and talking about Jacaranda, AFRA and the De Kocks. The deputy director enjoyed bouncing ideas off his beautiful and intelligent operative and now he looked at her thoughtfully.

'What would you do Jenni, if you wanted to mount an operation against South Africa, bearing in mind that you are a man like Hoyle?' He smiled bleakly. 'Someone with a knowledge of the country and what makes it tick? What would be your priorities in inflicting political unrest, chaos and terror; how would you try to convince the white population that their days are numbered, that the place is

312

falling apart?' The vivacious dark-haired girl was still flushed with their love making and her huge black eyes shone as she stared at him intently. She licked her lips and smiled faintly, tasting him there. The deputy director did not miss the inflection. Jennie recalled Jacaranda's latest reports and the boast by Hoyle of an attack on an important political figure, probably early in the New Year. She began to formulate her thoughts in concise sentences.

'I would go for a target which represents our country, our way of life and our political history. Something that would threaten our democracy and our very existence,' she said seriously.

The deputy director nodded. 'Go on,' he said encouragingly.

'I would choose some sort of special occasion to attack the government or what it stands for,' said Jenni, warming to the theme. Her thinking advanced swiftly and again she bore in mind the suspected target date of early in the New Year.

She tried to imagine Hoyle's rationale, attempting to get inside the mind of the man she had tried to kill. Hoyle knew South Africa well. He had lived and studied in Johannesburg, had used the system for his education, while all the time nurturing his hate so that now he was utilising the education that South Africa had given him to plot its downfall. Hoyle would look for a way of making the whites realise that their days were numbered, his target would be difficult and yet the attack must be dramatically effective.

A vague idea began to crystallise in her brain and then her thoughts continued to progress rapidly, her mind racing through possible avenues of approach, unaware of the fact that she had been silent for some minutes. Then her eyes widened with a sudden realisation and the deputy director leaned forward beside her staring into the eyes that did not see him.

He waited and then spoke quietly. 'Yes Jenni. What is it, what do you think, what do you see?'

A shudder went through the girl as she saw the possibility

313

clearly, almost like a prophesy of doom. It was as if she could see quite positively what AFRA was going to do and the fact that she could visualise the unfolding events frightened her because they seemed to be indisputably obvious and yet that was impossible. She had been right before on such hunches but never had she tested out something of such magnitude, such terrifying possibility. She heard herself speaking and could almost stand aside, watching herself, and the effect her words had on her lover. 'I think they might try to assassinate the State President during the Opening of Parliament in January.'

Relaxed in deep-cushioned luxury, Anderson was finishing his breakfast champagne and orange juice whilst reading over the outline of the Ajax plan, prepared by Hugh Francis and his team. Below, the rolling brown veld of Southern Africa unfolded in an endless panorama from over 36,000 feet. It looked to Anderson like a mottled brown carpet dotted with irregular splotches of green. But he knew that in reality it was far from featureless, knew well the bushveld, mountains and rivers of his native Rhodesia. This would be his first visit since a swift exit in 1974 pursued by the authorities. Now, however, he was more than welcome. He read on, relishing Francis's objective summary.

In Cape Town, usually on a Friday in the second half of January, the members of the Senate meet in their respective places of office early in the morning. The Secretary of this august body reads a proclamation summoning Parliament and makes an announcement of a formal nature. A judge of the Supreme Court, usually the Chief Justice, is then announced, and under authority of the State President, administers the oath to each member. It reads as follows. 'I do swear to be faithful to the Republic of South Africa and solemnly promise to perform my duties as a member of the Senate, to the best of my ability. So help me God.'

After this ritual, the judge retires from the Senate and the Secretary asks for nominations for a President of the Senate. When the president has been elected and conducted to his chair by the proposer and seconder, and congratulated by the leaders of both sides of the Senate, business is suspended. The Senate reconvenes shortly before noon and the President is dressed in his robes of State for the formal Opening of Parliament ceremony which takes place in the Senate Chamber. In the meantime, the State President and his wife, with an aide-de-camp in attendance, have left Government House in an open motor car escorted by mounted police. Sometimes a horse-drawn carriage is substituted and in recent years, an army escort of motor cyclists has also been used.

The route to the Houses of Parliament, via Government Avenue, Adderley Street, Darling Street and Parliament Street, is lined by troops. A guard of honour outside the Houses of Parliament and selected troops from the army, navy and airforce, line the steps. Policemen from several departments are in evidence in this area and riot police Task Force units appear in camouflage, although some are there clandestinely in plain clothes. The State President arrives at the Houses of Parliament traditionally a few minutes before noon and, as he alights, is greeted with a salute from the guard of honour, and at this point he waits at the bottom of the steps whilst the national anthem is played by the brass band of the South African Navy. At the entrance to the building, the State President and his wife are joined by the chiefs of the army, navy, air force and police and after perhaps another minute they all proceed into the Senate Chamber where a fanfare of trumpets heralds their arrival.

This moment is the most important on the South African political calendar. In the last few years the event has been covered by television and relayed live to homes throughout the country; it is watched by the most patriotic as it occurs but some seventy per cent of the white population would see a rerun on the six or eight o'clock news that evening.

The opportunity for an assassin would be very much appreciated by the South Africans, Anderson knew, but the breakdown of the event that AFRA researchers had compiled served to accentuate the importance. He had copies for each of the men, and the one woman, who would attend the Maseru conference. As he closed his briefcase the British Airways 747 began its descent for Harare, Zimbabwe; formerly Salisbury, Rhodesia. Anderson smiled, the face of Africa was changing and AFRA would assist in changing it even more.

Gerrit had asked for the Friday and Monday off and Rothman had agreed without comment; both he and Schwartz had been so glad to have had De Kock back ahead of schedule that he could have asked for a week and they'd have given it to him. Metricor (Cape) had advised them of the younger brother's death and there had been two suitably refined black-edged cards waiting on the desk when Gerrit walked into his office. He had worked flat out, catching up on the backlog that the two white men had left for him in his short absence and on the Thursday night he worked until nine o'clock before leaving the office – and his desk – neat and tidy and up to date. With him had gone the blue United Nations Passport which had arrived by ordinary air mail from London. He had posed for a picture during his visit to the AFRA offices and the passport itself was an original. Only the name and address was false.

For security reasons, he had told no-one where he was going and had just booked his tickets by telephoning the South African Airways office at the air terminal and then sent the messenger down with cash to pay for them. He left on the seven o'clock flight to Johannesburg on the

Friday morning and connected with an Air Zimbabwe flight at 11.15. The smiling black stewardess in the old Boeing 720 fan-jet told him that he'd be in Harare by lunchtime and Gerrit really enjoyed the ninety-five minute flight, drinking two vodka and appletisers and reading the latest copy of *Time* from cover to cover.

His departure from Windhoek had gone unnoticed by the Security Police who had lifted their surveillance two weeks previously. As he did not actually enter South Africa, his name was not picked up by the airport immigration authorities and so the Department of National Security did not become aware of the northward flight of a person in which their deputy director had a great interest. Had De Kock flown from Johannesburg direct to Maputo, his name would have been recorded automatically, because SAA co-ordinated all LAM and SAA passenger data on that route. This was not yet the case with Air Zimbabwe, however. AFRA had done their research well.

Gerrit found Harare airport rather like Windhoek's. The same flat, rolling bushland extended from the perimeter fences and the only difference was the existence of a gaggle of small camouflaged helicopters and the odd group of black soldiers wearing combat fatigues in the same olive and brown splotches. In Windhoek the helicopters were bigger and the uniforms brown. Apart from that there was little difference. Bearing in mind the three hour wait before the afternoon LAM flight to Maputo, he decided to take the bus into the city and have a look at the infamous Harare.

To South Africans of all colours, the Rhodesian bush war had been a sign of the times and a pointer to their own tenuous position on the southern tip of what was now almost a totally black continent. SAPA, the South African Press Association, sent regular war bulletins from their stringers in Salisbury to the sensation-hungry dailies in the Republic's major centres. Rarely a day had passed without some mention of terrorist atrocities or the kill-rate

317

that the Rhodesian security forces were exacting upon the enemy ranks. In fact, the war had been a bitter, often horrendous, conflict fought in often unspeakable conditions ranging from the sweltering tropical humidity of the Zambesi valley to the cold mists and rain of the north-eastern highlands close to the Mozambique border.

To the whites of Rhodesia the war had meant a severe weakening of what was a remarkably strong and self-sufficient economy because even with the aid from South Africa the conflict had cost the country in the region of one million dollars every day. Apart from this, all males between the ages of eighteen and forty-five had to endure the vicious chameleon-like changes of lifestyle that became an everyday occurrence and averaged out at one month in the army and six to eight weeks out towards the end of the war. Despite the maiming and killing of their limited youth, the rebel Rhodesians carried on until the eventual sell-out by the British at the Lancaster House conference which spelt the end of UDI and the beginning of Robert Mugabe's rule. To the white Rhodesian, the most heartrending factor of the entire war was that it had all been to no avail.

For the blacks the war had meant victory and majority rule after eight decades of the colonial yoke. After the Patriotic Front's victory in the elections the South Africans had looked on in stunned disbelief as a declared Marxist was set up as a leader of a previously convenient buffer zone on their northern border. Gerrit had read most of the pieces written on Rhodesia and had followed the South African press reports of the progress of the fledgling Zimbabwe which had started encouragingly but graduated into thinly veiled threats of late. His half-formed ideas and vivid imagination had conjured up a picture of Harare as being a semi war-torn city instead of the sort of quiet English style market town oddly reminiscent of those he had seen recently on the outskirts of London. The main difference was that Harare seemed more prosperous. Blacks, whites and coloureds strolled apparently happily together in the streets and the shops seemed to be well supplied with all sorts of goods. There were a few soldiers here and there and he had seen a lorry load of blacks in ill-fitting grey-green uniforms on the way in from the airport. They carried short automatic rifles on their shoulders and Gerrit recognised these from pictures as AK 47 Russian weapons. The blacks had been laughing and joking in their truck and one had given him the black-power salute. To Gerrit, Salisbury was not unlike Windhoek or even Cape Town without the sea but it seemed more English; suddenly he knew why there were no signs anywhere in Afrikaans.

In contrast to the orderliness of Harare airport, Maputo was an unkempt dustbowl of a place which Gerrit had heard only managed to keep going with the assistance of the South African Railways and Harbours Department. Admittedly he had read that in the Cape Argus recently. The rattling old Fokker F-27 Friendship only had twelve passengers on board, one of whom was a striking blonde girl who looked out of the window, seemingly fascinated by everything she saw. The Fokker prop-jet had refuelled and gone on to Lesotho after an eighty-minute delay and the blonde rejoined the flight after sitting close to Gerrit in the dirty, humid transit hall. There had been nothing to see except the featureless airfield and little sound except occasional bursts of rapid Portuguese and inarticulate English over the public address system. There had been soldiers here too, and one of them had stared insolently at the girl who totally ignored him. Five blacks and one Indian joined the flight to Maseru which was scheduled to arrive at 6.50 in the evening. LAM only did this round-trip once a week and nobody really knew whether the flights would keep to the schedule. There had been talk of cancelling the Lesotho run which could never be profitable on present bookings.

By the time the Friendship laboured in on its final approach to Maseru's tiny airport, Gerrit had experienced enough flying for one day. He looked out of the fogged-up

319

window as the Fokker wallowed down, clawing at the thin mountain air, its engines alternately revving harshly and backing off to a muted warble. In the mountains, not one kilometre from the landing strip, the shadows were lengthening, turning the inhospitable slopes into deep purples and reds; the late evening sun had already set and the last rays lit the sky with a fiery glow. It was a spectacular and crudely beautiful sight but largely lost on Gerrit. He had been flying all day, prescribing an elongated oval which had spanned almost four thousand kilometres of the bushveld, desert and semi-tropical scrubland of Southern Africa. Now he felt jaded as he collected his single suitcase in the cramped arrival and departure hall and walked outside to the little forecourt where a Volkswagen microbus waited; it was signwritten with the words Lesotho Hilton. The blonde was just ahead of him and the driver was stowing her two suitcases in the luggage compartment. There were no other passengers.

That evening, the eight Ajax operatives met together for the first time. Dinner in the hotel's comfortable à la carte restaurant was a relaxed affair and fairly late because Gerrit and the girl had showered and changed first. Ursula Hartmann looked fresh and immaculately groomed in a stunning black silk dress cut low to expose the tops of her lightly tanned breasts; she was obviously aware of the seven pairs of eyes that appraised her but remained aloof and politely detached. Anderson and Francis were casually dressed, tanned and healthy looking after two days of relaxation in the clear mountain sunshine but Manfred Meyer was as sallow-looking as ever as he greeted Gerrit like an old friend, gripping his hand and looking into his eyes with genuine pleasure. The other German, Krug, was very different, taciturn and reserved but he shook hands and bowed very slightly in the typically Aryan manner which Gerrit had noticed so recently in Nuremberg. The two men from Namibia were equally restrained, Van der Walt in sports jacket and slacks giving a cool firm handshake whilst the handsome, safari-suited Lucas

Lundonze merely smiled briefly and nodded, not even offering his hand. Gerrit noted that the girl watched Lucas covertly and licked her lips as if in anticipation.

The atmosphere remained cordial however, and Krug and Meyer drank sparingly while Francis failed to touch his glass at all. Anderson, Van der Walt and the black were soon onto the third bottle of wine and finished it before the main dish arrived. Uschi Hartmann still watched Lucas and declared her intentions by filling up his glass for him. To the rest it was obvious that the sophisticated blonde girl had chosen the black man for herself but if Lucas realised it he gave no sign.

In fact, Lucas had noticed the girl looking at him and had watched her covertly from the first moment he had set eyes on her. The state of arousal she engendered in him had caused him to squirm occasionally in his chair during the long meal and when her hand touched his as she handed him the glass of wine, an almost electric vibration seared his fingers. He had drunk almost an entire bottle of red wine and had eaten a huge steak and many chipped potatoes and the food and drink lay heavily on his stomach. When Anderson passed the snifter of brandy across to him he took it feeling confident and relaxed yet inwardly heated. As far as the company was concerned, they all seemed great guys to Lucas in his mild inebriation. For whites they were exceptional, he thought, and the woman was something else again, quite incredible. He had had a white woman once before but she had been a raddled Portuguese whore whom MPLA friends had supplied in Mozambique and had smelled terribly. He had done it with her but it had been as if she were an animal and he felt little better himself.

Anderson recognised that the team all needed time to wind down and get to know each other and thus no specifics were discussed and the operation was only mentioned once briefly by Francis who merely assured everyone that all systems were go and that they would sort out the finer details in the next two days. The dinner finally broke up around 11.30 and by then Lucas was slurring the odd word and was obviously feeling his drink; Anderson wondered just how they were going to handle him. It was obvious that the black would never forgive being even politely embarrassed and that he was trying desperately to remain in control of himself.

Concerned, Anderson watched as he stood and then Uschi Hartmann's arm went out and took Lucas's and he heard her soft assurance. 'I'll look after you Lucas, don't worry.' Her soft voice reached all of them and Lucas turned haughtily and then relaxed smiling into her face. The heat rose in him anew and he allowed her to lead him away from the table and mumbled goodnight to the others. His eyes took in the candle light and the black and white faces of other late diners a few of whom were dancing to the three-piece combo. He saw them all as a sort of blur.

The girl was surprisingly strong and she guided him to the lift and the doors closed on them and then seemed to open again almost immediately. They stepped out onto carpet which seemed unusually soft beneath his feet and he looked out of the corridor windows down on the lights of the main street of the dusty little city. He felt like a God.

He sensed her hands in his jacket pocket and she found his room key and then the door was open and she was guiding him into the warm, softly lit interior. Gently she steered him to the bed and he lay down and closed his eyes and she was gone and then the room seemed to spin and he felt the nausea rising in his stomach so that he struggled into a half-sitting position against the padded headboard. And then she was there again, back with a huge glass of iced water which he drank greedily. She opened the window and the fresh, cool night air revived him a little and then she went away and he heard her rummaging in her handbag and then water running again and she was back with two small white pills and a second glass.

'Take these Lucas, they work fast and you'll soon feel

better,' she said softly and he opened his eyes and looked into her beautiful face and took the tablets like a child.

He tried to stay awake but his eyes closed involuntarily and he seemed to doze for a while and then he felt her hands on him, gently moving over him and taking off his clothes. When he was naked he seemed to feel more awake and the breeze from the window felt good against his skin and then she pulled him upright and helped him off the bed and into the tiny bathroom. Lucas allowed himself to be carefully manhandled into the shower and Uschi adjusted the water to a pleasant lukewarm flow. 'I'll be back in a second,' she whispered.

After a minute the shower door opened and Lucas stared through a fine stream of water at the golden body. His eyes ran up from the slender legs over the small dark-blonde triangle of fine hair on her lower stomach, up past the narrow waist and over the firm pink-tipped breasts. Her hips and breasts were paler than the rest of her tanned skin and her whole body was firm and yet voluptuous like those Lucas had seen in the American magazines that he kept in his locker back in the base. As he stared at her she smiled and looked down at him and the warm water ran over him like gentle caressing fingers and he began to harden. Her eyes widened and she stepped into the shower with him.

Uschi Hartmann indulged herself completely with this wonderful black animal. She imagined him stalking through the jungle, loping along, muscles rippling and gun in hand with his comrades. He was a finely tuned killer, an incredible specimen of black manhood and she imagined herself at the mercy of him and his men, wantonly spread out for their pleasure. The fantasies continued as she stroked his smoothly muscled body, corded and solid from the thousands of kilometres he had walked, and marked with the scars of many battles. She kissed the gnarled stump of his right index finger and caressed his hairless mahogany coloured flanks, he smelled peppery and yet clean like a freshly washed dog and she took him in her mouth, revelling in the size and strength of him and finally she moved him to her and offered her own perfect body and he responded like the thoroughbred animal he was, thrusting into her like a wild thing until she gasped with pleasure and pain.

Before dawn, he slept exhausted and she left him, the muscles of her lower body aching where he had pounded her. She slept dreamlessly until ten and then awoke refreshed and showered luxuriously before joining the others by the swimming pool. Lucas was already there and he lay on a yellow canvas sun mattress wearing faded olive green shorts. The colour combination looked wonderful and she walked over to him and stared down at his body. He seemed to be sleeping but then he noticed her shadow and sat up smiling, motioning for her to lie next to him.

Anderson and Francis smiled with oddly fixed grins and Meyer looked over her head whilst Krug ignored her totally. Uschi didn't care because Wolfgang was impotent, she knew that because once after an ASG meeting he had plucked up courage and tried it with her. She had been happy to let him but the poor man just couldn't manage it. She smiled at them all, cool and confident. 'Did everyone sleep well?' she asked guilelessly and Ronald van der Walt laughed in genuine pleasure and broke the frozen atmosphere of the moment. Gerrit smiled too and spoke directly to the beautiful blonde girl whom they all secretly desired. 'Lucas ate an enormous breakfast,' he said. 'How's your appetite this morning Uschi?'

That evening they all met early in Anderson's penthouse and coffee was served. Gerrit stood by the window with Lucas and Van der Walt looking down over sleepy Maseru. Lesotho had previously been the British Protectorate of Basutoland and there was now a great deal of financial aid flowing in from the European Economic Community and FRIDA, The Federation for the Research and Development of Africa, which was very much EEC and World-Bank-sponsored. Still, Maseru itself was a tiny outpost of civilisation in what was really a very backward country. As in most African states one only had to drive a couple of kilometres out of the town centre, as Manfred and he had done this afternoon, to witness the poverty and filth. Gerrit smiled to himself. He wondered fleetingly what was happening to all the millions of dollars that were being sent to Lesotho annually. The Lesotho Bank was building a huge new office tower which could be seen clearly from his vantage point; as for the balance, he supposed the Minister of Finance and the rest of the cabinet did not stint themselves for creature comforts.

The Hilton was built on the ridge west of the town centre and the hotel's designers had tried to impart an indigenous atmosphere and a mountain cave type of interior which is so much a part of Lesotho history. The resulting cell-like concrete structure and massive vaulted lobby must have pleased the interior designers but the shuttered concrete and generally unfinished rusticity was a technique which had fallen short of authenticity. The cathedral-like hush which existed, at virtually any time of the day, was hardly in keeping with an international hotel. The rooms were quite luxurious however, and Anderson's top-floor penthouse suite had a couple of comfortable sofas and a boardroom table which could seat eight. After a few minutes Francis called the meeting to order and, in his soft English public school voice, began to outline the final details of Ajax. They all listened attentively, expressions wrapt.

That evening, the exporter Charles Drake dined with Anderson, Francis and Gerrit. The others were pursuing their own interests; Krug, Meyer and Van der Walt in the ten-pin bowling alley and Lucas and Uschi Hartmann within the more private confines of her room. The arrangements with Drake had been satisfactorily concluded and Gerrit would arrange with Tina for the safe storage of the arms once they reached Heim Import–Export in Cape Town. The decision had been made to include his sister.

The consignment, secreted within layers of handwoven

mohair rugs, would be freighted from Maseru on 5 January and the target date had been set for 23rd, a Friday of the same month. Ajax now had the green light in all departments and Anderson was delighted with progress.

The next day, Manfred Meyer and the other two Germans were to leave Lesotho on their return journey via Johannesburg to Europe. They would each travel on different airlines but Krug would be on the same South African Airways flight as Gerrit, to Frankfurt via Windhoek. Manfred would travel by Swissair to Zurich whilst Uschi Hartmann would go by British Airways to London. That Sunday night, after the bowling, Manfred and Gerrit sat in the bar talking idly of Germany and Tina. Both were secure in the knowledge that Ajax had a great chance of success and that there was at least the possibility of considerable damage being done to the hated racist system in South Africa. Neither had any serious qualms with regard to the risk factor of their own involvement.

CHAPTER 21

Henry Duvenhage was Pretoria's resident operative in Maseru and had lived there for fifteen years operating a successful business in imported farming equipment. The backbone of this was the Massey Fergusson tractor dealership for Lesotho, a company fronted by blacks but actually owned by Duvenhage. Henry was talking to an established contact, John Mungthlele, the assistant night manager at the Hilton. The two men sat in the coffee shop drinking Castle lagers and discussing the hotel guests, especially those from overseas. The meeting was a regular twice-weekly occurrence and Duvenhage always paid for the beers and often slipped Mungthlele a twenty rand note. Young John was thus more than happy to chat.

'Man but we've got a good looking chick in at the moment,' said John to Henry, rolling his eyes back into his head in the classical African gesture of amazement. 'She's the original ice maiden. A German with blonde hair and blue eyes and a body like you can't believe. She's been shacking up with a black guy, mean-looking sod who doesn't talk much, but it does however show you the superiority of the black man. In certain physical perform-ances our reputation is not exaggerated.' John paused for effect and imagined himself with the blonde girl, Christ he'd shoot his load before he got anywhere near her he'd be so excited.

Duvenhage smiled slightly trying to mask his annoyance. He could never manage to picture any white

327

woman sleeping with a kaffir and even the idea revolted and almost outraged him. Oh, the blacks were OK here in Maseru, he had quite a few black friends like old Percy from the bank with whom he drank regularly down at the Holiday Inn. He'd also laid quite a few of the local girls through the years and some of them had been outstanding like that little Miriam the waitress from the Italian restaurant, but somehow, in reverse, black on white, so to speak, it seemed to refuse to gel. He realised that his Afrikaaner upbringing back in the Freestate was responsible.

'She on her own then, John?' he enquired vaguely.

'No man, there seems to be a group of them,' said Mungthlele. 'Two other krauts and a couple of coloureds and two guys from England, although one looks like he could be ex-colonial; you can always tell because they tan so quickly. I'd say that he could be a Rhodesian, he's got that sort of clipped accent, a bit like yours but faster.' Duvenhage's interest quickened as John continued.

'They've had a few meals together and today they all locked themselves up in the Rhodesian's suite and we sent snacks and sandwiches up there twice, but no drinks. They must be having some sort of conference I'd say.' He paused, thinking. 'Oh, and they've got plenty of money man, hell they tipped the room service waiter five rand, no shortage of cash there.'

'Any locals come to see them?' asked Duvenhage.

'Not to my knowledge,' said John, 'but I can check that out with the waiters, they know all the locals and they'd remember.'

Duvenhage passed the twenty rand note swiftly across the table. He was not observed by any of the other diners; there couldn't have been more than a dozen of them in the whole place. 'You're a star, old Johnny boy,' he said brightly and the black smiled.

'I'll call you at your office tomorrow if there's anything else Mr Duvenhage,' said John, all politeness in his role of employee.

Duvenhage nodded. 'There'll be fifty bucks for you if you can get photocopies of their passports for me John. That should be no problem, eh?'

Gerrit casually watched the exchange from the adjoining bar where he and Manfred sat in a corner, partially concealed from view by a rustic concrete pillar. He recognised the unmistakable features of the Afrikaaner and knew that the young black man was on the hotel staff. Slowly he swallowed his drink, not listening to Manfred now, then he saw the twenty rand note flash across the table; it was a furtive move, not one which was supposed to be noticed although even had it been above board it would still have raised his suspicions. Gerrit pressed himself further into the corner and turned to Manfred, 'Let's see Anderson, quickly,' he said. 'I think we might have been rumbled.'

At about 10.30, Anderson phoned down to reception and asked for Mr Mungthlele by name. Mungthlele came on the line and Anderson reported a theft from his suite, some travellers cheques were missing, he said. Would Mr Mungthlele come up immediately.

Gerrit, Van der Walt and Anderson sat at the long table and Francis answered the door and ushered Mungthlele in. The young Basotho looked worried, visualising the general manager's reaction to the theft and cursing the fact that it had happened on his shift. He found it odd that Mr Anderson did not seem to be bothered or upset and then Mr Francis asked him to sit at the table, and held out the chair at one end. Francis took the chair at the other end and Mr Anderson and the two coloureds flanked him.

Francis offered him a drink and John began to wonder what was going on. He smiled uncertainly and asked for a scotch and water and the good-looking young coloured got up and got it from the little bar. Then they all sat again and John waited, curious and a little disconcerted.

'Good news, Mr Mungthlele,' said Francis in his most impressive courtroom voice. 'We've found the travellers cheques, they had slipped down the back of the couch in this wallet.' He gestured to the thick leather folder in front of him. It seemed to be completely full of notes. 'But I thank you for coming up so promptly and while you are here, there's something we would like to discuss with you.'

He sat back and placed his hands together in a steeple, his eyes bored into those of the young black. 'You know Mr Mungthlele, we've really enjoyed this short stay here in Lesotho, and we've especially enjoyed the Hilton, you have a fine hotel here.' He looked around the table at the other three men. 'I think we'll be back again before too long, eh chaps?' Anderson, Gerrit and Van der Walt nodded solemnly. 'However,' Francis continued in that beautifully modulated voice which John Mungthlele envied so much, 'we are here on very important business, business that could mean a great deal to your country.' He paused dramatically and even Anderson, who had seen these performances before, was impressed. Gerrit found himself hanging on every word. 'Do you follow me so far, Mr Mungthlele?'

John nodded, fascinated by the smooth authorative voice.

'Now we know that you've been talking to that Afrikaans gentleman,' Francis continued and Mungthlele's eyes widened. Gerrit thought of the phone call to Drake and the confirmation that the man described could be Henry Duvenhage, a wealthy local, who was known to work for the South African government.

Francis went on, 'We know that man might like to find out some details about us, eh. Is that not so John, may I call you John?'

Mungthlele nodded mutely.

'The position is,' Francis continued conversationally, 'that we do not want you to tell that man, or anybody else, anything about us or the people we have seen whilst we've been here. We know you have our passports in your safe and we realise that you could easily photocopy them on that nice new Minolta copier you've got down there in the front office.'

330

John Mungthlele was astounded, it was as if this young white man could read his mind. He squirmed in his seat, for once pleased that he had black skin because otherwise he would have been blushing furiously.

The aristocratic-looking barrister paused for effect and watched the young black's discomfort. Nobody spoke but the four men continued to stare at John who began to feel very uncomfortable. He realised that they expected him to say something.

'I wouldn't do anything like that, sir,' he mumbled. 'It's more than my job's worth.'

Francis smiled condescendingly. 'We hope not, John, we truly hope not,' he added quietly. 'Because if you were to do any such things, anything that might become harmful to our interests, we'd be sure to find out. You see, John, we have many friends here in Maseru, friends who have powerful connections.'

Gerrit marvelled at the innuendo, the impression of a vast network of nameless, faceless, determined men.

Francis's voice had now somehow become sinister. 'These friends would tell us you see, John, and then we would know where the information had originated from wouldn't we?'

Now all five men were under Francis's spell, the AFRA group staring hard at the young black, unconsciously taking on the character of those he was describing. Francis continued the assault.

'You do believe me, don't you John?'

The black nodded trying to summon outrage or even angry frustration at being held; subjected to this inquisition. He found himself unable to do so because he was frightened of Francis. John believed totally in what he had heard, he thought of Duvenhage and shuddered, imagining the consequences.

Francis began again in a more friendly tone. 'We're prepared to offer a little incentive to help you remember this conversation, would you like that?' he asked smilingly. Even though he realised that the worst was now over, John could not speak but he nodded again. 'We thought perhaps five hundred American dollars might help to keep our passports snug in your safe, John, until some of us leave tomorrow of course, would that be acceptable?'

For perhaps the tenth time the assistant night manager nodded mutely but this time he managed to speak. 'Yes sir, very acceptable sir, I promise I won't say anything else about you sir,' he muttered and inwardly cursed his stupidity for admitting that he had spoken to Duvenhage about the group.

Francis's eyebrows arched dramatically and he leaned forward and drew the fat leather document case towards him. John's eyes widened when he saw the thick wads of various currencies. 'What did you tell that man, John?' said Francis softly.

The young Basotho outlined the details of his conversation and confirmed Duvenhage's identity as a known South African agent.

Francis masked his concern at the permutation of risks. 'Does he know when we are leaving, John?' he asked casually.

'No sir,' said the young black, 'I didn't tell him that, sir, because you left your bookings open for twelve days, sir.'

Francis smiled and nodded. 'When did you say that you'd see him again, John?'

Gerrit and Van der Walt exchanged glances and Anderson looked stonily at the table top in front of him.

Emboldened, John spoke up brightly. 'I said I would contact him again when I had any further information, but he'll be in here again on Wednesday definitely. He always comes in on Sunday and Wednesday nights when I'm on duty; he likes to know about overseas guests, you see.'

When John Mungthlele had left, after a second and more sociable whisky, Anderson and Francis discussed the threat of Duvenhage's surveillance to the Ajax project. The two whites were sure of his allegiance but Gerrit was less certain that the black would keep quiet for very long.

He did, however, concede that it was unlikely that he would talk or do anything while any of them were still at the hotel. Francis and Anderson would be the last to leave on Tuesday morning; tomorrow was Monday and they would all be gone by midday. Not before time it seemed. Gerrit felt that the faster he could get back to Windhoek, the better.

Duvenhage had watched the news review on television which had been full of all sorts of crap about Israel and bloody Taiwan, a new trading partner of South Africa. He really had to admit that his country's television service was diabolical; technically it was superior but the programme content was dreadful. Thank God he was able to get some good videos from the States via a contact at the UN in Maseru and lately a few dirty ones at that. The local porn king was an Israeli who ran the shows for the sex-starved South Africans who came to gamble and screw the local hookers. Duvenhage had seen the Israeli's films because he always gave private showings to his cronies; often the prints were so scratched and patched up that one missed half the action.

Browsing through the Sunday papers, which were also full of garbage, Duvenhage sipped his second large whisky and thought about the group of foreigners that young John Mungthlele had told him about. He had considered telephoning Pretoria but there would only be some stupid duty officer on tonight, it being Sunday. He finished the second whisky and dismissed the thought, beginning to doze off in his comfortable leather armchair. Outside the french windows, the crickets chirped contentedly in the balmy night air and the faint burble of the swimming pool filter could be heard from the garden.

Duvenhage decided that he'd phone Pretoria in the morning, just to be on the safe side, but young John would get him those photocopies of the passports, which would go off to Johannesburg in the diplomatic bag on Tuesday morning's plane. They'd be in Pretoria by lunchtime of the same day.

As he drifted into sleep, Duvenhage realised that he'd have to rouse himself and get off to bed. Christ he couldn't drink like he used to. Two beers and a couple of scotches and he was buggered. As his mind wandered, vicarious thoughts began to enter his subconscious. The main erotic vision was one of a beautiful blonde girl being mounted by a rampant black man. In his shallow sleep Duvenhage erected, his mind presenting the picture with incredible clarity, so that he heard the gasp from the girl as the man entered her. The gasp was actually his own because the glass had slipped from his fingers spilling ice cubes into his lap.

Two days from the end of November, SAP eight battalion were still entrenched in the now solid heat and humidity of Katima Mulilo. The weather was bordering on the unbearable and daily salt tablets were issued to everyone. With the daytime humidity content often in the upper nineties, any liquid drunk sprang out immediately under arms and on foreheads. In the mess, men asked for beers off the shelf rather than the fridge because the cold ones just made them sweat more.

The young men of Reilly's platoon – he had been made a sergeant in October – were listless and bad tempered in the torrid heat. Such was their discomfort that they were even disinclined to play volleyball, the national game of white Caprivi, and spent their time-off in the shade, reading and grumbling about the oppressive, ever-present heat. Reilly himself suffered badly from the heat and spent most of his spare time sweating in his bunk in the barracks. It was pure hell in this Godawful eastern Caprivi and he couldn't wait for Christmas when they had ten days off back in the States. The wondrous stroke of luck came that morning, a Sunday, and was revealed by Lieutenant Bester at the church parade. Bester announced that they would be going to Cape Town in late January for a special duty, at this stage classified. Reilly and the others were quick to work out that they would only be back in Katima for two weeks before they'd get this second reprieve from insects, heat, absolute stinking shithouse weather and mind-boggling boredom.

The duty had not been revealed to NCOs either but there would be two platoons going and Bester had said that there was to be some precision drilling practice to be done before the occasion. Reilly surmised correctly that they were to be part of the State President's escort during the opening of parliament celebrations.

CHAPTER 22

Tina Heim received the letter from her brother in her Dusseldorf apartment and took it into the toilet to read, even though she was quite alone. Gerrit had taken no chances and had referred only vaguely to the possibility of her visiting Cape Town in January for another short holiday. Reference was also made to 'Christmas presents' which would unfortunately arrive too late for Christmas at Willi's. Could she try and make sure that there was someone there to receive them because he would hate them to be returned to sender? Gerrit and the AFRA planning committee had thought it highly unlikely that Pretoria would have been able to arrange a tap on Tina's home telephone in Dusseldorf but even so they had played safe and Gerrit indicated in the letter that she would receive a call between 9.30 and ten o'clock in the lobby of the Excelsior Hotel in downtown Dusseldorf. She must be there at 9.30 on the second Wednesday in December. Willi Heim would be at his office by then and Russell would be doing a relief day shift at the West London exchange for a friend from Sierra Leone. It would be no hassle for him because his course at the London School of Economics ended on Friday the 5th.

Mendelsohn was very anxious to obtain additional information on what he knew was an AFRA build-up for some operation out of the country. It could only be South

Africa, he felt this fact in his bones and it seemed Van Pittius had wind of it too because he telephoned twice weekly, pressing for details which Mendelsohn found it impossible to obtain.

In increasing desperation, he telephoned Hoyle at the AFRA offices saying that he had an amazing blue movie which they could show at his flat any day that following week. Any night that would suit Hoyle would be OK with him. Hoyle listened as Mendelsohn described the video tape which featured two fourteen-year-old Eurasian girls and a very well-built black man. Mendelsohn said that he knew Douglas would love it and he could invite the Haitian twins along again; they were always good for a laugh. As Jane would be in the Seychelles on a modelling assignment for the entire week, Hoyle agreed to spend Thursday evening with Mendelsohn. He had resolved to try and give up such indulgences but it would never work he knew; he thought back to the last occasion a few days after the fund-raising ball and his groin tightened in anticipation.

The young gynaecologist made an immediate telephone call to a reliable supplier of first-rate marijuana and watered-down LSD. That evening he contacted the twins who expressed delight at being invited again. Mendelsohn put down the receiver and rubbed his sweating palms together. He poured himself a large Glenfiddich and water and cursed the lousy situation he was in. This could be the last chance, he thought worriedly and groped for a valium in his desk drawer. Without it he knew he'd get no sleep that night.

It had been dark for two and a half hours and it was cold and wet when Hoyle stepped out of the AFRA Mercedes at seven o'clock on Thursday evening. He instructed the driver to return for him at two o'clock in the morning and hobbling fast on his new German alloy articulated leg, he reached Mendelsohn's porch and pressed the bell looking up eagerly to the dimly lit window on the second floor.

Hoyle had already enjoyed two whiskies in the privacy of his office and Mary, his secretary, had administered to him with great tenderness and considerable skill. She had brought him to the brink of his climax with her incredible mouth and he had been hard pressed to control himself and had just managed to stop her in time. As usual, she had asked no questions.

In the sumptuous apartment, Mendelsohn had laid out Eastern-style cushions on the deep-pile carpet and these were placed in front of his big 75cm colour television. Sandalwood incense burned in the half darkness and the large sitting room was warm from the central heating and a glowing imitation log fire which was actually fuelled by North Sea gas.

The girl who opened the door to Hoyle was blonde and blue eyed and had the lightly tanned skin of a Scandinavian. She wore a loosely fitting white kaftan which Hoyle could see right through because she was standing in front of the nearest table lamp. Mendelsohn stood behind her with the two Haitian girls who were similarly dressed in white cotton lounging pyjamas.

'This is Eva, Douglas. She's a patient of mine and a model. She loves this sort of evening, don't you sweetie.'

Eva turned to Mendelsohn and smiled and then looked at Hoyle, licking her lips in a profoundly provocative gesture. Hoyle's pulses quickened. Christ, he thought, three women. Thank God I saved it for later.

Aloud, he said to Mendelsohn, 'It seems as if you have surpassed yourself, David.'

They watched the video twice because it was so erotic. There had been plenty of champagne and a few joints and the girls had got very turned on and started to do all sorts of things to one another. First the two blacks had started on the Swedish girl and then she had gone down on Mendelsohn whilst Hoyle took her from the back. Then Mendelsohn had done the same with one of the Haitians and Hoyle had just lain there watching and drinking champagne and trying to recharge himself. He'd managed

338

it after about twenty minutes and after an age had exploded into the blonde girl's mouth whilst one of the twins held him trying to squeeze out every last drop from him. There had been more champagne, oddly sweet to taste, and then he remembered little except that there had seemed to be hands all over him and magically he erected once more. It was all incredible and seemed to go on forever.

Mendelsohn had taken very little champagne and had only pretended to smoke the joints. He watched Hoyle and waited until after eleven o'clock. The three girls were asleep in a black and white tangle in his huge bed where he had gone with them when Hoyle passed out. Now, Douglas lolled on the cream corduroy sofa, naked, his feet up on the marble coffee table, the painted alloy leg looking strangely obscene. He was conscious and occasionally sipped from a glass of champagne at his elbow whilst his good foot moved in time to the Jackson Browne song on the hi-fi. Douglas's eyes were closed but Mendelsohn began to talk quietly to him, asking him about AFRA's progress through the past year and what the prospects were for the next.

Hoyle muttered a few short curses and ground his teeth and then he sat almost upright and took a long draught from the flute of Moet et Chandon. Then he opened his eyes wide and spoke quite clearly. 'Ajax will do the trick,' he said. 'That will teach the white fascist bastards a lesson!'

Mendelsohn waited again and sipped his own champagne. Casually he lit another joint and hummed softly, idly to the soft song of Jackson Browne. When he spoke it was almost an aside. 'What's Ajax, Douglas?' he said softly.

Hoyle's foot stopped tapping and he slowly sat up and looked blankly at Mendelsohn. 'Don't you know about Ajax, David?' Mendelsohn said nothing but shook his head vaguely. Hoyle still looked at him and was about to say something when he paused and seemed to think about it. The reply, however, was very much as it had occurred within his mind and as such was the worst that Mendelsohn could have expected. 'If you don't know about Ajax, there must be a good reason, David.' He paused again and became almost brusque and very lucid. 'Sorry old man, I can't tell you any more.' As he sank back onto the sofa a small worm of suspicion stirred on the edge of his consciousness.

Mendelsohn picked up his joint and took a deep draw. His hands were steady, successfully masking his disappointment. 'That's alright Douglas, I know you'll tell me if and when you're ready.' Hoyle nodded, foot tapping once again. For the moment the matter was obviously closed but Mendelsohn had a sinking feeling that he'd been as close as he would ever get; in fact possibly a bit too close.

Van Pittius called him at home early on Sunday morning. Outside it was still black night and the wind was gusting in from the river, blowing the rain against the window panes. Mendelsohn cursed in half sleep and turned over, trying to ignore the soft buzz of the telephone. Eva stirred beside him and he closed his eyes and pressed himself against her wonderful firm buttocks. She murmured and moved back towards him but still the telephone went on and on. The radio alarm registered the time as 7.10 when Mendelsohn finally switched on the bedside light. For a winter weekend in London, such an hour was regarded as being half way through the night because sensible people would not even stir until after 9.30.

Mendelsohn, however, was used to being woken at all hours by patients, an unhappy fact which made it impossible for him to unplug the damned instrument and obliterate such invasions of his privacy as this. 'This is Dr Mendelsohn,' he said into the receiver.

Van Pittius' cloying yet clipped tones answered him. 'Good morning, dear doctor. Not so nice today though is it, eh. I'd rather be back in the old Transvaal at this time of year, in fact any time of year if it comes to that. Hell, but it must be bloody wonderful there right now, eh man?'

Mendelsohn did not comment but even in the soft bed, underneath his featherlight German duvet and warmed by the beautiful body of Eva, he felt the cold fear creep into the pit of his stomach. Van Pittius continued.

'Do you have anything new for me, doctor, any news of our friends in South Kensington?' Mendelsohn swallowed trying to lubricate his dry, foul-tasting mouth. 'Only a name Mr Van Pittius, just a name for the operation. I tried for other details with their number one man but he clammed up.'

'I see,' said Van Pittius softly, 'and the name, doctor?'

'It's Ajax,' said Mendelsohn hoarsely. 'I'm sorry, but that's all I've got. I tried as hard as I could,' he ended hopelessly, sounding like a schoolboy talking to his father and trying to explain a bad report. Van Pittius seemed to realise this and compounded the impression.

'Not very good, is it doctor, not very satisfactory at all.' A threatening tone was now evident in the hated voice and Mendelsohn shivered under his covers. 'I'll call again around mid-week, doctor. Perhaps then you'll manage to get us something else, eh? You know of course that my principals are most interested as to your progress.'

Van Pittius broke the connection without saying goodbye and Mendelsohn had an immediate mental image of faceless men in dark suits sitting in tall office buildings halfway across the globe. He lay there thinking of those men in Pretoria and the power they controlled, the vast wealth they had to draw from. How many press-ganged agents like himself did they have around the world? How many poor bastards who had committed some small transgression of their ludicrous rules and regulations like smuggling currency or gold? God almighty, it was his father's money and the old man should be allowed to do what he pleased with it in a so-called democratic Western society. But of course South Africa wasn't that at all, it was a fascist-inspired military dictatorship where the majority of the people held subservient positions whilst working their arses off for the good of the white minority.

The fear was still there in Mendelsohn when Eva stirred again beside him, sliding her hand up his leg, groping for him in the dark. She found him limp and tiny like a small boy and Mendelsohn reacted harshly, pushing her hand away.

'Can't you ever get enough? Christ, go to sleep and forget it, or go and sit on a bidet full of cold water,' he said roughly. Eva shrugged, she had been dreaming of the huge black in the video tape which they had watched again last night. The man was an incredible specimen with a thing like a donkey which made her wet just looking at it. Poor David was more than a little lacking in that area but he was pretty good when he was in the mood. Very imaginative. She suspected that he knew so much about women from his work that he knew just what to do to turn them on. She smiled to herself and rolled over. It was still dark outside and she could sleep for at least another three hours and perhaps David would feel better in the morning.

In fact, Mendelsohn did feel better and managed to service his healthy bedmate before breakfast. Later they sat in his study with the desk light on reading the Sunday papers and listening to the rain still lashing at the windows. It was daylight now, even though it might be a dull grey daylight, and things seemed better. He felt confident that he could get some further information out of AFRA and would try a more subtle approach. He looked out of the window and saw a tiny patch of blue sky appear for a few minutes and the rain seemed to be slackening. Van Pittius was right about one thing, the weather in the Transvaal would be far better at virtually any time of the year.

Christmas would be in only ten days' time and Mostert had bought a special present for his daughter. It was a Western Flyer bicycle with five gears, a carrier on the back and a basket up front. Little Janine was sure to love it.

342

They were to go out to the old folks' farm for Christmas lunch as usual and Mostert knew that Lorraine's mother would present her yearly spread of amazing proportions. There would be other children there; his brother-in-law's two boys and the little girl of Lorraine's divorced sister Angela. She was quite a looker, old Angie, and Mostert had caught her giving him the eyeball once or twice. So far he'd resisted temptation.

As he drove slowly home to Rondebosch in the heavy evening traffic on De Waal Drive, he looked up at the wonderful wooded mountain slopes on his righthand side under which were the red tile roofs and brilliant white walls of the university. The buildings seemed to snuggle into the base of the vast rocky bastion. Cecil Rhodes had apparently had a lot to do with the impressive styling of the building and had selected the site for this, the oldest seat of learning in South Africa. Mostert wondered what Rhodes would think now about this country that he had loved so much and from where he had gone north to found his own place in history. Now Rhodesia was gone and South-West Africa was bound to follow, within months perhaps. All that was left was South Africa, a country worth fighting for, if you were white of course. The blacks from up north, egged on and funded by their communist sponsors, wanted it naturally enough. They wanted the gold and the strategic minerals like uranium and ferro-chrome, magnesium and platinum. It was all there alright, but they'd never get it by violence now. Not with the new weapons that the Republic had these days. Nothing short of an all-out effort by Warsaw Pact or NATO forces would take this country now, Mostert thought. And even then the price would be high, even higher if the recently developed small nuclear devices were used.

Mostert crawled past the place where the bus had been attacked over seven months ago and looked down into the offside gutter as he always did when he passed this spot. For months there had been small pieces of glass scattered there from the shattered windows but now it seemed they had all been cleaned up or blown away by the ferocious Cape South Easter gales. As the Mazda was forced to a halt, he looked again and saw one tiny sliver glinting in the late afternoon light. It had been very quiet lately and the school boycotts had all but blown over. But undoubtedly the spark would still be there, dormant, yet nonetheless alive, and there would be more such attacks in the future. Mostert looked at the date on his watch dial; in just over two weeks it would be a new year.

Twelve hundred kilometres to the north, the deputy director for National Security was talking to London on one of his three telephones. The unfortunate recipient of his call was Jan Ludivicus van Pittius who sat in his small office in the Trafalgar Square embassy listening to a continual barrage of words from his superior in Pretoria.

The two men spoke in Afrikaans – itself a natural code even though the line was scrambled anyway – yet clear as a bell so that Van Pittius could hear the deputy director pause for breath, could note the inhalation before the next outburst. 'In God's name Van Pittius, I need results. I have to know what is happening in AFRA. I must have some idea of the size and nature of the force which is going to attack us and where it's coming from!' shouted the deputy director.

'Now listen carefully,' he continued in menacing tones, so that Van Pittius cringed back from the earpiece he held. 'I want you to tell Jacaranda that he has two weeks to come up with the goods, otherwise his mummy and daddy will be spending the Christmas holidays in Pretoria Central.' The deputy director gave a short laugh. 'I don't suppose they'd mind that though because the Jews don't celebrate Christmas anyway, do they.'

Van Pittius made no comment, knowing that it was fatal to interrupt the deputy director when he was giving an instruction. Sure enough the harsh voice resumed its monologue. 'I want you to tell Jacaranda that we know it's going to be Cape Town and in late January at that. Tell him that we think it's going to be some sort of an effort against the State President's opening of parliament celebrations. My people here think that's highly likely. Now if Jacaranda can make contact with one of the AFRA underlings and sort of mention in passing that he knows what's going on, something like 'Is Ajax on schedule for the 23rd of January?' or 'I wish I was going to Cape Town with Ajax, the weather there is glorious at this time of year' that sort of thing, you understand Van Pittius?'

This time Van Pittius replied, although he was appalled at the deputy director's crass suggestions. 'Yes sir,' was all he said.

The voice from Pretoria continued, 'You see, if he seems to know something about Ajax, they might take it as read that he knows the lot and start to discuss details with him.'

Van Pittius listened carefully and eventually replaced the receiver deferentially. He knew that he would have to force Mendelsohn and that the time was short, in fact critically so. He considered the effect of an obvious enquiry in AFRA by Mendelsohn. After January they wouldn't really need him any more anyway so they might as well go for broke now. Van Pittius smiled grimly to himself. Now it was his turn to put pressure on. He began to dial the Harley Street rooms.

Mendelsohn was appalled, as Van Pittius had expected him to be. He protested that it would be impossible to force the issue but Van Pittius reiterated the deputy director's threat and he had to relent, had to say he would try. Van Pittius gave him the details of what was known and suspected and things began to click together in Mendelsohn's mind. Van Pittius gave him twelve days. He had to have answers by the following Monday which would be two days before Christmas.

Alone in his apartment, Mendelsohn contemplated various actions, including suicide. It was a wet, blustery evening outside but he was ensconced as usual in warmth

345

and luxury. The practice was going so well that he now only took the cases that he wanted like the sterilisation of Eva. Everything was going wonderfully, everything except the dreadful business with Pretoria. He had considered running away, trying to make a new start in the States but he knew they'd find him there too, and anyway he couldn't just live there and forget about his mother and father who would surely suffer terribly in prison. He imagined how it would effect his younger sister Rachel, still living at home in Johannesburg and realised that he could never do it.

Mendelsohn's hand shook as he poured himself his third generous glass of Dimple Haig of the evening. He thought again of killing himself. He had a bag full of pills right here in his study and just a few of them would do the job admirably. He considered a handful of barbiturates washed down with a glass of Dimple and then into his bed for a long sleep, never to wake again. A cold sweat broke out on his forehead and he knew that he could never do it, he loved life too much and in any event he didn't have the courage.

Again he thought of moonlighting to America and it was the thought of this country that made him remember Mary Jefferson, Hoyle's coloured American secretary. She had always smiled at him in the AFRA offices and he'd considered her sexually on a few occasions but rejected the thought because of her closeness to Hoyle. An idea began to grow in his mind. He'd invite Mary out to dinner then take her back to the flat for a nightcap and a bit of grass perhaps. He was sure he could make it with her and after sex, women were at their most vulnerable and he could drop the hints as Van Pittius had suggested. Of course, there was a risk factor because she might mention the conversation to Hoyle who was perhaps already wary of the questions he had been asked. But Mendelsohn reckoned that it was likely that Mary had some sort of scene with her boss – probably ongoing from time to time. This might prove a good reason for her to

346

keep quiet about going out with him. He deduced it was worth the risk; he had no choice in the matter anyhow.

Mary agreed readily enough when he called her at the AFRA offices next morning and they set a date for Friday evening. Mendelsohn considered his strategy. He would collect her from her flat in Old Brompton Road and they could possibly start off in one of the wine bars or pubs in the area or go up to Motcomb's in Belgravia which was always good for impressing the ladies. Then they would go for dinner to Le Detour off High Street Kensington or Julie's in Holland Park. After that, if she felt like clubbing, they could go to Tramp or Wedgie's and then back to the flat in Chelsea. The next morning would be Saturday so the girl wouldn't have to go to work.

Sitting quietly with his customary end-of-the-day Glen-fiddich and waiting for Mary to bring in the ice and water, Hoyle had heard his private line ring in the adjoining office and Mary's soft drawl as she answered. He recognised surprised pleasure in her voice although he could hardly hear what she said. The word 'Yes' was mentioned once or twice and finally by straining his ears and sitting perfectly still he heard 'OK, David that would be really lovely. Yes, right I'll see you Friday.'

When she came in to the office he touched her and drew her to him as he sat at the desk, but sensed immediately that she was not altogether keen, was not aroused by his hands. Hoyle released her gently and looked into the girl's soft dark eyes.

'Who was that on the phone Mary?' he asked quietly. The openness of her face seemed to close up fractionally and a shadow crossed her eyes but her voice was calm.

'Just a friend Douglas, an old pal who asked me out to dinner on Friday.'

Hoyle nodded absently and broke his hold on the girl by reaching for his Waterford crystal whisky glass. This action seemed to part them quite naturally and Mary stepped back hesitantly, half turning towards the door.

'You can go Mary,' Hoyle said in the same gentle voice. 'It's time you had an early night.'

He sat for another half an hour in the silent office sipping the whisky and staring at the Hockneys on the wall. Recalling the evening with Mendelsohn and the three girls, he remembered that David had remained strangely sober and had asked those quite penetrating questions. Now, it seemed that he was going to take Mary out to dinner, perhaps press her about AFRA planning or even Ajax which she knew quite a bit about. Hoyle was suddenly sure that Mendelsohn was a threat, was suspicious of his large donation to AFRA funds. He would have to be stopped somehow, incapacitated, put out of the picture temporarily. Hoyle recoiled from the thought of physical violence; Reggie was the one to do the job, he'd done plenty of that sort of thing in Vietnam. Reggie could handle it; Hoyle reached for the telephone.

When Mendelsohn opened the door of the Porsche for Mary, she slid in gracefully, long legs slithering easily into the small passenger compartment. Mendelsohn was always pleased by women who could get into cars properly and she looked incredible in a dove grey chintz boiler suit with an aubergine scarf at the throat. She carried a wine-coloured shoulder bag and a sequined bunny jacket which matched her silver boots and her hair was softly brushed out into a halo-like Afro style which suited her perfectly. Mendelsohn was delighted that the girl had obviously dressed with care and he momentarily forgot the reason for this date as he smiled into her rather innocent face. The generous lips parted, exposing perfect white teeth which blazed against the scarlet lipstick.

'Lovely car, David,' she said admiringly.

Mendelsohn grinned back. 'The car suits you Mary, in fact it complements your outfit beautifully,' he said, gesturing across the silver paintwork of the bonnet.

The girl smiled again, a wonderfully genuine smile of

pleasure and Mendelsohn started the engine. He had a feeling it was going to be alright and the importance of the occasion had heightened his senses so that he could smell her perfume and the warm womanliness of her. The fragrance was Opium and on her it smelled terrific, Mendelsohn made a decision.

'I've got a reservation at Julie's,' he said. 'Would you like to go for a drink or should we go and eat right now?'

The girl looked deep into his eyes. 'I'm starving,' she said. The Porsche shot off down the Old Brompton Road towards Holland Park and Mendelsohn was surprised to discover that he had an erection.

It was a cold, wet night with the sort of misty drizzle that seldom stops during December in London but the subterranean basement of Julie's Restaurant was warm and welcoming and a huge log fire glowed in the old fashioned grate. They sat in elegantly worn, deep velvet couches and drank J & B and water and then the young maître'd' ushered them through into the dining room where their first courses sat steaming on a candlelit corner table. They had both chosen the speciality of the house which was game soup followed by roast rack of lamb with Provence herbs. Mendelsohn had ordered the Volnay Hospices de Beaune 1975 which was £27 a bottle and something of an indulgence but Mary exclaimed at the bouquet and sipped the wine appreciatively.

Mendelsohn was pleased that they had not bothered with the damp and crowded wine bars. They were summer places and often cold and draughty in this sort of weather. Julie's was an institution and, of course, he was known there which made a difference. One could sit quietly, as they were doing now, and drink in each other in relative privacy whilst eating superbly cooked, invariably simple dishes. After a wonderfully light soufflé to follow the lamb, Mendelsohn ordered some Stilton and the Crofts port for himself and a Courvoisier for Mary. The waiter brought a large flask of filter coffee and left them alone; Mendelsohn realised that he had rarely felt better in any woman's company.

The girl sat at ease opposite him, her huge brown eyes occasionally looking up into his as she ate delicately yet with a good appetite. Her soft, Southern States drawl was music to his ears and when he replied she seemed to hang onto every word he said so that he realised that she was highly receptive towards him. The excitement grew within him, and when he suggested a drink at his flat, she agreed immediately. He almost decided to open the discussion about Ajax there and then but resisted, waiting for later.

'Do you like grass Mary?' he asked suddenly. The girl showed no surprise. 'I only smoke it with very special people David,' she said softly.

Mendelsohn paid the bill of £69 without flinching and added a five pound tip. As they walked the short distance to the car, she pushed her arm through his and drew close to him so that her soft, springy, perfumed hair brushed his cheek. He felt himself grow erect again.

It was late on Wednesday evening when Hoyle had finally located Reggie and he hadn't got much sense out of him because the young American black had been out drinking with his West Indian cronies. But Reggie had called the following morning and gone straight into the offices in South Kensington where he and Hoyle were closeted together for an hour. Mary had been sent out to Hugh Francis' rooms in the City with a letter which could just as easily have been posted.

Reggie had said little and Hoyle had stressed that he didn't want Mendelsohn killed or maimed. 'Try and do something that will just keep him out of it for a while,' he had said. Reggie smiled to himself in the black drizzling night, one could never tell with such operations but it was always best to be on the safe side.

With the skeleton keys he had bought in Hong Kong last fall he opened the driver's door of the Porsche and slipped into the bucket seat. The car was parked about two hundred metres from the restaurant and it was dark and misty; the old London fog, thought Reggie as he pulled the catch for the bonnet. To the casual observer he was a young man having damp problems with his exotic car; there was even a can of Holt's Dampstart to hand to reinforce this impression.

Once inside the bonnet, Reggie took a penlight from the pocket of his leather jacket and quickly found the pipe to the brake master cylinder. Working deftly, he undid the jubilee clamp with a small screwdriver until the thin hose was loose on the nozzle. For good measure, he took a slender artist's knife and made three tiny vertical cuts in the pipe; after a few seconds minute beads of fluid seeped from the rubber.

Stepping back from the open bonnet he shook his head and cursed quite loudly. He took the spray can and opened the rear engine compartment with the catch inside the driver's door. Walking around to the back he sprayed fluid into the engine and fiddled about inside. Cursing again, he returned to the driver's seat and pretended to start the car without success. Finally he slammed bonnet and engine compartment closed and locked the driver's door. He stamped off towards Holland Park Avenue smiling underneath his outraged expression. Two or three pushes on the pedal and the fluid would be gone; then it would be curtains for Mr Mendelsohn. Poor Mary, he thought idly.

They settled in the car and fastened the safety harnesses and Mendelsohn tuned the stereo to Capital Radio. His hand brushed against the girl's thigh and she gently took it and pressed it to her firm right breast.

'Thank you for a wonderful dinner, David,' she said and pressed her lips below his left ear. He turned and kissed her and her lips opened, enveloping his with her soft, sweet mouth. Mendelsohn started the engine in a state of considerable excitement and accelerated fast down Portland Row towards Holland Park Avenue.

He loved the Porsche because it was one status symbol that he could enjoy on a daily basis and, even in London, a

Porsche was regarded as a sign of having arrived. Mendelsohn's was a two-year-old 911 SC Targa and had cost him almost £13,000 with 12,000 miles on the clock. The car had a few extras like electric windows and the stereo radio/cassette and it went like a dream and ran on the cheapest petrol he could buy.

It was a wonderful machine and Mendelsohn acknowledged this and relished the car as a thoroughbred. He kept it well serviced and, as he braked at the end of Portland Place, noted that the brakes seemed a little spongey. The alcohol and the closeness of the girl dispelled any doubts in Porsche technology and he dismissed the brake-fade as being due to moisture on the discs. It would soon disappear.

As he turned left into Holland Park Avenue, up towards Bayswater Road, he pressed the accelerator a little too hard and the car fishtailed on the wet, greasy surface. The traffic was thankfully light and Mendelsohn held the slide; fighting the delicate steering and light front end, unweighted but for the fifty litres of fuel. Mary squealed in mock terror and Mendelsohn flashed a grin at her feeling masterful and totally in control of his beautiful car. He accelerated again, flicking the wheel to the right, into the skid. Oddly, the Porsche failed to respond and continued its slide to the right, towards the central island at around 70 kph. Mary was frightened now and began to shout as Mendelsohn wrestled with the wheel to no avail. Suddenly, the rear wheels found purchase against the central kerbstones and, with the revs hitting 7000, the little car flashed across the westbound lane of Holland Park Avenue towards one of the old plane trees which grew from the pavements every fifty metres or so. Mendelsohn pressed the brake pedal to the floor but nothing happened.

This course of events occurred so swiftly, that neither he nor Mary Jefferson could even attempt to protect themselves from the impending impact. The forward motion of the Porsche caused the front suspension to be driven back towards the bulkhead, right through the luggage space under the bonnet on the driver's side. The transverse fuel tank behind the dashboard was built to withstand impacts but it ruptured on the right hand side when a severed steering rod drove up into it from the mangled suspension.

Both of Mendelsohn's legs were broken but he felt nothing except a sudden numbness. He tried ineffectually to open the door on his side but it was jammed and the electrics had ceased to operate so that he couldn't get the window down. Mary Jefferson had been held securely by the inertia belt and was shaken but unhurt, except for a horizontal gash across her forehead which caused blood to flow down into her eyes. She started to scream and tried to open her door without success and then suddenly, miraculously, a blade flashed down into the vinyl Targa roof and began to slash it open and then large black hands groped to tear the hole wider. A huge Jamaican railway porter reached inside the car and pulled at Mary as she fumbled in terror for her safety-belt release.

With the ignition still switched on, the power to the front lights shorted out from an exposed bulb filament across the few centimetres to the electrical junction box below the dashboard. The shattered side light was now only 5cm from the base of the broken fuel tank and, despite the soaking drizzle, the petrol ignited with a fearsome whoosh of sound.

Mary was hoisted clear and the Jamaican fell back clutching her and spinning away from the immediate inferno. But Mendelsohn was held by his crushed legs and still belted into his seat as the Porsche began to blaze furiously. With the Targa top cut open the supply of oxygen to the fire was plentiful and Mendelsohn was only able to utter one horrible scream which rose in pitch and intensity as the petrol fire blasted the hair from his head and shrivelled the skin off his exposed face. The big Jamaican tried to get close again but several onlookers held him back and they all watched in dreadful fascination as Mendelsohn's torso slumped forward, his shoulder harness having burnt through. The Porsche continued to burn for ten minutes and the body was little more than a charred log-like shape when the fire department eventually removed it thirty-five minutes after the accident.

The accident made front-page news in the national press next morning and when the nationality of the victim was determined, Reuters and SAPA's London stringer wired copy and black and white 8 x 10in photos of the burned out Porsche to *The Star* and the *Rand Daily Mail* in Johannesburg. *The Star's* second page caption that lunchtime read 'SA society doctor cremated alive in London.' Mendelsohn's father had a heart attack when he read it and he was taken to the Brenthurst Clinic in Johannesburg where he died seven hours later.

Mary was treated for shock in the nearby Charing Cross Hospital, on the Fulham Palace Road, and Hoyle collected her on the following day at five o'clock in the AFRA Mercedes. The girl was still drugged and grey with exhaustion from the horror of Mendelsohn's fiery death. Hoyle drew her to him like a child in the back of the big car but she did little more than mutter and moan in a tearful, incomprehensible reaction to shock.

Hoyle had been oddly upset by the news of Mendelsohn and kept recalling scenes with David and the Haitian twins. He remembered Mendelsohn's quiet confidence, his wonderful surgical abilities and his continued support for AFRA which had been more than generous. But he remembered, as he had on more than one occasion, their last conversation when Mendelsohn had casually mentioned Ajax. Conflicting thoughts crossed his mind as he clutched the sobbing coloured girl to him. Was it definite that Mendelsohn was working for the South Africans? he wondered, horrified now by his own suspicions. Could that have been the only reason for David's date with Mary? It seemed impossible but at the same time it was strange that Mendelsohn should only now take an interest in the girl when it had been fairly obvious all along that she fancied him. Hoyle had known about it and had noticed the way that Mary looked at the effeminate young gynaecologist. On a few occasions he had felt odd pangs of irrational jealousy when he'd noticed her attention and obvious admiration.

He would have to ask her what they had talked about when she had recovered enough to discuss it. His thoughts raced on. It was unlikely that Mendelsohn would have mentioned anything about Ajax in a restaurant. Rather he would have waited until he had Mary back at his flat, in the seduction chamber where he could go to work on her at leisure. Perhaps they would have spent the night together, smoked some dope or whatever. Hoyle could almost see it happening and wondered again why he had become so sure that something was amiss. Well, now she would have to go, especially if the Germans found out because there was no way they would risk any security leak. But how could they or anyone else find out? If she hadn't said anything or done anything, it may still be safe to keep her.

These thoughts rushed through Hoyle's brain as the Mercedes moved slowly up Holland Park Avenue in the heavy evening traffic. Mary looked out of the window and shuddered and Hoyle cursed the driver and shouted at him, asking why he had to choose this route. As they passed the charred tree where the Porsche had met its end, Mary began to whine hysterically and Hoyle had to kiss her to stop her. As always, her closeness aroused him instantly and her hands ran down his chest and into his lap, feeling for him with a terrible desperation. When they got to her flat, Hoyle knew he would have to stay and put her to bed. She needed him desperately and he knew he would respond without any problem, yet, he felt unclean and despised himself for taking advantage of the girl. Carnal thoughts at such a time were astounding, but he had read somewhere that they were not unusual. The Mercedes continued up Holland Park Avenue and Hoyle glanced back once at the blackened tree; Reggie had done his job alright.

CHAPTER 23

Six days before Christmas, on a Friday, the entire staff of Metricor's Windhoek office were air-freighted to Rothman's farm at Swatkopmund in an aircraft hired for the occasion. The pilot was a drinking friend of Rothman's and the small air-charter company was sometimes used by Metricor for short trips within Namibia. The charges were thus not excessive and Gerrit paid the account in advance as requested by Rothman. He noted that it was only a little more expensive by air per person than the return trip by conventional motor bus.

The annual Metricor Christmas barbeque was an affair which most of the company's employees would look forward to for months. For Gerrit, it was a duty to attend and a refusal would have been considered churlish if not bad manners. When the thirty-seven staff members boarded the old Dakota aircraft at Windhoek excitement was high and many of the passengers were artificially hyped-up due to a considerable intake of alcohol since lunchtime. It was now 3.30 and the flight was expected to take just under two hours. Rothman and his neighbours shared a good dirt landing strip at Goanikontes and, even if there should be a crisis, Swatkopmund's concrete strip was less than thirty kilometres distant.

Gerrit sat next to a young secretary from the sales department and the girl looked at him with searching sidelong glances. In the euphoria of near-independence for Namibia and the not inconsiderable amount of

Christmas spirit she had consumed, the girl pressed her thigh against his and continually flicked her long, thin blonde hair onto Gerrit's cheek. The hair smelled clean and slightly perfumed and the girl herself was bright and happy. Gerrit chatted amiably enough to begin with but his mind drifted away from the barrage of laughter and noise as the old aircraft droned along creakingly, fifteen thousand feet above the arid brown bushveld.

He thought of the telex communication with Tina on the previous evening. Again he had merely asked her to visit the Excelsior Hotel in Dusseldorf and await his call this very evening at 8.45 German time. That would be later tonight in South-West Africa at around 9.45. He would be down there in the bush, east of Swatkopmund, and the great fishing port of Walvis Bay which the South Africans still claimed as their territory under an old treaty they had conveniently resurrected. The strategic value of Walvis Bay was obvious and Gerrit had little doubt that the South Africans did not require it only for its proximity to the fishing grounds.

Russell would make the telephone contact with Tina as usual and pass on the decision of the AFRA executive in London. Tina was to travel to South Africa on the fifth of January on a pretext, to Willi, of having to sort out some finances and family matters. She would coincide her visit with the arrival of the consignment from Lesotho at Heim Import–Export's offices. Because she would be superficially, yet expertly, disguised and travelling on false documents, it was presumed that the South African authorities would be unaware of her arrival. A safe house had been arranged for the Lesotho hardware with a coloured UMSA operative who still lived in the virtually white reclaimed area of Signal Hill which had previously been a Cape Malay community. This man, Daniel Malan, would secrete the arms away safely in a tiny cellar, dug under the hard-packed earth of his backyard. He would personally collect the consignment in one of his VW Combi panel vans from the despatch department of

Heim Import–Export's warehouse in Buiterkant Street in the city centre.

The Ajax equipment would be stowed inside a container of other goods but the individual packing cases would be labelled 'Handicrafts from Lesotho.' Malan's small transport company was long-established in the Cape area and it was unlikely that there would be any problem with the collection. In any case, Tina would be there to supervise the operation if necessary.

Her cover story to the Heim Cape Town office was that she had ordered some special curios for friends in Germany. It would be told as follows: there was a boat leaving within the next few days for Hamburg and Tina had arranged with her old friend Malan to run the cases down to the docks for her. She did not want to bother the Heim transport manager with this small matter and Dannie Malan was almost like family and was doing her a favour. This was the story and although the reasoning was a bit weak, Gerrit thought that it would hold up. With luck, Tina would handle the matter with her usual casual efficiency and Willi would never hear about it.

The Dakota began to lose height for Goanikontes and below, the picturesque rugged semi-desert of the South-West African veld was lit with the evening sun. As the old plane banked gently, the Atlantic could be glimpsed as a metallic copper streak on the horizon and a darker smudge marked the sprawl of buildings that was Swakopmund. Beside Gerrit, the secretary giggled and slumped theatrically against him. The babble of excited voices rose into a crescendo as the engine drone subsided and the girl, already mildly drunk, turned and looked into Gerrit's face.

'You were in another world, weren't you Gerrit?' she said softly. 'I spoke to you a few times but you didn't answer. You must have been sleeping with your eyes open.'

Gerrit smiled at her, she was actually quite attractive. 'Sorry, Nola,' he said gently, 'I was in a dream, too many vodkas I guess.' He moved against the softness of her upper arm and bent closer. 'It should be a good party, shouldn't it, it's the first one I've been on.'

Nola Streicher smiled back without guile. 'I'll make sure you enjoy yourself, Gerrit. From what I hear, you practically run Metricor.' Her lips were close to his ear and Gerrit could smell her breath, fresh, and faintly flavoured with gin and tonic. He pressed against her arm again and she turned so that the softness of her breast brushed his forearm. AFRA was forgotten momentarily.

A week later, on the day after Christmas, Manfred met with Wolfgang Krug and Uschi Hartmann in a student jazz club in West Berlin. They were to travel to South Africa separately and once there, would stay in different hotels; Krug in the Heerengracht on the Foreshore and Manfred in the nearby Capetonian. Uschi Hartmann would be ensconced in the luxurious Inn on the Square in the centre of the city. Manfred and Krug were to arrive on 12 January and the girl on the 14th. Russell had phoned Manfred a week earlier at three o'clock in the morning to say that Tina would be going on holiday to visit relatives. Manfred then knew that she would be with them on the Ajax strike. The thought of her made the heat swell in his groin although it would be highly unlikely that they would have any chance to see each other socially. But in just two weeks they would definitely be going. Ajax was on and they were committed to the attack on the 23rd. He knew it would be no easy task and accepted that some of them might die. Naturally, he could not imagine that he personally would be a casualty. All he could think of was the opportunity to knock the racists off their perch of complacency.

In Pretoria, the New Year's party had been in progress for four hours. The house in which the celebrations were taking place was set high on Waterkloof Ridge overlooking the city and was owned by a leading industrialist who had made millions out of Japanese car franchises. For him the passing year had been his best ever and on the third day of the New Year he was leaving for a ski-ing holiday in Switzerland with his entire family; five children, wife, mother-in-law and two African maids.

The deputy director leaned against the rattan bar on the elegant patio and sipped his seventh double Ballantine of the evening. Inside, Jenni Theron was dancing with a young effeminate-looking man who was a successful hairdresser and well-known Pretoria socialite. The man was dressed in very tight white satin trousers and a white silk shirt without a collar and as he moved he thrust his hips forward so that his groin was clearly visible to the onlookers. With his blonde hair and tanned skin, the young man could be described as being pretty but the deputy director detested him for his high, whining voice and fluttering hands. He could dance well though, that one had to admit.

The deputy director turned away and peered deep into the amber lights of his whisky. It had been a phenomenal year for South Africa. The gold price had almost quadrupled itself before falling back to around $600; a figure which had made the Republic many additional billions in foreign exchange and should continue to so do in this coming year. He'd heard on the grapevine that the mines were being held back as far as production was concerned and had only been running at 60 per cent capacity for the last few months. There was heady talk too that the Americans might reintroduce the gold standard, tying the dollar to gold and revaluing it upwards to anything between $1500 and $2500 per ounce. Of course South Africa could make gold a strategic weapon if she wanted by selling a sizeable portion of her gold production on the open market to single buyers like one of the Arab states. Perhaps that might just happen in the year ahead, the deputy director mused. It would serve the West and particularly America a long-owed lesson. He smiled grimly into his glass and considered Europe's oil reserves of around a hundred days and America's paltry eighteen months.

Because she was already exchanging gold for oil with the Saudis, South Africa had amassed sixteen years' reserves, even taking into account the projected rate of industrial expansion. That did not count the Sasol oil-from-coal plants which were really churning out oil now and there were still another two plants to be opened in the next decade. On top of all this, the government-sponsored oil-search rigs had recently discovered rich gas deposits off the Cape coast around Mossel Bay. Oh yes, thought the deputy director, the old Republic could look after herself very well these days and in a few years he reckoned that she would be able to point two fingers at the rest of the world. The fucking Russians included.

Although current South African lifestyle was still incredible, he'd seen the signs of an inflationary spiral reflected in property prices, new car sales and heavy retail spending prior to Christmas; up some 25 per cent on the previous year. But the blokes at the Reserve Bank knew exactly what they were doing and were keeping a careful rein on the economy, the gold production hold being a typical example. They'd allow expansion to happen slowly and methodically and, if the PM's idea of a Constellation of Southern African States came to fruition in the next decade, South Africa could become literally the power-house of Africa. Already, both industrially and commercially, the recent advances had been stupendous.

The deputy director felt happier now and just a little drunk as he surveyed the mass of gyrating bodies in the large playroom which was being used as a discotheque. But then the AFRA problem rose suddenly in his mind and even the sight of Jenni's firm buttocks jerking erotically failed to dispel the odd butterfly feeling in his stomach.

He recalled his great irritation at the untimely death of Mendelsohn. On the telex of the following morning,

Trafalgar Square had reported that the girl who had escaped Jacaranda's fiery fate was none other than Hoyle's secretary. The deputy director therefore deduced that Mendelsohn had been going for it, had been trying hard, and perhaps only a few more days would have been necessary to get the Ajax information he so badly needed. Now, because the stupid Jew had fried himself in his fancy motor car, they couldn't get any closer. But the operation would still be on. Since Jenni had come up with that startling intuition in his office, the deputy director had no doubt whatsoever that they would be coming and that the target would very likely be the State President. Well, there'd be a warm reception waiting and he had meetings on strategy with the powers that be in the police and the army in two days' time. If Ajax materialised, South Africa would be ready.

There had been that odd report from the security police agent in Lesotho who had said that some Germans and a black and a couple of coloureds had been staying in the Maseru Hilton for a few days for some kind of conference with an Englishman and a Rhodesian. The SP's local man Duvenhage had sent copies of all the names and registration documents but there had been no records of any of them. The passport photographs would have been useful, because nobody could fake those if they were carrying the documents with them, but Maseru had been unable to come up with copies as they had in the past. The deputy director made a mental note to check whether De Kock was out of Windhoek that weekend and whether Trafalgar Square could find out if any of the top AFRA boys had been on a trip. The seed of an idea began to germinate in his mind.

Reilly and Cohen had developed their friendship to the extent that they arranged to see each other during their Christmas leave in Johannesburg. The heavily laden Hercules had landed at Waterkloof on the evening of 23

December and now, incredibly, it was already New Year's Day and they would be going back to the border on the 3rd. To the jubilant young troopers and constables in the aircraft that day, the ten days back home had seemed like the pot of gold at the end of the rainbow. They were returning into the arms of their families and loved ones, bronzed, hard and healthy; seasoned young heroes, some of whom had been bloodied in the defence of their country.

Reilly found it hard to sleep in his soft bed and kept waking at first light every morning, heart thumping as he imagined himself late for parade. He had been out to a few parties and today he was going to Cohen's place in Highlands North for a lunchtime barbecue. With him would go Dede Ross, the nice bubbly little redhead he'd met in a disco on his last R and R in September. She just loved it and in fact, had bloody nearly worn him out in the last few days.

In his time away at the border, Cohen had changed very much for the better. No longer was he the spineless-looking, studious youth who had left his anxious parents in the early months of the previous year. Military life suited Cohen and he secretly identified his positive feelings for border life with the legendary Sabra brigades in Israel. He'd even thought of going there when he finished his two year stint. Cohen's fertile imagination conjured up pictures of himself bronzed by the Israeli sun and dressed in a neat olive green uniform. He would live and work side by side with beautiful Sabra girls in tight shorts and half-open blouses and at night he would guard the kibbutz against the loathsome Fedayeen and Al Fatah insurgents. By day they would work in the healthy outdoors, in orchards and vineyards and dig fortifications and irrigation ditches. It would be a wonderful life where everything was shared, including the girls.

This vision of paradise contrasted sharply with the concrete jungle of Johannesburg that was waiting for him after his police duty. What was worse, was the position in his uncle's firm of accountants from where he would be released to attend courses at the university. He would qualify to become the holder of a minor position in a world of little grey men. The more he considered the problem the more determined he became that Israel offered a legitimate excuse because he was a Jew and he would be defending the Jewish State. He resolved to write to the embassy in Johannesburg, before he went back to the operational area, and apply to join a kibbutz.

At 12.30 Patrick Reilly arrived at Cohen's in his mother's yellow Renault 5. With him was the small yet voluptuous redhead whom Cohen had met a few days earlier. Dede wore brief red satin running shorts and a tight T-shirt and nothing else that Cohen could see, or indeed wanted to see. Other young people arrived before one o'clock and the girls, mostly nubile young Jewesses, were open in their admiration of Cohen and Reilly, both of whom wore their camouflage police shorts and matching caps. The barbecue was a great success and much beer and wine was drunk whilst Cohen's mother fussed around with steaks and salad. Some of the young Jewish youths, who had managed to evade national service in some way, were obviously envious of the macho image projected by Cohen and Reilly. Cohen felt proud and very manly and his girl, Della Silberman, clutched his arm and looked at him with adoration. Cohen couldn't resist it, he glanced across to Reilly who lay on a sun lounger with Dede's head resting on his thighs.

'It'll be good to be back, eh Patrick?' he said loudly.

Reilly nodded and smiled. 'You can say that again Selwyn,' he replied. Strangely enough, he actually meant it.

The Ajax equipment reached Lesotho on schedule from Mozambique. It was packed in wooden cases stencilled with the General Electric intertwined GC logo and addressed to Charles Drake's weaving company in Maseru. Uschi Hartmann had made a request to Helmut Gerber, the ASG chairman, to include a handgun in the consignment and Gerber had complied and added a couple of Walther P 38 automatics to the list. The pistols were packed with the other arms and there were fifty rounds of Norma soft-nose 9mm parabellum ammunition for each gun.

The consignment was passed through customs at Maseru without a second glance and Drake sent three of his workers to collect it. Later that night he unpacked the arms himself, feeling very uncomfortable because they were to be repacked in a case bearing his company name. Once they were included with the basketwork, soapstone carvings and various rugs and wallhangings he was consigning to Cape Town, the container would weigh in the region of 1100kg. On top and underneath would go the heavy karakul rugs which would absorb any knocks and superficial damage to the actual cases in which the arms were packed.

Drake perspired freely in the mild Lesotho night as he manhandled the three crates into the big container. Their wooden sides had been restamped and the General Electric logo had been obliterated with a felt-tip marker. The long metal-bound boxes now bore the legend Charles Drake Rug Weaving and Handicrafts, Box MS 291 Maseru, Kingdom of Lesotho. After he had completed the job with the aid of a small block and tackle, Drake walked to the back of his long workroom which was an ex-British Army Nissen hut. He entered his office and opened the refrigerator, removing a Castle lager. The beer was ice cold and as he took the first long draught, sweat sprang out on his brow and under his arms. He breathed deeply, feeling a sense of foreboding which he tried to dispel with a second long swallow. He looked out into the dimly lit workroom and saw the container, huge and almost menacing in the shadows. Well, he'd done his bit. The rest was up to AFRA.

In the Karoo at midday in January, the temperature averages 30°C; around 90°F. Inside the Le Roux homestead all the blinds were drawn and the shutters closed to keep out the sweltering heat. The ancient house was dark and silent, yet still it was oppressively warm and Sarel le Roux lay on top of his bed, perspiring moderately from his exertions and from nervous tension. Beside him, Sylvie Venter sprawled in sleep, her hair damp around her brow and temples from their lovemaking.

Sarel's parents were away, holidaying at the family cottage near Wilderness on the coast, and he was joining them later that day. In the meantime, he had taken the opportunity to drive into Oudtshoorn before breakfast and collect Sylvie. He planned to drop her off again on the way through Wilderness after lunch.

The young policeman leaned on one elbow and looked down at the naked girl beside him. He gently drew back the sheet which covered her thighs and appraised the tanned body which was creamy white in two strips in the region of her breasts and lower stomach. Sylvie was of medium height and slim with an athlete's build but her body was firm and ripe and her high breasts generous and pink-tipped. The now tangled hair was a thick and lustrous ebony mass which spilled over the damp pillow which she clutched to her cheek and it grew thickly too in a dense triangle at the base of her flat stomach. The girl's eyes were closed and a faint smile played on the corners of her mouth. She slept like a child and breathed faintly, hardly moving the rumpled sheets.

Looking at her Sarel grew erect again and gently rolled her over onto her back. With great care, he pushed her legs apart and moved on top of her, spreading her thighs and guiding himself slowly into her warm wetness. Sylvie's body accepted him readily, seeming to draw him inside her with an incredible involuntary mobility. Her eyelids fluttered and then she murmured and moved against him, thrusting upward with her hips and pulling him down towards her. Their bodies slid against each other in an easy rhythm, slippery with sweat, and as Sarel gradually worked towards his climax he thought again of how much he would miss this beautiful wanton girl. They had known each other from childhood and played together, discovering each other's bodies fully when she was fourteen and he only a year older. Since then, they had seen each other regularly and he knew as he climaxed inside her that he loved this girl, wanted her for himself, hated the thought of the other men that he knew she had while he was away on the stinking border. He wouldn't be back home for at least three months and Sylvie couldn't wait that long, much as she might cry when he left her today. Le Roux cursed aloud as he shuddered on top of the girl and she sobbed and writhed beneath his hard body and clutched at him in a long moan of ecstasy.

Gerrit left Windhoek for Cape Town by road on the morning of 16 January. He travelled in a rented Volkswagen Golf, taking only a canvas hold-all of clothes, some R3000 in travellers cheques and the UN passport. He had told Rothman that he had urgent family business to attend to in Cape Town which concerned his brother's death and certain possessions including a small piece of property in dispute. Rothman had smiled knowingly.

'You go for it, Gerrit boy. Don't let any other buggers get hold of what is rightfully yours, I'm sure you've got family for Africa down there, all waiting to get their hands on the loot, eh?' he said. Feeling generously disposed towards young De Kock he had taken the key from the bottom drawer of his desk. 'Use the company flat if you need it, Gerrit. It's empty right now and you know where it is, eh?'

Gerrit had smiled and nodded and thanked Rothman who had waved him away unconcernedly. He had made a copy of the key two weeks earlier.

In early January South Africa and South-West Africa are still basically enjoying the Christmas recess. Many schools do not reopen until the middle of the month and most businesses are not fully operational until the last week of January. The population moves reluctantly into the New Year seeming to loathe to return to work in the heat of midsummer. So it was not surprising that Rothman agreed readily to Gerrit's request because, although Metricor had been back at work officially since the 5th, there was nothing urgent or outstanding to do in January and he and Schwartz had managed to play golf on two afternoons during the first week. Gerrit had said that he'd be back in Windhoek, no later than the 29th and his heart had fluttered alarmingly when he made the statement so that he'd felt it necessary to add the words 'all being well' even though he had no intention of ever returning to Windhoek or Metricor.

Lucas Lundonze again chose the Zulu alias of Abel Mtlanga but this time the old Volkswagen was fitted with CY number plates denoting its registration as being from the municipal area of Bellville, a suburb adjacent to black and coloured townships north-east of Cape Town. Lucas's passbook still listed him as being born in Christiana in South Africa but new residency stamps had been added for Langa, the black location near Bellville. All his papers were in order and he left Windhoek about eighteen hours before Gerrit.

Ronald Van der Walt, using his Harris Koopman alias, travelled south as co-driver in a frozen fish transporter from Walvis Bay on the afternoon of the 17th. Each of the three Ajax operatives passed into South African territory without incident and headed for the rendezvous point in Langa where a small house belonging to UMSA 'sleepers' had been made available for their use by the Cape Town contact man Dannie Malan.

CHAPTER 24

Manfred Meyer's experience with arms was limited. By studying in Berlin, he too had evaded the German Federal Republic's military call-up but on the day after New Year he travelled down with Wolfgang Krug and Uschi Hartmann to the ASG's secret camp and firing range at Zweisel. There he would try out the weapons they were to use. Manfred had fired the rifles and thrown a few grenades and had finally tried a Walther P 38 automatic pistol which had seemed like an extension of his arm. Surprisingly enough, he was quite accurate with the weighty double-action weapon and Uschi was pleased that she had included two for the operation.

Now, as he sat in the bar in the Capetonian Hotel on the second Wednesday in January, Manfred realised a few prickles of doubt about Ajax and the motives of AFRA itself. South Africa seemed to have changed markedly in the years of his absence and although the politics were obviously still all wrong, there was little obvious oppression that he had seen in the two days since his arrival. Perhaps it's because I'm changing with age, he thought, becoming more mellow with advancing years. He looked around the pleasant bar and noted the two coloured girls drinking orange highballs over in one corner. One of them stared at him directly and smiled, displaying missing front teeth. Manfred looked away almost embarrassed as he recalled a discussion with Tina about the reasons that coloured girls had their front teeth removed. He glanced towards the corner again and saw the girl still watching him and without warning he became semi-aroused sitting there in the bar, as he pictured her in action upon him.

He'd spent a little time walking around the Foreshore and Adderley Street that morning and had seen only contented looking well-dressed people of various colours. Some were obviously on holiday and all the shops seemed to be very busy. Undoubtedly, the country was immensely wealthy and all population groups seemed to be enjoying the prosperity, especially the whites of course. There was merchandise on display to choose from which rivalled even that of Berlin or Frankfurt; it was a different Cape Town to the one he had left in 1974. His impression of the country had started when the Lufthansa 747 had touched down at Jan Smuts Airport, Johannesburg. He had passed through immigration without any problems, collected his luggage and carried it through on a trolley to domestic departures in the adjoining building. The South African Airways airbus to Cape Town had been full of happy, bronzed people who were confident and affluent looking and in total contrast to the few pallid-looking Germans who had left the freezing drabness of Frankfurt am Main. Manfred had appraised these South Africans and had decided that more than the weather was involved in their positive outlook on life.

Together with all the other Ajax members, he had embarked on a simple disguise for entrance to South Africa. His hair was now very short and bleached to a strawberry-blonde colour and his moustache had been removed. He wore gold-framed, green-lensed teardrop sunglasses and a double-breasted navy blazer and lightweight grey flannels. His passport was in the name of Joachim Scholtz and his place of birth listed as Hanover. The passport bore stamps for the United States, Japan and South America. Herr Scholtz was listed as a thirty-three year old chemical engineer now resident in Westphalia. His reason for visiting South Africa was recorded as vacation on the entry visa.

Uschi Hartmann had arrived on Swissair from Zurich and surrendered a French passport to the appreciative immigration officer. Her blonde hair was trimmed to a pleasing bell shape around her face and colour rinsed to a light chestnut shade and she wore a simple yet elegant cream trouser suit. Over her shoulder was slung a Nikon FE camera and she carried a Christian Dior travel bag in natural tan calfskin. The immigration officer thought that she was the best-looking bird he'd seen all week and he'd had a busy week at that.

Uschi's eyes, behind the huge goggle sunglasses from Yves St Laurent, were frankly appraising as she looked at the young blond Afrikaaner official in his crisp white shirt and blue and gold epaulettes. Surprisingly he addressed her in reasonable French and she replied in the same language, smiling with apparent pleasure.

'Enjoy your stay, madamoiselle,' he had said with a friendly grin.

'Oh, monsieur, I expect to,' Uschi had replied. The name in her passport showed her to be Yvette Bellegarde from Versaille; occupation marketing executive and purpose of visit, business.

Krug had come in on South African Airways from Frankfurt and entered the country just as easily as the other two on a passport listing him as Pieter Hirschfeld from Nuremburg. The three had made contact by telephone at their respective hotels on the morning of the 15th; they spoke German and merely exchanged four words. 'Hello, all well; goodbye.' There had been a message at the Inn on the Square for Miss Bellegarde which simply said that the Cape Town office had called to say that the samples had arrived and that the provincial sales managers would be arriving on the 18th and would like a meeting as soon as it might be convenient.

Tina had arrived from Frankfurt on 9 January and had successfully intercepted the container at Heim's. The armaments were now safely cached in Dannie Malan's backyard cellar and Tina was staying at the President

Hotel in Seapoint where she was registered as Frau Ingrid Gruber of Hamburg. Her hair was now worn up in a severe auburn tinted roll and her eyes bore blue-grey contact lenses and were devoid of make-up. Her clothes were austere and unflattering and she wore a padded body belt which filled out her waistline making her shapeless and stolid looking. Steel rimmed plain lensed spectacles completed the changes which were amazing and quite horrifying to Tina. It was as if she were looking into the future and seeing herself in fifteen or twenty years' time.

By early January, South African military intelligence had estimated that there were upwards of five thousand SWAPO insurgents within the borders of South-West Africa. Their handwriting was definitely recognisable and followed clear patterns based on the intimidation of the local population. It was known that 90 per cent of SWAPO recruits were Ovambos, many of whom were born in Angola. The border between that country and South-West Africa bisected the football-shaped territory which is Ovamboland almost equally but the Jati strip was the real border. This one kilometre wide, cleared belt of no-man's land was a killing ground where anything that moved was shot; animals being regular victims. This chicken run for SWAPO was overflown by Alouette helicopter gunships and South African Impala jet fighters which supplemented the regular police and army patrols and OPs.

During the past month, South Africa had boasted on national television and radio of the sizeable losses it had inflicted on the insurgents. Some 150 terrorists were liquidated in the first week of the New Year and the officer commanding the vast operational area was confident that even greater advances against the enemy were inevitable in the months ahead.

A basic SWAPO problem, of benefit to the South Africans, was that the average recruit was not up to the standard of earlier volunteers such as Lucas Lundonze and Nicholas Mohapi. Furthermore, odd behavioural patterns had developed among the freedom fighters, and reports of witchcraft and superstition were rife. SWAPO had made recent efforts to convince the local Ovambo tribesmen that they, the Freedom Fighters, were unaffected by the bullets of the South African soldiers. In order to preserve this myth, platoon commanders would risk further lives in retrieving dead and wounded after actions with the SA army. Despite such nonsensical practices however, it was only the South African presence in the territory which prevented a SWAPO dictatorship gaining control overnight. Undoubtedly, the Pretoria government were working towards a black takeover of the territory still known as South-West Africa but their intention was to place in power an administration positively disposed towards themselves. They had all but given up trying to keep the United Nations happy at the same time.

Pretoria had little faith in the traditional idea of a United Nations peacekeeping force and the South African Army despised this casual pot-pourri of soldiers to such an extent that the government feared open warfare might break out between its forces and those of the UN. The overall long term plan, on the South African side, was for some combination of the Cape Corps – a coloured battalion – and the clandestine three-four and three-five battalions. These, with the Ovambo battalion, would ideally make up the army of the new Namibia.

The problems frustrating Pretoria in this regard were the same as those confronting SWAPO in its efforts to put together a united force. Within the borders of South-West Africa, thirty-nine different dialects were in common use and a future Namibian parliament would have to take some note of each of them to be legitimate and democratic. SWAPO had little conscience about this but other stumbling blocks for the so-called liberation army were the lack of unity amongst the various tribal groups, each of which had their own jealously guarded traditions, ideals and unique lifestyles.

This suited the South Africans because Pretoria's military strategists had never regarded the individual African as any kind of a threat to their sovereignty. They did however admit that a concerted effort by a united black force would constitute a very different kettle of fish whether from within the Republic itself, in the form of passive down-tools by the black workforce, or an attack from outside the country's borders. The bloody wars with the Zulus were permanently lodged in the Afrikaaners' memory traces and it was thus very obviously in the interests of South Africa to dissuade any unification of black aspirations. Although the war in Ovamboland and the Caprivi was costing the South African government in excess of US $1,500,000 every day, the country could afford it. Glutted with gold revenues and a still booming economy, white South Africans enjoyed the finest lifestyle per capita of any people in the world and even the blacks were becoming affluent in comparison to their contemporaries in the militant countries to the north.

Douglas Hoyle knew all this and he fretted and worried over the improving situation of the South African blacks and the correspondingly dying nationalistic fervour of the increasingly westernised worker in that hated State. Hoyle was writing his publisher's editorial for the first issue of *Confront* to appear in the New Year which was destined for the shelves at the end of January. Everything was put to bed except his piece and he longed to find some loophole in the increasingly clever South African system of buttering up the black worker in order that he might continue to support the white society. The following issue would feature the Ajax strike and Hoyle had already prepared the background to his leader in advance of the action. He smiled to himself as he imagined what a scoop this would represent to any of the international news magazines or national dailies. Ajax would do the trick. Ajax could stir the blacks from their complacency and drive them forward eventually to conquer the white fascists.

Hoyle lay back in his soft leather chair and stared at the David Hockney on the wall which predictably portrayed a man in a swimming pool. He sipped his Chivas Regal and water and visualised the preparation being made, even at this very moment, halfway across the world in Cape Town. In five days' time it would be the 23rd and Ajax would strike. Outside it was grey and cold in South Kensington but in the Cape it would be balmy and warm. A new sun was about to rise and a new fire would soon burn across the southern tip of Africa.

Gerrit's disguise was basic yet effective. He had bleached and dyed his hair to the unnatural titian shade which is typical of certain Cape coloureds and it had been frizzed out in the popular Afro fashion. Wearing sunglasses, blue denims and a T-shirt bearing the legend 'I love Cape Town' he had set out to reconnoitre the block of flats above the French Colonial Bank on the corner of Parliament Street and Spin Street in the city centre. He entered the building through the side entrance in Parliament Street and took the service lift to the eleventh floor where Metricor kept a sizeable flat for overseas directors who periodically visited the office in Cape Town. The apartment was seldom used and it was highly unlikely that anyone could be in residence during this period in January and Rothman had said it would be empty. But Gerrit trembled as he took the duplicate Yale key, made from the original borrowed from Rothman's desk drawer in Windhoek and now unexpectedly also in his pocket.

The time was close to midday as he knocked briskly on the door, reasoning that, even should the place be in use, the chances were that the occupants would be out at this time. The Ajax strike would consist of various phases and this flat represented just one of them; nonetheless it was strategically very important. Silently, Gerrit inserted the key in the lock, turned it and pushed the door open. He stepped quickly inside and saw that the apartment showed no signs of recent occupation. Had it done so, he would have left the pot plant he carried under his arm with the compliment slip from Metricor, Cape Town, which bore an indecipherable signature. It was a lame excuse but it would have got him in and out again quickly, before the recipient could reason out the likelihood of such a gift.

Gerrit crossed to the window and looked down across the narrow street to the steps of the Parliament Building diagonally opposite. On the corner directly opposite was the Cultural History Museum which he had last visited as a child on a day trip with other standard-three pupils from his primary school in Goodwood. The angle down to the steps was quite sharp, well over to the left and at ninety degrees, but he knew this should not trouble Wolfgang who apparently was able to hit a ping-pong ball at one hundred yards with the Unique automatic calibre .22. The range here would be less than fifty and at such a short distance, Krug could group five shots within five centimetres. It wouldn't take him longer than the same number of seconds to do it either, and then he'd be gone, into the lift which Manfred would be holding open, and away.

As he stared down into the busy street, Gerrit could imagine the soft lead .22 bullets slamming into the bulldog head of the South African State President. The man was old, almost seventy, and in poor health having suffered some sort of a heart ailment early in the last year. He would be unlikely to survive the attack and with luck hundreds and later millions would see him struck down on the steps of the parliament in their Mother City. The blow for liberation in Azania would be considerable but that was not all they had planned – there were to be other diversions.

CHAPTER 25

Mostert was making advanced preparations for the defence of the State President during the celebrations on the 23rd. The narrow streets of the central city area were a natural bottleneck, an ambusher's paradise, he thought morosely. He had been told by the commandant that an attack of some sort was expected by an AFRA terrorist group but no further details were available and the security police had nothing concrete to go on. Pretoria was naturally shitting themselves and there were to be a lot of plain clothes policemen in the crowd along the official route. There had even been talk of using a disguised policeman instead of the State President but that had been rejected because of the television coverage. Nobody could survive an appraisal under their telephoto lenses which were reportedly able to pick out the blackheads in facial skin, never mind the features themselves.

In any event, Pretoria thought it would be cowardly to bow to the threat of AFRA, even though they suspected the planning of a strike. There had been pompous statements about the security forces of the Republic being able to defend their State President, despite the enemy pitched against him. That was all very well, thought Mostert. But if the buggers were clever about it – and he theorised that they would have to be to be making the attempt – then they could be anywhere at any time and, furthermore, would very likely split their forces. It could be an absolute bloodbath. Mostert grimaced to himself imagining the masses of people, many of them women and children, exposed to the ravages of a modern terrorist attack. Not for the first time in his life, he now doubted the wisdom of his superiors. They were behaving predictably like pig-headed Boers. Like their forefathers had in the bloody Zulu Wars. And plenty had died then too.

Police reinforcements were being drawn from all parts of the Cape Province and even a few from the operational area. At least those boys would be used to being shot at and might react better than the local mob if it came to a shoot-out with AFRA, Mostert considered. It all depended on how the insurgents would arrange their strike. If he was them, he'd be disguised and appearing as an ordinary holidaymaker complete with cameras and all that rubbish. You couldn't search every gadget bag or handbag. Suddenly, the idea struck Mostert. What if some of them were women with handbags full of sodding grenades. His mood blackened as he pondered the worsening possibilities.

In the blazing heat of midday Reilly's platoon climbed aboard the C 130 Hercules for the two and a half hour flight to DF Malan airport, Cape Town. At M'pacha in the Eastern Caprivi, the temperature was 32°C and the men's clean camouflage fatigues were sweat-soaked by the time they settled on the canvas benches in the gloomy interior of the big prop-jet aircraft. When the engines were started and they began to roll, a semblance of air conditioning brought blessed relief as cool air blew over their wet faces. Reilly and Cohen chattered happily. At least this was better than the boredom of Katima Mulilo, and with any luck they'd have a day off in Cape Town after the parade.

Krug had hired the Datsun pick-up from a company called Rent-a-Truck. He had given his false name and paid a cash deposit for a week in advance and they hadn't even asked for his international driver's licence which was also a forgery. He'd gone in to the rental firm's offices wearing Bermuda shorts and a T-shirt and said he wanted the pick-up for surfing. This was a fairly common request and there had been no problems. In fact the Datsun would be driven by Dannie Malan while Lucas and Ronald van der Walt would ride in the back. They would not be equipped with surfboards but would wear dirty white overalls and crouch uncomfortably among paint drums and ladders. However, their journey would not be of long duration. Underneath the tatty tarpaulins there would also be a dozen one litre wine bottles filled with a milky viscous liquid. There too would be two AK 47 rifles and plenty of ammunition; the ASG in Berlin had doubled up on the AFRA requisition and sent six sixty-shot magazines.

The two coloureds and the SWAPO operative would make their attack at 11.30 precisely and their target was to be the old police station in Seapoint, some five kilometres from the city centre where the State President's parade would take place. Lucas and Ronald would be used as a feint, to divert attention from the target area and cause a few troops and police units to be diverted. It was not expected that this ploy would be believed by the authorities but a certain amount of confusion would be created and this was all the Ajax members wanted. The real strike was scheduled for a few minutes before twelve and was a three-pronged move which would leave little margin for error.

The AFRA executive had decided that it would be too risky to use coloureds or blacks in close proximity to the presidential cavalcade. It was expected that they would be searched by police or army units and might even be prevented from getting anywhere near the steps of parliament. For fear that the South Africans might cancel the parade, AFRA had planned the diversionary attack to be well out of the city centre even though the central police station was a tempting target. The actual attack on the State President would be carried out totally by the whites and supported by Tina de Kock who looked as white as anybody else. It was reasoned that they would be able to get close up in the crowds with relatively little risk of discovery. Until it was too late.

On the evening of the 21st, the Ajax members communicated together by telephone, Uschi Hartmann being the spokeswoman for the German contingent and Gerrit de Kock representing the coloureds and single black member. Everything was one hundred per cent ready and the escape routes were planned. The day prior to the attack was to be spent in relaxation and Uschi, Manfred and Wolfgang would go to the beach. Tina planned to relax and read in her hotel room, and Gerrit, Ronald and Lucas would remain in Langa at the house where Dannie Malan would join them for lunch. On the morning of the 23rd they would all rise early, rested and ready.

Since Major Vosloo's disappearance somewhere off Hout Bay, Sergeant David Mortimer had been made warrant officer and had assumed temporary command of SAP Seapoint. Mortimer was young, only twenty-nine, and his future in the police was assured. He secretly hoped that his promotion to lieutenant would come through during the early part of the New Year and that, resultingly, he might become permanent commander of Seapoint. For this reason, Mortimer had been working hard, running the busy station like clockwork and cosseting the wealthy Seapoint public by reacting promptly to their every complaint. Pleasant noises had been made on his behalf by the local ratepayers' association and everything looked good. As he sat in Vosloo's chair on the morning of the 23rd of January, Mortimer relaxed and congratulated himself on his recent swift advance. He felt a little guilty that his good fortune had, to some extent, been at the expense of poor old Hennie Vosloo but comforted himself by thinking that the major had been old and close to retirement. It had happened a bit sooner than it would have done, that was all.

380

Outside it was a beautiful day and so far the morning had been uneventful, even peaceful; probably because a lot of people were in town watching the State President's parade. Now it was 11.15 and he was finishing his third coffee of the morning whilst rereading a docket about an attempted break-in at the opulent San Lorenzo apartments down on the beachfront. He'd gone down there himself and the owner, a rich divorced Jewess, had brought him coffee and little cakes. She'd prattled on about her jewels and furs and how she must install a safe, otherwise the insurance company wouldn't cover her. Mortimer had listened and looked at her tanned legs, dramatically exposed in tight denim shorts. Her top half had been outstanding too and she'd leaned forward when she'd seen him looking. It had been a pleasant little hour, well spent in the line of duty.

Mortimer's recollections were interrupted by a loud muffled explosion outside the window followed closely by a second and third. Suddenly, thick oily flames seemed to cling to the very glass of the panes and then the window shattered and an object exploded in a fiery ball against the burglar bars. Flaming trails spattered across the office and several splashes landed on Mortimer's desk causing papers and cardboard dockets to burst into flames. The young officer leapt to his feet and ran to the door. As he reached the corridor to the charge office the horrifying chatter of Kalashnikov assault rifles echoed through the empty passage and someone started to scream horribly. Terrified, Mortimer reeled back through the smoke into his office, trying to find the R1 rifle which he kept behind the door.

Ronald's first three throws had fallen short but Lucas had got the range with his first lob and then they'd both got a couple more of the makeshift fire bombs into the police station. The bath tub napalm had set the old wooden building burning furiously and Lucas knew that all those inside would have to come out pretty soon. He picked up the AK almost casually as a black constable appeared in the charge office doorway, pulling at his pistol holster and coughing heavily.

Lucas, Ronald and Daniel wore cotton Balaclava-type hoods and painter's overalls. They had parked the Datsun right outside the station and Lucas rested the AK on the cab roof with the action set on automatic fire. Ronald sat on the floor and both of them fired together as the black policeman appeared. The range was not more than fifteen metres.

As some twenty bullets from the two AKs scythed through the chest and stomach of Bantu Constable Alpheus Temba, Tina was in a taxi approaching the Foreshore-end of Adderley Street. She was dressed in a drab khaki slack-suit and wore a huge greyish sunhat and black goggle sunglasses. Over her shoulder was a voluminous canvas bag and on her feet she wore low-heel, lace-up mocassins. She carried an Olympus OM 2 camera with a 300mm telephoto lens and a long cane-handled sun umbrella. The taxi driver had not given her a second look and had immediately classed her as just another oddball tourist.

When Tina saw the thick crowds at the end of Adderley Street, she asked the driver to stop. 'I'll walk from here,' she said, affecting a harsh German accent.

The driver nodded. 'That'll be four rands, madame,' he said. 'You going to watch the parade?'

'*Ja*,' said Tina brusquely and paid the cabbie. Then she walked off determinedly through the crowds on the pavement. She had fifteen minutes in which to get into position and the time was 11.35.

The sun was high and Tina sweated slightly as she forced her way through the jostling crowds who seemed to be in a mood of holidaylike euphoria. The shoulder bag was not too heavy, considering the fact that it contained four fragmentation grenades. The KL6s were of East German manufacture and looked like slightly ovoid tennis balls made of grey plastic and having a small ring at one end. Each contained around nine hundred steel ball-bearings the size of a small pea and on hard ground a single grenade was deadly at anything up to 120 metres radius from the explosions centre. The other eight KL6s had been shared between the Ajax operatives. Uschi and Gerrit both had two, and one each of the M82/7 phosphorus grenades. Manfred and Wolfgang Krug carried the same and the diversionary group had the balance between them; hidden in their overalls and in the dashboard compartment of the Datsun pick-up.

Daniel had personally distributed the grenades and the two Walther pistols in carefully packaged parcels, gift-wrapped and delivered to the four hotels, on the previous evening. They each weighed about the same as a basket of fruit, or a half dozen bottles of wine, and with the security in South African hotels being almost non-existent, they had been sent up to the respective rooms and received immediately. It had all been so very simple.

Late in the afternoon on 16 January, the deputy director had received delayed, but nonetheless positive, news from London about some of the top AFRA brass being out of the UK during the time of the meeting at the Lesotho Hilton. It could have been coincidence but the deputy director had already established that De Kock too had been away from Windhoek. He instructed Jenni Theron to enquire from Metricor, Windhoek as to the present whereabouts of De Kock. When she reported that he was on an additional week's leave and that his destination was known to be Cape Town, the deputy director felt quite suddenly that they were getting much warmer.

Further enquiries established that De Kock had not used his company car for the trip and it could not be established from Pretoria whether he had flown or driven to Cape Town. South African Airways had no record of De Kock as a passenger and none of the car-hire companies held a rental agreement in his name. But Jenni felt convinced that De Kock was in some way involved in

383

the Ajax operation and asked the deputy director if she could fly to Windhoek and circulate his photograph to air-charter firms, public and private bus companies and car-hire offices. The deputy director agreed to let her go and she left on the evening of the 18th on the South African Airways 747 SP, bound for Frankfurt.

By midday on the 19th Jenni had a good lead. A young coloured man answering the description of De Kock had rented a white VW Golf GLS from Hertz's central city office in Windhoek. The man had said he was a diplomat and had offered a UN passport but no licence. The registration number of the VW was SW 174392 and by three o'clock that same afternoon, every policeman and traffic officer in Cape Town had the number written in his pocket book. But the Golf was not to feature in the Ajax operation itself and was not planned to be used until the getaway from Cape Town. It was securely locked in a lean-to shack in Langa township.

By 20 of January, the Cape Town Police had begun a house-to-house search for the vehicle and on the afternoon of the 22nd a young African constable actually passed within two metres of the lean-to without even considering that the car could be inside it. His lack of imagination was to be a fatal factor for a number of people within the following forty-eight hours.

The day had started badly for Jacobus van Vuuren Malan, the ageing politician who was South Africa's State President. Malan's career had been long and hard and for the duration of Hitler's War the English speaking government of his country, under General Jan Smuts, had imprisoned him and fellow sympathisers of the Nazi regime. Malan was a member of the Ossewabrandwag and the Broederbond (Brotherhood) two age-old ultra right-wing Afrikaaner political movements which had been reborn with the rise to power of the National Party in 1948. The State President was a taciturn man with dyed-in-the-wool principles and he disagreed often with the more liberal policies of Prime Minister Pieter Botha and his flamboyant younger Minister of Foreign Affairs, Roelof 'Pik' Botha.

He had awoken at 5.45 in the large yellowwood bed in his official residence, The Townhouse. The beautiful old Cape Dutch building stood behind the Houses of Parliament, deep in the heart of the Mother City and the Malans had lived in it for three and a half years. Both Jacobus and his wife loved the house dearly and relished every moment behind its high white walls where they would entertain occasional foreign dignitaries and cabinet ministers. In the twilight of his political career, Malan was more than happy just to wander in the garden or sit out on the broad shaded *stoep* drinking brandy, which his doctors continually tried to make him give up.

A servant had brought coffee and rusks at six o'clock and the State President had remained in his bed and drunk the strong brew. He had arisen at 6.10 precisely to a drawn bath, and towels bearing his personal crest were laid out neatly for him in the spacious bathroom which adjoined the bedroom. The old statesman completed his ablutions and was shaved and dressed in a silk gown before his wife so much as stirred from her deep slumber. He felt a little nervous, as he always did on State occasions and today's Opening of Parliament was the most important date in his official calendar.

President Malan ate his soft-boiled egg as he listened to the eight o'clock news on Radio Good Hope. The newsreader reported the opening of parliament by the State President the Honourable Jacobus Malan and mentioned that, as last year, the ceremony and parade would be televised live. Impala jet fighters were to fly low over the city and there would be much pomp and ceremony as usual. Malan chewed on a piece of toast and ruminated on the fact that this would be his last year in national politics, although the office of State President was really a non-political appointment. His retirement was imminent due to ill health and in the past year he had suffered two minor heart attacks, the last only five months ago in late August. Before parliament had closed for the Christmas recess he had told the Prime Minister that he would have to step down soon.

This morning, the faint burning pain under his heart was there again and he'd noted a slight breathlessness when he'd stood up too quickly to get out of the bath. He knew well enough that he would probably not live out the next couple of years but the realisation did not trouble him because he'd had a full and active life and one which he felt had benefited his beloved country, South Africa. By ten o'clock he was dressed in official morning clothes and the embroidered blue and gold sash of office was draped diagonally across his chest. His coloured butler Cedric was brushing the silk top hat, and all the paraphernalia of white gloves and his mace of office were laid out ready for eleven o'clock when his personal bodyguard would arrive. Malan lit a small cigar and puffed distractedly as he considered all the fuss and bother he would have to go through within the next two hours. It was all too much he thought, and grimaced as his wife rushed past with cream on her face and curlers bristling from her bluish-white hair.

The old open Daimler was a relic of British colonial days and had been given to Prime Minister Smuts back in the thirties. As he walked out into the forecourt of the Townhouse where the beautiful old vehicle was parked, the State President looked up at the great bulk of Table Mountain; Mother Mountain as he always thought of it. Above the massive green and grey slopes was the wonderful tablecloth of fluffy white cloud and beyond that a sky of infinite blue. The colour was a pale cornflower and Malan thought that it would signify a strong off-shore breeze later in the day. He knew his Cape weather, having been born near Paarl in the winelands seventy years and eight months ago to this very day, 23 January.

As the trumpet fanfare began and the four bands of the

police, army, navy and airforce began their repertoire of ceremonial marches, an odd flutter of fear gripped the State President. He shook it off and when the gleaming black Daimler turned out of the Townhouse gates into Government Avenue, he waved regally to the crowds. As always, he loved the cheering and glanced sideways at his wife Hettie, resplendent in a white costume and huge picture hat. She was a strong and vigorous woman and she smiled happily acknowledging the adulation of the crowd. She's going to miss all this, thought Malan, as the car began its slow journey up Adderley Street.

At 11.45 on the morning of 23 January, Uschi Hartmann spotted Tina de Kock on the opposite side of the road from her own position outside the government offices in Parliament Street. The coloured girl had managed to get as close to the steps of the Houses of Parliament as possible, right in the corner of the alleyway alongside the Cultural History Museum. Uschi could hardly recognise Tina, she certainly didn't look coloured and her clothes looked awful. More like a blowsy German matron, like the friends of her mother's back home in Dusseldorf.

In contrast, Uschi wore a tight towelling sweater and white jeans and carried a big raffia beach bag and her Nikon. Her hair was enclosed in a white turban and she wore a pink celluloid tennis visor and her sunglasses. She was barefoot and looked pretty and harmless and the young policeman in camouflage uniform right in front of her had noted her presence for all the wrong reasons. The nearest one was actually pressing himself back against her so that she could feel his hard hip against her thigh and his upper arm brushing her breast as he rigidly held his rifle. She'd moved a bit and then kept still, letting him touch against her because she was inwardly very excited and more than a little aroused by what was about to happen in the narrow street.

Five minutes earlier, and almost ten minutes behind

schedule due to a hurried conference on the attack in Seapoint, the cavalcade had left the State President's residence behind the Houses of Parliament. The procession had started on its slow looping journey up Government Avenue and into Adderley Street amid a fanfare of trumpets and loud cheering. The State President and his retinue would travel up Adderley Street to the statue of Jan van Riebeeck, founder of the Cape Colony, circle the statue and return again down Adderley Street and into Bureau Street, finally turning right into Parliament Street to the Houses of Parliament where the cortège would halt to allow the State President to dismount. Uschi and the others knew the details by heart and were expecting there to be upwards of fifteen hundred armed soldiers and police in the President's guard. At the procession's head would be some three dozen motorcyclists followed by mounted police and immediately behind them would be the official car. All along the route were armed police and army units and outside the Houses of Parliament a cordon of police would surround the old man and his wife closely as they walked up the steps of the parliament building.

Gerrit's role was purely defensive and he was to take no part in the actual attack. His position was close to the corner of Spin Street and Parliament Street, some twenty metres from the side entrance to Parliament Chambers, the apartment block from where Wolfgang would fire. Should Wolfgang and Manfred be discovered and have any trouble getting out of the building, Gerrit was to clear the entrance with grenades and then disappear, ducking across Church Square to Plein Street. If he was pursued he was to try and lose himself in the vast Parkade parking garage but the confusion was expected to be such that each of them could escape without too much trouble. Wolfgang's rifle would make scarcely any sound and the direction of fire would be hard to pinpoint in the mêlée after the grenades were thrown.

Wearing a flat white cap and sunglasses, Gerrit stood and sweated slightly in the bright sunshine. He glanced at his watch and noted the time: 11.55. Already there was a craning of necks towards the corner of Bureau and Adderley Streets where the cavalcade would reappear and he could hear continuous faint cheering coming gradually closer from the direction of Adderley Street which was blocked off from all traffic except the procession. Now that the time had come Gerrit's mood was calm and almost dreamlike. He had felt qualms over the fact that Tina would be involved directly in the attack for he feared for the life of his beautiful sister and had doubted her ability to throw the grenades. Wolfgang had told them that it might be best to try and roll them between the legs of the soldiers in front; all you had to do was pull out the ring, wait three seconds and then get rid of the thing. It was child's play, he had said.

Gerrit wondered whether he would be able to throw the horrible devices in these streets, filled with innocent spectators, many of whom were black and coloured. He looked up over the old and time-honoured buildings at the clear blue sky under which he had been born twenty-eight years earlier and saw the seagulls wheeling high up, the sun glinting on the pristine whiteness of their wings. The dream that had disturbed his sleep in Nuremberg returned and he trembled suddenly, despite the heat as he recalled his own violent end and the way in which he had awoken, sweating and terrified. Now it was all happening for real and in minutes there would be death and carnage on these very streets just as he had dreamed. Something inside Gerrit's well organised and restrained mind broke without warning and he began to cry openly as his brain flashed images of shattered bodies and maimed children across his subconscious.

The images crystallised and became real and he began to shout incoherently so that people around him stared and moved away. Finally he slumped against the wall of the French Colonial Bank and began to cry brokenly in great shuddering sobs. A young blond policeman in camouflage uniform moved towards him enquiringly noting the coloured boy's hands thrust deeply into the pockets of his denim bush jacket. He seemed to be holding something inside his pockets and the constable felt the first stirrings of alarm. As he reached the young coloured, the procession turned the corner of Adderley Street and started up the short single block of Bureau Street. The time was 12.07 and parliament was about to be opened in the Fairest Cape in all the world.

Reilly was acting purely on his own initiative but at the last briefing session that morning, they had all been told to act immediately against anyone looking even slightly suspicious. Lieutenant Bester was some distance away from his and Cohen's positions on the corner of Spin and Parliament Street being some thirty men down the line, almost opposite the steps of the Houses of Parliament. Cohen too broke ranks and joined Reilly as he walked quickly towards the young coloured. Both unshouldered the 9mm machine carbines they carried and cocked them in one smooth single action.

The coloured was still slumped against the wall, clutching the objects of some sort concealed deep within the pockets of his jacket. Reilly was very suspicious now and the adrenalin coursed through his bloodstream so that he seemed to see everything with great clarity and each little sound seemed louder. They had heard news of the attack on Seapoint SAP only minutes earlier and the grapevine had it that four men were dead and the police station was still burning. There was no news of the terrorists that had attacked the station but units of the Cape Town Riot Police had been detached from the State President's guard and had gone to investigate. It was suspected that this attack had been a diversionary tactic for the main thrust against the State President himself.

Gerrit de Kock looked up from his broken, head-bowed position against the wall of the bank and he saw the polished brown boots and camouflage-clad legs. He raised his eyes higher and there was the black hole of the gun barrel pointing at his face and it was all just like in the dream. The similarity was such that he smiled, imagining that he would wake and that this terror he felt could not possibly be real. The blond hair and the blue eyes were there too, and the young soldier was tanned and handsome. It was all so real, just like it had been in the last dream, but the dialogue was different. Harsh and bitter, the voice like a whiplash.

'Turn around and put your hands on the wall!' shouted Reilly whilst Cohen covered him from the left flank. The coloured failed to move but seemed to mouth something under his breath and Reilly moved in to search him, wanting to turn him around and kick his legs out so that he would be immobile, spread-eagled against the wall.

'Quickly now man, come on, turn around fast and get your hands up on that wall!' he shouted again, his finger on the trigger of the machine carbine. Something snapped in Gerrit's brain and suddenly, all the emotion he had felt was replaced by the hate which had been buried in his subconscious since he was old enough to realise his secondary position in the strata of South African society.

'Fuck you, you racist bastard!' he screamed into Reilly's face and pulled one of the fragmentation grenades from his pocket. Before Reilly could move, Gerrit plucked out the ring from the grenade and held it out at arm's length so that it was only inches from the young corporal's face.

Few had seen this exchange and the State President's car had already turned the corner into Parliament Street and was slowing to pull up beside the steps of the House. What followed happened so quickly that witnesses, who were afterwards asked to recall the action, could not get the sequence of events in the correct order.

Reilly recoiled from the grenade involuntarily and Cohen shot Gerrit in the chest with a three second burst which spun the coloured around. The grenade dropped to the pavement and rolled into the gutter and Reilly kicked it as hard as he could, sending it skittering away from the crowds of massed spectators on the corner. Some of these onlookers saw this last act of the drama and most heard the shots. Instinctively many threw themselves flat, as did Reilly and Cohen both of them screaming 'Get down, get down!' The KL6 was partially underneath a parked police Landrover and some twenty-five metres from the corner when it exploded. It detonated with a loud throbbing bang which echoed through the narrow streets, reminding many of those watching the parade of the cannon which was fired daily at noon from Cape Town castle but which had already sounded some ten minutes earlier.

Gerrit's last thought as the bullets struck him was one of total disbelief. It was exactly like the dream except that he had not woken up sweating and shuddering with reaction. Instead he was quite calm in the knowledge that he was going to die. The 9mm bullets had slammed into his chest and right shoulder and forced him around so that his face pressed against the white plaster of the wall of the bank building. He had felt nothing more than a series of rapid blows and then a hot numbing ache deep within his chest which seemed to be expanding gradually making it difficult to breathe. As if in a dream, he watched the white plaster wall, with its miniscule cracks and imperfections, slide past his line of vision as he gradually slithered down onto his knees. It all seemed to take ages and his nose and left cheek were pressed hard against the wall which felt cool and pleasant in contrast to the burning sensation in his chest. As his knees reached the pavement, the slight pain and discomfort began to lessen so that it seemed almost as if he were losing consciousness under an anaesthetic. Then his eyes closed and he couldn't see the wall anymore and he slid further away and seemed to be drifting into darkness, thick and impenetrable. Strangely, he felt no fear.

Shrapnel from the grenade struck down a middle-aged coloured woman and a white teenage girl and shattered the plate-glass window on the mezzanine floor of the bank where the staff were watching the proceedings. Several people were badly cut by flying fragments but Reilly's speedy action had prevented ghastly injury to many more and the Landrover, now sitting drunkenly on shredded tyres, had taken much of the blast. Reilly and Cohen were unharmed although their ears were ringing. As they climbed to their feet, people began to scream and shout and the injured woman's blood flowed profusely onto the warm paving stones.

As the State President and his wife stepped out of the open Daimler limousine, Cohen's short burst of sub-machine gun fire stuttered harshly into the politely poised silence. For an instant the old man stood still, his plump matronly wife clutching his arm, and then the grenade went off and everybody seemed to move at once. Acting on previous orders, the cordon of Task Force police closed in on the old couple and manhandled them to the ground before piling unceremoniously on top of their bodies.

Nervously, Wolfgang Krug squinted through the Japanese Tasco telescopic sight and tried to centre the crosshairs on his target. Disturbed by the sudden burst of sub-machine gun fire he released a shot at the silvery head of the State President as- it disappeared under a mass of military fatigues. The bullet thudded solidly into a policeman's buttock and then the target was obliterated. Krug cursed and drew back from the window, flinging the .22 rifle to the floor.

Outside in the corridor, Manfred had heard the soft plop of the silenced rifle through the open apartment door and his heart turned over sickeningly as he stood, immobile, finger pressed on the 'door open' button of the lift. Then Wolfgang was pushing past him shouting and cursing. 'Come on, it's a screw-up!' he screamed in German. 'Let's get the hell out of here! Quickly!'

In the street the crowd began to surge forward towards the Parliament steps, some women crying and screaming because they thought the State President was dead. The police and army guard units turned to force them back and it was then that Sarel le Roux saw the pretty girl in the beach gear step back and take something from her bag. She seemed to fiddle with it and then the grey egg-shaped object was rolling out from under the legs of the police cordon towards the mass of bodies protecting the State president at the bottom of the steps. The thing was about the size of a small ostrich egg and, as time seemed to stand still, Sarel recalled the hundreds he had eaten in his mother's omelettes on the farm at De Rust. Without further thought, he flung himself forwards and dived onto the object, covering it with his body. He lay still, his face against the warm tarmac and nothing happened and then a great surging blow hit him in the stomach. He was whisked away and he saw the sky for a fraction of a second before redness rushed in to swallow everything up.

Small pieces from the central area of Sarel le Roux's body were showered over the crowd who fell back in revulsion. The main part of his disembowelled trunk flopped loosely back onto the road surface, smoking, and the shocked television cameraman who shakingly focused on it failed to notice a red mist coating his lens.

Tina de Kock recoiled like the rest of the onlookers, realising that everything was hopeless and that their attempt had failed. A great fear rose within her because she knew that something had happened to Gerrit. It could only have been him involved in the firing and grenade blast around the corner. She turned and shuffled away through the crowd, the canvas bag still on her shoulder and the umbrella under her arm.

Uschi had seen the young policeman dive forward and then she had melted back into the crowd, hearing the muffled explosion and the screams. But Sarel le Roux seemed to have been the only one to have observed her actions and Uschi was unmolested as she pushed her way up Parliament Street, hand held to her mouth as if in horror. She turned towards the open building site at the end of the street where the crowds were already lighter;

somehow she would have to evade the cordons they would throw up to surround the whole central city area.

Manfred and Wolfgang attempted to walk casually out of the side entrance of Parliament Chambers into Spin Street, but there were several police and army men within metres of the doorway. Some were bending over Gerrit's body whilst others held back the curious crowd and then a dark-looking young policeman looked up and noted the direction of Manfred's gaze and must have read the expression on his face. He immediately shouted and stood up cocking his weapon.

'You two, stay right where you are, hands on the wall!'

Manfred froze immediately but Wolfgang cursed and began to run, in a jinking movement down the street. The young policeman raised his gun and a burst of shots rang out and Wolfgang stumbled and fell. Manfred pulled the Walther from his belt and fired it three times at the group of soldiers and police and then began running, leaping over Wolfgang's body, terror and adrenalin forcing him to weave and dodge as shots pursued him. Something plucked at his sleeve and then he was round the corner of the building and into Plein Street running blindly in the direction of the railway station.

Lieutenant Bester had been close to Le Roux and had seen the direction from which the grenade had appeared. He crouched on the road, cradling the head of the shattered body and tears ran unnoticed down his cheeks. All around him, people were milling about and screaming and his men were having trouble keeping control of the situation. The State President had been bundled away into the Houses of Parliament while the balance of the Task Force escort covered the surrounding buildings with rifles and sub-machine guns. At least the old man was safe, thought Bester as he sat with Sarel Le Roux's blood soaking into his lap unaware that the television cameras were still focused on this terrible real-life drama. Clarity returned suddenly to his shocked brain and he recalled the good-looking young girl with the straw bag, right there in the front row on the pavement. She had been standing behind young Du Plessis, Christ, he thought, it could have been her. Bester stood up and shouted orders and men began running. Within minutes he had organised search teams and Uschi Hartmann's description was being circulated.

In accordance with instructions radioed by Bester, Mostert's Riot Police units set up road blocks within a two kilometre circle of a point centred on Parliament Street. On the north-eastern side, the huge mass of Table Mountain formed a natural barrier but this only accounted for a section of the gigantic circle. It would have to be a house-to-house search and they'd close the net slowly and carefully as they moved in. Nobody knew how many of them they were looking for but they'd get the bastards. Mostert swore foully under his breath and cocked his R1 rifle, shouting to his men and running for his Landrover.

By the time Warrant Officer Mortimer had managed to find his R1 rifle in the smoke-filled office, Constable Temba had been dead for over seventy seconds. As he staggered into the charge office Mortimer saw old Sergeant van Aarde slumped in one corner, blood welling down the front of his uniform from several holes in his chest. Lucas had left the Datsun and run up the short brick driveway to empty his second sixty-shot magazine through the charge office door. Van Aarde had tried to raise his old .38 service revolver but the AK bullets had stitched a ragged line across his barrel chest, blasting him back against the wall. The black then tossed in a phosphorus grenade for good measure.

Lucas was back in the rear of the Datsun by the time Mortimer stumbled through into the blazing charge office. The young police officer took in the bloody chaos and his brain registered horrific gory details like the fact that

Sergeant van Aarde had soiled himself in death and coughed up great gouts of thick lung blood which had spattered over the cream painted walls. Constable Temba's body was spread-eagled on the linoleum floor and his intestines bulged obscenely from his shattered abdomen. Mortimer noted in revulsion that they were bluish-white and very thick and it seemed impossible that they had all been contained within the torn stomach walls. The smell was sweet and foul, like an abbatoir.

In rage and terror he fought his way onto the tiny front verandah of the old police station gripping the rifle, his eyes streaming from the smoke. He was just in time to see a grey Datsun pick-up pulling away from the kerb rapidly and he threw up the R1 and managed three hysterical shots before the vehicle disappeared from view, turning right and uphill towards the mountain. Mortimer began to weep as he lowered his rifle. Behind him the ceiling fell in with a muted roar and a blast of hot air struck his back. The charge office was enveloped in vicious oily flames as the fire took hold of the dry softboard panels. The bodies of Temba and Van Aarde were consumed in less than a minute. Mortimer ran down the driveway into the road as he heard the first sirens in the distance.

Unbeknown to Mortimer, the last bullet from the R1 had found a target. Fired low at the fast-moving truck, it had struck the tailgate and passed on through the thin steel, flattening out slightly with the impact. The, 7.62mm round, still travelling at some 2500 feet per second, crashed into Ronald van der Walt as he sat tensed in the rear of the Datsun clutching the left hand door pillar of the cab for support. The bullet entered his body through the right hip and blasted up through the coloured's pelvic girdle and spine, mushrooming as it did so into a rounded miniature battering ram that pushed bone and flesh before it. Ronald's body was slammed against the rear of the cab and his heart stopped instantaneously. He had felt little more than a heavy blow before ceasing to exist.

Shocked, Lucas grabbed Daniel's AK and reloaded

both weapons from the canvas sack at his feet. He knew that they would have less chance of escape now that the surviving policeman had seen them. It would all depend on whether they could make it back to Loader Street up on Signal Hill. In the narrow back streets of the Malay Quarter they planned to ditch the Datsun, discard the overalls and pickup the escape vehicle – Daniel's VW Combi which was fuelled up and ready to go. Daniel had the keys in his pocket and Lucas wished he would go faster because they had to try and get through onto the N2 to travel east along the coast, before any road blocks went up in that direction.

Manfred ran on in desperation, heart thumping and lungs burning with the agony of drawing each breath. Behind him, Cohen and Reilly thundered along, boots hammering on the pavement with the machine carbines swinging madly from their shoulders. Blood soaked the left side of Reilly's shirt where a bullet from Manfred's pistol had grooved a shallow channel through his bicep. But although the arm had stiffened up, he felt no pain. All he could think of was catching the bastard terrorist, they couldn't allow him to escape.

Mad, disjointed thoughts raced through Manfred's brain as he charged on blindly across Church Square towards the Plein Street parking garage, an area they had picked out as a possible refuge in the event of pursuit. As he ran, Manfred considered the hopelessness of his position and tears began to course down his cheeks. He knew somehow that he had no chance of escape. Felt positive that he was going to die and that this whole master-plan, all the effort, had been in vain. But he ran on and as he reached the entrance to the multi-storey car park he heard shouting from behind and then a young, strong-looking man appeared suddenly in front of him, holding up his hands and blocking the path to the ramp. The Walther was still clutched in Manfred's right hand and he raised it instinctively and fired without aiming at point blank range, the bullet bowling the man over. He ran on, labouring upwards now on to the concrete ramp and then there was a popping noise from behind him and his legs were knocked from under him. He fell headlong, dropping the pistol.

Running ahead of Reilly, Cohen had dropped flat when he saw the terrorist shoot the young man who had tried to bar his way. He sighted the sub-machine gun at the legs of the fugitive who was about sixty metres away and still running steadily. The short-barrelled weapon stuttered and rose up from right to left but the terrorist stumbled, and then fell, rolling back down the upward ramp of the Parkade. As Cohen got to his feet, Reilly passed him, running on strongly towards the two fallen men, his machine carbine held across his body and his left arm slickly red with blood.

Reilly was incensed and as he reached the writhing terrorist he lifted the hand machine carbine, his fingers curled around the trigger. The weapon was cocked and ready to fire and Reilly pointed it at the terrorist's face, looking down on the man who stared up at him in fear and pain. The terrorist shook his head and threw his hands up in front of his face and the crowd of onlookers who had gathered, watched spellbound. Somewhere close by, a woman screamed shrilly, but Cohen had reached Reilly and dived forward pushing the barrel of the sub-machine gun downwards towards the pavement.

'Don't shoot Patrick, don't do it!' he shouted urgently and Reilly slowly relaxed his grip and shook his head, trembling with reaction. The hate was etched deeply into the lines of his face as he stared down at the wounded man.

'You're a fucking lucky bastard,' he mouthed slowly. 'My friend here's a soft little bugger, so you'll live a little longer.' Then he smiled grimly. 'But you'll swing, my friend, no doubt about that. We don't mess about with animals like you in this country, we just put them down like mad dogs.'

Manfred heard the words and felt the hate in rising

terror. Despite a resolve to the contrary, he began to prattle about rights, describing himself as a soldier, a guerilla fighter of the Azanian Freedom Revolutionary Army. Cohen immediately noted the German accent. Reilly laughed harshly and moved forward again quickly driving the metal butt of the sub-machine gun into the terrorist's face, smashing teeth and lips with a short cruel swipe. Manfred fell back stunned, feeling faint and tasting blood salty on his tongue. He managed to sit up again but his legs were numb and he knew that he would be unable to rise. His mind reeled as he heard the young policemen's voices talking loudly above him and he felt a great and terrible loneliness as he realised that everything was lost.

The great dream of striking a blow for the oppressed blacks of this beautiful country had failed totally. Then the pain came properly, in sudden waves, deep in the bones of his shattered legs. He screamed hoarsely and fainted, slumping back on to the warm paving stones.

When he awoke, still in shock, he realised that he was lying on a stretcher and sensed a man with a white coat kneeling beside him. He felt the prick of a needle and a lifting sensation and then he was inside a dim, cave-like place with canvas sides and an odd smell of oil and plastic. He closed his eyes, the morphine making him sleepy and heard the voices all around him; he didn't recognise the language at first and then it came back to him. It was Afrikaans, the bastard form of Dutch spoken in South Africa which had developed from the early settlers in the country. Gerrit had spoken to Hoyle in this tongue in London. It seemed a lifetime ago.

As the big Puma helicopter thundered into life, Manfred's reason returned and with it a sense of rationale. He knew he was finished and that they would probably torture and then hang him after a show trial that would expose all the AFRA planning. The pain in his legs had subsided and he could taste some sort of antiseptic fluid on his swollen lips where the doctor had swabbed them. A strong wind blew through the open door of the big helicopter as it rose into the air and Manfred realised that he was lying very close to the opening. Bright technicolour images of his life flashed across his brain as he lay with eyes closed in the shuddering cabin of the big machine. He thought of his childhood and the parents he had not seen for five years. He recalled odd snatches of pleasant annual holidays at Sylt on Germany's northern sea when he was still in junior school and the little hotel at Westerland, which had since become a jet-set resort. He remembered his father's arms lifting him high above the rushing surf and the way the summers had seemed so long and golden; endless, wonderful days.

He opened his eyes gradually and looked up through slitted lids at the canvas-padded roof of the cabin. Turning his head slowly left and right he could see only the pilot and co-pilot and then the two camouflaged uniformed figures of the young policeman further down the fuselage. Having made the decision, he tensed himself and carefully began to move his hands under the red blanket which covered him. The tubular alloy stretcher was held firmly to the floor by four clamps. Manfred was belted to it with canvas webbing straps and he fumbled gently with the buckles at his chest and thighs, feeling little more than a dull ache in his lower legs. Because of the pain-relieving morphine, his movements were deliberate, yet slow, and it took him three long minutes to manage the buckles. Once free he summoned his strength again and opened his eyes again, to turn his head and check on his captors. They were talking quietly and had been joined by the doctor, still in his white coat. The medic was bending over the blond policeman who had struck Manfred in the mouth and doing something to his arm. Manfred was glad that he had shot him.

In the cockpit, flight lieutenant Andre de Beer held the Puma steady on his course south along the coast for Simonstown, the South African naval base in False Bay. His superiors had decided to ferry the wounded terrorist there to avoid the press or any abortive rescue attempt by

401

the rest of the Ajax group, the numbers of which were still unknown. At Simonstown there was an efficient base hospital but police surgeons were to fly out from Cape Town to meet the Puma. All de Beer had to do was get the bastard there safely.

He was flying at three hundred feet, a height which enabled him to see the sunbathers down below on the beach at Muizenberg. They'd gone out over the mountain and Constantia and had passed over Kenilworth race course where he'd been last Saturday. De Beer looked ahead and could see the Police Alouette, a tiny dot in the distance. That would be the one carrying the medics, he thought absently and then Muizenberg was behind them and Fish Hoek coming up ahead with Simonstown just across the bay. De Beer looked down through the plexiglass and saw a girl sunbathing naked in the garden of a house close to the shoreline. As the Puma thundered towards her, she grabbed a towel and covered herself, but not before he had determined that she was a genuine redhead. He smiled to himself and then pandemonium broke out behind as someone began to curse horribly in German.

Manfred made his bid, knowing as he did so that there would only be one chance. It was a supreme effort and involved heaving himself off the stretcher with his right hand so that he rolled onto his stomach where he used his left arm to propel him in a continuing roll towards the door. The fact that he was still inside the thick blanket seemed to help but the door had a slight lip and he came to a stop against it, desperately trying to heave himself over. The pain from his legs was terrible and he cursed loudly, the words seeming to give him extra strength. Quite suddenly he was over the door sill and falling, and then something grabbed his legs and he was wrenched about by the slipstream and the downward thrust of the rotor blades. The agony from his shattered, grating bones made him scream and yell with pain and terror.

Unbelieving, Cohen had seen the red blanketed figure

402

suddenly roll towards the open door and stop momentarily, held by the low sill. He had dived forwards just as the terrorist heaved himself upwards and over the tiny barrier and without thinking had grabbed for his trailing leg. The weight of the man drew him forwards and outwards and he grasped frantically at the door frame to save himself but his hand could not find sufficient purchase. He had to let go of the terrible deadweight pulling him out and teetered on the edge of the doorway, buffeted by the slipstream which sucked at him. Then Reilly grabbed for him from behind and he was drawn back into the relative silence of the cabin, trembling with reaction. Cohen had soiled himself but he didn't care and he and Reilly laughed madly together with relief.

Silently Manfred cartwheeled down from the helicopter and de Beer caught a glimpse of him as he wheeled left, banking the big machine now that the two policemen were safely back inside. With his body floating free, Manfred noted a great lessening of the agony in his leg and his mind was surprisingly clear as he fell to his death. Myriad thoughts rushed through his mind and Tina's face flashed into his last seconds of life as his eyes registered glimpses of golden sand and blue sea. One kaleidoscope impression revealed a girl with red hair staring upwards with mouth open and then she was gone as his body turned for the last time and thudded into the hard packed sand only metres from the tideline. The impact broke his spine in two places and the cold water of the Atlantic rushed forward surrounding the limp corpse as if trying to draw it back into the ocean.

De Beer spun the Puma down, no longer noticing the naked redhead who was running towards the terrorist's body. His thoughts were on the retribution that would be exacted upon him by his superiors. But how was he to know that the bastard was awake after all that morphine that the doctor had pumped into him? The bloody policemen should have guarded the bastard, and he'd nearly taken one of them with him. The shit would really

403

have hit the fan if that had happened. As for the open door, the SAAF always flew that way on short hops. It was just bad luck that the silly bastard had decided to throw himself out. It was the first time in De Beer's eleven years' experience that anyone had ever fallen from an aircraft.

Lucas and Daniel reached the old Malay Quarter after nineteen minutes' driving. They had seen various police vehicles and fire engines travelling in the opposite direction but none had paid them any attention. This was due to the fact that Sergeant Mortimer had fainted from temporary asphyxiation and had not yet reported the grey Datsun truck which they were about to discard. They stopped in a quiet alley, shed their painters' overalls and left them in the Datsun with Ronald's body. Then they walked the two blocks through the narrow streets to Malan's house in Loader Street. To confound police roadblocks they then drove back towards Seapoint on the coast road, with the two AKs and the remaining grenades in the back of the van covered with jackets and a large holdall containing money, travellers cheques and two changes of clothing for each of them.

The plan was to head along the coast to Llandudno and then cross the mountain to Hout Bay, carrying on across the narrow neck of the peninsula via Chapman's Peak to Fish Hoek. From there, the intention was to drive out on the N2 East via Mossel Bay and Knysna to Port Elizabeth. Daniel's friends in the coloured township of Gelvandale would put them up for the night and they'd go on next morning in another vehicle to Grahamstown, East London and finally independent Transkei where they would be given political asylum, food and new identities.

It was a long trek but Lucas thought that they might make it. In the back of the VW was a large consignment of cheap Cape wine due for delivery to a licensed liquor store in Gelvendale and all the necessary papers were to hand in

Daniel's plastic attache case which lay beside him on the front seat. After clearing Cape Town they would ditch the AKs somewhere in the country but Lucas intended to hang onto them until he was sure that they wouldn't have to fight their way through any roadblocks. The South African police would not expect the Ajax fugitives to take this route but both men knew that there would be blanket roadblocks around the Cape for a distance of two or three hundred kilometres within a few hours. But it would take the police a while to get organised and so right now they had a good chance; the first hour's drive would be the biggest risk period.

The old panel van chugged through Green Point approaching Main Road Seapoint. Lucas tensed when he saw camouflaged figures and blue lights up ahead but the roadblock was set up on the opposite side of the road and they were waved through after a cursory glance. Daniel's vans were reasonably well known around the Cape Town suburbs and the coloured even greeted the young warrant officer on the roadblock saucily.

'What's up man, you got a problem or what?' he asked.

The officer looked grim and Lucas thought for one horrible moment that Daniel had overplayed it. 'Just get moving, *Skollie* or I'll turn you round and send you *fokking* off back where you came from. Stay on Main Road and get on through Seapoint quickly. Now move it.'

'OK, boss man,' said Daniel ingratiatingly and the VW moved off, now only two blocks from where they had hit the police station. There were police everywhere here and Lucas grinned at Daniel from the passenger seat. 'A real hornet's nest, eh Danny? A bloody shame that Ronald got it.'

The coloured glanced sideways as he drove on calmly. 'Yes, it is. He was a good man, old Ronald, didn't say much but he was a tough fighter. He and his men did a great job on that bus on De Waal Drive last year.' Daniel lapsed into silence. So far, so good he thought.

Lucas opened a Black Label can from the six-pack at his

feet and handed it to Daniel. Then he popped another and lifted it in greeting to his companion. Daniel smiled sideways at the black man. He's as hard as nails this bugger, he thought. 'Cheers,' said Lucas and took a long pull at the beer. 'Yey, that tastes good,' he said rubbing his mouth with the back of his hand. 'I wonder how the others have done'.

In a matter of minutes Uschi managed to get out of the immediate vicinity of the parliament buildings without being accosted. She walked briskly through the Botanical Gardens listening to the clamour of whistles and sirens behind her. Once in Queen Victoria Street, she walked quickly up the short hill to Orange Street, turned left and headed for the Mount Nelson Hotel, only ten minutes' walk away. On her shoulder was the beachbag, still containing her Walther P 38 pistol and the remainder of the grenades and as she reached the imposing colonial entrance of the hotel two police Landrovers careered past, filled with uniformed figures clutching rifles and sub-machine guns. If they noted the slim girl in the beach clothes, they paid her no attention and she walked briskly up the driveway and into the lobby, approaching the reception desk confidently. She had told nobody in the group of her escape route and each member had been left to work out their own. Uschi thoroughly approved of this policy.

'Do you have a room for me?' she said politely. 'My things are at the air terminal downtown but I was taking a walk around looking for this hotel. It's just for a few nights.' She stopped speaking and looked around in admiration at the old Cape Dutch and English furnishings of the lobby. 'This place is so beautiful, like a storybook. I'd really love to stay here.'

The young coloured clerk smiled and nodded. 'We can fix you up, madam. Would you like me to call a taxi to collect your things?'

Uschi smiled at him winningly. 'Give me a minute to

freshen up and then I'll take a taxi down to the terminal and get my stuff. In the meantime, I'll sign your register, my name is Angela Kaufmann.'

It was late afternoon when Tina eventually made it back to the Hotel President in Seapoint. She had been unable to get a taxi for hours because the entire city centre seethed with pressmen and photographers interviewing any eye witnesses to the attempt on the life of the State President. The police had been everywhere, stopping and searching coloureds and blacks and even some whites but her disguise held up and none of them gave her a second glance. She had wandered about in the streets of the city following the excited crowds, dazed and emotionally shattered by the loss of Gerrit. Her suspicions that he was dead were confirmed when she bought the late afternoon edition of the *Cape Argus* which bore screaming banner headlines. 'Terrorist Attack' filling some one third of the front page. She had read the leading piece with trepidation.

The paper said that one of the four dead terrorists was thought to have been an AFRA operative identified as Gerrit de Kock, a Cape coloured until recently resident in Windhoek. The department of National Security confirmed that De Kock had been under their surveillance and the police were anxious to interview his sister Mrs Tina Heim, now living in West Germany but thought to be presently in Cape Town on a visit. The paper also said that two other terrorists had been killed, one being a second coloured man thought to be a member of the banned Unity Movement of South Africa, a group suspected of being responsible for the bus attack in De Waal Drive last year. This man had been shot whilst escaping from the Seapoint Police Station which had been attacked and set on fire by a diversionary terrorist group. The third terrorist killed was Manfred Meyer, a West German citizen who had been deported from South Africa in 1974 for offences in contravention of the Immorality Act. Meyer was known to have entered South Africa under a false name and had been staying at the Capetonian Hotel. The security police suspected that Pieter Kirschfeld, the other AFRA operative killed in the attack, had also gained entry to the Republic in the same way and police were searching all hotels and boarding houses in the Cape Town area to interview foreign nationals.

The article had gone on to say that the police had been aided in their task by the television film of the proceedings which was being studied by operatives of the security police and the Department of National Security; a spokesman said that the authorities were confident that the remainder of the terrorist force would be apprehended in the very near future. Three policemen had been killed and five other people had been injured in the attack, one of them very seriously.

Tina sat in her hotel room drinking neat brandy and looking out over the sloping lawns to the rocky beach. The evening was fine and the sky lit with the orange red light which promised a wonderful Cape sunset within a couple of hours. Seemingly with great regret, Tina dragged her eyes away from the view and back to the television set on the dressing table. The time was almost six o'clock and she watched, mesmerised, as the sweep hand on the screen moved around to the hour.

The news bulletin was almost entirely devoted to the attempted assassination of the State President, an event which had been filmed by three cameras. The announcer was serious as he asked all viewers with suspect heart conditions or emotionally unstable dispositions to refrain from watching the film which would follow. Tina watched spellbound, dreading the next few minutes. First there were close-ups of the crowd and Tina saw her own staring face behind the goggle sunglasses and clearly noted Uschi hovering behind the row of policemen on the opposite side of the road. When the camera had zeroed in on the scuffle in front of the steps of the House, she bent closer to the set and then the young policeman's body had been thrown up into the air like a sack of potatoes and the film had gone an odd reddish colour. The close-up of the body after the explosion was so horrific that Tina rushed to the bathroom and vomited up the neat spirit in hot gut-wrenching surges.

After the news was finished she switched off the set and slowly removed her clothes. Then she turned back the covers of the double bed and crawled between the sheets clutching a water glass full of brandy. Her mind was blank from the horror of the film but she knew they would be coming for her soon and lay back against the padded headboard drinking steadily from the glass but scarcely tasting the strong liquor. She felt she had nothing further to live for because the two men who mattered most in her life were dead. In her mind she had already rejected her planned escape route which was very unlikely to succeed now anyway. She would be unable to face a police inquisition and the trial that would follow and now knew what she would have to do. Slowly she rose as if sleep walking, and chained and bolted the door of the room. She then returned to the bed, taking the big straw bag which she had carried all day. No thoughts of Willi entered her mind.

Tina took a long gulp of brandy and then searched in the bag for one of the fragmentation grenades. She took the smooth grey plastic device from the bag and clutched it to her naked breasts. Little passed through her mind, and all she was concerned with was the strength required to actually pull the ring from the grenade. She closed her eyes and her hands were wet as they slid over the slippery oval shape. But soon her fingers found the ring and she pulled firmly at it, yet it failed to move. She pulled again, harder, and then it came away quite suddenly and she held the grenade to her chest tightly, with both hands. Her lips moved in silent prayer and then there was an enormous flash which she saw for a split-second as a red glow from behind her closed eyelids. In a millisecond there was nothing.

The SATV film was relayed by satellite, to every major news service in the world. The reaction was the same in most Western countries: one of outrage. Somehow, the real-life drama played out by the elegant, silver-haired statesman and his young saviour brought home, yet again, the horror of international terrorism. Jacobus van Vuuren Malan gave the best performance of his long career with a speech in English to the hushed House after he had recovered from the attack. The old man's voice broke with emotion and tears rolled down his cheeks as they did in homes from Manchester to Miami where the TV film was seen. In South Africa, the mood of the public was such that the government requested new sweeping powers to combat urban terrorism and these were voted through parliament without delay. Sarel le Roux was honoured as a hero and posthumously awarded the Africa Star, for bravery above and beyond the call of duty.

Le Roux had done more for South Africa's image with his last act than anyone since Professor Christiaan Barnard's first transplant, and the effects of his sacrifice rebounded around the world, sometimes with violent results. In London, the AFRA offices were stoned and a twenty-four hour police cordon was set up to prevent National Front demonstrators from breaking in and burning the place down. Even Peter Hain's anti-apartheid movement rejected the AFRA attack as 'a solution too terrible to comprehend'. On 24 January, Hoyle stayed away from the office and he and Jane slipped quietly out of the country the next day, heading for Sardinia and the tranquil privacy of a friend's villa. Anderson was left in charge in South Kensington but Hoyle had a feeling that the gravy train had finally stopped; that AFRA's days were numbered. It was incredible that public opinion had swung so markedly against them because of the dramatic suicidal act of one young policeman. There had been no word from Gerber at the ASG in Berlin and Hoyle had not attempted to make contact with his German allies.

Looking at the whole thing philosophically, thought

Hoyle, he was not in too bad a position. Whether AFRA would continue or not, after all the storm clouds blew over, Hoyle would still have £300,000 in a numbered account at Credit Suisse in Geneva. This was not a fortune by any means, but carefully invested it would provide him with an adequate income for the rest of his life, and Jane was still earning very well. As the Iberia DC 8 cleared a thick bank of cumulus and emerged into the bright sunlight of a beautiful winter afternoon, Hoyle sipped at his Chivas Regal and soda and smiled at his wife. She clutched his arm tightly to the envy of a number of male passengers in the adjacent seats. Things could be worse, thought Hoyle.

At 9.30 pm on 24 January, Jenni Theron lay on her back in the deputy director's bed looking up at the slatted pine ceiling above her. Her employer slept on his face beside her and she flinched at the bubbling snores which escaped his half-open lips at regular intervals. There was to be an in-depth investigation into the AFRA affair because everyone realised that, had it not been for young le Roux, the State President would have been dead, or at best, severely wounded. The young policeman had saved not only old Van Vuuren Malan but many others in the vicinity of the grenade from horrible injury and the deputy director had received his parents and some girlfriend of his at the office that very afternoon. Afterwards, the deputy director had drunk half a bottle of Ballantine's and then they'd come back to the flat. Jenni sensed a change in the wind.

Perhaps it might be time to try for a transfer to the other crowd, she thought. She'd met the handsome young director of the National Intelligence Service at a recent cocktail party and had felt his eyes run over her body. Quietly she slipped out of bed and ran to the shower in the adjoining bathroom. She closed the door softly and turned on the taps. As the powerful water jets buffeted her body

411

she smiled with her eyes tightly closed. It may yet turn out to be a good year, she thought.

Lucas and Daniel ditched the AKs and grenades near Humansdorp without leaving the N2. It was close to evening and Daniel kept watch whilst Lucas carefully wiped the weapons and threw them into a deep drainage culvert which flowed under the national road. Two hours' drive further on, they were stopped by Riot Police at a road block some thirty kilometres from Port Elizabeth and had to submit to a thorough search of the van. Their papers passed scrutiny however and they were allowed to continue. Thirty-two hours later they crossed the border into Transkei.

Uschi had never returned to the Mount Nelson but had merely used the registration routine to secure a taxi. Once in the cab she directed the driver to the Inn on the Square where her baggage was waiting at the porter's desk. From there they drove to an address in Bishopscourt on the slopes of the mountain above De Waal Drive. As the taxi drew up in the forecourt of the old double-storey mansion the front door opened and an elderly woman ran out to greet Uschi.

'*Meine kleine Uschi,*' she said excitedly. '*Gott, wie du grosse gerworden bist.*'

Uschi smiled back and paid off the cab. '*Tante Rosa,*' she said softly, 'yes it's been a long time.' She embraced the older woman and then the two of them walked arm in arm into the house.

Uschi had made her plans well and the utilisation of her godparents, who had been resident in the Cape for the last eight years, was a stroke of great good fortune. After supper that evening, she telephoned her parents and told them that she had arrived as planned in South Africa and would be there with *Tante* Rosa and *Onkel* Hubert for the next three or four weeks. After that she'd use the Lufthansa ticket that the ASG had given her which showed that she had travelled to South Africa on 18 January. The ticket was an open return and a passport with the same name of Heike Schmidt displayed an entry stamp from immigration at Jan Smuts airport on the 19th. The first thing Uschi did when she had a moment alone was to burn the French Yvette Bellegarde passport and the Swissair return ticket. She destroyed them in the tiny fireplace in her bedroom under the eaves of the old Cape Dutch house and flushed the remains down the toilet next door. She removed every scrap of ash. Yvette Bellegarde had ceased to exist.

In the light of what had happened to the others, especially poor Tina who must have been in terrible desperation, Uschi planned to lie low for at least a week. Her parents had telephoned and ranted on about her being in South Africa, a dangerous and terrible country. They had watched the film of the attempted assassination on television and had been appalled that their wilful daughter would probably be in Cape Town at that time. Uschi's mother whined lengthily about taking care and eventually Uschi had handed the receiver to *Tante* Rosa so that the older woman could reassure her mother that she was quite safe. After an early supper Uschi went to bed and lay awake for a while reviewing the events of the past twenty-four hours. Gerrit, Tina, Manfred, Wolfgang and Ronald were all dead. She thought of Lucas and his muscular black body and the peppery animal smell of him and she wished in that moment that he was there, that she could have him inside her.

As she drifted into sleep, she hoped that Lucas would make it. Perhaps one day they might meet again, though she doubted it. She dreamed of him, a black panther-like figure stalking through the jungle, muscles rippling and eyes burning in the half light. Lucas was an animal, he would survive.

Uschi spent much of her time sunbathing in the huge

413

grounds of the old house in Bishopscourt. After eight days her body was tanned a deep golden colour and she had washed the auburn dye from her hair, telling *Tante* Rosa that she preferred the natural blonde shade. Her godmother approved and Uschi was pampered and spoiled by the wealthy old couple. Sometimes they went out to dinner in the evening but most of the time Uschi remained at home, swimming and occasionally playing tennis with David, the eldest son of the next door household. He was in his second year of medicine at the University of Cape Town and some five years younger than Uschi, but after their second meeting she allowed him to touch her in the changing-room in his garden. The night after that they went out to a raucous student pub in Rondebosch and she allowed him to make love to her in the back of his Alfa Romeo. He was hurried and inexperienced by Uschi's standards but she reached climax and derived some satisfaction.

On a Sunday, two days before she was scheduled to leave South Africa, David took her on a picnic trip up onto the mountain above Kirstenbosch. They drank chilled white wine and ate cold crayfish tails and later walked hand in hand in the beautiful botanical gardens. With the excuse of having drunk too much wine, Uschi ran off alone into the undergrowth in search of somewhere to relieve herself. The young South African student was surprised, but nothing about this beautiful German girl was normal and he accepted her reason and sat waiting on a stone bench, staring out over Table Bay and wondering how he was going to live without her.

Uschi had brought with her the big beach bag which she had kept locked in the suitcase in her room. From it she took the Walther pistol and the remaining grenades and buried them a few metres apart in the dead leaves and humus of the mountainside. Then she ran back laughing to David and kissed him on the cheek.

'I feel wonderful,' she said mischievously. 'Don't you want to kiss me David?' The young man stared at her, wondering at the power she seemed to hold over him. He drew her to him and kissed her long and lingeringly and then they walked off down the mountain, arms around each other's waists.

Six months after Uschi Hartmann had returned without incident to Berlin, an old coloured gardener was raking the deep carpet of dead leaves in a remote part of the Kirstenbosch Botanical Gardens high up on the southwest flank of Table Mountain. His rake touched on something solid and he dug about and recovered the Walther pistol. Hefting the rusty weapon in his hand, the old man wondered if he should try to sell it in the township or give it in to the police. He decided on the former course of action but when the rake revealed other egg-shaped objects which looked strangely sinister and dangerous, he lost his nerve and reported the find to his superior who in turn called the police at Wynberg. Mostert was there within the hour together with a colleague from the Security Police. The grenades were identified as the same type which had been used in the attack on the State President and were similar to five found by children in a culvert under the N2 near Humansdorp in the Eastern Cape.

The AK rifles which had been found with the grenades at Humansdorp were proved to be the weapons used in the assault on SAP Seapoint. Mostert had a feeling that the chapter had ended and that the white girl whom Bester had seen had somehow buried this cache up here on the mountain. She was undoubtedly long gone now; Mostert could feel this fact in his bones. He looked out over Table Bay and the grey mists which were sweeping in from the sea. It was pouring with rain and bitterly cold and he slithered on the muddy pathway as he made his way down to the little office of the curator of the Kirstenbosch Botanical Gardens.

For the last six months it had been quiet and just lately,

since June, the weather had been really appalling. So much for the Fairest Cape in all the world, he thought and grimaced as he turned the Landrover downhill towards the city which lay damp, yet protected, in the lee of the huge mountain.